PURE
DELIGHTS

PURE DELIGHTS

STELLA CAMERON

KENSINGTON BOOKS

For Jerry, my excellent friend.

"One ought, every day at least, to hear a little song, read a good poem, see a fine picture, and, if it were possible, to speak a few reasonable words."

Johann Wolfgang von Goethe

Dear Reader,

I wanted to be an actress. I also wanted to be an opera singer, a concert pianist, a ballerina, a painter and a surgeon.

Abject shyness kept me from as much as approaching the stage. My sister was the one born with the marvelous voice. I had an appendectomy shortly after starting piano lessons and nobody remembered to send me back after I'd recovered. My family decided I was too tall to be a dancer. And, yep, my sister can really paint. I still think I might have made a good surgeon, but . . .

I never actually told anyone I wanted to be a writer—I just wrote. Writing was my own and I needed no permission or approval. On paper, the rebel in me that I successfully hide most of the time is free to pop out and say the darndest things. I've always been an observer rather than a player—of any game—and it's the watcher in me that makes writing so natural, so exciting and such a driving force in my life.

I'm a wife, a mother, a daughter, a friend . . . and a writer. In that order. Joseph Campbell talked about the importance of following one's bliss. He was right. But equally important to me is the challenge of keeping the little pieces of my particular bliss in the right sequence.

I hope you love the book!

Stella Cameron

Prologue

His rubber soles made no sound on the fire escape. When the time came, he would climb up this way again and it would all be so easy. Tonight must be the last trip to the lighted windows on the top floor of the building in Seattle's Pioneer Square district . . . until he was told to go through with the plan.

Midnight. A muggy July midnight when voices and music reached his ears in spurts from hot rooms with the oldest views in town.

Below him, the streets were still alive. Only the careless, the stupid or the drunk loitered. The rest kept their distance from buildings with dark, humid alleys between, and walked in groups and with purpose.

He heard the strident strains of the Dixieland band at the Central Tavern and the wail of a police siren on the waterfront, beneath the viaduct. From Elliott Bay came the bellow of a ferry boat's horn.

One more flight of metal steps took him to the platform outside the top-floor windows.

She trusted everyone. He'd heard her tell the crazy old woman on the ground floor not to be so paranoid about locking doors. 'Friends never invade your space, Mary,' she'd said with that sickeningly earnest way she had about her. "If an enemy wants to get at you, locks won't stop them."

Locks might not stop her enemies, but open doors and windows made their job so much simpler.

There were flowers in pots on the fire-escape landing. He crept around them and flattened himself against the wall outside the window. Slowly, he edged close enough to see into the room beyond . . . the bedroom.

She wasn't there, but he heard the sound of running water and knew it meant she was showering in the tiny bathroom. Steam would be clouding the single mirror and coating shiny, white enameled walls with dripping moisture.

He knew every inch of the two floors where she lived—intimately. He had touched everything that was hers. He knew what she kept in every drawer in her bedroom. He knew the sizes of everything she kept in every drawer in her bedroom. He knew each bottle and jar in the medicine cabinet and on the counter in her bathroom. He knew that on the rare occasions when she remembered, her perfume was AnaisAnais.

The flowers in the pots were a kind that smelled exotic at night. Some sort of lily.

AnaisAnais was exotic on her skin. The scent of the flowers made him see her white skin and imagine her smoothing perfume onto places hidden by the plain clothes she wore over silk, and satin, and lace.

The water stopped running.

He could leave now—ought to leave now. He'd proven again that there would be no problem when he came to do what he'd eventually have to do.

She was singing. She always sang in the shower and around the apartment when she thought she was alone. Almost always she thought she was alone. Her voice didn't fit. She was cool and smooth and remote. When she sang, her voice made him think of dark, warm, moist places where living things entwined and the scents were carnal.

He should leave now.

She came out of the bathroom.

A white towel hid all but a hint of her black hair. Without glasses, those deep blue eyes wouldn't see any shifting shadows beyond mirror-dark windows.

A white robe, belted at her narrow waist, reached only the tops of her smooth, naked thighs. The drab clothes she wore by day were a sly disguise used to hide what really lay beneath . . . silk, and satin, and lace . . . and soft skin.

He must leave now.

"Friends never invade your space," she'd said. He wasn't her friend.

She unwound the towel from her black hair and shook it loose.

She untied the belt of the robe and turned away.

He frowned and tore at a thumbnail with his teeth.

When she tossed aside the robe, her damp black hair settled on her white shoulders. Her back was long and straight, her hips rounded, rounded as no one would guess who hadn't seen her without the sly, drab clothes.

Something furry and lithe shot past his legs. Aagh. He clapped a hand over his mouth and trapped the scream inside his head.

Her cat. She touched the cat, stroked the cat the way she pretended she didn't want to be stroked herself.

Sly.

The cat hissed and he saw its fur rise along its scrawny spine. Arching its back, drawing its lips back from tiny, needle-sharp teeth, it hissed and hissed, then let out a high, thin yowl.

She heard that sound.

The singing stopped and he saw her start toward the window.

Firm, round breasts tipped pale pink.

Black hair where her white thighs met.

Coming to the window.

His rubber soles made no sound on the fire escape.

One

She had the face of a goddamn nun.

For as long as Tobias Quinn could remember, the woman who stood before him had seemed remote, silent, watchful and holy enough to shrivel an ivory elephant's balls.

She made him nervous.

Nervous wasn't something Tobias allowed anyone to make him feel—for long.

Paris Delight wasn't a big woman—or a small woman. She was thin, or at least he'd always thought of her as thin; a thin child, a thin teenager and still thin when she'd ignored his advice and left to wander around Europe on her own.

She favored shapeless, nondescript clothing in dark colors. That was nothing new, either.

He cleared his throat.

She used one index finger to push her glasses up.

This was evidently her workroom as well as a living space on the lower floor of a two-story apartment at the top of the building. She made jewelry or some such thing. The high workbench in front of her was of rough, gray wood—utilitarian but elegant in a way. Wooden furniture, each piece obviously unique and expertly fashioned, stood on age-bleached wooden floors devoid of carpets. The only color in sight was the glowing blue of a blown glass vase filled with purple and yellow irises, and the hodgepodge of black, white, and orange that was a scrawny cat curled into a ball on a window sill.

Music from concealed speakers filled the room's airy spaces with the beautiful, breathy sound of a flute skimming above a bass guitar. The music soared and wooden-bladed fans spun— and the black-haired woman stood quite still. Still, intent and hostile.

Tobias cleared his throat again. "It's hot," he said, splaying a hand over his chest on top of his cotton shirt. "Seattle isn't supposed to be this hot—ever. Not by eight in the evening. Not even at the end of July."

Paris's response was to lower her thick, black lashes.

The pale, quiet kid who watched from the edges of whatever was going on. That's how he remembered her. Tonight she seemed to be watching again, only from the center this time. Oh, boy, was she ever in the center of what was going on for him now. *Bull's-eye.* Only she didn't know it . . . yet.

Tobias tried again. He said, "I let myself in."

Using skinny-nosed pliers, Paris held what appeared to be a piece of polished bone. Deftly, she placed the bone into a space in a partially constructed piece of silver jewelry and set down the pliers.

She didn't like him. Had never liked him. But he was going to persuade her to pretend she'd changed her mind.

"Why did you come here?" she asked, bending over the bench to examine several more pieces of bone.

The jocular approach was always worth a try. He said, "Because I knew you must be missing me," and plastered on a smile.

Paris looked slowly up at him. Behind her round glasses, her eyes were dark-blue and impossible to read. She said, "You've got to be joking."

What he'd come here to accomplish was no joke. "Why?" he asked. "You and I go back a long way."

Her straight black hair was pulled severely away from a heart-shaped hairline and secured at her nape with a rubber band. No self-respecting strand would have the temerity to pop free, but Paris smoothed the spot above each ear as if checking for stragglers.

"We do, y'know," Tobias persisted. His smile was beginning to hurt. "I remember when you were born."

"I doubt it," she said shortly. "You were seven. Seven-year-old boys aren't interested in babies."

"How do you know? You were never a seven-year-old boy."

He thought the corners of her mouth flickered.

"Go on," he said. "Smile. It'll do you good. You were always too serious."

"You know absolutely nothing about me," she told him in that unexpectedly earthy voice of hers. "You never knew anything about me and you didn't want to. I'm of no interest to you."

This showed signs of going badly. "How long have you lived here?"

A slowly inhaled breath raised her indistinct breasts beneath a loose, rust-colored gauze dress. "In Pioneer Square?" The question was rhetorical. "Six years. Since I got back from Europe."

"That long?" That sounded as if time had flown by while he hadn't thought about her. Close to true, but not an impression that would help his cause tonight. "I suppose it must be. Of course it is. You were"—he snapped his fingers—"twenty-three. Am I right?"

"Six from twenty-nine is twenty-three," she said. "Why are you here?"

Mmm. He could just spit it out and wait for the explosion—if Paris Delight was capable of any sort of explosion. He said, "How's your little business going?"

There was the slightest hesitation before she said, "My little business is just fine, thank you."

"Still making bangles and things?"

"I rarely make *bangles,* as you call them. I work primarily on privately commissioned pieces of jewelry."

"Nigel said something about that," he said of his younger brother. "And things for markets and so on."

She raised her glasses to rub the corners of her eyes. "Not markets and so on. I design limited editions for local galleries. High-end galleries. Are we done with the cross-examination?"

"The door downstairs—the one to the street—it isn't locked."

Once more she took a slow breath. "No, it isn't."

"How many people live in this building?"

She took her glasses off, gathered a handful of rust-colored gauze and polished lenses with complete, frowning absorption.

"How many—"

"Seven. Sometimes eight. Sometimes more."

He indicated the door he'd used to enter the lower floor of her two-floor apartment. "That isn't locked, either."

"No."

"Anyone could come off the street, up here and walk right in on you."

"I noticed."

He had to smile. "Meaning me? I'm not exactly anyone, Paris. You and I grew up side by side."

She threaded the wire arms of her glasses around her ears and poked, a little ferociously, he thought, at the nose piece. "We grew up in the same general vicinity. We were never side by side—unless you were passing me by. I don't think you ever noticed me on those occasions." The lift of her pointed chin gave him a clear view of her sharp, oval jaw and slender, white neck. *"Why* are you here?"

"I came to see you." Damn, she was going to be really difficult. "For old times' sake."

"Garbage."

"Garbage?" he echoed.

"Absolutely."

The flute music ebbed and flowed and she stared unblinkingly up into his eyes. Her skin was the kind they put in cosmetic ads—the kind that didn't need any cosmetics—which was just as well because she certainly didn't use any. Paris Delight of the fanciful, vaguely lush name, made personal simplicity an art.

"Do you know all the people in this building well?"

Her lips came together and he noted the lower lip was full and that she had a way of sucking it in slightly. "I know everyone most of the time," she said finally.

"It isn't right for a woman to live alone here. I'm amazed your grandfather hasn't put a stop to it." Now *that* was a clever approach.

"I'm not a kid, Tobias. And I don't live alone."

For an instant his mind went blank. "Not alone?" He surveyed her narrowly. "Who lives with you?"

"Next question?" she asked without inflection.

If she was living with a man, he was dead in the water. "You ought to lock the door to your apartment and the door to the street."

"The intercom doesn't work."

He took a moment to make a connection before saying, "Then fix it. Better yet, move out of this crumbling pile of stones."

"I like this crumbling pile of stones. I *love* it." The faintest trace of color rose over her high cheekbones. "I *absolutely* love it. If I could choose anywhere in the entire world to live, this would be it. I'm never, ever going to move from the Pioneer Square area and I'm sick of people telling me—"

"Okay, okay." He held both palms aloft. "I get the message."

"This is prime real estate," she continued as if he'd never spoken. "Do you have any idea how much it's worth?"

"Yes, of course." As Seattle's leading developer, he ought know better than anyone.

"There are thousands of people who would give a great d to get their hands on two floors and a roof garden slap b in the middle of Pioneer Square. And I'm never moving o

"Right."

"You aren't welcome here, Tobias."

Funny, she must have used his name hundreds of time he had no recollection of actually hearing her say it t tonight. "I may not be welcome, but you're going to be came."

"I doubt that."

"Trust me."

She gave him an incredulous stare and produced a sheet of thin felt from a shelf beneath the bench. This she spread over her work. "I try to avoid being rude," she told him, rubbing her hands on a rag and walking to the middle of the room with its exposed, red brick walls. "You were a troublemaking little boy and a nasty pubescent person. You grew up into a supercilious teenager and an arrogant young man. I could go on, but I won't. We both know you don't have many secrets from me."

Tobias whistled soundlessly and let his eyes follow the dark wooden beams that traversed the space beneath an open, vaulted ceiling lined with cedar boards.

"I don't trust you," Paris said. "And I don't like you. You shouldn't have come here and you know it. Please leave."

Pushing his hands into his pockets, Tobias wiggled his bare toes inside warm leather deck shoes. He'd considered every possible way to get himself out of the bind he was in and they'd all evaporated—except one. He had to have Paris Delight's help and he had to have it now. Without it, he stood to lose a great deal of money and that might not be the worst that could happen. His reputation could go right down the toilet, too.

"Please go—"

"I need your help," he said simply. "That's why I came. To ask you to help me."

She stood close to him now. The top of her head was on a level with his mouth. She must be five-foot-eight, or even nine. But her bone structure was small and, with her translucently pale skin and unblinking deep blue eyes, the awful gauze dress made her appear wraithlike, a collection of bones inside a shapeless drape.

"Will you help me?" he asked her and touched her upper arm.

She leaped away. "It's too late."

Her response startled him. How could she possibly know, unless . . . Damn, the old man had already contacted her after all.

"Look, I know what you've probably been told about me, but I deny it. I deny it categorically."

"Hah!" she said. No one word should be able to convey that much disgust. "You have incredible nerve."

"I don't like begging," he said with complete honesty. "But I'll beg if you want me to."

"I want you to go away. Men like you make me nervous."

He made *her* nervous? "I'm a very honorable man."

"Hah!"

Dammit.

Paris stalked to a rocking chair fashioned from twined willow wands and sat down. Using her bare toes, she rocked back and forth and fixed him with a burning dark gaze.

"You'll get splinters in your feet," he commented distractedly. She was not going to deter him. "You ought to wear shoes."

The chair swung more furiously.

Tobias pulled a stool away from a low, square table and sat down facing her. "Give me a chance. That's all I ask. Let me explain my side of things, then decide if I deserve a chance to prove I'm not some sort of monster."

"You need therapy. People like you can be helped if they really want to be."

"What—?" Whatever happened, he mustn't lose his temper or his head. "How exactly would my seeing a therapist help?" Old man Delight had to be shut up and stopped, in that order.

"There's a difference between . . . between passionate involvement and an insane drive to . . . to *possess.*"

Coming from a woman whose blood temperature probably ran at sublukewarm, those were wild words. "I'm a passionate man," he said. "When I set out to accomplish something, it becomes a passion. I wouldn't call that insane."

Paris stopped rocking. Beneath the dipping hem of her dress she hooked a slim foot behind the other ankle. "When a man keeps . . . When he keeps forcing himself where he's already been told he's not wanted, that's not normal. Overwhelming the weak to satisfy an enormous . . . enormous *appetite,* is . . .

It's wrong, that's all, and there's nothing I can do to change the truth in that."

"You've got it all wrong."

"I've got it absolutely right. I got it from the mouth of the person best qualified to know."

Pops Delight. Shit! That old bastard had poisoned Paris's mind. That also meant he was probably to blame for the rumors that were beginning to circulate—ever so discreetly—through Seattle's business community.

"Paris, just listen to me. I—"

"No. No, I can't listen to you. I put family loyalty before anything else in my life. That's a habit I don't intend to break."

Evidently she didn't smell danger even when it got real close. "You said you avoid being rude," he said coolly. "You're being rude."

She shook her head slightly. "You're still arrogant. You think because you're some sort of hard hitter in this town you can push people like me—and my family—around."

"Your family and mine started out together," he shot back. "Our grandfathers were partners."

"They surely didn't stay partners, did they?" Her fine nostrils flared. "By the time your grandfather died, they hadn't spoken to each other in years."

"Because your grandfather was, and is, a jealous, hard-headed . . ." He closed his mouth, but knew it was already too late.

"Go on," she said. "Finish what you started."

"This is ridiculous." Tobias stood up and walked around her to an open sash window. "I didn't come here to argue with you about a dead feud."

Paris didn't respond.

Absently, Tobias noted how clean she kept her windows and that there were big clay pots filled with an unlikely mix of cottage garden flowers on the fire escape outside. Marigolds and white stocks, magenta nicotiana, multicolored sweet Williams and pinks. Vines crowded with huge, unfurling white flowers spilled down from the landing above. He could smell a subtle, lilylike scent.

He had to make Paris see his point of view. He said, "Look—"

"This amazes me." She cut him off. "I can honestly tell you that if someone had asked me what was least likely to happen today, I wouldn't even have *thought* of a visit from you."

"Thanks."

"Well, why would I? We haven't seen each other in years. And you've already admitted you're only here because you want something from me."

"Yes," he said, focusing on the rangy cat that had risen slowly to stand with all four feet together and its back arched like a croquet hoop.

"And we know what you want and why I won't do it."

"Yes," he said through his teeth. "We know why you *think* you won't do it. I'm going to change your mind."

"*No*. Absolutely, *no*. You have a problem. You've admitted it. What you haven't admitted is how serious it is. You are a sick man."

He turned sharply. "What the hell do you mean by that?"

"I've already told you."

From the back, he saw that her tightly restrained hair was thick. It shone blue-black in the failing light. Tobias considered before saying, "Why don't you tell me about my sickness again? I seem to have missed the full impact of your diagnosis."

"I'm tired," she told him. "Talk to someone who understands the kind of control problems you've got. I'm not qualified to help you."

"Pops talked to you, didn't he?"

She became still, then twisted to look back at him. "Pops?"

"Yes, Pops. Your sainted grandfather. The man we already spoke—"

"I know who my grandfather is. What does he have to do with this discussion?"

"When you were a little girl," he said. "Even when you were very young, I thought you were . . . *deep.*" At least he'd stopped himself from saying, *difficult.*

In this light her eyes were royal blue. "Go on, Tobias," she said.

Some would say Paris Delight was beautiful. Tobias frowned at the thought. Her face was delicate, with an ethereal quality.

The realization that she was waiting for him to continue disconcerted him. He considered stroking the cat, but changed his mind. "Pops is wrong," he said, too loudly. "The old buzz . . . He can be very persuasive, but he's wrong."

Paris stared at him.

"The only reason he's making my life hell over this is because he can't let go of the past."

"Don't say nasty things to me about Pops." There was steel in her words now.

He'd rehearsed and rehearsed this meeting and not one line had come out as planned. "He's standing in my way—the way of progress, that is," he amended quickly. "Because he refuses to put aside an argument he had with a man who died *ten years ago,* for God's sake—he will *not* listen to reason."

She shook her head slowly and blinked. "I have no idea what you're talking about."

"Yes, you do. He's primed you. He told you what to say if I came here. He's sitting up there in that damned valley he thinks he owns and he's interfering with progress that *needs* to take place."

The rocking chair creaked and she got up. "You're here to talk about Pops?"

"Yes." He wrinkled his forehead. "And you've got the whole thing one hundred percent wrong. I'm not trying to control anyone. I paid for something and now I want to use it. Do you see anything unfair in that?"

"I—"

"*Do* you?"

She puffed up her cheeks and let the air escape.

"Paris," Tobias persisted. "Do you disagree that I've got a right to use the land I bought from Pops?"

For an instant she appeared bewildered. Then she said, "What land did you buy?"

"Oh, come *on.*" No wonder his grandfather, then his father had given up on the Delights. "Give me anything, but don't give me the ignorant act. That old . . . Before my grandfather and my dad were killed, Delight wouldn't part with a thimbleful of his precious Skagit Valley *black gold.*"

"Pops lives on that land," Paris said, but there was uncertainty in her voice now. "That's where he's lived for thirty years. He loves it there."

"My grandfather should never have allowed the middle section of that land parcel to go," Tobias said grimly.

"*Allowed* it to go?" She moved closer. "Pops bought the parcel with him. They were partners. Pops gave your grandfather the largest share."

"That's rich." He bowed his head and held back his anger. "Pops wanted the water rights so badly, he talked grandfather out of the whole, goddamn midsection. Jesus Christ. Every time I think about it I can't believe he could have been that trusting."

"*Trusting?*"

"Yeah, trusting. He never thought Pops would build that frig— Who would have expected a supposedly sane man to build a minicastle slap bang in the middle of one of the best stretches of farmland in the state and *sit on it?*"

"This conversation is definitely over."

"It definitely is not over. You need to know the full story."

She backed away. "Please leave."

"He didn't tell you he's sold everything but the acre he lives on, did he?"

"You're lying," Paris said. She made a move toward the door.

Tobias walked deliberately to the far side of the room where several rough-glazed earthenware pots stood on a collection of small tables of various heights. He picked up a squat round pot and turned it upside down.

"Why would Pops sell his land?"

He glanced up quickly. Her arms were pressed to her sides. "Because he needed the money," he told her.

"No. No, that's not true. How could it be?"

Tobias felt a shifting uneasiness. "He's old, Paris. It's not unusual for an old man to get to a point where he needs to start realizing capital from various sources."

"Everything but *one* acre?"

"Yeah. Should be plenty for him, though."

"Pops doesn't like . . . He's very private."

So private he thought he should be allowed to take money for land, then threaten retaliation if the buyer wanted to develop it. "Paris, just listen to me, okay? Hear me out. The two of us can help Pops through this. His pride's getting in the way of what's best—for everyone."

"I need to talk to him."

"Yes." Their eyes met and for the first time he knew they were both thinking the same thing. Tobias said, "I've got access to a ham radio." A ham radio was the only way Pops Delight had communicated with the outside world for five years.

"Pops wouldn't sell his land."

He felt uncomfortable when he said, "He has sold it. He's been selling it to me in lots for seven years. Now he won't . . . He won't leave my people alone to do their jobs. And he's making threats."

"What kind of threats?"

Telling her the threats were vague but that someone was leaking rumors that he was heading for financial ruin and he blamed her grandfather wasn't likely to get him what he wanted.

"What?" she pressed.

"Threats that I'd rather not talk about directly. I came here with a plan. You've always been Pops' favorite."

"Forget it," she said. "If you think he'd put up with me interfering with his business affairs, you're mistaken."

"Of course he wouldn't. But if he thought you and I . . ." His tongue felt suddenly thick.

Paris's right hand went to her cheek. She didn't look twenty-nine, Tobias decided; in fact, barefoot and devoid of makeup, she looked much as she had as a teenager.

He began again. "Pops is a strong-minded man and I respect that. But you always did know how to soften him up. If you told him you and I were, er, *friends,* he'd stop thinking of me as—"

"*Friends?* We're not friends."

He would push through to the end and be done with it. "I

came to ask you to tell your grandfather you and I are involved."

"*Involved?*" Her husky voice rose.

"Yes," he said, and knew he was blustering. "*Involved.* As in, *deeply* involved. This isn't just for me. It's for you and everyone else in your family and mine. We have to deal with this and move on. It won't be for long, just till Pops agrees to stop setting those damn wolves of his on my surveyors and doing whatever else he says he's getting ready to do—"

"Stop!" She closed her eyes. "Stop this. First, Pops doesn't have wolves. They're part wolf and part German shepherd and very sweet."

"Not when they're coming over a fence at you," he muttered. "I don't want to argue. Tell Pops we're in love and—"

"*What?*"

Tobias winced. "Tell Pops we're in love and we think there may be something for the two of us in the future." Hell, it sounded even worse than when he'd first thought the idea up. "All I need is a diversion to get his mind off—"

"You're sick."

Tobias massaged his temples. "For God's Sake, Paris. I'm not a snake and you know I'm not asking you to actually *marry* me."

"You—"

A single rap on the door made Paris stop.

"Paris?" a voice called. "You in?" The door opened and a tall woman with blue-gray hair strode in. "There you are, you poor darling. I came just as soon as I could get away. I'm on again after the intermission, so I mustn't be long. Why didn't you *tell* me?"

"I'm fine," Paris said. If possible, she turned even paler. "We'll talk about it later, okay, Sam."

"Samantha, if you don't mind, darling," the woman said. She held a pair of black sling-backed pumps by their straps. "I'm having one of my days. One of my weeks, actually. Last night I really thought I wasn't going to manage to go on at all. I couldn't get in the mood. Now, I want the details. Wormwood said the police aren't interested."

It was clear the woman hadn't noticed Tobias. He watched

Paris intently. There was something she didn't want said in front of him.

"Sam," she said. "This isn't a good time."

"I *know*, darling. That's why I came just as soon as I heard— Samantha, dear, all right? You shouldn't have kept this from me. I'm going to find a way to help. We all are." She dropped the pumps and swept off her very realistic blue-gray wig. "Let me sit down and rest my poor feet. Then you're going to tell me *everything.*"

Paris drew herself up very straight. "Sam, I've got company."

"Oh." The woman swung around and saw Tobias. "Oh, hell, why didn't you say so?"

"I'm saying so now," Paris told her. "This is Tobias Quinn."

He looked into the expertly, and heavily, made-up face of a man with a blond crew cut. The tight, black silk suit, trimmed at the neck with rhinestones, must have set him back more than a bit.

Tobias was confronted with the odd spectacle of a man in drag who looked as if he'd like to kill him.

"Who the hell are you?" Sam—or Samantha said.

"Tobias Quinn." Somebody ought to take Paris's life in hand, but it wasn't going to be him.

"Quinn," the man said, advancing in his black fishnet tights. "Do I remember that name?"

"Possibly," Paris said, entirely too sweetly. "Tobias is my sister's husband."

Two

"*Ex*-husband," Tobias said, looking not at Sam but directly into Paris's eyes. "My ex-wife and I have been divorced for two years."

He had actually come in here and suggested she pretend they were "involved." Paris made herself look steadily back at him while she said, "Sam and I are very old friends."

"Very," Sam said. He radiated hostility. "You okay, Paris?"

She couldn't help smiling—until she realized that Tobias did, indeed, appear predatory. "I'm fine," she murmured. The man she'd once thought she loved had narrowed his gray eyes to slits and fastened his attention on Sam.

"Do you make a habit of letting yourself in here?" Tobias asked.

Paris bristled but before she could respond, Sam advanced and assumed the stance of a man ready to fight. "You're Cynthia's husband," he said, his voice flat and menacing.

"Ex-husband," Tobias said. He set down the pot he'd been holding and braced his feet apart. "I thought I already told you that."

"The guy who—"

"*Sam!*" Paris implored. "There's nothing you need worry about here." All she needed was to have Sam start spouting all the intimate details Cynthia had unwisely shared about her marriage.

Undeterred, Sam hooked a thumb in Paris's direction. "This lady is a very dear friend of mine. She doesn't look happy and I've got a hunch it's more than some punk forger that's making her that way."

"Sam—"

"Leave this to me," he ordered, flashing her a warning with green-shadowed blue eyes. "We look after each other down here, Mr. Quinn. Weirdos like you aren't welcome."

Paris played her fingers over her mouth. Tobias's expression showed clearly that he didn't regard himself as the weirdo in the room.

"What's this about forgers, Paris?" he asked. "Are you in some sort of trouble?"

"Oh, the boy's quick," Sam said, snorting. "Someone's copied your collection and cost you an entire season's take and he wants to know if you're in *some sort of trouble.*"

Paris cast Tobias an amused glance—and saw that he was anything but amused. "Tobias was just leaving," she said. "Weren't you?"

"Not until I'm sure you're all right."

She opened her mouth, but couldn't form words. He was right when he said they'd known each other since she was born. But Tobias Quinn had never, ever shown any inclination to consider her as anything but a shadow in his existence, a shadow he wouldn't miss if it disappeared.

"What happened?" he continued. "Someone came here and copied your work?"

"This is not the time to discuss my personal affairs," she told him. To Sam, she said, "You'd better get back. The intermission's got to be about over."

"Intermission from what?" Tobias asked suddenly.

"The revue at the Blue Door," Paris said quickly. "Get going, Sam. *Please.*"

"They'll cover for me. Lips can go on first."

"I think the lady just told you to get out," Tobias said, and there was absolutely no doubt that he looked mean.

A mental picture of Tobias landing a punch on Sam's scarlet painted mouth was more than Paris could tolerate. She went to Sam's side and threaded her arm through his. "Come on," she said. "I'm absolutely fine. Of course, I'm going to be a total wreck when all this really sinks in. That's when we'll all have to have a powwow." She steered him to the door, picking up the shoes he'd dropped on the way. "I'll come over to the club later. Tell the others to stick around."

"Wormwood was gibbering, poor old fart," Sam said, still straining to look back at Tobias. "He said that hag up at Fables threatened to spread the story all over town if you don't take the whole collection out of circulation."

"It wasn't quite that straightforward, but I'll be okay." The very last thing she would ever have wanted was for Tobias Quinn to hear that she was in deep professional trouble—particularly after what he'd just told her. Not that she believed his tales about Pops.

Sam went, grumbling, from the apartment and she shut the door behind him.

"Do you make a habit of hanging out with transvestites?"

"Oh, that's *it.*" Making fists, she marched across the room and whipped the cover from her workbench. "That kind of ignorance isn't worth bothering with, but maybe you can learn something. Sam's not a transvestite. He's a female impersonator and an extraordinary one."

"Are all your friends like him?"

"No." There was no way she'd be able to concentrate now. "Some people might say most of my other friends are strange."

In the silence that followed she gave in to the urge to study him—thoroughly. He'd only got better-looking, damn it. And there was something that hadn't changed at all; her throat still tightened at the sight of him and her heart beat faster and all the little muscles low in her belly wound into thrilled coils.

He smiled. For as long as she could remember, a smile from Tobias, albeit invariably an accident on his part, had been able to reduce her insides to mush.

"When did you get to be so lovely, Paris?"

She drew in a breath and it stuck in the middle of her chest. Damn him. His kind had a sixth sense when it came to gauging a woman's reaction to them. Not that her reaction would be different from most women's.

"I mean it," he said, as if reading her mind. He pushed his hands into the pockets of his jeans and walked lazily to stand on the opposite side of the bench from her. "I used to think you were a prissy, colorless little thing."

"Thank you very much."

"Not at all. It takes a strong man to admit he was wrong. I was wrong."

She smoothed a piece of polished black tourmaline. Captured in quartz, it glowed mysteriously. This man was mysterious—and he was dangerous. She had an expert witness to that fact.

"I can't help you," she told him.

"Look at me," he told her, and when she did, he said, "I think we should help each other, don't you? It appears we're both in trouble."

Tobias was well over six feet tall, leanly muscular and possessed of an aura of barely restrained energy. And he was, as anyone who had ever known him would agree, an unconventional maverick. His thick, dark hair was drawn back from a peaked hairline into a tail at his nape. The sharp angles of his face held wicked slants, slants where his brows flared and where his cheekbones stood out prominently, and in the shadows that slashed beneath those cheekbones. A thin white scar showed above one brow. His eyes were the dark gray of pewter.

The single gold hoop in his left ear reminded anyone in doubt that Tobias Quinn, mastermind behind the biggest, most daring development schemes Seattle had seen in the past ten years, made his own rules.

"Am I right, Paris?" he asked softly.

The bows of his upper lip were sharply defined. The firm lower lip was fuller and when he spoke he revealed the slightest overlap of the eye teeth. Paris had spent many a girlish—and not-so-girlish—hour mesmerized by the thought of Tobias's mouth.

She wasn't girlish at all anymore.

"Paris?"

She flicked her gaze to his. "You and I have nothing in common." Why did she still have a tiny part of her that wished it weren't so?

He reached out and settled a big hand on top of hers on the workbench.

She didn't pull away.

"How's Emma?"

His question surprised Paris. "Wonderful."

"Still holed-up at the Four Seasons?"

"She's at the Alexis, not the Four Seasons," she told him of her grandmother. "And she's not holed up, as you put it. She likes her freedom and a hotel suite gives her that. She hates cooking. Always has. Room service makes sure she doesn't have to cook anymore. And she can come and go whenever she wants to."

"Bit tough to do that with a drawbridge always up, huh?"

She went to pull her hand away but he closed his fingers around hers. "Sorry." He lowered his head and looked up from under dark, spiky lashes. "I like Emma. Actually, I've missed seeing her. All I meant was that I don't blame her for walking out on Pops when he decided to fill the moat and keep the draw bridge up. Bit confining, wouldn't you say?"

Paris didn't want to talk about this, to Tobias or anyone else. Her grandparents' separation still caused her pain.

"Will you help me, Paris?"

"No."

"Geez." He closed his eyes and grimaced. "What's it going to take? If you won't help me make him see reason, I'm going to have to get a court order for him to cease and desist. You won't like that."

No. But she didn't, for an instant, believe Tobias would do such a thing.

Suddenly he said, "What did you think I was asking you for when I first came here tonight?"

Paris drew in a sharp breath and felt her face grow hot. "I— nothing. I didn't know why you were here."

"Oh, come on." Propping his elbows on the bench, he lifted her hand and held it in both of his. With the tips of his fingers, he played with the tips of hers. "You can fess up. What did you think I wanted?"

The tips of her fingers were slightly rough from her work. The tips of Tobias's fingers were rougher. The effect of the friction between their skins made itself felt all the way to those tiny muscles deep in Paris's belly—and lower.

He bent her hand back and traced the lines on the palm. "What, Paris? You can tell me."

She watched his lips forming words, and his eyes as they followed the movement of his forefinger over her palm.

"Who lives here with you?"

Paris ran her tongue over the dry roof of her mouth. "No one you know."

"A man?"

"A man," she agreed.

"Your lover?"

She tried to jerk her hand away.

Tobias laughed and tightened his grip. He was too strong for her.

"Not your lover." He grinned in just the way she'd remembered. "Am I right?"

"You think you can seduce any woman you want to, don't you?" she said. "I know all about you, Tobias. You're trying to seduce me now."

"Me?" His flaring brows rose innocently over widened eyes. "How could you suggest such a thing of me. I'm a man of honor." Still smiling at her, he bent his head and blew softly across her vulnerable palm.

Paris shuddered. She shuddered and shut her eyes. The sensation was raw and for an outrageous exquisite instant she felt as if she were naked and his breath bathed her heated body.

"That's enough," she snapped, opening her eyes and tugged against his grasp until he let go. "A man of honor who drove his wife away after three years of marriage."

The smile left his face instantly. "We won't talk about Cynthia."

What on earth had she been thinking of, to let him wind his way around her senses for even a moment? "If you thought Cynthia was the way to get Pops to do what you want, you wouldn't be here," she said, furious with herself. "You still want Cynthia, don't you?"

He crossed his arms on the bench. "What makes you say that?"

Paris wasn't comfortable with him so close, but she wouldn't give him the satisfaction of thinking he could frighten her away. "Cynthia and I tell each other everything, Tobias. I know how often she hears from you."

He shook his head very slowly from side to side.

"It's absolutely pointless for you to pretend otherwise. You didn't contest the divorce because you didn't have a leg to stand on. And we both know why, don't we?"

"I don't think you know anything about what happened with Cynthia and me," he said softly, so softly, Paris's stomach flipped over.

"Can you tell me you haven't tried to get back together with her?"

He looked steadily into her eyes. "Why didn't I notice that you're beautiful?" he said. "It's not like me to miss details like that."

"You're changing the subject."

"You're right. Help me with Pops."

"No."

Tobias sighed. The only part of his face that wasn't entirely perfect was his nose, which bore the evidence of having been broken during a childhood baseball game up in the Skagit Valley. That had been when Pops and Emma were together and still happy, and Paris's mother was alive—and Tobias's grandfather, and his father, Lester. Tobias's step-mother and his step-brother, Nigel, had also been there, of course. Not too much later, Paris's mother had died. Then her father, Maurice, met and married Beryl, Cynthia's mother.

"What *are* you thinking about?" Tobias asked.

"How you broke your nose," Paris said and pressed her lips together.

He smiled thinly. "Long time ago."

"Long time," Paris agreed. Cynthia was just about the same age as Paris. Maurice had adopted Cynthia and the two girls had slowly become close friends.

"Used to be great when our folks got along, didn't it?"

"I guess so," she said, but knew she missed those days. "Things change and we have to move on." Maurice and Beryl had eventually moved to Idaho to run a food co-op. Then Pops and Emma had announced that they were disowning their only son on the grounds that he had bad taste in second wives and that he was "terminally boring."

"You and I could make ourselves responsible for pulling the families together again, Paris."

She only half-heard what he said. Cynthia was the beautiful, flamboyant one. Everything about her was larger than life, from her masses of red-blond hair and her turquoise eyes, to her marvelous, voluptuous body. Cynthia was the one all the boys had wanted to date and, later, wanted to marry. Even when Paris hadn't seen her sister for weeks, she could hear her marvelous, uninhibited laugh and visualize the way she walked—the way she grabbed the attention of any man who saw her.

Tobias had staked his claim to Cynthia when she was fifteen and he was twenty-two. He'd seriously told Maurice that he knew she was too young, but that he could wait. He'd waited far longer than expected—until Cynthia had grown tired of New York where she'd worked in some peon's position for a women's magazine while she tried to sell the mysteries she wrote.

"It could be great again, Paris," Tobias said earnestly. "All it's going to take is a united front from you and me. They'll all fall into line if they see we've got something going."

Paris looked into his clear gray eyes and saw the darker shadow of his black lashes. Cynthia had lived and breathed Tobias Quinn. All she'd talked about was how he made her feel and how she never wanted to stop feeling him make her feel that way.

He'd taken her love and twisted it. Two years had passed since the divorce and Cynthia was her old, flamboyant self. There was a great deal about her sister's lifestyle that worried Paris, in particular her obsessive preoccupation with her own overt sexuality, but at least she seemed happy. Paris wouldn't let Tobias interfere with that.

"She won't have you back," she told him.

His expression grew blank.

"Cynthia's writing again. She's got a marvelous series going about a hard-boiled Seattle cop. This one's going to fly. Don't interfere anymore, Tobias. Go away and leave her alone."

"You don't understand," he said, straightening. "I'm not . . . I'm not here about anything to do with Cynthia. When I walked in here, I . . . Well, take it any way you want to for now, but corny as it sounds, I'm not sure I ever really saw you before tonight."

It took all of Paris's willpower not to catch his words and take them to her heart.

He splayed a hand over his chest in a gesture she remembered him using since forever. "Forget I said that," he told her. "It doesn't matter—not now, anyway. Join me in putting a foolish old disagreement to bed, Paris."

His chest was broad and dark hair showed at the open neck of his rough, blue cotton shirt. He was drawn in shades of darkness—all of them dangerous, all of them compelling. She saw him in minute detail and felt the disintegration of the barrier she'd started building as a girl of fifteen, when she'd seen how he looked at Cynthia.

"Tell Pops we're in love, Paris," he said very quietly. "Who knows, maybe we were meant to come together like this. Maybe we can make the myth come true."

His words seeped in. "Damn you," she whispered. "Damn you, Tobias Quinn, for the manipulative swine you are."

"Hey—"

"No. No! I will not lie to my grandfather. Cynthia's right. You're an arrogant son of a bitch who never for one moment doubts that he can make any woman jump if he wants her to."

"Cynthia—"

"Don't you say one bad word about Cynthia. You made her suffer the way no human being should suffer. She ought to have made sure you suffered just as much. She should have seen you in jail."

"In jail?" He screwed up his face. "What the hell do you mean, in jail?"

"What I say." Paris marched around the bench and made to pass him. His hand shot out to grab her arm. "Oh, you're very good at manhandling women, aren't you," she said. "That makes you feel like a really big man."

"Goddamn it! Will you listen to me?"

"Listen to you pretend you didn't almost destroy my sister with your demands? Listen to you deny that you're an animal disguised as a man?" She paused for a breath. "Listen to you try to say you haven't been hounding her to come back to you ever since the divorce?"

"Yes," he hissed, the lines of his face saturnine. "Yes, I want you to listen to me say all those things."

Paris pried his fingers from her arm and rushed to open the door. "If I didn't love my sister, I'd tell her you came here tonight. I won't because it would hurt and frighten her. She's told me all about you, Tobias, and not a word of it is pretty."

"I'll bet. And now you're going to listen to my side."

"Out!" she ordered, and waited until he slowly approached. When he stood looking down at her in the doorway, she said, "You almost destroyed Cynthia with your demands. Now you're trying to use sex to make me come to heel. You are despicable."

"I wasn't using *sex*, for God's sake. I—"

"You use sex for everything," she cut in. "You're addicted to sex and that's why Cynthia left you. Get out."

He let her push him out onto the landing. "This is only the first round," he told her. "I'll be back."

"Not if I see you coming. If you do, I'll make sure some of the people whose opinions you value so highly know all about your perversion."

"Perversion?"

"Perversion, yes. Any man who forces his wife to walk around naked in front of him every minute of the time he's with her is perverted."

His mouth worked, but he made no sound.

"Finally speechless? You made her cook your meals naked and wash dishes naked." Her throat tightened and she fought to swallow. "And only a pervert makes his wife have sex several times a night in every sick way he can dream up."

Tobias found his voice. "Are you going to list those ways for me?" he asked.

His mood had become dangerous. Paris was beyond caring. "That would turn you on, wouldn't it? Well, I don't know all the ways, but you do."

"Tell me. Tell me one."

She thought frantically. "Well . . . Making her dress up like a schoolgirl and watch dirty movies, and . . ." Her face glowed with embarrassment.

"Go on," he said silkily. "Or are you really as much of a prude as billed?"

"No, I'm not." Her eyes prickled. "You liked to pretend you were seducing a schoolgirl and you made her do all the things on those disgusting movies."

"What things?"

"You took her clothes off and then you made her . . ."

"What did I make her do?" His face was rigid, the lines beside his mouth white.

"She had to get down on her knees and in front of you while you kept on watching, and . . . and . . ." She could not say it.

"And suck my cock?" He pulled the door from her hands. "Is that what I made her do?"

Paris pressed her hands to her face and turned away.

"Glad you're not a prude," Tobias said behind her. "I bet the worst part was when I sucked her back—*hard*—right? Sorry I don't have time to stick around for a full fucking evaluation. Later, okay, babe?" The floorboards creaked beneath his retreating feet.

The door slammed and she heard him call, "Later, Paris. I'll be back."

Three

Nigel Quinn rested his elbows on the wet bar. He clamped the phone to his ear with one hand and used the other to support his head.

"I told you," he said, feeling the too-familiar clenching in his gut. "Give me a little more time and we'll both win. I've got to have more time." He heard the desperation in his own voice. Desperation was bad; these people fed on it, and the fuller they got, the meaner they got.

The guy on the other end of the line was thinking and smoking. Nigel heard the indrawn breath and pictured one colorless eye narrowed as its owner dragged on a cigarette.

"Nice place you got there," the man rasped at last. "Gotta be worth three mil? Maybe four?"

More, Nigel thought. "How would I know?" he asked. "It isn't mine."

"So how come you use it like it was your own pad?"

"It belongs to a good friend," Nigel lied. "He doesn't use it most of the time. He let's me drop in when I'm in Seattle."

A smoky laugh grated along the line. "Don't fuck with me,

kid," the man said. "You know what happens to guys who fuck with Piggy."

"I'm not . . . I'm straight with you," Nigel said, but he was sweating.

"The fuck you are." Piggy coughed. "The fancy pad belongs to your brother. He moved out after his divorce and never got around to selling the place. Tobias lives on a houseboat these days. What the fuck kind of name is *To-bi-as*? The way I see it, all you gotta do is go to *Tobias* and say, 'I need a loan, big brother. Gimme the money I need or you're gonna find you was mistaken about your only brother.' Tell him that."

Tobias must never find out exactly what had happened to Nigel in Vegas. "Mistaken how?"

The laugh came again. "Mistaken in thinking you was his only brother. When you turn up as his only sister instead, that is."

Nigel flinched and instinctively cradled his crotch. The son of a bitch would do it and enjoy the exercise. He leaned farther over the wet bar. His legs threatened to give out and he needed to puke.

"Don't mind me," Piggy said. "I don't mean nothin'. Just get a little carried away sometimes. Comes of havin' too big an imagination. My old lady used to say I was born with more imagination than was good for a boy." He laughed and went into spasms of coughing before managing to continue, "There's a few bitches around what thinks my imagination's good, though. Never met a bitch who couldn't be persuaded to say how good it is."

Nigel pictured Piggy. Short and approximately as wide as he was tall. Thick sandy hair, slicked straight back, grew low on his forehead, but he had no eyebrows, just a shiny, bulbous overhang to his little, colorless eyes. He also had no neck. His fat face sat on his bulging collar, and he seemed to melt downward, shoulders to arms to wide hips and short legs. But Piggy's most memorable features were his hands. Pink and devoid of hair, they resembled clusters of stubby water balloons, but they fanned cards or dispensed blows with equal finesse.

And Piggy had a master's touch with a knife.

"So how's your love life?" Piggy asked. "Still seein'—"

"My love life is my affair," Nigel said. "Give me a couple more weeks to get the money together. Tell your people I'm good for it."

"I could." There was another suck on a cigarette. "Geez, I bet you and your lady friend really get it on in that pool *Tobias's* got there."

Nigel's brain computed Piggy's words slowly. The wet bar was in the basement of Tobias's multistoried Lake Washington home. Beyond a wall of glass, terraced lawns swept down to the moon-slicked surface of the lake. Bordering the lawns on either side, naturally forested slopes rose to a road that snaked along the ridge behind the cove Tobias had bought as the perfect private bowl to hold his fabulous house.

Between the wet bar and the glass wall lay Tobias's indoor swimming pool.

Sweat broke out on Nigel's face and ran between his shoulder blades. The little shit could see him. He was out there watching.

Nigel straightened up slowly and stared outside.

"Hi," Piggy said. "Miracles of modern science, huh? Wonderful what you can do with a cellular phone and the right kind of binoculars. How about a nice, friendly wave?"

"Where are you, dammit?"

"What does it matter? I been here before. How d'ya think I knew all about the place? I just gotta get through t'you that we can always find you. There ain't no point runnin' again, 'cause we'll find you again. And next time we won't waste time talkin'. Okay?"

Nigel fought for breath. He scanned the dark vista on the other side of the glass.

"I asked if that's okay," Piggy said, too softly.

"Okay," Nigel managed to say. "Two weeks. Give me two weeks and I'll get it for you."

"One week."

"I've got to have two." Two weeks and a hell of a lot of luck.

"You got ten days, kiddo."

Too much had to happen. Too many pieces had to fall into place just right. And he couldn't make any mistakes or Piggy and his nameless boss would have to stand in line to castrate Nigel Quinn.

"Ten days," Piggy repeated.

What he needed had already been offered—in exchange for the right kind of "favor." He only had to agree to obtain and provide certain information for a certain party and the money would start to flow. But could it all happen quickly enough? Probably, if he worked hard and fast and kissed the right ass—not his favorite pastimes.

"D'you hear me, kiddo?"

Nigel pursed his lips and said, "Twelve days."

"I ain't no fuckin' pawnbroker. Ten. I'll let you know where we'll make the pickup."

Any more argument would be pointless. "Yeah." With a little help from a lovely lady, he could pull out of this mess with a fat cushion to spare. "I'll be expecting to—"

The line went dead.

Nigel muttered, "Break your bleeding neck in the woods, Piggy," and hung up. Mentally, he visualized Piggy's head snapping off his beefy shoulders. A happy thought.

Less happy was the sure knowledge that the fat little man who moved so surprisingly swiftly and silently could still be out there watching.

Nigel started for the steps that led down to the exposed aggregate surrounding the pool. The flip of a switch would unfurl sun blinds inside the glass roof and walls.

He didn't make it to the control panel before a distant hum warned that a garage door was opening on the top floor. The driveway ran down to a phalanx of five garages that formed the only front entrance to the house. High, white stuccoed walls arched from either side of the garages to separate the property from the outside world. Where the walls ended, the sheer, forested slopes took over. Too bad Tobias hadn't figured out that only law-abiding men were kept out by walls and cliffs.

Glancing back through the windows, Nigel changed his mind about closing the blinds that were almost never used. They wouldn't keep anyone out, either, and they could become an unwelcome sign to Tobias—if he should be on the lake—that something was seriously wrong. Nigel's future depended on keeping up the pretense that although he'd made some poor judgment calls, everything in his world was more or less under control. If he could pull off that lie, and squeeze enough money—a very great deal of money—out of the man who wanted to pay for something Nigel hoped to give him, he could pick up what he'd been forced to abandon in Vegas a few months earlier. He'd have to set up shop somewhere fresh. Reno, maybe. Hell, he might even try his hand in New York. If there was one business with no frontiers it was the business of sex—sex and providing it in whatever way the customer's little heart desired.

Footsteps sounded on the metal spiral staircase leading down to the basement, and the key to ensuring Nigel's happy future came into view.

Backless, bronze, high-heeled sandals rang on the steps. Long, elegant legs made their slow, calculated descent. Encased in shimmering ivory hose all the way up to a clinging, peachy silk sarong skirt that could have doubled as a handkerchief without bulging out any pockets, these were the kind of female legs wet dreams were made of.

Despite the probability that—with the aid of "the right kind of binoculars,"—a pair of albino eyes could very well be watching every move he made, Nigel eyed those approaching legs and felt the precise instant when his dick announced the alert. By the time lush hips came into view, his equipment was approaching code red, and with the arrival of the lady's big, beautiful breasts, the firing button was begging to be pressed.

She came to him silently and began unbuttoning his shirt.

"This isn't a good idea," he told her.

"It's what you need," she said, and stripped off the shirt. "Did you stop by the store?"

"Yeah. I got what you wanted." And what he wanted, without wasting another minute, was to discuss the man with the money, the man who could buy Nigel's peace—his *life*. He had to convince this woman to do some persuasive talking for him.

She smiled at him and pushed the tip of her pink tongue between her teeth.

There was no reason not to deal with business and pleasure at more or less the same time.

Her mouth was full, and painted the same shade of peach as her skirt and short silk tank top. The top pulled over her erect nipples and left an inch of midriff bare.

Her tongue darted suggestively in and out. Just once he'd like to kiss her, but on the occasions when he'd tried, she'd averted her face and told him mouths were filthy.

Bending, she nibbled one of his nipples and dipped her hands into his crotch to support his balls and deftly gauge his readiness for her.

"Like what you feel?" he asked, trying to catch her ear in his teeth. He knew better than to restrain her at this point. She'd either leave marks on him, or walk away in a rage. "Is it hard enough now?"

Rather than answer, she straightened and went to Tobias's Nautilus gym. She turned to face Nigel, reached up to grasp a bar in both hands, and pulled.

For a moment, he watched the tank top hitch up as she extended her arms, then relax as she pulled the bar down.

The second time her arms rose, Nigel pushed the top above her bare breasts and kept on watching them move until he threatened to come in his pants.

"Tobias might decide to come back," he said, having difficulty drawing a full breath.

"Leave the fairy tales to me, lover," she said. "You're the one who told me your brother won't come here while you're in residence. I bet you he's with someone on that cozy little houseboat of his right now. So we don't have anything to worry about, do we?"

She was right. Nigel said, "No—nothing." Nothing except the possible presence somewhere outside of a man who'd have his hand inside his own pants by now.

He couldn't take it anymore. At the next extension of her arms, Nigel palmed her breasts and pushed them together. When she panted and arched her back, he caught her nipples in the V of his index and middle fingers and sucked them in turn. He was still sucking when she released the bar and skimmed the top off.

Nigel let her go and she walked slowly, hips swinging, toward the windows. He opened his mouth to shout for her to stay away, but brought his teeth snapping together. She'd only ask questions he couldn't answer.

"Start the video," she said, running her hands up her thighs, pinching her nipples, clasping her hands behind her neck and thrusting out her breasts—watching herself in the windows.

Nigel almost felt sorry for Piggy.

Doing as she requested, he pushed in a cassette and adjusted the reception on the big-screen TV at one end of the pool. The woman whose almost life-sized image appeared wore her blond hair in pigtails. Her demure white blouse and short pleated skirt gave her a schoolgirl look—until her face came into close focus. Despite the actress's youth, her expression was only a sultry, pouting parody of innocence.

Nigel could take or leave the movies, but for the lady who'd moved to lean on a towel rack beside the pool—where she had a better view of the screen—sleazy videos had a definite correlation with great sex.

She watched while the woman on the screen made ineffectual attempts to stop two men from taking off her schoolgirl white blouse and revealing oversized breasts restrained by a demure brassiere. Then she looked over her shoulder at Nigel and said, "Come here."

The men relieved the wriggling woman of the bra.

Nigel stopped watching the screen. Instead, he concentrated on watching his fingers untie the peach sarong skirt. She had her back to him. When the skirt fell, she crossed her arms on the towel rack and rocked her hips slowly from side to side.

Naked but for her high-heeled bronze sandals and shimmering, lace-topped ivory stockings, the woman offered up the most perfect bare ass he'd ever seen.

"Now," she demanded with her eyes fixed on the screen. *"Now."*

Nigel obliged. Sliding his arms under hers and using his grasp on her breasts as an anchor, he drove into her from behind. In that moment, as she convulsed around him, he thought once more of Piggy, grinned, and pounded even harder. When his climax broke, he forgot how much more arousing these games had been when Cynthia Delight Quinn had still been his brother's wife.

Four

Midnight at the Blue Door. Used perfume vied with used air for scent-of-the-night honors. Smoke drew a hazy gray-purple lens over the single spotlight on a small stage.

Spilled beer and greasy fingerprints marred round tabletops reminiscent of clear plastic cookies with shells and coins suspended where chocolate chips might have been. Through the plastic, green metal pedestals and patrons' legs were mildly distorted.

"Lips is really on tonight," Sam told Paris, morosely watching the thin, exceedingly tall bald man who whistled his way through a rendition of "Fifty Ways to Leave Your Lover."

Paris couldn't concentrate. Each time the front door opened she glanced over her shoulder, toward the dark alley outside the little club that was her second home. Mist had risen in the night's heat and she'd hurried to the Door over cobbles turned shiny black under the streetlights. The same mist seeped into the crowded room to mingle with smoke and turn the whole brew to a humid soup.

"She does love me, y'know," Sam said indistinctly—in the act of draining a coffee cup. "She's just got this hang-up about being independent."

Someone had chosen her. Fiddling with her glass of white wine, Paris looked at the door again. Someone had picked her out from all the other jewelry designers in the area and decided to ruin her business.

Random?

Or something deeper, more sinister?

Impersonal? A chance encounter with something she'd made that led to this . . . this *person* deciding he or she could make copies of Paris's jewelry and not get caught?

Or an act of jealousy or hate? A deliberate attempt to snuff out her career just when her designs had become sought after?

A piercing run of notes from the whistler, and Mrs. Lips's thunderous accompaniment on the piano, made Paris flinch.

"Look at her," Sam said, balancing on the back two legs of his chair. The black silk skirt rode up to reveal decidedly muscular and masculine thighs inside the fishnet stockings.

Sam wasn't talking about Lips's blue-eyed blond wife at the piano. "Ginna's a knockout," Paris said honestly, following Sam's intense stare to the willowy, glistening-skinned woman who owned the Blue Door. Ginna slipped between tables, smiling and chatting and bending here and there to whisper in a patron's ear while she delivered drinks. "And she does love you, Sam."

"No accounting for some people's tastes." The man who sat to Paris's left, facing Sam, spoke without inflection. Wormwood, the painter who lived in two of Paris's spare rooms, was brown. Brown hair and eyes, leathery skin stained by too much sun and loose, mud-colored shirt and slacks. He could be thirty or fifty—none of them knew or could tell.

Sam spared him a flat, blue glare. "Remember that piece of wisdom every time someone doesn't buy your zebra-striped john seats."

Wormwood's thin smile—revealing yellowed teeth—was predictable. "Touché, friend." A mild man, he rarely baited as he'd just baited Sam, and he always backed away from an argument. "I don't paint john seats. Furniture, remember. Chairs, tables, chests."

"Yeah," Sam said, his eyes returning to Ginna. "Forget I said that. I'm not myself. I asked her to marry me again tonight."

Wormwood and Paris folded their arms simultaneously and waited.

"She refused me again."

Paris drew in a breath.

"Women can be skittish," Wormwood said.

Sam, still crowned by his blue-gray wig, curled a lip in disgust. "What d'you know about women? Never remember seeing you with one."

Paris leaned to clasp his flexed forearm. "Wormwood's only trying to help," she told Sam. "Maybe if you quit asking, Ginna would come to the decision she wanted to marry you all on her own."

"We've been together for two years." Sam and Ginna lived on the floor beneath Paris's apartment. "She says she's happy the way things are."

"Shit," Wormwood said under his breath. "Here comes our favorite coffee king."

Paris didn't have to turn around to know it was Conrad, her adoring shadow and another neighbor, who approached.

"Hi, people." Conrad, almost thirtyish, almost handsome in a darkly smooth way, gave his customary greeting before swinging a chair around to mount the seat saddle-fashion. "Crowd's thinning out early tonight. Just as well."

By day Conrad operated an espresso stand conveniently near the Cow Chip Cookie shop. By night he tended bar at the Blue Door. Between those sessions he painted—with modestly increasing success—which Paris suspected was at the base of disillusioned Wormwood's dislike.

"Why is it just as well the crowd's leaving?" Preoccupied, Sam's question of Conrad didn't really require an answer. "Ginna needs the business."

"Business is great around here," Conrad said earnestly, his brown eyes shining. He gripped the back of his chair with big-knuckled hands. "But we've got to figure out what to do about Paris. The fewer ears around for that, the better."

Paris hunched lower in her seat, retracting her head turtle-fashion into the cowl neck of the black cotton sweater she'd pulled on before leaving her apartment.

Wormwood leaned over the table and patted her folded arms. "Relax, love," he said. "Conrad's right. We're going to find a way to catch this bastard."

"Thanks." Paris smiled. She knew what it cost Wormwood to give any credit to Conrad.

To a smattering of applause, the last live act of the evening drew to a close. The Blue Door was famous for its quirky performers.

"I guess Lips and his lady aren't joining us tonight," Paris commented.

Arm in arm, the woman craning her neck to smile up into her husband's face, the Lipses slipped away through a back door from the stage directly outside. They were also permanent residents of the building where Paris lived. She'd known them for four years but neither husband nor wife had ever revealed having other names.

When the back door swung shut Sam gave a theatrical sigh. "Such slavish mutual adoration makes you want to . . . *puke,* doesn't it?"

There was a short, uncomfortable silence before Ginna's favorite—and Paris's—Kenny G's acrobatic sax scaled the air and bounced off exposed red brick walls adorned with a blown glass frieze of yellow sunflowers, orange poppies and cavorting pink nudes.

Paris moved with the music and met Wormwood's eyes. He raised his brows. She knew he shared her thought that Sam wished he and Ginna were joined by more than a comfortable arrangement.

Laughing and jostling, a group at the next table got up to file out. Another burst of hot, damp air entered the room in their wake.

"So," Conrad said. "Paris has got big problems. We need a plan."

A hand settled on Paris's shoulder. She jumped and twisted around.

"Hi. I told you I'd be right back."

Paris looked into Tobias Quinn's disturbing gray eyes.

"Speak of the devil," Sam said clearly.

"Were you?" Tobias asked, equally clearly but without taking his gaze from Paris's.

"We sure were." Sam's voice vibrated with hostility. "Conrad said Paris's got problems. And here you are."

"And here I am," Tobias agreed blithely. "Ready to be of assistance to one of my oldest and dearest friends."

Paris felt like a butterfly on a board watching the pin approach. "This is Tobias Quinn," she said in a small voice. She already regretted telling Sam about Tobias's connection to Cynthia. Paris looked hard at Sam now, willing him not to make any reference to what he'd heard at her apartment. "Tobias's family and mine used to have a business connection." Next to Paris, Cynthia was probably Conrad's ideal woman. No point in giving the volatile boy an excuse to rattle any imaginary sabers.

"That's nice," Sam said, still truculent. He pushed his coffee cup away with enough force to crash it into Paris's glass.

"Who is this guy?" Conrad asked, visibly bristling at something he didn't expect—the appearance of a man who might get in the way of his own attempts to pursue Paris.

"You heard the lady," Tobias said with a mildness Paris knew was deceptive. "We're old friends. And we've got business to discuss."

He had her corralled. If she protested, there'd be the kind of fuss and attention she was determined to avoid. "How did you know where to find me?" she asked him, turning her head so the others wouldn't see the coldness in her eyes.

Tobias's lean face—all bold angles and sharp-edged shadows in the dim light—remained relaxed and smiling. "*You* told me. Don't you remember, darling? You said you were coming here later."

Darling? She'd gone from the nonentity he never noticed to *darling*—because he wanted something from her. But he had truly just pulled off another coup in the surprise department. When he'd slammed her door on his way out she'd have sworn he was mad enough to take much longer to come back.

Paris collected herself and unzipped her own smile. "So, I did tell you." She swept an arm to encompass the whole club. "What do you think of the Blue Door?"

Raising his slashing brows, he glanced around. "Well, if you like—"

"Yes," Paris said, cutting him off. "Marvelous, isn't it? I love this place. The fact that my best friends—who also happen to be my neighbors—meet here probably helps, but this is just about the most comfortable place in the world to me."

"Really?"

"*Really,*" Conrad said. "Glad to meet you. I'm sure you'll understand if Paris isn't available to talk business with you now. She's had a shock and we need—"

"*Conrad.*" Paris frowned at her self-appointed champion. "Tobias isn't interested in my little problems."

Paris felt Ginna approach before she actually looked up into the woman's classically sculpted face. Ginna's gorgeous smile, a white flash against a flawless complexion that glowed like rich coffee, was directed at . . . Tobias?

"Whether he's interested or not isn't the point." Sam slowly allowed the front legs of his chair to meet the wooden floor again. "Let us take care of this, Paris."

"*Tobias Quinn.*" Ginna's mellow, husky voice, heavy with pleasure, flowed over the tension. "Welcome. I'm honored to have you here. Sit down. Sit down." She took one of the chairs vacated nearby and placed it between Sam and Paris. "Be comfortable. What'll you have to drink?"

Silence fell on the group.

Tobias shook the hand Ginna offered, then leaned to kiss her cheek. "Good to be here. And good to see you, Ginna. I'll have a beer . . . Ballard Bitter?"

"You've got it." Ginna made to leave but turned back to lean over Paris. "You hanging in there?"

Paris patted the hand Ginna rested on her shoulder. "I'll be okay." Just feeling surrounded by people who cared eased the fear.

"We'll make sure you're more than okay," Ginna said. "We're going to help you through this." She slipped away in the direction of the bar with Sam following every fluid move.

When she was far enough away not to hear, Sam asked Tobias, "How do you know Ginna?"

With an offhand gesture Tobias said, "Met at some downtown business meeting." A navy sweater covered his shirt now. He sat between Sam and Paris and bestowed his smile, a smile that was vaguely wicked even when he tried for ingenuity, on all sides. "So, fill me in on what's happening," he said. "I already know a few general details, but I had to leave Paris's before she finished telling me the story." He turned absolutely innocent eyes on her.

Paris stared back, unerringly found her glass and took a long, tepid swallow—still staring at him.

He hooked his arms over the back of his chair. "I gather the police haven't been helpful."

"Not interested," Wormwood said, surprising Paris. "You can imagine how much spare time they've got, with everything that goes on down here."

"None, I guess," Tobias agreed. "Doesn't excuse indifference though, does it?"

Ginna returned with the beer and immediately left to help another customer.

"Murder and rape probably interest the cops more than someone ripping off jewelry designs," Sam said.

"That's why we've got to come up with some way to put a cap on this ourselves," Conrad said. "Fables. That's the place on—"

"Western," Tobias put in, leaning forward, solemn concentration in every line of his face and body. "Very upscale. I know the place."

"They take Paris's consignment pieces—a lot of them," Conrad said.

"Did," Paris commented without intending to say anything.

"Because they think some of the pieces aren't yours?"

She bowed her head. This wasn't something she wanted to talk to him about.

"That's not it," Wormwood said. "Someone copied a lot of the pieces that were for sale at Fables—and at Bits of Seattle on Second. They copied them and sold them in quantity to low-end gift places."

Paris closed her eyes and pressed them with her fingers.

"Good copies?" Tobias asked.

"Good enough for a customer who'd bought one of the real things to recognize and complain," Wormwood continued, more loquacious than Paris ever remembered—but he was being drawn out by an expert at getting what he wanted, they all were.

"So the stores with the real thing want to return the merchandise?"

"Bits of Seattle say they'll work with Paris," Wormwood said. "They'll lower the prices and warn customers. Fables wants Paris to take everything back."

"And pay any customers who return purchases," Sam said.

Tobias took Paris's hand from her face and held it. She could either let him keep on holding it—on his unyielding thigh—or snatch it away and risk her friends' reactions.

She left her hand on his thigh.

"Fables can't legally ask you to pay the customers," Tobias told her and, for a foolish moment, she almost believed he sincerely cared. "You did everything in good faith."

"Their not very subtle suggestion is that I made the cheap versions and sold them' myself." She made a fist inside his hand but rather than letting go, he rubbed her wrist slowly back and forth on worn denim. Her next breath didn't come easily. "If I don't want that suggestion to filter all over Seattle, I'll go along with the request—with no arguments."

"Shit," Tobias said quietly.

"Yeah, *shit,*" Conrad echoed. "Paris can't afford the loss."

"Tobias really doesn't want to know about it," Paris told him hastily.

"Sure I do. You know I do."

He pried open her fist and threaded their fingers together.

"She's doing well," Conrad continued, looking at Tobias as if he were an old and trusted friend. "Or she was. With the commissioned pieces and the consignments, another year or two would establish her. But it's tough to make enough headway to have a cushion. For buying materials and coping with anything unexpected—like this."

"Paris has as good as lost most of a year's work," Wormwood put in. "She'll hold on and bring out a new line in a few months. But we're afraid the same thing could happen again."

"Wouldn't it solve the problem if the fakes were bought out?"

"I said I was going to do that," Paris said. Her head began to ache and she longed to go to sleep and forget. "Fables said it was too late. Look, I don't want to talk anymore."

Conrad bumped his chair closer to the table. "We've got to make a move, Paris. The first thing I think we should do is—"

"Not now," she cut in. "Thanks, guys, but I want to be at it early in the morning. I'm going to cut out, okay?"

"Of course it's okay." Conrad slapped his palms on the plastic tabletop and stood up. "Come on, I'll take you."

"No need," Paris insisted. "You aren't off work yet."

"Ginna won't—"

"I'd come," Wormwood said, hunching his shoulders. "But I'm meeting someone."

"Hot date?" Sam began to rise. "I'll go with you, Paris—"

"Stay where you are," Tobias said, all affable reason. "I need a few words with the lady anyway."

A rush of cold sent goose bumps up her spine. Just as quickly, heat washed her skin. "I do not need a bodyguard, thank you," she said distinctly. "This is my area of my town and I'll go alone. But thank you all very much."

Tobias, pulling her up with him, gave her no choice but to stand. "There are times when it's kind to put your friends' feelings first," he said, playfully tweaking a strand of her escaped hair. "Carry on, folks. She's in safe hands."

Five

In safe hands?

The instant the club's door closed behind them, Paris pulled her hand from Tobias's. She started along Post Alley toward home.

He promptly caught up, rested an arm around her shoulders, and walked close enough at her side to make sure their hips brushed.

"I really don't need this," she said through her teeth.

Tobias laughed softly. "But I really do. Humor me."

The mist had thickened to fine, cool rain. Paris took off her glasses and blinked against the moisture. She walked doggedly, totally aware of the man beside her. Breaking away and running would hardly keep her dignity intact.

Dignity in Tobias Quinn's presence shouldn't matter.

It mattered a great deal.

"No woman should be walking alone in this area at night." The gravelly quality of his voice was subtly different. "I particularly don't like to think of *you* doing it here. Or anywhere else in the city—or in any city."

"So much tender concern," she said, disliking the snappish

note she struck. "You're quite an actor. Must be useful in your kind of business."

"*My* kind of—"

"How *do* you know Ginna?"

"I already answered that question."

"The only business meetings Ginna attends are area merchants' meetings. She wouldn't be at the kind of meetings you attend."

"Drop it."

She tried to pull away, only to find herself held more firmly. "I'm intrigued," she told him. "Did you two know each other sometime in the past?"

Tobias sighed, long and deep. "It's not my policy to discuss tenants."

Paris stopped. "Tenants?"

He moved her on. "I guess you'd say I'm Ginna's landlord. I own the building. We met when I was invited to one of those merchants' events you mentioned."

Irritation flexed muscles in Paris's jaw. "Why didn't I think of that. You probably own the whole block."

"Property and property development are my business."

She paused again. "You *do* own the whole block?"

"Let's talk about more important things."

So, he did own it. And God knew how much more property he owned. Paris shook her head. Quinn, as Tobias's company was called, had certainly done more than well since the days when their grandfathers had started out together in land speculation. Pops had made out well enough—particularly with the fortune Emma brought into their marriage. But Sam Quinn—Tobias's grandfather—had gone on to found an impressive empire.

"Tell me you won't go out alone at night here anymore."

She snorted and ignored the request.

Tobias shook her slightly. "Paris? Say it."

"Don't be ridiculous. I'm almost home. You can leave me and be on your way with a good conscience now."

They'd turned onto Yesler Way and reached the wrought-iron

pergola at the south end of Pioneer Place Park. Triple-globed streetlights cast a yellow-white wash over brick paving.

A grunt came from the pergola and Tobias turned her deliberately toward the row of sleeping bodies on benches protected by the ornate shelter.

"Hardly with a good conscience," he murmured. "I'm seeing you home. And I'm asking you to let me talk to you. No games, Paris. No tricks. This is serious. I wouldn't be here if it wasn't."

She stopped herself from telling him some things didn't need to be said.

They walked on, crossing Yesler to First Avenue in silence.

His big arm pressured her shoulders. Not an unpleasant pressure. Just an unfamiliar, inappropriate pressure.

This was the one man in the world she should absolutely refuse to see. Beneath the smooth exterior he'd cultivated lay a dark power. She might not be sophisticated, but she knew seething sexuality when she felt it.

And this was the one man in the world she absolutely wanted to see.

Paris swallowed, then kept her mouth open to breathe.

Wanting Tobias Quinn was wrong.

She didn't want him. How could she? She hadn't seen him in years—or thought about him. Not really.

She did want him.

She had thought about him.

How, or why, were questions she couldn't answer. She *could* identify guilt when it hit like a blow.

"You like it down here, don't you?"

"Uh-huh," Paris said. "Absolutely."

A shape rose from a doorway and shuffled toward them. Tobias skillfully skirted the man, who carried on his way.

Rock music blasted from the Colour Box. Steamed windows turned customers to fuzzy, swaying, glass and bottle-tilting shapes.

Another block and Paris turned the corner at South Main. "Home, sweet home," she said, arriving in front of her building. She wiped the lenses of her glasses on her sleeve and pulled

them back on. "Thanks very much. Watch out for yourself going home."

"I don't want to keep pushing, Paris."

In the act of opening the street door, she stopped. "I can't
talk to you anymore."

"Why?"

"You know why."

"I know why you think you can't. Look at me."

Slowly, Paris turned around. She stood at the top of the three
steps leading down to the sidewalk. Tobias's face was turned
up to hers, his features sharply defined in the harsh light of
the streetlamp.

His eyes were narrowed against the rain. Black hair had fallen
over his brow. Pressed shut, his wide mouth with its uptilted
corners looked hard . . . and as if it needed other lips to make
it warm and soft . . .

"If you won't talk to me, will you please just listen?" His teeth
shone a little, and the pale planes over his cheekbones.
"Please?"

Paris did what she always did when she didn't want to say
what she wanted to say. She bowed her head and said nothing.

In the silence, she felt Tobias move, heard his feet on the
steps. "Thank you," he said and waited until she raised her
face again. "I promise you won't regret it."

"I wish I believed you." Resigned, confused, heavy inside with
some muddled longing she didn't intend to identify, Paris
opened the door and walked into the hallway.

No light showed under the door belonging to Mary—the elderly woman who lived on the ground floor—or under any of
the doors Paris passed as she climbed the flights of stairs to her
apartment.

Tobias climbed right behind her.

Everyone else, except Lips and his wife, was still at the Blue
Door and probably wouldn't return for hours. Wormwood—
whom they speculated had a secret male friend he visited most
nights—might not be back at all.

When Paris hesitated before her own door, Tobias reached
around her and pushed it open. "Before we go any farther,"

he said, following her inside and shutting the door again while she switched on a light. "I apologize for talking to you the way I did when I was here before."

"You mean you apologize for talking about the things you made my sister do?" She turned cold again.

Tobias stared unblinkingly at her. "Is your . . . Is the person you live with at home?"

She kicked off her shoes. "I don't live with a person. A person lives in my home. He has two rooms I don't use and no, he's not here."

He turned his face sharply away, but not before she saw the faintest of smiles curve his mouth.

The knowledge that she wasn't really "living" with a man pleased him. Why, *damn* it? A chiding voice in her head said, *he's only pleased because he's getting what he wants—a chance to push for your cooperation without interruption.*

"You never wore shoes as a kid, either," he said.

Wordlessly, Paris went to her rocking chair. She stared at her workbench, at the shelves laden with tools beneath. Working would help her shut out thought.

"That's another thing you did. Ignored me."

"You didn't talk to me," she said, tilting her head to look at him. "Cynthia's over you now."

He passed her and stood near a window. "Good."

"Cynthia doesn't live here."

"I didn't suppose she did."

"Didn't you? You do know she's an equal owner of this apartment?"

"Equal with you? Yes. Emma gave it to the pair of you. I never understood why, since Cynthia isn't really related to her."

"Cynthia's my sister. My father's daughter."

"Not by blood."

She used her toes on the floor to rock the chair. She could hardly blame him for not understanding how she felt about needing to take care of Cynthia—when allowed to do so. "Dad adopted Cynthia after he married Beryl. That made us sisters as far as I'm concerned. She's the only sister I've got and I care about her." Emma hadn't wanted Cynthia's name on the apartment deed. Paris had insisted and she was still glad her grand-mother had finally agreed.

"As I already told you, Cynthia has nothing to do with my coming to you."

No, he'd come to ask her to pretend the two of them were in love! "I hope what you suggested you do want was a joke." It had to be.

"I'd like to help you with this forgery thing."

"I'm managing just fine." Surely he didn't believe he could manipulate her with phony concern.

"You aren't managing at all. You're foundering."

Paris shot to her feet. "Don't tell me what I am. Or what I'm *not.* You've got about ten seconds. Then I want you out of here. I need to work."

He regarded her for what felt like far longer than ten seconds. "You're really hurting, aren't you? And—nice as they are—your friends can't help. Can they?"

The empty chair continued to rock. Paris bent to stop it.

"Can they?" Tobias prodded.

When she straightened, he was closer, close enough for her to see the start of dark stubble on his jaw. She said, "They care. That helps," and swallowed loud enough for them both to hear.

His gaze went to her throat and rested there.

There was the subtlest shifting of air and atmosphere between them. Paris stood very still, held as if the tension between them was a sharp blade on smooth skin—the slightest move would cut.

Tobias looked from her neck to her mouth, to her eyes and back to the pulsing place in her throat. She had imagined him kissing her there—imagined it again now.

Letting her breath hiss out, she bowed her head. Guilt was more than a blow. Guilt almost buckled her knees.

"You always did that, too."

Paris closed her eyes.

"And that."

"What?"

"Hid your face and closed your eyes when you wanted to get away from something," Tobias told her.

"You don't know what I'm feeling. You never did. Why would you? It didn't matter to you."

"Did you want it to matter to me?"

"No!" She did look at him now. "Damn, you, Tobias. Your ego was huge when you were a nasty little boy and it's only gotten bigger."

"Now that I'm a nasty man?"

"You said it."

He grinned, suddenly and infectiously. "Remember the time you pinched Nigel so hard he cried?"

Paris couldn't stop her own smile. "He kicked one of Pops' dogs."

"Nigel never forgave you, y'know."

She chuckled. "I know. How is he?"

The grin slipped a little. "Still trying to grow up. But he's okay. I hope."

Nigel Quinn wasn't a subject that interested Paris. She said, "Good," and went to look out of a window at the dark shapes of rooftops and buildings against a sky that would lighten in only a few hours.

"Do you remember my dad?" Tobias said.

"Of course. We were all sad when he drowned—and your grandfather and step-mom, of course."

"So was I. I still am."

Paris had been in Europe when it happened. She'd had no concept of how the accident off some Caribbean island might have affected Tobias or Nigel and, when she got back to the States, the event had seemed like family history.

"Dad left something unfinished. He wanted to build an agricultural college. It was very important to him."

Lester Quinn—a busy man rarely at family gatherings—had become a distant memory to Paris.

"Maybe Pops mentioned it? Or your own father?"

"You know my dad was never interested in the business." He'd tried for a while but once her mother had died and he'd married Beryl, the efforts had stopped.

"How's the food co-op going?"

"Fine, as far as I know."

"And Pops never said anything about the college?"

"Pops doesn't talk about your family anymore, Tobias. Not since the . . . Not since he decided to sell his interest in the business." How strange to think that Quinn had once been Delight & Quinn.

"Of course not." Tobias came to stand at her shoulder. "You remind me of my dad."

She glanced up at him and quickly back at the much safer skyline. "What a funny thing to say."

"Not really. He was a dreamer. So are you."

A streak of orange and white hurtled down the fire escape from the top story and arrived in front of Paris. Grasping twin hooks at the bottom of the window, she hauled it up enough for her cat to leap past.

Paris shivered and Tobias immediately closed the window. "These windows don't lock."

"You're obsessed with locks."

"Anyone could come up the fire escape and get in."

"They could. They haven't yet. And I don't intend to spend any time worrying about it."

Tobias sighed. "You worry me."

"I can't imagine why. We're strangers."

"You know better than that. What's with the cat?"

"Aldonza?" Paris glanced at her disdainful calico critter. The animal had assumed her electrocuted cartoon cat stance. With teeth bared, hissing, she aimed slitted eyes at Tobias.

"As in *Man of La Mancha?*" he asked.

"What else? She doesn't think much of men."

"Figures."

Still spitting, Aldonza stalked away, apparently on her extended claws.

"I think maybe I understand why you like this place."

She kept her attention on the sky.

"You can dream here, can't you?"

Tensed muscles in Paris's back relaxed a little. "Yes. Yes, I can. Are you still in that beautiful house of yours?" The beautiful, extravagant house where he'd lived with Cynthia.

"Rarely. I've got a houseboat on Union Bay."

That surprised her. "Sounds cozy."

"It is. Unfortunately I haven't been featured on a radio talk show."

Paris smiled. "Sleepless in Seattle?" She had an instant picture of Tom Hanks alone in his comfortable houseboat receiving mail from countless women wanting to keep him company. "You're hardly the kind of man who has difficulty with loneliness."

"How do you know?"

"You're the most handsome man I've . . ." *Hell.* She shut her eyes. "I'm tired. You should go."

His laugh worked its way under her skin, into her nerves. She felt as if his laugh found her thoughts. He said, "Did you start to pay me a compliment, ma'am?"

"Forget it."

"No way. Thank you. You've made my night. You're pretty gorgeous yourself."

This began to remind her of a scene from a movie—one she was in the process of helping make. "Your dad wanted to build an agricultural college?" She wanted safe ground.

"Yes. He believed we need to move back toward our roots in this country. He thought there were great areas in Washington State where—with the right kind of training and incentive— young people could get excited about the land again."

"Farming? Surely we already know that the small farms are a thing of the past—mostly."

"Oh, he wasn't thinking only of small farms. He wanted a place where people could learn the most up-to-date methods of land management—on a big scale and on a small scale. And he wanted it to be accessible on a trade-school basis. Dad thought we were getting too far away from teaching usable skills—that we'd lost respect for them."

"I wish I'd known him better," Paris said thoughtfully. "Maybe you'll be able to carry out his dream."

"Maybe, I—"

"Tobias, I'm . . . This has been a tough day. One of several tough days."

His hand, settling on the back of her neck, jarred Paris to her toes and twisted a lot of points on the way.

"Let me help you," he said softly, turning her gently toward him and looping his fingers about her throat. "I'd like to. I'd really like to."

Paris kept her eyes downcast. "Thank you. But, no."

"Why?" His thumbs made small circles on her collarbones beneath the neck of her sweater. "I owe you for all the times I made fun of you when we were kids."

His attempt at humor didn't work. "You don't owe me anything." She was grateful for the sweater. Without a bra under her dress he might have seen how her nipples hardened at his touch—at the brush of his breath on her brow.

He was big and solid—and so very much a man.

Paris shivered.

"Cold?" he asked.

"No."

"What did the police say?"

She felt disoriented.

"Did they say they'd question the shop-owners who bought the copies?"

"They already have. No leads."

He rocked her slightly. "There must be invoices."

"You don't understand the way some of these things are done. It can be informal. A cheap invoice from a generic book. Handwritten. No printed name or address."

"And that's the way it was?"

She nodded. "I'm tired."

"I know." He took off her glasses and set them on the windowsill. She didn't try to stop him "I'm going to help you, Paris. I'm not going to let you refuse."

She shook her head.

"*Yes.*" His thumbs came up under her chin, drawing her face toward his. "A good private investigator. And I'll deal with the people at Fables, they'll—"

"No. No, Tobias. Thank you, but I can't"—she made the mistake of looking into his eyes—"I can't," she finished faintly.

In the pale glow of a single lamp his eyes were dark silver. Pewter. The gray of the sky in a gathering storm.

His gaze shifted from her eyes to her mouth and her lips parted.

Tobias breathed in slowly and angled his face over hers. His eyes closed and then he kissed her.

His mouth was firm and mobile and cool—cool, then warmer—but so very tender. Slanting carefully across her lips, the pressure of his kiss urged her to reach for more, to meet him.

Paris raised her hands hesitantly to his chest, flattened her fingers and palms where she could feel the contours of his muscles—and the hard beat of his heart.

He smoothed her shoulders, her back, lifted the bottom of her sweater and settled his hands at her waist. Heat shot into her flesh, speared an almost forgotten path into her belly.

"No." Paris jerked her head back. A shudder passed the length of her spine. "No." She touched trembling fingers to his lips, then to her own. "This is so strange. It's wrong."

Rather than release her, Tobias drew Paris closer. This time his kisses found the space between her brows, then her eyes when they closed. "If it's strange, it's the kind of strange we're going to enjoy," he whispered. "And it's not wrong, Blue. It's finally right."

Blue? He'd called her that when they were kids together. She'd never known why. Still didn't.

He laughed aloud. Why not. There was nobody to hear him up here. A chimney on a rooftop opposite Paris's apartment was his screen. Finding a new place to watch her from had helped cool his impatience. Word for him to make his move had to come soon.

Seeing Quinn with her had been a shock.

Paris wasn't stopping him from mauling her. The fools were slobbering over each other like junior highschoolers.

He would have figured the Quinn guy for a smoother performance. Not that this development was anything he'd planned on. Neither had the man with the money—whoever he was. Shit, he'd like to know who was paying him to teach that bitch a lesson.

Rain misted the lenses of the night glasses and he wiped them on his sleeve.

It wasn't his fault Quinn had shown up. It was hers. Anger swelled, making him suck in great gulps of air through his mouth. His head began to ache. He hated it when his head ached and he hated what caused his head to ache even more.

She made his head ache.

Fake.

Drab, baggy clothes over skimpy satin and lace.

She was leading the Quinn guy on the way she led others on. Pretending to be pure and shy.

All an act.

He knew what she really wanted.

Sometimes she didn't wear a bra. He knew that. He knew so much about her.

Why didn't Quinn take her clothes off.

His dick pressed against his zipper. Yeah, he'd like to watch Quinn undress pure, sweet Paris.

Not that Quinn would give her what she was going to get when he finally made his own move.

The glasses shook and he steadied them by pressing his elbows to his sides.

Kissing again. Looking at each other again.

Quinn's cock must be busting out of his jeans by now.

He cupped his own crotch and groaned.

Women like her wanted one thing and they wanted it hard and long and every way. And they liked pain. The quiet ones were always excited by pain.

He would give her pain. And she'd beg for more.

And the man with the money would pay him for his good times.

She kept drawing away from Quinn, bowing her head in that way that could make a man want to sink his fingers into her hair and pull until she screamed.

Teasing bitch.

"Squeeze her tits, Quinn," he muttered. "You poor fool."

When the time came, he'd squeeze them. Bite them. He'd do all the

*things pure Paris dreamed of behind her hot, quiet eyes. She knew they
were going to be together, but she didn't know how—or when.*

The room was ready.

Everything he needed—wanted—was ready.

How much longer would he have to wait for the go-ahead?

*Her ass was sweet. Round and sweet and white and begging for
pain.*

*He'd make himself wait. Tease her like she'd teased him. Then she'd
be his as often as he decided he wanted her.*

Rain ran under his collar and between his shoulder blades.

The pain in his head seared like fire behind his eyes.

Quinn hadn't been expected—not like this.

Thud. Thud. Thud. The pain began to turn his stomach.

She would pay for this.

Every detail of what he'd seen must be remembered and repeated.

Through the pain, an idea formed.

*This could be made to work for them. It could make it all easier. God,
why hadn't he thought of it right off. He was going to really clean up
when he told the money man what he had in mind.*

Thud, thud, thud.

He grimaced at the thumping and squinted through the glasses.

They were just sitting on the windowsill now. Side by side.

Cute.

*He'd always known there might be something difficult to deal with
after the fun was finally over.*

Bodies were a friggin' nuisance afterwards.

He laughed again, and cradled his thundering temples.

With a little luck, someone else could be left "holding" the body now.

Tobias covered her hand on the sill. "Are you as surprised
as I am?" he asked, staring straight ahead.

"More, I should think." What was happening to her? She was
the level-headed one, the woman who never gave in to whims.
How long had it been since Michael . . . ? "Would you like
some coffee before you go?" Michael was a subject best left
alone.

"You keep talking about me leaving," Tobias said mildly. He

took her fingers to his lips and looked at her while he kissed them. "I don't want to go anywhere."

Her stomach made a suicidal dive.

He laughed. "Don't look so stricken. I don't have any intention of trying to drag you off to bed . . . Yet."

Heat washed her cheeks.

Tobias laughed again. "I don't think I ever saw you do that. It's pretty. Is there anyone else, Paris?"

The question surprised her. She said, "No," without considering she might prefer to be less direct. She didn't add, *not anymore.*

"Good."

"Look, I don't think—"

"I do. Will you please think about allowing me to help you?"

She blinked rapidly. He'd made her forget. While he'd kissed her and held her, he'd made her stop thinking about the disaster rolling in, gathering speed.

"Will you?"

"I . . ." She *needed* help, dammit. "I'll think about it." Could Cynthia have exaggerated? Made it all up, even? Cynthia was the writer, the one with the imagination.

Overwhelmed by wretched guilt once more, Paris stood up. "Thank you for being so kind." She was disloyal.

"You make it easy to be kind. I want you to have your dreams."

He hadn't forced himself on her. He'd been sweetly sensual— and she still ached with wanting him. Smiling, she urged him to his feet. "I hope you get your dreams, too. Build the college. Your dad's college. That's your dream, isn't it?"

"It's . . ." His chest expanded and he exhaled slowly. "It's a dream that's become a necessity. I'm glad you understand that."

"I do. That's how I feel about my work, too."

"So you'll help me?"

Paris smiled questioningly at him.

"You'll help me?" he repeated. "You'll go to Pops?"

The skin on her face felt suddenly too small. "Go to Pops?

You mean . . . I thought the college was something . . . else. I thought . . ."

"You thought right." Urgency radiated from him. "Honestly, Paris. This—you and me tonight. This isn't anything I expected. But I told you I need your help with getting Pops off my back. Off my men's backs."

She stood very straight. "I thought you wanted to help *me*. Didn't you say that?"

"Yes. And I do. I will."

"You planned to soften me up." Folding her arms tightly about herself, she turned away. "God, I feel such a fool. Why on earth would I think you'd have anything to do with me unless I had something you wanted?"

"No! No, Paris. Please, believe me. I—"

"You planned every move. You swallowed your own rage at what I said to you and went to the Door to find me. And you pulled off exactly what you set out to pull off."

"The hell I did! Why would I think I could do that?"

Because he'd known how she'd loved him from when she was a gangly teenager, but she wouldn't give him the satisfaction of hearing her tell him. "An agricultural college to keep young people close to the land? How quaint. When exactly would you do something like that? After you finish ruining the land my poor old grandfather has loved for thirty years?"

"Damn it." Frustration loaded his voice. "And damn you, all of you Delights. Unreasonable to a man—and woman."

"Because we don't like being used." She hurried to open the door. "Yet again we part on a sour note, *friend.*"

"Have it your way. But we aren't through."

"Let me guess. You'll be back."

"You're damn right I will."

"Please don't start swearing at me again."

He drew level. "You've got this so wrong, you're going to be embarrassed."

"I doubt it."

"That land your *poor old grandfather* loves is exactly where I'm going to build that college. And student housing. And a town.

And everything else my father intended when he bought in the first place."

Paris's mouth dropped open.

"Yes," he said, walking to the top of the stairs. "I'm going to do it and you're going to help me."

"Over my dead body."

Paris saw a movement behind Tobias and peered into the gloom.

"If necessary," Tobias said, turning and walking into Wormwood.

Distracted, Paris asked, *"What* did you say?"

Dodging around her roommate, Tobias left without replying.

"Well," Wormwood said steering her back into the apartment and closing the door. "Don't give that another thought, dear. I'm sure your Mr. Quinn didn't mean what he said."

Six

A stiff breeze gusted up from Elliott Bay, drove gutter grit in eddies along the early morning streets. Discarded paper debris from the previous night swirled and slapped into railings and walls—rolled into doorways where sleepers still lay shrouded in bedrolls.

The early morning rain had cooled the city, but more heat was promised before the day was out.

Paris hurried on her way. She thought vaguely that she must have slept, at least for an hour or so.

Sleep or no sleep, she was a woman with a mission. If she didn't catch Grandma Emma before she took off on whatever quest she undoubtedly had set for the day, the opportunity would be lost until tomorrow.

Grandma Emma had very definite ideas and rules about her own schedule. Freedom at all costs. Tobias Quinn—damn him—had been right about one thing. The day Pops decided to fill the moat around his little castle home in the Skagit valley—and to keep the drawbridge almost permanently raised—had been the day Emma Delight left for Seattle.

That had happened months ago and Pops hadn't allowed visitors since.

No one had spoken to him.

Except Emma. And—despite protests to the contrary—Paris was convinced Emma *had* and *did* talk regularly to Pops.

Few people were abroad at six in the morning. A harassed-looking man gulping espresso with a designer-dressed toddler in tow marched determinedly toward the daycare center on Spring. Delivery trucks slid in and out of alleys behind businesses. The scent of freshly baked cinnamon rolls floated from nearby.

A typical summer-in-Seattle morning.

Nothing about the morning was typical for Paris.

Too agitated—and too raw inside—to be tired, she reached Madison Street and made her way quickly uphill to the Alexis Hotel and its condominium suites next door.

Inside the building, Paris hesitated in front of the elevator. She'd finally messed-up big time.

Paris the peace-maker.

Paris the one who could be trusted.

Paris, the one who had stoically watched her sister marry Tobias and never once let her own longing for him show.

Cynthia wasn't strong the way Paris was strong. Their father had been kindly—if worriedly—tolerant of his adopted daughter's repeated scrapes. Cynthia's mother had ignored them, as had Pops. Emma, tight-lipped on the subject, had silently withdrawn from the granddaughter she'd been forced to accept.

Paris grew up wanting to make Cynthia happier. If she was happier, she wouldn't look for trouble just to make everyone prove they'd keep on loving her even if she was bad.

Crying.

Cynthia sprawled facedown on top of her bed and sobbed, "They hate me," into her crossed arms.

Rain spattered the diamond-paned windows in the pretty bedroom the two girls shared. The day was one of Paris's favorite kind. She loved looking out on the dripping trees.

"Let's go for a walk," she said. She'd like to hold Cynthia but she

*knew better than to try. "We could walk down to the store and I'll buy
you that magazine you wanted."*

*"S'raining" thirteen-year-old Cynthia said, sniffing loudly. "It'll
mess up my hair."*

*Paris looked at Cynthia's red-blond curls and tugged at one of her
own braids. "Okay. D'you want me to go get it for you?" She couldn't
bear the sobbing.*

*"I guess. That dumb old Mrs. Purvis didn't have to tell Grandma
Emma she saw me try to take it. I'd already put it back. Everyone hates
me."*

"No, they don't. And I don't. I love you."

Cynthia hiccuped and cried afresh.

"I do," Paris insisted. "And I'm always going to be your best friend."

"You are?"

"Yes."

"You promise? No matter what I do?"

"I promise."

Paris had never forgotten that promise. But a few hours earlier she'd allowed herself to respond to the man Cynthia had
divorced.

"Ma'am? Are you okay?"

She started and looked into the face of a hotel waiter who
held open the elevator door. "Fine," she said, stepping inside
as he got out.

The door closed again and she punched a button, hunching
her shoulders beneath the black cotton jacket she wore over a
baggy shirt and jeans.

What a fool.

A little sexual promise had been enough to topple her. A
little sexual promise from the only man she'd ever truly fanta-
sized about.

From Tobias Quinn.

A kiss.

Several kisses . . . His hands at her neck, on her back, caressing her waist through thin gauze.

She shuddered.

And she'd do it all again. "Oh, *God.*" Scrubbing at her face, she absorbed the soft thud of the elevator's arrival at the designated floor.

Having responded to her buzz on the entrance intercom, Emma Delight waited at her open door. Comfortably solid in a poppy-colored silk suit, Emma's shrewd green eyes took in her granddaughter's faintly disheveled appearance. Emma looked at Paris's tumbling coiffure and touched her own stylishly casual white hair.

"Morning, Emma," Paris said, stuffing her hands into her jacket pockets. "Hope you've got some coffee left."

"Mm," Emma said noncommittally. "In the pot. On the table beside the couch." Emma truly lived the life of a well-heeled nomad. Constantly on the move. Gathering nothing remotely homey about her in her expensive rented suite. And everything she ate or drank was prepared by someone else. Here, in what she currently called home, she went strictly room service.

Paris corralled a spare cup from the kitchenette and went to pour coffee from the hotel pot in the burgundy and rose living room. "It's not decaffeinated, is it?" she asked, suspiciously eyeing the colored dot on top of the pot.

"Brown dot," Emma said as if reading Paris's mind. "Regular. I'm not completely in my dotage yet."

"Some people never touch caffeine." Now she was here, Paris didn't know where to begin. "It's supposed to be bad for all sorts of things."

"If you're one of the people who drink a lot of it, it may be."

"Huh?" Paris paused in the act of sinking into the couch, then slumped all the way down and drank before asking, "What did you just say, Emma?"

"Maybe caffeine is bad for some people. You look like hell."

"Thanks." Emma could always be relied upon to say exactly what she thought. *"You* look terrific. Got plans for the day?"

"I have plans for every day. You know that. What's the matter with you? You haven't combed your hair. Are you losing weight? You're already too thin, my girl."

Letting her head fall back against the couch, Paris rested her cup on her lap and stared at the ceiling.

"Paris—"

"Where are you going?"

"That's none of your business."

Paris smiled a little. Emma—who had devoted most of her adult life to one man's whims—had spent the months of her separation from her husband doing what she wanted to, when she wanted to. And she steadfastly refused to discuss *anything* she did.

"How's Pops?" Paris asked casually.

"How should I know?"

The answer was entirely too quick. Paris scooted straighter, blew hair away from her eyes and downed the rest of her coffee.

She poured another cup.

"Something's wrong with you," Emma said, her voice rising. "You look *really* terrible."

"So you've told me." Paris studied Emma's pretty, softly made-up face. "I'm never going to be a fashion plate like you, Grandma."

Emma's "Hmph" restated her dislike of being called a grandmother, even by her beloved Paris.

"I've written to Pops a dozen times since you moved out. He hasn't answered once."

"Doubt if he got the letters. Probably never picks anything up from the Post Office box. Anyway, he wouldn't write any letters back. Hates them. Hasn't put a word on paper since he sold the business."

Paris blinked stinging eyes. "He ought to have a phone."

"He wouldn't answer it if he did."

"This is all getting out of hand, Emma," Paris said, deliberately stern. "I tracked down a ham radio operator and tried to make contact."

"Really?"

As if Emma could fool anyone into believing she didn't care. "Yes, really," Paris said. "The guy said Pops wouldn't respond."

"Sounds likely."

Paris smacked her cup down on the tray, spraying drops of coffee over white damask. "D'you know what I think?"

For the first time, Emma's serene mask slipped slightly.

"What?" She ran her tongue over lipstick the exact shade of the silk suit.

"I think Pops is dead and you're not telling me because you know I'll be distraught and you can't stand emotion."

Emma's eyes opened wide. Her finely arched brows shot upward. "That's the silliest thing I've ever heard. I *like* emotion. I'm very emotional."

"So you don't mind telling me Pops is dead?"

"He's *not* dead."

Paris contained a smile. "How do you know?"

"I . . . I just *do* know."

"Someone's seen him and told you?"

Emma smoothed the hair at her nape upward. "No."

Tears, filling her eyes, shocked Paris. She fumbled in her pocket for a tissue, pressed it to her nose and sniffed.

"Oh," Emma said, crossing quickly to sit beside Paris on the burgundy couch. "Something's very wrong with you. I know it is. Tell me, dear."

"I need . . . I need to talk to Pops. I miss him. And I'm worried about him."

"There, there," Emma said, patting Paris's shoulder and drawing her against a substantial bosom. "He loves and misses you, too."

Paris grew quite still. "How do you know?"

Emma sighed gustily. "Because he tells me he does. There. Now are you satisfied? You already know your grandfather is sorting some things out and he's decided to do it completely on his own."

On his ornery own. "He's trying to make you go back to him, isn't he? This business of shutting himself away from the world—and from me—is all part of his plot to get his own way with you, isn't it?"

"Don't ask me questions like that."

Blowing her nose, Paris pulled away from Emma. "You two are behaving like children."

"Don't you *dare*—" Emma scrambled to her feet. "We are adults, my girl. Regardless of what you believe, people don't necessarily return to second childhoods as they get older. Your grandfather and I have had some serious problems in our marriage. Those problems are as real to me at seventy as they were at forty. The difference is that I'm *not going to take it anymore.* Understand?"

"Yes," Paris said in a small voice. "Sorry. But I don't see why Pops is punishing me because you won't do what he wants. I need to talk to him."

"Talk to me."

More tears threatened. Lack of sleep had to be the reason. Lack of sleep and memories of last night—of the fool she'd made of herself—were too vivid.

"Is this really important, Paris?"

She nodded.

"He'll be mad at me."

"If you arrange for me to talk to him?"

It was Emma's turn to nod.

"I thought you weren't taking anymore of that—of caring about what he wants or what he does."

Emma lifted the receiver on a phone atop the kitchenette counter and dialed.

"You said he didn't have a phone."

"He doesn't." Emma held up a hand. "A ham operator has to patch me through to him."

"And you pretended you hadn't done this before."

Ignoring Paris, Emma spoke briefly, giving Pops call code and her name, then holding the receiver tightly with both hands while she waited. "Yes," she said at last. "It's me, Edward . . . No, nothing. I'm absolutely fine. Paris is with me."

Emma screwed up her eyes and Paris could hear an angry masculine voice thundering along the line.

"She's crying," Emma said, tugging the hem of her jacket down and bracing her feet more firmly. "And I will not listen to you if you shout. There's something wrong with her. She won't tell me. Only you . . . Yes, I know I told you she was all right, but that was before this morning."

Paris made to get up but Emma waved for her to stay where she was.

"Yes, Edward," Emma said. "I've told you what will have to

happen . . . No. No, and I haven't changed my mind, either. Edward, this is not the time for this. Paris is with me."

There was a pause, then Emma took the phone from her ear and looked at Paris. "Your grandfather says he's perfectly fine. To quote him: he is always perfectly fine. He's not interested in dealing with *hysterical* females anymore"—Emma's mouth tightened to almost nothing—"so if you just want to cry in his ear he'd rather you didn't."

Paris surged to her feet. "Some things never change. Really, if Pops weren't my father's father I wouldn't *want* anything to do with him. And I'm *not* hysterical."

"No, dear," Emma murmured, smiling faintly as she pressed the phone to her ear once more. "Yes, Edward, I know. Sometimes the truth hurts, doesn't it? Yes . . . Here she is."

Paris all but snatched the receiver from her grandmother's hands. "Pops? Is that you?"

"One fool for a descendant is quite enough, missy."

Blinking rapidly, Paris realized she'd forgotten exactly what she'd intended to say. "What does that mean?" she asked.

"Your fool father. Biggest disappointment of my life. You took after your mother—God rest her soul. And thank God for that. Don't go soft and stupid on me now."

Relief at hearing her hard-headed favorite relative's voice blunted a rush of annoyance.

"Darn it, Paris! What's eating you?"

"Pops—"

"Speak *up*," he roared. "I've got perfectly good ears but I can't hear mewling whispers."

She smiled and wrinkled her nose at Emma who looked quizzical. "You're punishing people who love you, Pops," Paris said. "That's mean."

"Mean? *Mean?* When a man gets to be my age—almost eighty, in case you've forgotten—he's earned the right to make decisions and stick to 'em. If that's being what you call *mean*, then so be it."

"Okay." Anger was starting to cancel out relief. "If my lady-like language annoys you, let's get down to something you may understand. You're being a shit, Pops. Does that—"

A chuckle stopped her. "Emma still there?"

"Of course."

"*Whooee,* she'll have something to say about her sweet Paris using foul language."

Paris decided against mentioning that what she'd said had been pretty mild. "I'm glad you're okay," she told him. "Something else made me come here this morning and push Emma into letting me talk to you."

"What?"

She remembered exactly what she'd intended to say. It needed work.

"*What?*" Pops repeated sharply.

"Is everything going well for you up there?"

"Wonderful."

"You're eating properly, and—"

"You didn't call to discuss my domestic situation."

Not entirely true. "Is something . . . Are you being bothered by anything at the moment? Anything that's not to do with the family?"

There was silence.

Emma came closer and mouthed, "What's he saying?"

Paris shook her head. "Pops? You haven't . . . You aren't doing something . . . Geez."

"Spit it out."

"Would anyone outside the family have any reason to say your behavior—over some—*business* matter—was unreasonable?"

"Riddles," Pops said, but he sounded less sure of himself. "You'll have to be straighter than that, missy. Who's been telling you things about me?"

"Oh, that doesn't matter. I just want to be sure you aren't . . . I want to be sure the rumors I've heard are wrong." When Pops didn't respond, she continued, "Did you sell all your land? Everything but one acre?"

The question sounded ludicrous.

Emma's quickly averted gaze suggested Paris had hit a sensitive issue.

"Who told you that?" Pops asked, his voice cracking with barely contained rage. "Who's been talking to you?"

"Is it true?" Paris persisted.

"I . . . I understood none of that land would be developed."

Paris slumped onto a barstool by the counter. "You have sold it."

Emma took the seat Paris had vacated on the couch and studied her twined hands.

"Pops, are you in financial trouble?"

"Hell, no . . . No. And I'm not ready to have you watching over me like I was senile."

"You sold every bit of all that land. When?"

"Over the past—seven years. Not that I need to explain myself to you or anyone else."

Paris's heart began to thump hard. "Who did you sell it to?" Tobias hadn't lied—at least not about everything.

"That's none of your damn business, missy."

"If you didn't need the money, what made you do such a thing?" Paris asked miserably.

He was silent for so long she was afraid he'd severed the connection.

"Pops?"

"I did . . . Don't you tell your grandmother, but I did need the money. Or I thought I did. It doesn't matter now. That . . . Aw, *hell*, I've been taken advantage of."

"Meaning?"

"Meaning that—that—he didn't play the game right. Not straight."

"They're starting to develop that land, aren't they, Pops? And you're trying to stop them." She felt sick.

"I understood there'd *be* no development."

Paris traced the little beige tiles on the counter top and tried to think calmly. "Why would anyone buy property if they didn't intend to use it? Why would you *think* anyone would do that?"

Pops coughed and muttered something about drinking water, then he said, "Park site. That's what I understood. The land would be used for a park site. But not for a long time. A tax write-off. That's what I thought it was all about."

Gradually, Paris began to understand. "You mean you were told . . . You were told your land would eventually become a park but now they're trying to—"

"Yes. Yes, that's exactly what I mean. They think they can bulldoze a foolish old man. Only I'm not *that* old and I'm no fool."

"I see." Whatever happened, no one in the family must find out she'd responded to Tobias. They'd never forgive her and she'd never get over the shame. "Pops, what can I do to help you?"

"I don't need any help."

"But they've got every right to do whatever they want to do, don't they? You have actually signed papers? You've sold the land and taken money for it?"

"Yes, damn it. And I'm not sorry. I can take care of myself."

Paris longed to rest her warm forehead on the cool tile and close her eyes. Emma must have known this was going on, yet she'd done nothing to stop it. Not that Pops would have listened if he hadn't wanted to. Emma came from money and continued to receive extensive income from family trusts. Giving Paris and Cynthia a valuable apartment had been a simple gift in Emma's eyes. Even in times when few women held their own purse strings, Emma had firmly and apparently wisely controlled hers. On the other hand, Pops had evidently been tricked into losing his grip on a good portion of what he'd prized so dearly—his land.

Sometimes damage control was the only solution. "Pops, I think I've got an idea." She needed more time to think her way through this. Using Tobias's scheme was out of the question because of Cynthia, but there had to be a way to compromise. "Why don't I go to the people who bought the land?"

"Never."

She rolled her eyes. "To suggest we work together."

"*Never*, I tell you. I've got things to do here."

"Pops, don't hang up. I'll talk to Tobias and suggest—"

"How did . . ." Pops's breathing was alarmingly labored. "Of course. I should have known it. Like father, like son. Any son of Sam Quinn's would be just as conniving as that son of a bitch."

Paris sat up very straight. She'd never heard Pops sound quite so enraged—or quite so strange. "Tobias is Sam's grandson, not his son. Lester was—"

"I know who's who in that no-good family. What difference does it make? All the same. Take it from me."

The tone of Pops's voice unnerved Paris. "If we offered to work with them, rather than against them, don't you—"

"I *will not.*"

"Pops, listen to me. I'll speak to Tobias for you, and—"

"Stay away from him. He's a liar and a cheat, the same as his father. Sam lied and cheated. He lied to me—"

"Pops—"

"You listen to me, missy. I've been wronged. I was wronged years ago—years before you were born. Now they're wronging me again. And it was *my* turn, this time. D'you understand? *My* turn."

"I don't understand."

"Well, understand this. And I've already as good as told *him* as much. If anything changes here, it'll kill me."

Paris swiveled to look at Emma. "Don't say that, Pops." Arms crossed, Emma appeared serene.

"I will say it, missy. I'm going to make him very sorry he decided to tangle with me. And I'll *die* before I give in to Tobias Quinn."

Seven

"You're a hard man to find, big brother."

At the sound of his half-brother's voice behind him, Tobias handed a clipboard to the building-site foreman, ironed irritation from his own features and turned around.

Nigel's bright blue eyes sparkled with apparent pleasure. "God, it's good to see you. Even if I was on the verge of hiring an investigator to track you down."

Tobias had been expecting a visit from boyishly handsome Nigel. "No one else seems to have trouble finding me." His secretary knew Tobias would be at the university District office project until noon.

"It's taken *hours,*" Nigel said. His dark lashes were spiky, his brown hair tousled. The picture of a charming, trustworthy, loyal sibling.

Looks were deceiving.

Nigel Quinn cheated.

He lied.

He used others and didn't give a damn about a single human being other than himself.

He was here because he was in trouble and needed help.

And he had slept with his brother's ex-wife—had slept with her when she was still his *wife*.

And, most galling of all, Nigel thought he'd fooled Tobias, which translated into: Nigel thought Tobias was a fool.

"What's up?" Tobias asked neutrally. This wasn't a great day for Nigel to try anything. Tobias's latest encounter with Paris Delight had upset more than his plans for dealing with her grandfather. The encounter had upset Tobias, period. He couldn't keep the woman out of his mind, and other parts of his anatomy insisted on reacting to the stimulus. He was working too hard. He needed a diversion, a soft, sexy female diversion—one who didn't resemble a big-eyed waif and who didn't mess with his mind. *Waifs?* Only *real* women interested him.

Nigel seemed to be having difficulty coming up with an answer to Tobias's question.

"You had a reason for coming here?" he said shortly. One *real* woman. And soon.

"There's something I wanted to talk to you about." Nigel, dressed in a dark green Armani suit, khaki dress shirt and hand-painted green and rust-colored silk tie, frowned around as if deeply interested in his surroundings. "Apartments?"

Tobias indicated a board headed with the word, QUINN, in six-inch-high letters. "Brooklyn Tower. Fifteen-stories—luxury office suites," he said, reading aloud. And he thought, *how are you going to ask me? What lie will you make up to explain why you need to borrow money? Big money?*

"Have I told you how much I appreciate the loan of the house?"

No, he hadn't. Tobias said, "I'm not using it." He wasn't certain he ever intended to use the house again.

"I've had a lot of time to think, over there. All that space and all that time alone seem to make me edgy. I've been looking at some rough stuff about myself."

Looking at rough stuff—or *doing* rough stuff in what had once been Tobias and Cynthia's bedroom and anywhere else in the house that appealed? Possibly doing it *with* Cynthia, who liked her sex rough? Tobias kept his expression impassive. All about them, men and women came and went, threading through the maze of huge forms placed in preparation for pouring foundations. Unlike most of his competitors, he liked to keep a personal eye on each stage of a project.

"You probably find it hard to believe I've been soul-searching."

"I think we'd better find somewhere else to talk," Tobias said, wishing he didn't know he was being set up. He checked his watch. "Bit early for lunch, I suppose."

"Not for me," Nigel said quickly. "Come on. I'll buy. It's been too long."

Like never. Tobias wondered if anyone would guess Nigel was thirty-three—only three years younger than his brother.

Nigel was already walking away, his steps sure and springy. Tobias followed, acknowledging workers as he went. He handed his hardhat in and caught up with Nigel on the sidewalk. The younger man was shorter by some inches, a fact that had been one more source of friction between them when they were teenagers. Lots of spare time to work out had bulked Nigel up in recent years. He now came close to matching Tobias's mature physique.

Late morning sun made the most of Nigel's tan. Striding beside Tobias he was the picture of handsome, healthy success.

"I'm in trouble, Toby."

Tobias almost stood still. "Yami Yami should be pretty empty. Japanese and Chinese. Okay?"

"Great. Anything's great."

"We'll go there." Tobias kept moving and silently swore that he wouldn't be taken in by whatever game Nigel had decided to play this time.

A few University of Washington summer students straggled along, Birkenstocks scuffing, backs bent under the weight of book packs. The area seemed blessedly and unusually quiet.

The restaurant was only a block east of Brooklyn, on University Way. Bamboo shades were lowered against the sun but Tobias could see there were few customers inside.

"Fully licensed," Nigel said absently, pushing open the heavy glass door. "I could use a drink."

They took a table for four, near the window, and sat side-by-side with their backs to the wall. Unspoken was the idea that this way they'd see anyone who got close enough to hear what they said.

"Vodka martini," Nigel told the waitress.

Tobias ordered a Pepsi and waited until they were alone again before he said, "What kind of trouble?"

Nigel opened the plastic-coated menu and stared.

"What kind of trouble?" Tobias repeated.

"I'm lost," Nigel muttered. "Cast adrift." His hands shook a little and he raised one to push back his hair. "I'm not going anywhere, Toby, and I'm scared stiff."

The drinks arrived. Tobias glanced at Nigel and told the waitress, "We're not ready to order. Give us a few minutes."

"I know you probably never thought the day would come, but it has," Nigel continued. "I'm too old to be trying to find myself anymore. It's time for me to settle down and consider myself *found*, for God's sake." He spanned the rim of his martini glass and lifted it to his lips.

Tobias chased one half-formed thought after another. Either this was a different Nigel, or this was the same Nigel with a very different patter.

"Say something," Nigel said, swallowing liquor. "It took all the guts I've got to come here and tell you this."

"I'm listening. I'll listen for as long as you want to talk."

The door opened to admit a lone customer who headed for a distant corner. Overhead, round white paper lanterns swayed gently in the current of warm air from the street. Nigel watched the lanterns and his expression became distant.

"I'm listening," Tobias prompted.

"Let me in." Nigel swiveled in his chair and looked intently at Tobias. "Bring me into Quinn and make me part of it."

Whatever he'd expected, it hadn't been this. "You want—"

"Yes. *Yes.* I know I've always said I wasn't interested. I've said a lot worse. But I've changed. I'm older."

Older and in debt up to his ears. The rumors had been discreetly dropped in Tobias's lap. And suggested reasons for the debt hadn't been pretty. Gambling, drugs, women, mob problems and a trail leading back to whatever Nigel had run away from in Las Vegas.

Tobias shifted his sweating glass on the shiny wooden table top. The talk about Nigel was becoming a professional embarrassment.

"What do you think?" Nigel asked urgently.

He thought his brother needed access to enough money to keep his creditors at bay—the ones all over Seattle, and elsewhere.

"We'd make—"

The waitress's return halted Nigel and he said, "I'll have the Kung Pau Chicken."

"Same, please," Tobias said.

"We'd make a hell of a team," Nigel said, barely moving his lips. "You *need* a right hand man you can trust. I can be that man."

Tobias lifted his drink, leaving a wet ring on the table. There were times when shock tactics seemed the only course. "You're in debt," he said quietly.

Nigel flinched but kept his eyes on Tobias's.

"Aren't you?"

"Yes."

Muscles in Tobias's gut began to relax. "Big debt."

"I've made some dumb mistakes. I don't want to make them again."

Honesty had been Nigel's lifelong short suit. Confronted with a facsimile of it now, Tobias felt mildly disoriented. "You've come to me pretending you want to work in the business because you want to soften me up for a big loan. Right?"

"*Wrong, Goddammit!*" Nigel slammed down his empty martini glass. He glanced around and lowered his voice. "You always think the worst of me. The whole family always did think the worst of me. You asked me a question and I answered you. I was straight, Toby. *Straight.* I may be here because I owe money and I need—no, dammit, I *want* to get clear—but it's more than that. I know it's time to clean up my act."

Tobias studied the other man's face. Nigel had turned a

shade paler under his tan. An unusual, fierce glitter hardened his blue eyes.

"Look, I made a mess of things in Las Vegas, okay?"

"Why didn't you just tell me that when you came back? Why did you pretend you were bored with whatever you'd been doing and wanted a change?"

The chicken arrived and Nigel ordered another vodka martini.

"I was ashamed," he said when they were alone again. "Is that so hard to understand? You're a fantastic success. You've been on your way to being a fantastic success for as long as anyone can remember. I took a cash settlement from you to be *out* of Quinn. I left with enough of a stake to carve out a helluva good niche somewhere."

Tobias didn't want to think about the vast sum Nigel had evidently squandered.

"I've made lousy choices and I've failed," Nigel continued. "Do you blame me for not wanting to spill my guts to you?"

"No." Tobias stripped the paper covering from his chopsticks and separated the cheap wooden pieces. "How much do you need now?"

Nigel pushed his plate away. "You aren't listening . . Or you aren't hearing me. I *don't* want a loan. I want a *job*. I want a job I can build on. Don't you like the idea of having me around, Toby? Is that it? Isn't there room for me at Quinn?"

Their father had dreamed of both his sons coming into the business. Their grandfather had had the same dream.

"All right," Nigel said, averting his eyes. "Sorry. I shouldn't have asked. I blew my chance years ago when I took the money and bailed out. Forget it." He started to get up.

Tobias grasped his arm. "Sit down."

"I don't want pity."

"Good. You won't be getting any. Sit *down*." He had to try seeing this through his father's and grandfather's eyes—as an opportunity to save Nigel from himself. "Tell me what you see yourself doing at Quinn."

Nigel dropped back into his chair, propped an elbow on the table and supported his brow on a fist. "I saw myself learning from you. I may have failed on my own, but with you I can learn to succeed. I believe that."

"You want to learn the business? That's what you're telling me?"

"Yes." Nigel turned toward Tobias once more. "Put me on the payroll. You've been giving me an allowance, now I want to *earn* it. Make me your assistant-to, or whatever it's called. Or an assistant to your assistant-to if that's what that woman in your offices already is."

"Gladys is my secretary. I don't have an assistant." And he'd never wanted one. "You don't know squat about what we do and I don't have time to give lectures. If we do this thing you're going to have to learn by watching and listening."

Nigel leaned closer. "I can *do* that. And I'll study the company, Toby. You've got my word, I'll work at being useful to you."

Despite his misgivings, Tobias smiled. "You'll have to give me time to get used to the new Nigel, y'know."

"You're a bloody saint to give me the chance. But I've changed. Honest to God, I've changed."

"We'll have to talk salary." They both knew the rules—they'd been dictated by Nigel the day he walked away. Tobias controlled Quinn. "You'll have to tell me what you need to get out of . . . You'll have to tell me how much you need."

"I'm paying things off. I'm not in great shape but I'm managing on the allowance."

"Working with me is going to make you worth more than that."

Nigel slumped against the back of his chair and rubbed his mouth. "Does this mean the answer's yes?"

Tobias thought about Cynthia. That discussion could come later. He said, "Yes."

"You'll take me on?"

"Yes. You start tomorrow. Seven-thirty sharp. A.M. Ditch the shiny shoes and wear something that looks good in mud."

"God!" Nigel found Tobias's hand and pumped. "You won't be sorry, I promise. I'm going to make you proud . . . I'm going to make you *glad* you agreed to this."

"I'll be rooting for that." And, after all, what did he have to lose?

Eight

"You said *lunch.*" Cynthia Delight Quinn could make a little word like "lunch" sound so much . . . bigger.

Paris sent her adopted sister a look meant to warn against further complaints and stood near the open doors to the terrace outside Cynthia's too-expensive sixteenth-floor condominium.

"Lunch yesterday, if we're going to get technical." Cynthia was difficult to intimidate. "This is almost time for dinner on the day *after* you were supposed to come." Dangling a bottle of white wine by the neck and with the stems of two glasses jutting between fingers of the same hand, she passed Paris and stepped into the sunshine.

Yesterday. Today. Hours and days had begun to run together for Paris. Had it only been the day before yesterday when first her world started to fall apart and then Tobias Quinn had showed up to all but complete the job?

Cynthia, her red-gold hair afire in the setting sun, sat in a white wrought-iron chair and crossed legs clad in silver tights. She arranged the bottle and glasses on a small table beside her.

Between her breasts, a damp spot showed through her matching silver leotard.

"Been working out?" Paris asked. Business hadn't been the only excuse for her not showing up until now. Deciding what and how much to tell Cynthia had taken time.

"I work out every afternoon." Flashing a shrewd turquoise glance at Paris, Cynthia picked up the bottle. "Something's going on, isn't it?"

Hovering in the doorway, Paris waited until she was handed a glass and said, "Too much. Sorry about yesterday. I did call, though."

"Mmm. And I forgive you, love. I'm a demanding hussy. Hate to wait for anyone."

One of the privileges of gorgeous women—people rarely did keep them waiting. "Are you still writing?" Paris asked.

"Am I ever!" Cynthia stretched out her impossibly long and very lovely legs and crossed her ankles. "Big sister, dear, *this* is going to be the one. The *big* one."

Heights terrified Paris. Even being this close to the terrace sickened her. She sat on the floor facing Cynthia, who refused to as much as acknowledge her sister's fear of high places. They were both twenty-nine but Paris's birthday came two months before Cynthia's, hence "big sister."

"I know you think all I do is indulge myself while you work your fingers to the bone," Cynthia continued. "But I'm going to surprise you one day. And it'll be soon. If there's one thing that's hot, it's mysteries set in Seattle."

Paris sipped the wine and found it too sweet. "Seattle, huh?"

"Yup. Don't ask me anymore questions. Talking about a story always takes the guts out of writing it. Once it's told, it's told."

"You're the writer. I'll take your word for it. What does this place cost you?"

Cynthia's apricot-glossed lips pursed. "A lot. I don't ask you about your expenses, Paris."

"As far as what it costs me to live goes, you know them. More or less. Taxes and utilities. It's your apartment, too."

"The taxes must be pretty crippling."

"They aren't low."

"You can't expect me to pay taxes on that place, Paris. I can't afford it."

She shouldn't have mentioned the obviously exorbitant lifestyle Cynthia insisted upon. "I manage fine." Or she'd been managing fine until her next year's income became threatened. Paris knew the answer before she said, "You *could* come and live with me."

Those marvelous turquoise eyes, rimmed by dark lashes, rolled with as much eloquence as any finely delivered expletive.

"Okay, okay. I know you hate the place."

A visible shudder racked Cynthia. "It's so . . . so . . . *Tacky.* I mean . . . Not the way you've done the place up, of course. That's really quite . . . charming. But the *building.* Those streets at night. Well, I'll tell you, love, there's no way I'd want to come and go down there after dark. And I don't have to remind you I'm a night person. I'd *suffocate* trapped inside at night."

"Right." No point explaining how Paris had never felt freer than she did in and around her home.

"And those *people* you have to tolerate tramping up and down the same stairs. My God!"

"I like those people. And they think *you* like them, too. Conrad thinks you walk on water."

Cynthia rested the back of a wrist on her brow and drank. *"Conrad!* Don't expect me to be excited because some bartender's got the hots for me. Let's not talk about it now. I worked like a dog all day on the book. Then I worked out. My mind needs some free space to roam around in." She waved her glass in Paris's direction. "When's the last time you bought new clothes. You drag that brown gauze thing out every summer."

Paris smiled. "Actually, this is a new brown gauze thing. Clothes don't mean much to me."

"I know." The two words were laden with disapproval. "To think my only bearable family member walks around looking like a charity case."

"This wasn't free," Paris said defensively. "I *like* it."

Cynthia made a snuffling sound into her wine glass and wiggled a forefinger. "You, big sister, were buying your clothes at

Goodwill when it *wasn't* the thing for every rich teenager to do."

"I could never see wasting money on things that aren't important."

"You're hopeless." Cynthia sighed. "But don't forget I was the one who kept Grandma Emma and my dear mother off your back about it."

Paris chuckled. "It was you, wasn't it. I haven't forgotten." She pushed up her glasses and rubbed her eyes. "Oh, I haven't thought about that in years. The sight of you, in name-brand everything, defending me . . . Funny. You'd get mad at them. Then, when you got me alone, you'd get mad at *me*. You never managed to change my taste, did you?"

"I sure didn't. You're still a mess."

"If you say so." Paris stretched her neck from side to side.

"You look a bit tired, love," Cynthia murmured. "Not sleeping? Or overdoing it for the next collection?"

Paris wasn't ready to tell that tale of woe again, not just yet. She said, "Guess who came to see me a couple of nights ago?"

"Can't imagine. Someone who's kept you up ever since?"

"Funny girl," Paris said, wrinkling her nose. "Actually it was your ex-husband."

Cynthia spilled wine all over her leotard. "Shit!" She jolted upright in her seat. "What the hell are you talking about?"

"Tobias Quinn walked into my apartment. Night before last, to be precise."

"You've got to be kidding." Long fingers, tipped by apricot-painted nails, splayed over the spreading dampness from the wine. *"Tobias?* Why in God's name would he go to see *you."*

She would not allow herself to think that Cynthia might be amazed by the prospect of any man like Tobias Quinn giving Paris a second glance.

"Paris? Come *on.* You've shocked the life out of me." She smiled tentatively. "You're joking, aren't you? That would be your idea of a joke. Subtle. So subtle it makes no sense."

It was Paris's turn to smile. "Thanks for the compliment. I'm not joking. He showed up at the apartment. Didn't call first.

Nothing. Just came and started telling me everything he thought was wrong with my home—with where I work and live."

Cynthia grunted. "Well, that's a first. Something Tobias and I agree on. But that can't be why he came."

Caution would be everything from here on. "He wanted something." Paris felt herself turning pink. "My help."

Total blankness wiped Cynthia's face smooth. "Your help? What with? Let me guess. He's met some woman he wants you to make jewelry for."

Paris didn't miss the shadow in Cynthia's lovely eyes. "No." So it did still hurt—having to give up on Tobias. "Very logical guess, but wrong. He's having some sort of disagreement with Pops."

The blank expression returned.

"Evidently Pops is trying to stop Quinn from developing the land surrounding his."

Clearly baffled, Cynthia shook her head. "Pops's land? Tobias can't do that."

"Tobias's land. Over the years, Pops has sold everything but one acre—the acre he's living on—to Quinn. Now Tobias wants to use it."

Cynthia didn't reply for so long Paris grew edgy and drank the wine despite its cloying taste.

"That *man!*" Cynthia pushed to her feet. She went to the railing and stood facing Elliott Bay.

Fixing her eyes on the distance, Paris got up and joined her sister. On the corner of Broad and Second, Cynthia's apartment complex soared above the buildings separating it from the waterfront. On the far side of the bay the gray peaks of the Olympic Mountains spiked a purple and red streaked sky. Paris concentrated on the sun's final titian glitter upon the water, and the bright balloon spinnakers on a scattering of sailboats. She could not look down.

"That man is impossible," Cynthia muttered.

"You mean Pops?"

Breeze tossed Cynthia's luxuriant hair. *"Tobias.* Is he ever going to leave us alone?" She braced her hands on the railing, hunched her shoulders and swayed forward.

Paris knew better than to warn Cynthia not to lean too far over the railing. "Pops has threatened to set the dogs on the Quinn surveyors."

"I hope he does it."

"It's Tobias's land."

"*Why* did he want it? And *why* would Pops sell it to him?"

"Pops sold it for the money," Paris said in a small voice. "Tobias says he wants it for something his dad always intended to build up there."

"*Garbage.*" Cynthia looked over her shoulder at Paris. "He wanted it because he wants everything that's ours."

There had never been any doubt that when Maurice married Beryl her little daughter became a member of the Delight clan. Paris was glad Cynthia still felt the strong bond. Emma's luke-warm attitude toward Cynthia was the one blight on an other-wise happy situation, but fortunately Cynthia seemed oblivious to the older woman's ambivalence.

"Why did Tobias come to you?"

"For help."

"That doesn't make sense."

Total recall had never been one of Paris's gifts—until now. She saw Tobias's spearing gray eyes and the flare of black brow, the sweep of flamboyantly carved bone, the curve of expressive lips . . . She saw the man as clearly as if he stood before her.

"Paris? Did you hear me?"

She released the breath she'd held. "Yes. He wanted me to speak to Pops for him." There. That was all that needed to be said. Cynthia knew about Tobias's visit, but the embarrassing details hadn't been revealed.

Cynthia faced Paris and leaned a curvaceous hip against the railing. She crossed her arms. "I don't believe that man's gall. You mean he came and asked you to persuade Pops to stop interfering with his damn building plans? That's it, isn't it?"

"Yes."

"*Bastard.*"

A defensive flare caught Paris by surprise. "He did buy the land, Cynthia."

"And why do you think he did that? I'll tell you why—because he hates all of us and he took advantage of an old man, that's why."

Paris considered what Pops had told her but decided there was no point in mentioning either her conversation with him—she'd promised she wouldn't tell a soul—or the fact that Cynthia's theory was very close to Pops's.

"Oh, love." Cynthia enfolded Paris in one of her rare, but smothering hugs. "It must have been horrible for you to see Tobias like that. What a shock. You never liked him, did you?"

Paris didn't respond.

"And he really put you off your stride. Poor you. You shouldn't have wasted almost two days being upset by *him.*"

"He was only part of it," Paris mumbled against Cynthia's rose-scented shoulder. "Someone's been selling cheap copies of my designs."

Slowly, Cynthia's grip loosened. She stepped far enough away to see Paris's face but continued to hold her arms. "That's bad, isn't it? Oh, Paris . . . Do you mean like *forging?*"

Paris bowed her head. "Exactly. Forging. And ruining everything I've worked for in the process. Devaluing everything."

By the time she'd finished telling Cynthia every detail of what had happened in the past two days—omitting only the truth about Tobias's suggestion, and what had transpired between them later—by then, Cynthia had led her back into the apartment.

They'd settled at opposite ends of a white leather sofa in Cynthia's spacious office. Only one light—a white sphere suspended inside a tall, clear glass tube—chased the room's gathering shadows. Atop a blond wooden desk, an amber cursor blinked on a darkened computer screen. Tidy piles of papers corroborated that Cynthia had indeed returned to her writing after a long hiatus.

Paris kicked off her sandals and pulled her legs up beneath her gauze skirts. "So that's that," she said, resting her chin on her knees. "No leads. And the police don't seem to want to know. Not that I blame them particularly."

"Well, I do," Cynthia said darkly. "You can bet your socks

they'd have wanted to know if Mr. Tobias Quinn was doing the complaining."

The connection escaped Paris. "That's another story, Cynthia."

"Is it?"

"Well, of course it is."

"Hm."

"Look, I'm going to be all right." Focus had so often eluded Cynthia. The last thing Paris wanted was to distract her from a fresh attempt to publish one of her mysteries. "I shouldn't have bothered you with any of this."

"Yes you should." Cynthia was vehement. "We've got a pact, remember. We tell each other everything. *Everything.*"

A little warmth crawled into Paris's tensed muscles. "A pact," she agreed. For a long time she'd felt a chasm between them. Growing closer again would make her a happy woman. "So, I have told you. Now I don't want you worrying about me for even a moment. I'm a big girl and I can look after myself."

"You sound like a line in a bad play. And you're wrong. You, love, are too damn trusting. And *too* damn innocent. If you hadn't been, that creep Michael couldn't have pushed you around the—"

"Not now," Paris said simply.

"No," Cynthia agreed. "Of course not. Sorry. Anyway, the point is that you don't *look* for the dark side in people, so they take advantage of you."

"I don't think I'm following you."

"Tobias, of course."

"I refused to help him."

"He'll be back."

He'd already been back. "I don't think so." Paris didn't like bending the truth.

"Doesn't anything strike you as odd?"

Paris snorted. "Never mind odd. My whole life is *crazy* right now."

"What about the timing? First a major move is made to put you out of business. If you can't get things back on track—which is probably going to mean you'll need someone to stake you financially for a bit—you're going to go down the tube."

"I can't get anyone to stake me," Paris said miserably. "Even if I could stand to ask. You never have any money. And I wouldn't dare ask Pops or Emma because they'd probably tell me to go into a *nice* business. I can't even get a loan from the bank."

Unspoken between them was the fact that the Main Street property couldn't be used as collateral without Cynthia's cooperation.

Cynthia covered her face and looked at Paris through her fingers. "We could sell the place. You could take your share and find a small apartment. Or a little condo. Somewhere nice and safe. You'd have plenty of money left over to weather this unpleasantness"

Stupid tears pricked at Paris's eyes. She did not have time to turn into a labile idiot. "One day I'll be able to pay you for your share of the apartment," she said.

"That's not the point." Cynthia dropped her hands and anger sparked in her beautiful eyes. "You *know* that's not the point. I'm not *rich*. We both know I stretch my means a bit. To be honest, I dare not mortgage the one asset I own free and clear . . . Half-own, that is."

"I can't leave," Paris whispered. "I know you don't understand, but my life is there. Among the people you can't stand and in the place you detest. I *love* it all. I don't think I could work anywhere else."

Cynthia sighed. "I know," she said quietly. "Everyone who knows anything about you knows—including Tobias."

This constant returning to Tobias irritated Paris. "Why would he care?"

"Insurance," Cynthia said. "In case you refused him."

Paris lifted her head and frowned.

"Don't you see? I know him, Paris. He's devious and cruel. How long has he been buying Pops's land?"

"Years."

"Hah! Like the poisonous snake he is. Pulling it under his rock, bit by bit. Then he struck. And when Pops made a fuss,

Tobias looked around for help and settled on you. After all, you're Pops's favorite."

"I don't see what—"

"*Think.* I know you're good, but why would someone single out just your work to copy? To make you vulnerable, that's why. I think Tobias is behind it. Yes, that's exactly what I think."

Paris could only stare at Cynthia.

"I know it sounds fantastic, but I spend a lot of my life looking at motives, remember. You could say this is all a fabrication of my writer's mind, but I don't think so. Tobias has always been a man for contingency plans. How do you think he became the number one developer in this town?"

"Cynthia—"

"Let me finish. His contingency plan was to make you vulnerable before he ever came to you—on the very day you found out you were being ripped off, in case you haven't noticed. That way, if you refused what he asked you to do, he could come back and say he'd found out what happened to you."

He hadn't needed to. He'd been told.

"Then, he could offer to help you. He'd wait a decent interval before reminding you of the price. Oh, take it from me, he can be very charming and very persuasive."

Paris could attest to that. "I don't know if I buy your whole theory, but he isn't going to get what he wants. In fact, I may let him know we think he'd stoop to anything to make me cooperate."

"No!" Cynthia leaned toward Paris. "Absolutely *not,* love. You are not to talk to him at all. We don't want to warn him we may be on to him."

"Cynthia—"

"*No,* Paris. Of course I could be all wet, but what if I'm not? What if he did try to groom you to be his patsy? Wouldn't you like to know that?"

"Y—yes." Surely he wouldn't go that far.

"Right. So let him make the next move. Did he tell you he'd be back? After you said you wouldn't talk to Pops?"

"Well . . ."

Cynthia threw up her hands. "I knew it! That piece of slime.

You wait and see. He'll come back and say he wants to help you."

Slowly, Paris lowered her feet until they met the cool, pale, polished wooden floor. She filled her lungs carefully, all the way to the top.

"He will," Cynthia insisted. "I—"

"He already has."

Nine

The shit had really hit the fan.

Tobias slung his tux jacket over one shoulder and watched Nigel's cream Lexus slip away into the night.

Two days from hell had been followed by this night from hell. Only Nigel's enthusiasm for learning about the business had provided a potential bright spot.

Pulling his black tie loose as he went, Tobias walked down the ramp toward wooden docks where the houseboat community was moored.

Someone was trying to slit his professional throat and there was only one candidate for the office of slitter: Pops Delight. Tonight, during a fund-raising black-tie dinner at the Westin, Tobias became the enraged witness to the power of innuendo.

The word slinking around the lush corridors of Seattle's Successful was that through a doomed major move, Quinn could be staring into the jaws of financial ruin.

Tobias thought longingly of diving, naked, into the lake. Tension mounted—a boiling fever beneath his hard-learned exterior control.

The grumble of a dinghy outboard cut through the gentle

suck and swoosh of water under docks and piers. A white moon twinkle-toed a swath over choppy ripples. The smells were good—the best. Honeyed flowers frothing from wooden barrels, tar, fraying wood, worn hemp and the distinctive scent of a hot but purely Seattle breeze.

Damn, it was hot.

Tobias walked to the entrance to his dock and leaned to rest crossed arms on a railing. All around him he felt the subdued life of the water dwellers. Few lights showed. One in the morning on a week night was serious sleep time for most of these people.

Wind chimes plinked coyly from a nearby floating doorway. Tobias bent his head and listened. Might be magic on any other night.

"Sorry to hear about the, er—well, sorry, anyway, fella."

Cornell Millerton, president of one of the most prestigeous merchant banks on the west coast had delivered his anonymous commiseration in front of at least ten men and women Tobias could not afford to have rattled—not if the rattling had his name attached.

And, when he'd aimed a puzzled smile around the group he'd met one sympathetic nod after another.

Damn.

He whistled soundlessly into a fist.

"Sometimes we just have to cut our losses and run, boy."

The sharp blue eyes of Gunter Williams, another Seattle area developer, hadn't conveyed either sympathy or goodwill.

"This Skagit Valley mess," Roberta McClellan of McClellan, Gerston and McClellan had whispered conspiratorially to Tobias and his long-time friend and mentor in the business, Bill Bowie. *"The partners discussed it this afternoon. There's talk of confidence in Quinn getting a teensy bit shaky."*

While his stomach had clenched, he'd given the woman his most cocksure grin, and assured her—with complete honesty— that Quinn was in absolutely terrific shape.

Bill hadn't covered his concern quite quickly enough before uttering some platitude about gossip blowing over. They both understood the importance of client confidence in a high-ticket industry where a single mistake could take a business out.

Tobias had done what he'd rarely done with Bill Bowie. He'd lied and insisted he didn't have a clue what all the chatter was about.

But he knew. Finally, after sitting up in his precious valley for years—like a gray spider guarding a sumptuous pie—Pops Delight had discovered no one shivered at the sight of a gray spider anymore. The man to whom Pops had slowly sold almost all the pie wanted to start eating it.

Tobias staightened and turned to rest his back on the railings. He hadn't twisted Pops's arm to sell. Piece by piece the old man had *offered* the land to him. Now Pops had the money and Tobias wasn't supposed to want to touch a damn shovelful of the dirt the money had bought.

Throughout yesterday and today, with Nigel doggedly trudging in his wake, Tobias had walked, driven and walked some more among highly paid professionals whose time—and, therefore, salary—was being *wasted*.

The breeze didn't do a thing to cool him. Blood pounded at his temples. He tore off his tie and balled it inside one fist. A drink might at least rub the edges off his rage.

He strode rapidly toward home, his shoes clipping the boards sharply. There had been other remarks tonight, remarks that suggested someone had given Pops a little extra useful information to leak: Tobias Quinn was desperate enough to go begging assistance from the old man's granddaughter.

Cold bitch. Always had been, Always would be. He'd like to . . . Yeah, he'd like to see what it would take to warm her up. Sanctimonious little tease. She'd wanted him to kiss her as much as he'd wanted it. The curl in his belly turned from tight, to tight fire. She'd wanted more than his kisses. He knew an aroused woman when he saw one—felt one—*smelled* one.

Her scent. Some sort of exotic lily or fragrant crushed herb? The spider's lily. Moisture-stroked smooth and sensuously pale. Unfurling its luscious petals in invitation until it could draw in the one hungry victim it had prayed for a chance to entice.

And he'd done it. He'd given that chance.

But he'd barely sipped at the edges of those petals before the lily decided he'd tasted enough to give her power over him.

Tomorrow he'd be paying another visit to Main Street. This time his mission would be to deliver a warning.

He walked onto the side deck of his two-story houseboat and skirted the housing, fishing in his pockets for keys as he went.

The antique porch swing by the front door moved gently to and fro, rocked by a toe that cleared the deck by an inch with each sweep.

His shirt shone blue-white in the darkness.

Paris said, "Surprise," and pushed herself backward on the swing again.

"I'm not fond of surprises."

She just bet he wasn't fond of this surprise. "Shocked you, huh?" He didn't look shocked. He looked . . . inscrutable. In the faint glow from a light beside the door, his face was exactly as her mind had painted it a hundred times since he'd arrived, uninvited, in her apartment.

His lips parted and she heard him draw a breath. "I don't shock easily. How did you get here?"

"By car."

"Hm."

"In the building where I live we own two old ones between all of us. Cuts down on expenses and parking problems."

"How quaintly cozy."

"How condescending you are."

"Still a granola girl to the bone." He unlocked his door and opened it. "You can report that I'm still standing, walking and talking—*and* in business. Good night."

Paris got to her feet and quickly followed Tobias. "It only seemed polite to return your visits," she told him. He was closing the door as she put her hand on it. "I wanted to come last night but it took awhile to find out your address." And when she'd left Cynthia's it had been too late to make enquiries.

He bowed his head. "Forgive me if I seem rude, Paris. But I'm tired and I don't feel like visitors."

"I'm tired and I don't really feel like visiting. But you and I have a few things to talk about."

"Oh, I don't think so." When he looked at her, there was ice in his gray eyes. Every boldly drawn line in his face stood out sharp and taut. His hair, drawn back from its vaguely devilish peak, reminded her of pirates. The faint glitter of the single gold earring caught her eye. A dangerous maverick.

"You believe you can always be the one in control, don't you?" she asked him. This was one time when his subtle power wouldn't intimidate her. "When we were children, you proclaimed yourself the leader. You haven't changed."

"We've both changed. In every way imaginable. If you've got any sense you'll get the hell away from my door and back into your little commune car."

"That sounds like a threat."

"Take it anyway you like, kid. Unlike some people, I believe in honesty. In my present mood I could be very bad for your health."

Paris forced her shoulders to stay down and pushed the door open wider. "I've had all my booster shots." Her heart leaped at the menace she felt beneath his civilized exterior but she turned sideways to walk past him into a large, unexpectedly informal room.

"It would be a good idea for you to leave." Tobias left the door open and threw his tuxedo jacket and tie over an old sea chest that doubled as a table beside a brown leather sofa worn shiny and dark by use.

Surrounded by book-lined walls and more brown leather furniture, Paris pressed trembling hands to her sides and stood her ground.

"Quinn has never done better than it's doing now," he said and crossed his arms. "It'll take more than a few lying rumors to topple us. There isn't a developer in the northwest who wouldn't kill to be in my position."

She began to get the butterfly-under-glass feeling again. "I don't know anything about rumors and I didn't come to talk about your profit-and-loss statements. Please close the door."

"Lady, there's only one possible reason for you to be here

and we both know what it is. God, you must have thought I was
Santa Claus when I walked into your apartment."

Paris sniffed, but didn't smell alcohol—not that that always
meant someone hadn't drunk too much.

He pointed into the night. "You're not getting anything else
to use against me. Go home."

Paris gathered her courage and shut the door for him. "I
waited out there a long time. I'll leave when I get what I came
for."

His laugh chilled her soul. "Well, well. A woman who knows
what she wants—or what she thinks she wants," he said, making
a slow circle around her. With his head inclined, he studied
every angle of Paris until his eyes fired her skin the way the
heat wave had failed to do. "Okay, here I am. And here you
are. D'you want what you came for fast? Rough? Without any
finesse? Or shall we pretend—make-believe. You want to go
through the polite rituals, Paris? How about a drink?"

She couldn't swallow. She told him, "I don't want a drink."

"I do."

His hand, snaking out to close on her wrist, made her flinch
and draw back.

"I'm not going to bite you," he said, thinning his lips in a
way that had nothing to do with smiling. *"Yet."* He drew her
into a small but very well-equipped kitchen and picked up a
glass with his free hand.

Quiet she might be. A little limited in social experience she
might also be. But Paris knew what Tobias implied. "I'm not Cynthia," she said, raising her chin and trying to pull free. "Sexual
harassment isn't going to work with me."

"You certainly aren't Cynthia," he told her, smiling frankly
now. He released her wrist so suddenly, she staggered before
catching her balance. "She's got bigger breasts."

Paris's face flamed. "You're despicable. And you're predictable."

"This is so interesting," he said. "You and I have said more
to each other in a week than we did in years of growing up
together."

Ice cubes tumbled into Tobias's glass from an ice maker on

the door of a black refrigerator. "Sure you won't join me?" He raised a bottle of scotch and one black eyebrow at the same time.

She shook her head.

"You scored a point or two tonight," he said. "I'll give you and your granddaddy that much satisfaction."

"I haven't begun . . . So far I haven't *scored* anything I wanted here. And you've lost points with me, Tobias. Not that you ever cared about my opinion."

He poured his drink, lifted the glass to his lips and speared her with his unwavering glacial stare.

"You're trying to take advantage of my grandfather."

Never looking away for an instant, he took a long, slow swallow. "He's been spreading lies about me," he told her. "And now you've decided to join forces and use the fact that I approached you to your own advantage. Pops is trying to bring me down. He won't make it. *I* will get what I want because it's mine. You can tell him *that*. And you can tell him not to meddle with a business he never had the guts to become a major league player in."

Paris's hands sweated. She rubbed her palms on her skirt. "Pops doesn't talk to anyone so he can't *spread* lies. You thought you could use me to help you victimize him." She didn't dare parade Cynthia's theory about Tobias's involvement in Paris's own troubles, not until there was at least some shred of proof. "*You* lied to him."

"Did I?" Black silk would slide off his voice. "Why don't we go and get comfortable, sweetheart. I'm truly fascinated by all this. I wouldn't want to miss a word."

"I don't have to get comfortable, thank you."

"No?" Again he made his insolent assessment. This time muscles flickered in his jaw and he reached out to run a finger down the side of her face.

Paris held quite still.

"What's the perfume?"

The question surprised her. "*AnaisAnais.*" And she guiltily remembered putting it on, knowing she was doing so because she was coming here.

"It reminds me of lilies." His fingers followed the line of her jaw to the point of her chin. "Something exotic. Does that fit? Underneath all the dowdy cotton, are you exotic, Paris?"

"My breasts are smaller than Cynthia's," she told him defiantly and, at the same time, felt the weight of that flesh, the sear and tensing of arousal. "And I'm not the kind of woman who can be scared into doing things she detests."

The finger made a slow descent of her throat. "Things you detest? Are we back to my kinky sexual demands on your lily-white sister?" He smiled again and watched his fingertip meet the V-neck of her blouse—at its deep center—and sweep, at such an exquisitely leisurely pace, over the top of one breast. He said, "No. I'm wrong. Cynthia's not the lily. You are. Soft and white . . . and waiting to lure me into your dark, hidden center. Or you would be if you weren't frigid. Are you frigid? If you detest sex I suppose you probably are."

"Stop it." With each sharp breath her breasts rose under his scrutiny. The ice in his eyes was becoming something quite different. "Give it up. That's all I want to tell you. And playing these sick little games of yours won't get to me. You will not get away with what you've tried to do."

"Because you're going to stop me?" He set down his glass, took his other hand from her skin. Gradually, he backed her from the kitchen to the bottom of an open wooden staircase leading to the upper floor. "Because you're going to take advantage of the fact that I—stupidly I now admit—I came to you for help?"

He really was convincing. "You told Pops one thing and did another."

"I never told Pops anything, Paris."

She faltered at the speed of his retort.

"My lawyer dealt with the land transactions. I haven't spoken to Pops—or rather he hasn't spoken directly to me in years."

"Whose fault is that?"

"It wasn't *mine.*"

The motion of his body toward her sent Paris's ankle against the bottom step. She sat down with a thud. "You said that land was going to be used for a park."

With a hand on each banister, Tobias leaned over her. "I did not say the land would be a park."

Paris trained her eyes on his flat belly. "Yes, you did. And you said it would become some sort of tax write-off."

"*No*, I did not say it would be a tax write-off. I didn't say what I intended to do with it, period. I bought it. End of story. And that's the way it's going to be written."

"We—"

"You are going to *get out of my way.*" Keeping his grip on the banisters, he dropped to one knee between her feet. His face was inches from hers. "You and that . . . You and Pops will leak no more rumors about me. Do we understand each other?"

"I . . . We haven't."

"Yes, you have. And you came here tonight for two reasons. You wanted to see if I'd trip up and tell you how much damage you've already done. And you wanted to gather some more ammunition. Let me guess what you'll tell Pops for his next release. How I forced myself on you? Is that what you're after?"

Any show of fear excited men like Tobias Quinn. Cynthia had told her all about that. "We both know I don't interest you physically," she said. "Did anyone ever tell you that really strong men—men who are strong inside as well as outside—they don't use muscle to force themselves on women."

His laugh made Paris jump. "No man, strong or otherwise, could force you to do anything. You're made of stone. And you're one hell of an actress."

She was no actress and she hated confrontation. "What I am doesn't matter to you. And what you think of me doesn't matter to me. Leave Pops alone. Do you understand me? He's old and he"—she hadn't even told Emma what Pops had said about not wanting to live if the development went ahead—"He's old. Don't try to punish him for an argument he had with men who . . . Just don't."

"He's shooting at my employees."

She gasped. "No . . . Pops wouldn't. He wouldn't."

"He *does*. Every day. They can't work."

"Pops hasn't shot a gun since he gave up . . . hunting." Oh, *no*.

"Hunting birds? Yes, of course. I remember. That's what he's supposedly shooting at now. Right over the heads of my people. And it's going to *stop.* "

He remained where he was, braced over her, near enough for her to see the pattern of dark hair on his chest through the fine white shirt. And the faint beard stubble she'd seen on his jaw when he'd taken her home from the Blue Door.

She'd touched his face that night, stroked his face.

He was warm. Even in the heat of the night, the warmth from his body smote her, wound about her as if they were pressed together, skin-to-skin.

Paris looked hesitantly up into his eyes.

His pupils dilated.

His lips parted and Paris's own mouth opened a fraction.

Without warning, Tobias brought his other knee down between Paris's feet, forcing her legs apart. He drove his hands into her hair with enough force to snap the band she'd used to hold it back.

"What do you feel about me?" he asked in a hoarse whisper. "The man? *Me?*"

Paris started to shake her head but he held it fast.

"*Say* it. Say I repel and attract you at the same time. Tell me you hate my guts but you can't look at me without wondering what it would be like to sleep with me."

The space around them had become a vacuum. Tobias seemed to grow larger and she was shrinking.

With the heels of his hands he clamped the sides of her face. His fingers made tight, painful circles on her scalp.

"Tell me." He brushed his mouth across hers. "*Tell* me."

"Stop it." She scarcely heard her own voice.

"*Say* it."

Paris groped until she held his wrists. Her eyes closed.

His mouth, when it opened hers, was hot and hard and insistent.

In the middle of all the clamoring drive to respond she heard the clear reminder that this man only wanted to use her. She heard it and shut it out.

Tobias's tongue should not be where it was. She should not meet it, welcome it.

He pressed her down on the hard edges of the stairs and cradled her head on a forearm. Paris arched her back away from the painful wood and Tobias's big hand pushed inside her blouse to cover a breast.

"I want you," he muttered. Buttons tore from the blouse and he tugged the fabric aside. "You excite me, Blue. God help me, you excite me."

Blue.

His lips and tongue replaced his fingers on her breast.

Paris tossed against the dart of sweet sensation. She writhed at the pull low inside her body when he rubbed a beard-roughened cheek on the very tip of her nipple.

Tobias pushed her knees farther apart, bunched her skirts about her hips, stroked her legs from calf, under sensitive knee and aching thigh to her bottom inside her panties.

His lips left her breast. She heard his zipper part, felt the iron velvet of the head of his erection through thin silk.

Hard fire.

Burning steel.

He ripped the silk away.

"Tobias!" She opened her eyes. A sheen of sweat coated his brow and the pirate's hair fell, unruly, to his shoulders. She wanted him, but she didn't want what would come afterward. Paris pushed on his chest with both hands. *"Tobias!"*

"Yes. Yes, Blue." His strength forcing against her hands, bent her elbows and brought him even closer.

"Don't," she told him through chattering teeth. With a desperate shove, Paris forced herself up a stair. It . . . The contact was broken.

Tobias's darkened, unfocused eyes opened.

"Stop it. Please stop. I don't want this."

He only grew heavier, pressed her until she almost cried out from the jab of the stairs at her back.

"Let me get up," she begged, desperately clawing at his shoulders. "Please let me up."

The focus snapped back into sleet gray.

"Please."

His mouth worked, then he said, "You don't have to plead, Goddammit."

Paris cringed and struggled.

Abruptly, the pressure left her. Tobias spun away and stood with his back to her.

"That's not what I wanted," she said, pulling her blouse together, tugging her skirts over her legs. "It's not. It's not. No, it's—"

"*Shut* up." His shoulders heaved. "Be quiet. Please, be quiet."

She stood up on legs that shook. "I didn't mean to—"

"Don't talk, Paris."

"You don't repel and . . . Oh, God."

Paris rushed to throw open the door. In seconds she heard Tobias's footsteps behind her. She ran, not caring that the blouse flew away from her breasts.

He kept coming.

Her breath escaped in sobs and returning air seared her throat and lungs.

The ancient white Buick wasn't worth locking. Once inside, she turned the key in the ignition and almost fainted with relief when the engine rumbled to life.

Yanking the wheel, she swerved the vehicle away from the steep bank opposite the docks and pulled on the headlights. The glare picked out Tobias. He loomed at the top of the ramp leading to the docks. By the time Paris drew level he'd begun to turn back toward the houseboats.

Bottled force.

Now Paris knew the threat that lay in uncorking that bottle.

Ten

Bill Bowie was a self-made man, and a man who'd made himself very nicely.

Bill Bowie was a man of few words, and the words he did utter were to-the-point.

Bill had two passions in life—business and Vivian Estes.

Of average height, at something more than forty-five he was built like a long-distance runner, all steel tendon and lean muscle. His thin, white-blond crewcut and sailor's wind-bronzed skin put a bleached glitter into pale blue eyes.

Bill Bowie never wasted money-making time, yet he was in Tobias's office in the middle of a working morning and they had no business to conduct. That was unusual. Vivian Estes was at Bill's side. That wasn't unusual.

"Nigel around?" Bill asked, nodding at Tobias's elderly secretary who still took notes the way he liked them taken—by hand.

"He's gone up north to check things out for me."

"Good." With one hand at a waist any man would be thrilled to get close to, Bill ushered his tall, black-haired, olive-skinned lover to a chair. "I want to talk to you about Nigel," he told Tobias.

"Someone ought to." Gladys, the secretary who'd joined Quinn as an office girl back in Sam Quinn's time, was a mistress of theatrical asides.

Tobias pretended not to hear her. "Nigel's really trying to clean up his act."

"He's trying to clean up," Gladys said, running the tip of her pencil along the spiral binding of her notebook. "I doubt if his act's what he's got in mind."

Tobias rose slowly from his desk. He'd long ago given up on intimidating Gladys into submission. "Do you suppose you could get some espresso sent in?"

Gladys got up and yanked at the belt on her pink and white striped shirtwaist dress. She was a woman who did not believe in artifice. Her hair was in the yellowed phase of gray and cut ruthlessly short around a florid face.

"If you two would tell Gladys what you want?" Tobias suggested.

"Nothin' for me, thank you," Vivian said, turning her impossibly green gaze on Gladys and smiling. "Bill likes an Americano, don't you, sweets?"

Bill said, "Yes," and looked at Vivian with the kind of simmering adoration he had never lavished on anything or anyone else.

"Americano," Gladys said, wrinkling her shiny nose and jotting notes. "And a tall-double-skinny-nothing for Mr. Quinn, I shouldn't be surprised. Anyone for an iced mocha with whipped cream and a cinnamon stick? Fat-free bagels? Sugar-free muffins?"

"Two Americanos will do nicely, Gladys," Tobias said, catching Bill's grin. "And thank you very much for doing that for us."

When the door closed behind Gladys, Bill said, "Why do you put up with that female?"

"Because Tobias has a good and true heart," Vivian answered in her voice like dark, warm honey. "Unlike you, sweets, he understands tradition and respect for institutions." Vivian, about whom almost nothing was known except her New Orleans origins, flashed a smile guaranteed to dissolve bones.

"Gladys is certainly an institution around here," Tobias said. "And she's a fantastic secretary. She's also absolutely loyal to me. That lady would take on tigers to protect yours truly."

"She isn't too thrilled about Nigel moving in."

Tobias wasn't certain he could keep himself from snapping at the next person to get under his skin today. "Nigel isn't moving in, Bill. He's trying to make a life for himself."

"I don't trust him."

Shit. Did anyone really believe *he* was ready to completely trust Nigel? "Nigel is my brother."

"Half-brother."

"We had the same father and I want to give him a chance."

Bill went to stand beside Vivian. "I've never understood why you insist on staying in this place."

"I like the area." On Stewart Street, with a view down the busy hill into the gaudy, teeming heart of Pike Place Market as well as a great overlook of the waterfront and bay, Tobias felt about his cluttered five floors of offices the way he felt about a comfortable pair of shoes—deeply attached.

"I like it here, too," Vivian said. "Bill wouldn't be comfortable among all the others."

Tobias frowned and said, "All the others?"

Vivian indicated the more than century-old exposed brick walls, heavy beams and worn wooden floors. "Others," she said. "A lot of lives have passed this way."

"Let's get down to it," Bill said quickly. He sought Vivian's hand and held it atop the shoulder of her tangerine-colored linen dress. Everything about the woman moved with fluid, irresistible grace, including the way she raised her unreadable eyes to Bill's.

No one met Vivian Estes and failed to be mesmerized. Tobias unwillingly took his gaze from the almost Eastern set of her perfect features. A rich, beautiful woman from New Orleans who was said to practice *unusual* arts. As big a mystery as the woman herself was her single-minded adoration of conservative Bill—and the fact that he tolerated and clearly liked being openly adored by Vivian. She went with him everywhere—had for ten years.

"I've ignored all the talk, Tobias," Bill said. "Until now. It's getting dangerous now."

The talk about him could get a whole lot worse after his out-of-control animal performance with Paris last night. "I can handle it. But thanks for—"

"You aren't handling it." Bill turned to a drafting table and idly unrolled a blueprint. "Nigel's being hounded by the mob. It's all over town."

Tobias dropped back into his chair. "What's all over town is an exaggeration of the truth. Nigel's in debt but he's paying it off."

Bill bent over to examine a drawing more closely. "You're paying it off, you mean. I bet he's the highest paid gofer in history."

"Wrong. Nigel made it clear he doesn't want any favors from me. Just a chance to learn the business, and I'm giving it to him. He may become very valuable to me. In the meantime I'm paying him a good salary."

"You bought him off years ago."

Tobias swallowed and caught Vivian's eye. She turned her mouth down sympathetically. He thinned his own lips and said, "You don't give an inch, my friend."

"No. But I *am* your friend. And because I am I want to make sure nothing happens to you. There are men—and women—in this town who would love to see you go down. They'd be happy to shovel the dirt in on top of you."

"That was true before Nigel showed up again."

"Nigel's an added complication at this point." Bill tapped the paper. "What d'you think about this? I've been asked to bid, too."

The blueprint was of a proposed downtown condominium complex. "I think we could be getting overbuilt. But there shouldn't be any difficulty arranging the right marriage. The money's there." He and Bill shared a unique friendship. They competed, sometimes fiercely, but never without respect.

Bill sniffed and rolled the print again. "Did you go to the Delight woman's place?"

Tobias felt again the sensation of having been punched in the gut. The same sensation had assaulted him again and again through the early morning hours, waking him each time he slid into sleep.

He'd never wanted a woman more than he'd wanted Paris when she'd come to him. And he'd never felt more self-disgust than he'd felt after he'd sent her running into the night—running from *him*.

"That was a lousy idea," Bill said.

Tobias closed his eyes tightly for an instant, then pushed back from his desk. "Pops started working on my reputation before I talked to Paris."

"He sure did," Bill agreed. "And he was doing very nicely without any help from you."

She could just have mentioned his visit to Pops in passing. "I don't know how he managed to put the word out so fast. It was only three—no, four days ago. When I spoke to her."

Tobias didn't miss the glance that passed between Bill and Vivian. "What?" he asked, looking from one to the other. "You know something I don't, right?"

"Listen to Bill," Vivian said in her gentle drawl. "You're too close to all this, Tobias. Too involved and emotional. Something's not right and we don't mean just Pops Delight."

"No," Bill said. "Pops is a spiteful old man with a grudge. Probably because he didn't do as well as your grandfather. But think about it—does he have the contacts it would take to stir up the kind of furor that's getting to you?"

"It's not getting to me."

"If it keeps up, it will. You need to watch your back."

Vivian rose and approached Tobias. "You're important to Bill and me." She smoothed the backs of cool fingers over his brow. "You're gonna need to keep right on lookin' in front of you. Bill's gonna be the eyes in the back of your head, friend."

Tobias caught and held her hand. "I appreciate the concern, but I do think I can take care of one ornery old man and his pellet gun."

Vivian withdrew her hand, pushed her long, straight black hair behind her shoulder and turned away from Tobias. She said, "He's not getting it, Bill. Tell him."

Bill went to Tobias's desk and supported his weight on his

knuckles. "Someone right here—someone we rub shoulders with in this business—definitely someone at that cozy little gathering at the Westin last night—is out to get you."

For several seconds Tobias listened to the whir of a wooden-bladed fan overhead. "Competition isn't anything new," he said finally. "If Pops deliberately feeds false rumors about how my deal with him is crippling me, the appropriate ears will be happy to listen."

"Will *you* listen?" Bill said, leaning farther over the desk. "This wasn't Pops's idea. Don't you see that? He wouldn't have thought of doing this—this way—without help. Someone is out to get you big time. One of our *friends* went to Pops Delight and sold him a scheme. That same friend is coaching the old man every step of the way."

"You gotta find him," Vivian said.

"Fast," Bill said. "Before he gets whatever he's really after."

The second strong Americano—the one Bill would have drunk if he'd stayed till it arrived—slid down Tobias's throat untasted.

If he'd thought beyond an old family feud he wouldn't have needed Bill and Vivian to tell him the obvious.

One by one, Tobias made a mental check through names and connections.

"Mr. Quinn," Gladys called from her desk outside his open door. "I'm taking a two-hour lunch."

"Hour and a quarter," he responded out of habit.

"Hour and three-quarters."

Usually they settled on one and a half. Today Tobias said, "Yeah. Fine. Hold the martinis to three."

"I'll try." Gladys's desk drawers slammed shut.

From his post in front of the windows he heard her leave, on her way—as she was at this time every day—to mass at a church near the Seattle Center.

The Skagit plans hadn't become public knowledge until he'd started hiring for the project. At that point he'd already been warned off by Pops.

"Get the hell off that land or I'll make you wish you had," had been the succinct message delivered via a ham operator.

The threat had surprised Tobias at first. Then he'd decided the old man was probably getting a little funny.

Snarling dogs and whatever had been repeatedly fired over the heads of his men were anything but funny. Going to Paris had been a desperate measure that seemed like a good idea at the time.

Hell, had it been such a terrible idea?

Tobias smiled slightly. The most terrible part about seeing Paris again was that he'd taken so long to do it. Not that she'd welcome him with open arms if he ever showed up again.

Everything else about his visit had been a bad idea. Every word he'd spoken to her had been wrong. What he'd done and—even worse—what he'd almost done last night made him want to erase the memory completely.

He looked at his hands and felt suddenly cold. There had to be a way to apologize to Paris and then put the incident behind them.

On the floors below him, more than a hundred men and women—the best of the best at what they did—went about Quinn's affairs. Across town in his second office building twice as many people worked. The company had long ago become too big for him to know everyone by name.

What Bill had failed to say was that for his theory to make sense, the details of Tobias's dispute with Delight would need to have been revealed to a competitor by someone inside Quinn.

He wasn't a damn detective.

"Knock, knock."

No. Tobias closed his eyes and prayed that voice had been an evil trick of his imagination.

"You look as if you could use some company."

"Not yours, Cynthia." He didn't turn around. "I don't know who let you in here, but you can find your own way back out."

"I found my own way in. And you aren't being very nice."

The door closed softly.

Her high heels tapped a leisurely path toward him. Tobias

didn't have to look at Cynthia to see the swing of her hips with that walk.

She said, "It's so good to see you," in the breathy voice he'd found such a turn-on for more years than he wanted to remember wasting.

"Still fascinated by your old view?" Cynthia stood beside him. Tobias focused on the mysteriously European-style cookery clutter in the corner windows of *Sur La Table*.

Her fingertips brushed the hair at his temple. He fought an urge to flinch.

"We don't have to be enemies anymore, Tobias."

A half-sideways glance in her direction gave him a different "old view" that was also still fascinating. Cynthia chose her clothes to showcase her beautiful body. The stretchy white lace camisole she wore under an unbuttoned white linen jacket was *all* she wore under the jacket.

He'd actually told Paris she had smaller breasts than Cynthia . . . *Why* would he say a crude thing like that to a woman like Paris Delight?

Tobias jerked his head away from Cynthia's hand.

"I want to talk to you," she said.

"I don't want to talk to you." He looked at her marvelous face, then directly at her full breasts. Large dark nipples showed distinctly inside the tight top. "Maybe you shouldn't be on the streets in that," he suggested. "Better button up the jacket as you leave. And that's going to be now."

Cynthia shrugged out of the jacket and draped it over her forearms. "Paris is in trouble," she told him. "And she's angry."

If he'd expected her to say anything it certainly hadn't been about Paris. "I'm sorry to hear that," he said, deliberately noncommittal. Surely Paris hadn't told Cynthia about . . .

"She called me last night."

Abruptly, Tobias turned away from her and returned to his chair.

Cynthia made her undulating way to sit on the corner of his desk and cross her legs. "Remember how I used to come and visit you here?" She tilted her head back and laughed. "While dear old Gladys was at Mass?"

He remembered.

Vividly.

She ran the toe of her shoe along the side of his thigh. "Ever miss the possibility of one of my little surprises."

"Cynthia—"

"I wonder where Gladys thought I was when she came in and couldn't see me." Her toe made the return journey.

"Gladys is no fool. She knew you were under my desk. Have we finished reminiscing?"

"I used to love—"

"*That's* enough."

"While you tried to pretend my head wasn't in your lap."

"Ah, yeah." There were points in his anatomy that didn't seem to recall that he detested this woman. "That was in another life."

"Okay." A sigh necessitated an adjustment of the camisole. "Paris's call surprised me."

"Is it unusual for her to call you these days?" Now he was stalling.

Cynthia spread her jacket over her skimpy skirt and tucked it under her legs. With a faintest of smiles she bent closer. "Just making sure you don't accuse me of trying to distract you again."

Keeping his gaze above her collarbones wasn't easy. "Are you thinking of getting to the point anytime soon."

"I sympathize with you about Pops, you know."

He looked directly into her eyes.

"When Paris called she told me how you stopped by her place last week and asked her to speak to Pops for you."

"Did she?"

"Paris tells me everything."

Silly Paris.

"She said you want her to put in a good word for you with Pops."

Why would Paris tell Cynthia a slightly skewed version of the truth? "I did visit Paris."

Cynthia laughed, showing her perfect teeth. "Prickly as ever, isn't she?" Crossing her arms under her breasts had the effect she wanted.

"Paris is . . ."

"Paris is Paris," Cynthia thoughtfully finished for him, before he could scramble for, and possibly find the wrong thing to say. "But when she mentioned you, she made me think. She won't really admit it, but the truth is Paris is in financial trouble. She's had an awful shock. Some creep's been making cheap copies of her jewelry and now none of her customers want to touch her stuff. Not this year's anyway. She needs a loan to get her through."

Tobias shifted in his seat. Evidently Paris had felt compelled to tell her adopted sister about the encounter without revealing much about what had been said. And he'd lay odds Cynthia had no inkling about either his second visit to Paris's apartment or the disaster at his houseboat. He propped his elbows on the arms of his chair and tapped his fingertips together.

Cynthia pouted—the old you're-not-giving-me-enough-attention pout—then turned her mouth down as if she'd somehow forgotten herself for a moment. "She doesn't know where to turn. There's no one to ask."

"You just said she isn't admitting she needs a loan."

"I said not *really*," she told him, sounding petulant. "You always insisted on picking apart what I say."

"That hardly matters anymore."

She tossed her hair. "No. Anyway, I'm not here about me. I'm here about Paris. I did offer to help her but she refused. For as long as I can remember, Paris has felt threatened by me. I'm sure she turned me down because she couldn't bring herself to accept."

If memory served, the shoe might well be on the other foot. "I never thought of Paris as the jealous type."

"Oh, not exactly *jealous*. Just intimidated perhaps. Not that I can understand why she should be." Cynthia's rosy gold hair swished again and she arched her back. "But I'd like to help her. So I thought of you, Tobias. I don't know how much money she needs but couldn't you offer to help her?"

"How would I do that? Wouldn't she want to know *why* I was offering?"

Cynthia reached for his hand.

Tobias dropped his arms to his sides.

"I'm not going to *bite* you," she said, her voice catching effectively. "Paris told me Pops sold you all kinds of land and now he's trying to stop you from building on it."

"I don't make the connection here."

"It's simple. I agree with you that Pops is a nasty old coot. God knows why Emma stayed with him as long as she did."

Tobias squinted at her. "So?"

"So, I don't think Pops should be allowed to stand in your way. If you weren't so decent, you'd serve him with one of those—those—you know what I mean."

"Restraining orders?"

She jabbed a long, painted fingernail in his direction. "That's it. But you're not doing it for old times' sake. I know you."

That had been the problem, she *hadn't* known him. "Whatever you say." The rumor mongers would have a field day with Tobias serving an order on "poor old Pops Delight."

"Don't you see? This can all work out perfectly. Paris is the one person who can get Pops to listen. If she tells him to give you a break, he probably will."

"Paris doesn't want to do that."

"But she could change her mind if you do something to make her want to trust you. Why don't you go and tell her you've found out about her problems and you'd like to help her. If she tries to refuse, *insist*. Then if you wait and let her be the one to mention Pops again I bet she'll offer to talk to him for you."

Tobias shook his head. "This is quite some scenario you've worked out. What I don't get is why. What's your angle, Cynthia?"

Her brilliant eyes filled with tears and she averted her face. "I've made a lot of mistakes," she said. "Maybe I regret some of them."

Cynthia and regret? Together? Another unique concept.

"Damn you, Tobias. You can be so hard."

He looked at her and wished he felt something other than indifference. "You made me the way I am with you. There was a time when you had me on a platter—heart and soul, lady. It wasn't enough for you."

Slipping from the desk, she went to her knees beside his chair

and took his unresponsive hand to her face. "I don't expect
you to believe this, but I still care about you, Tobias. I do know
what I lost—what *we* lost."

Gently, he disentangled his fingers from hers.

"Sometimes I . . . Well, sometimes I wish things were different, that's all."

He wanted her gone before Gladys came back.

"I've grown up a lot. I've learned I have to let go of some
things."

"We all do. Get up, Cynthia."

"I . . . I wish I could feel you forgave me."

"Get up."

She did as he asked. "You never give an inch, do you?"

"I don't have any idea what I'm supposed to give an inch
about. Do you want me to run through the reasons we got
divorced and then absolve you? Or do you want to run through
them? Can we just get on with this and let me get back to work?"

"*Yes!* Damn you, yes. Use your wits with Paris. That's my message to you."

His eyes ran upward over the lacy pattern of the camisole, over
the heaving swell of her all-but-naked breasts, to her moist,
parted lips and wetly glinting eyes. "You make absolutely no
sense."

"She's wanted you since we were kids! She used to . . . She
watched you all the time, for Chrissakes. Then, when she saw
I had you, no man could fill your shoes for her."

He opened his mouth, and closed it again.

"Don't tell me you never knew. No man could be that oblivious."

Amazed at the outrageousness of her suggestion, Tobias
shook his head. "She detested me."

"That was an act. I tried not to believe you'd be difficult to
convince. Look, three years ago she finally let a man into her
life. Michael. An actor. Tall, dark, good-looking—very much
like you, if you didn't examine him too closely. Paris wouldn't
have given him a second look if she hadn't been searching for
another Tobias Quinn."

"Where is this coming from?"

"Open your *mind* for once. Michael had charisma. Because he was as close as she could get to a man like you, Paris supported him for *two years* while he was getting off the ground in the theater locally."

Tobias felt an unaccustomed squeezing in his gut. "What happened?" Not that Paris Delight's love affairs interested him.

"He got a big break. Went to New York. Then he let Paris know there was no room for her in his success story."

"Bastard."

Cynthia's finely arched brows rose. "I think she·missed the kid more than him in the end."

He had to ask, "Kid?"

"Michael had been married. He had a little boy. Paris got very attached to him. I think she really started to think of herself as his mother, or some such stupid thing."

"You would think that was stupid."

She tossed her jacket over her shoulder. "Don't start on that with me. That *is* history." Her hand went to her flat stomach, a stomach she'd made very clear would never be distorted by pregnancy. Only she'd waited until after they were married to make that announcement. "Anyway, she's over most of it—the guy, for sure."

He wanted her to leave—*now.* "Why are you telling me all this?"

"At this moment I'm not sure why. I heard something in Paris's voice last night. I guess that's what made me decide to come here. I wish I hadn't." She swung away from him. "Okay, I'm going."

He pushed to his feet. "What did you hear in her voice?"

"Nothing you want to know about."

"I want to know."

She looked at him over her shoulder. "Paris is still in love with you."

Eleven

"There you are, Blue," Tobias said.

Paris's head whipped toward him and she dropped the bag of oranges she'd just bought.

The bag split.

"Hell." Tobias stopped Paris from scrambling between the crush of passing Pike Place Market shoppers to rescue rolling fruit. "Stay where you are. I'll get it," he shouted over the din.

Fish peddlers yelled at laughing customers and tossed huge salmon into their hands while a man with an open violin case before him coaxed a Paganini concerto from his tired instrument.

"How many were there?" Tobias asked the stall-keeper who came to help. "Give me the same again."

"There's nothing wrong with those," Paris said.

Tobias tossed the fruit into a nearby garbage can. "They're ruined." He took out his wallet. "And it was my fault for shocking you."

"You didn't shock me. You surprised me. That was a waste. A little bruised fruit never hurt anyone."

He settled a hand on her shoulder. "I think *you're* a little bruised, Miss Granola." She was trembling, dammit.

"I've never seen you in the market before."

"That's because I don't come here," he told her, making way for a woman wearing a crown of balloons. "I'm only here now because I finally got one of your bodyguards to say this was where I might find you."

Today her black hair was a loose, shiny mass. He'd forgotten how it tended to spring away from her face in damp weather, or on humid days like today. She poked at the bridge of her glasses. "I don't know why you would come looking for me. You didn't say anything about . . . Who did you talk to?"

"The gentleman in brown at your apartment was the only one who didn't seem to think I was Jack the Ripper. The bartender from the Blue Door—Conrad? He told me to get lost. And your buddy Samantha threatened to do nasty things to me if I didn't butt out."

A hint of pink sprang into her cheeks. "Sam's very protective."

"Why should he think I'm a threat?" It was his turn to feel uncomfortable. "I assume he has no reason to think I'm a threat. Or does he?"

"No."

"The lady on the first floor—the one with pink hair and a party hat—she wanted to talk, but only about what I might need for the next costume party I plan to throw."

"Mary's eighty-five and she still runs a party-goods store." There was no mistaking how much Paris did not want to talk to him. "Costumes. Decorations. Magic tricks. Favors. Has done for thirty years. Excuse me, please."

"Absolutely not." Passing money to the stall-keeper, he accepted the replacement bag of oranges the man held over mountains of produce. "Give me your bag."

"I can manage, thank you."

Tobias unhooked the canvas bag from her thin wrist. "It's making marks." He touched the red ring on her skin and promptly wished he hadn't. She all but leaped away. "Yeah, well, I guess I don't blame you."

He got a view of the top of her head. She said, "I need to finish my shopping."

"Okay if I tag along?"

She dug her teeth into her bottom lip.

"I work just up there, y'know." He pointed in the general direction of the hill that rose in front of his building. "But I never think to come down and buy any of this wonderful fresh stuff. I probably glow in the dark. I live on things you can put in the microwave. Educate me in the mysteries of the market. Maybe you can do a good deed and save my arteries." His boyish smile usually warmed the coldest female heart.

Paris didn't smile back.

"Which way?" With a hand at her elbow, he waited.

Indecision intensified her blush before she moved, suddenly and determinedly, away from him. Tobias caught up.

At the next stall she pulled a worn brown wallet from the pocket of her full, dark green skirt. She bought yellow and green peppers, a leek and a handful of pea pods.

When she stood with her purchases in her hands, he opened the bag for her to drop them in and said, "Will you have dinner with me tonight?"

Her response was to yank back her shopping bag and hurry away.

He reached her as she entered a small shop where the air was heavy with the scents of myriad spices. "Will you?" he asked, sidestepping other shoppers in a narrow aisle.

"No."

"We need to talk."

She took a jar of sun-dried tomatoes from a shelf and attempted to go around him.

"I said we need to talk."

"I doubt it."

When she dodged the other way, he cut her off again. "Give me a chance, Blue. Please."

"Why do you call me that?"

She glared into his face. Tobias looked back and felt his damned insides flip over. "Don't you know?" He wasn't about to explain now—here. "What could it hurt? Having dinner with me, I mean?"

Behind the round glasses that were exactly right for her,

Paris's eyes told him exactly what—or who—she thought might be hurt by getting anywhere near him.

"Paris—"

"I've missed several work sessions and I've got a lot of catching up to do." With that, she marched past him and went to pay for her goddamn sun-dried tomatoes.

Flowers caught his eye. In buckets outside the store. He strode to a showy display of white lilies with red centers and bought two bunches. The woman who sold them wrapped pink paper around cellophane and tied the bouquet together with red ribbon.

Tobias turned in time to see Paris zip by at a trot. Once more he caught up. This time he stuffed the flowers into her hands, stopping her in midstride. He planted his feet apart and his fists on his hips beneath the suit jacket that wasn't helping his overheated blood.

The market bustle swelled about them. *"Seattle Post Intelligencer,"* came the yell from the Read All About It newsstand. *"New York Times! Seattle Times! We've got the Times!"*

"I thought you'd like the lilies," Tobias said, letting his hands slide into his pockets.

Paris looked from him to the flowers and back again.

"They remind me of that stuff you wear," he said and looked heavenward. Why not just go ahead and remind her—blow-by-blow—of what he'd said and done last night, and bury any chance he had of doing what he'd been trying to think of a way to do ever since?

"It's after five and it's hot," he told her.

"I noticed."

"Why don't we go somewhere and have a drink. There's—"

"No."

"Oh, for—Give me a break, will you? Coffee, then? Would you come and have some coffee with me? *Please?*"

"We seem to say *please* to each other a lot."

Was that a crack in the armor? "Yeah. You don't have any reason to say *please*. I do. So could we? Have coffee?"

She turned away, her skirts filling with the hot wind, and then turned back. "Coffee?"

"Yeah. Coffee."

"Where?"

"Seattle's Best? In Post Alley?"

Her head bowed, but she nodded. "Okay. But it can't take long."

Once more he relieved her of the bag. "Not long, I promise you." As long as he could persuade her to stay. "You look tired . . ." He set his teeth together and ushered her across the cobbled street choked with overheated shoppers, jockeying vehicles and yelling stall-keepers. At least he hadn't added that she probably needed more sleep than she'd got last night.

When they climbed Pine Street, Tobias resisted the temptation to take her arm once more. "Even the wind's hot," he said, his attention caught by a swaying hanging basket of pink ivy geraniums and trailing ferns.

With one accord they turned right into Post Alley where the red and white awnings of the coffee shop flapped. "Outside?" he asked.

Paris nodded and sat at a table in the shade of the facing brick wall. "Just black coffee, please," she said before he could ask what she wanted.

When he returned, after checking regularly to make sure Paris hadn't fled, she silently wrapped her hands around the red paper cup he set before her.

"So," he said, pulling up a chair. "How has your day been?"

She blinked at him. "Fine."

"Good." He took a swallow of his own coffee. "Good."

Her hands were slender but capable, the nails short and unvarnished. Nothing like Cynthia's.

Tobias drank again. "Sometimes . . . Do things ever . . ." He turned up a palm. "Do things ever get *away* from you?"

The wind tossed her long hair across her face. He didn't hear what she said as she used both hands to pull it behind her neck.

"Excuse me, Paris?"

"I said things get away from all of us sometimes."

Her skin was pale. The linen blouse she wore was a lighter shade of green than the skirt. "You're a gracious woman."

"I don't know what you want from me."

"Nothing," he said reflexively. "Just . . . Don't you like being told you're gracious?"

Her lips pursed and he could almost feel the gentle brush of her breath on his face. She rested her left hand on the table and seemed unaware that if he moved the small finger on his own right hand—just a fraction—they'd touch.

Paris is still in love with you.

He was trying to work out Cynthia's motive for that bizarre suggestion. One thing had been implicit; if he told Paris about Cynthia's visit, he'd only deal a blow to his own cause.

What would it be like to be loved by Paris Delight?

The curve of her neck and shoulder looked oddly vulnerable to him.

Loving or being loved was something he'd put behind him—not as an impossibility, but as a definite improbability. If he did ever fall in love again it sure as hell wouldn't be with a Delight.

"I had a lousy day yesterday," he said. "Things haven't been easy lately."

"I know the feeling."

"When I got back to Union Bay last night—"

"No."

He bent closer. "No?"

"No. I don't want to talk about it."

"AnaisAnais," he murmured. "That's what it was called."

She clamped her hands back on the cup.

"Look. About last night."

"I shouldn't have come."

"I'd been to a dinner at the Westin." As if she cared where he'd been. "All day I watched men stand around when they should have been working. Then I was at the Westin listening to people whisper about how that's what I was spending my time doing these days."

Paris took off her glasses and set them down. "How would they know?" She massaged her brow.

"They were told. Do you have a headache?"

"You mean your employees talk about you?"

"Maybe . . . *No.* I mean Pops . . . Forget it. Do you have a headache?"

"I think I do."

Women. "Either you do or you don't."

"Are we done here?"

"I was just trying to explain why I behaved . . . I'm not the way I seemed last night."

"Okay."

He took off his suit jacket and hung it over the back of the chair. "It is *not* okay. It is definitely anything but okay."

"Don't shout."

Tobias loosened his tie, then dragged it all the way off and undid the top button on his shirt. "I never shout," he said through his teeth.

"People are looking at us."

"Maybe we're worth looking at."

"I want to leave now," she said, sounding utterly miserable. "Don't you understand that I'm embarrassed?"

"Because *I* behaved like an animal with you?"

She scanned the area rapidly. "I'm not . . . I've never been like that."

"Like *what?*"

Her shoulders came up. "Easily . . ." She averted her face.

"Easily upset?"

"You know that's not what I mean."

Could he just come up with the right words and be done with it? "The things that happened—"

"That wasn't normal for me," she said in a rush.

"No, no, I'm sure it wasn't. But I want you to know I said the first things that came into my head. I wasn't thinking."

"You were angry. So was I."

She was trying to make it easier for him, so why wasn't it working? "I don't know what made me make that dumb remark about your breasts."

"Please!"

"I've got to tell you, Paris. Why would I say your breasts were smaller than Cynthia's?"

Her eyes were huge.

"I want you to know I didn't mean it. I mean it isn't important."

The hand that picked up her glasses shook. "Stop it," she whispered. "People will hear."

"Some men are really into big . . . No, I mean some men are really big on . . . Those things don't matter to me."

She started to get up.

"You have absolutely nothing to be embarrassed about, Paris."

When she picked up her shopping bag her chair started to tip backwards.

Tobias caught the chair. "Please don't go. I'm doing this very badly. Honestly, Paris, I think you've got beautiful breasts."

With a hissed, "How could you?" she broke into a run and dashed away.

Tobias looked from her flying skirts, directly into the amused face of a man at the next table.

The lilies rested beside Paris's almost untasted coffee.

Tobias muttered, "Fuck," and rested his closed eyes on the heels of his hands.

Paris headed where she usually headed when she needed to calm down—to the waterfront. By the time she stood opposite South Main, her heart had slowed and each breath no longer burned her lungs and throat.

She waited for the trolley to make its turn and trundle upward on the tracks that passed her place on their way to the International District.

The bag of fruit and vegetables weighed heavily on her shoulder. The lights changed and she crossed under the viaduct.

Why had he come looking for her?

Why had he deliberately set out to humiliate her?

Why couldn't she put him out of her mind?

The front door wasn't completely closed. Paris pushed it open to be confronted by Conrad, in a muscle-revealing black T-shirt, sitting on the bottom step of the stairs.

He jumped up. "Holy *shit*, Paris. We were organizing search parties."

The door to Mary's apartment stood open. The sound of an

old video of Guy Lombardo leading a New Year's Eve celebration from the Waldorf Astoria in New York blared forth.

Wormwood sat several stairs above Conrad. "I told them you could take care of yourself," he said, rubbing at his red nose with the back of a hand.

Conrad wouldn't be subdued. "Quinn came here. Did that arrogant sonuvabitch track you down? When Wormwood let it slip that he'd told him—"

"*Can* it," Wormwood interrupted and sneezed. "She's okay. Just like I said she would be."

"You have a cold?" Paris asked.

"Maybe."

"Paris!" Sam, sartorially splendid in a red shantung suit, tasteful gold Anne Klein pin and matching earrings, erupted from Mary's apartment and seized Paris's arm. "Did that smarmy bastard find you?" He pulled her through the door into the streamer-festooned mayhem that was a duplicate of the showrooms at Does-R-Us, Mary's Pike Place shop.

"I told them he was lovely, dear," Mary said, noisily enjoying her afternoon glass of sherry. Paris would have described the color of her hair as blush, not pink, and she was wearing a shiny green hat with a shamrock on the bill. "He said he thought he just might have a really big affair in mind before long. What do you think about that?"

"I told him to get the hell out of here and stay out," Sam announced loudly enough to almost drown out Lombardo. He wore red stockings to match the suit but—as was his pre-performance habit—no shoes or wig.

Ginna sat beside Mary on a cabbage rose-patterned couch. She said, "I keep telling Sam he doesn't have to worry about Tobias. The man's a pillar of the community." She smiled widely. "And what a pillar, I say."

Paris looked from one face to the next. "Why are you all here?"

"Because we're worried about *you,*" Sam said. He sounded furious. "We know what that guy did to Cynthia. He's not right in the head, Paris. Not right at all. Now he's following you around and we don't like it."

Conrad had entered the room behind Paris and he stood with a powerful arm around her shoulders. *"Did* he find you?"

Wormwood stuck his head around the door. "See you later, people."

"You shouldn't have told him where Paris was going," Conrad said.

"The guy seems harmless to me," Wormwood commented. "I can't figure out what all the fuss is about. I gotta go."

Mary swung one end of the green feather boa she wore. "An *interesting* affair was what he said. An affair to remember."

"Subtle," Sam said, glaring at the place where Wormwood had been. "He's sick, I tell you. Some grub's gnawed into his twisted brain and made him fixate on you, Paris. The idea of having an affair with his ex-wife's sister turns the creep on."

"Oh, please." Paris sank to the edge of a red Chinese chest and rotated her aching neck. "You are blowing this thing completely out of proportion."

"He *didn't* find you?" Conrad asked hopefully, dropping to his haunches in front of her.

"Actually . . . Yes, Tobias found me. And, no, he didn't try to take me to see his etchings." There'd been framed photographs on the walls at the houseboat. Harbor scenes and San Juan Islands sunsets, from what her muddled recollections suggested.

"It's been years since I did a wedding," Mary said dreamily. Small and bony, her movements were unexpectedly graceful. "A bit of sparkle. That's what I like to see at a wedding. You'll look lovely in white, Paris. Silver sequins and net. I always did love net. And what's wrong with plastic champagne glasses, that's what I'd like to know?"

Paris met Ginna's eyes and they shook their heads in unison.

"Okay," Sam said, all business. "Enough of this. What did he want?"

To talk about my breasts. Paris winced. "I really appreciate the concern. You're family and I love you all. But you're overreacting. There's some old family business that's come up and Tobias wanted to talk to me about it."

"I told you, Sam," Ginna caroled.

"He had to track you down to the market to talk about a

piece of old family business." Sam didn't sound convinced. "It couldn't wait until he could reach you by phone like normal people do?"

"Maybe this isn't our business," Ginna suggested. "Tobias Quinn is a very respected man in this town. And, if everything's all right with you, Paris, I've got to get back to the club."

"Everything's peachy with me." She'd left the lilies behind.

Ginna got up and approached Paris. She stood in front of her and ducked her head. "You and I are old friends," she said, for Paris's ears alone. "Old friends hold each other up when the going gets rough. I'm ready to start holding anytime, Paris."

"I know," Paris murmured, smiling gratefully. "I'll let you know if I need your arms. Thanks, Ginna."

"You're too . . ." Ginna frowned. She settled her hands on Paris's shoulders and shook her gently. "You're decent. Maybe too decent."

Paris smiled and gently removed Ginna's hands. "I'm not the saint you think I am," she told her. "Go on. Get to work. Customers will be waiting."

"Uh-huh." Ginna's eyes were troubled, but she held out a hand to Conrad. "Come on, buddy. It's show time. Time for us to peddle gins and grins."

"Yeah, show time," Sam agreed, gathering his wig and shoes. "You coming down later, Paris?"

"Don't watch the door. It depends on how much I get done."

When they'd filed out and she was left with Mary, Paris said, "So you thought Tobias was nice?"

"Lovely, dear," Mary said and winked. "He was certainly in a dither about finding you."

Paris left the old lady and slowly climbed the stairs toward her own apartment. The question was *why* had Tobias been so anxious to find her?

On the second floor, the door to the Lipses' apartment stood open. Draped in a satin dressing gown that reached the midpoint on his long, thin thighs, Lips himself lounged against the jamb. "You didn't get whipped off for a harem, then?"

"No," Paris said, starting up the next flight. "Although that might make an interesting change of pace."

"What you need is a good man in your life," Lips said. "You ask my missus. You'll never hear her say she's looking for a change of pace."

Paris looked down on the top of Lips's shiny head. "I'll take your word for it." She'd have to because Mrs. Lips never made a comment without whispering it to her husband and getting clearance first.

The silence inside her own apartment was a blessed relief. Once the fans were moving and both windows had been raised to let in the evening scents from the flowers outside, Paris went into her green and white kitchen to put away her purchases.

Eating could wait. Forever, from the way she felt now.

Using a rubber band from the stash inside an old Arm and Hammer Baking Soda can, she wound her hair into a single braid and made her way to the workbench.

She snapped on the adjustable lamp and swung it down. The new collection showcased crocheted and braided wires—silver and gold—and unique pieces of bone, crystals or gems. Only the methods employed and weights of the materials were a departure for Paris. Her style would flow through every piece but the difficulty in duplicating the focal points should make them more challenging to copy.

Something felt different.

Covering work in progress with a sheet of felt was her own idiosyncrasy. The black felt had been moved, ruckled against the block that held needle files.

Paris flipped the felt aside and stood in the curved cut-out section of the bench. The silver wire neckpiece she'd almost completed lay where she'd left it. The flowing, almost beardlike waves curled downward from a solid band to surround a teardrop-shaped amethyst.

All the tools she'd been using had been brushed to the left side of the bench.

The skin on her spine tightened. Tapping brought her head up. Aldonza, on her back legs, chased an insect across a windowpane.

Someone had been here and moved her tools.

Someone had swept the surface of the bench clean of filings

and had done so in a hurry. Rather than being tipped directly into the leather skin bag suspended especially to receive the debris, silver and gold dust and minute metal chips littered the floor.

Someone had rushed to clean a space, had dragged the shavings over the jutting benchpin where pieces of jewelry under construction were secured, and let the glinting fragments fall.

Aldonza tired of bug torture and jumped down. She strolled toward Paris, her eyes glowing in the workbench lamp.

Paris rubbed her arms through the sleeves of her thin cotton blouse.

Someone had touched her work.

Aldonza arched and rubbed around her legs.

Paris rested a forefinger on the teardrop of amethyst. Helpless. What could she say? That she thought someone had come in and *looked* at her jewelry?

The cat's claws tapped on the floor. She shot from her place by Paris's feet and batted a ball of crumpled paper toward the low, square table in the middle of the room, then back again.

Absently, Paris used a toe to kick the paper, and watched the cat pounce to capture her new prey.

Whoever had been here might still be here.

Everyone but Mary and the Lipses had left. Mary was too old for these things and the Lipses didn't seem to take Paris's dilemma very seriously.

She gathered Aldonza into her arms and tossed the wad of paper on top of the bench.

They always said you shouldn't confront an intruder.

Running away from her home was out of the question.

A passageway led from the left side of the main room to the two rooms Wormwood used. Paris opened the first, the one where he painted, and felt emptiness among the pieces of work in various stages of completion. The second room contained the futon where he slept when he did sleep there, a cloakroom-style coatrack supporting what few clothes he owned and several wooden packing crates. His bathroom was clean and also quite empty.

Stairs at the far end of the passage led up to the floor where

Paris slept and where a second bedroom was unused. All still and silent.

Another flight of stairs rose to the roof garden.

Still clutching a complaining Aldonza, Paris cautiously emerged beneath a royal blue sky runneled with purple and gray.

This place was her joy and her nemesis.

The sky thrilled her—the sense of freedom.

The low parapets surrounding the area represented a wall of magnets bent on dragging her to them and tossing her over into wailing oblivion.

Paris drew a breath and relaxed. In the center of the roof were her cold frames. Here she raised flowers for the pots Sam placed on the fire escape landings. An oval of tall, waving bamboo clumps in large planting boxes created a playpen for Paris, giving her room to enjoy her air and sky and plants, but screening out the sucking parapets—and the drop beyond.

Nothing moved but the rustling bamboo.

She backed toward the stairs again and, once she was inside, bolted the heavy door. If an intruder lurked in some corner beyond the bamboo, he'd have to reveal himself and in doing so would give Paris plenty of time to get help.

She was alone.

Relief left the ache of tensed muscle in its wake. Aldonza wriggled and hissed when Paris hugged her.

Back in the workroom, a warm draft slipped through the open door leading to the rest of the building.

The latch must have failed to catch.

Paris's stomach clenched again. She hurried to shut the door tightly, let Aldonza leap away and returned to the bench.

Everything was exactly as she'd found it when she got home and pulled back the felt.

But . . . not as she'd left it a few minutes earlier.

The ball of paper wasn't there.

Twelve

The telephone on the table beside her rang four times before Paris lifted the receiver. "Yes?" The room had grown almost dark. She must have been rocking in her favorite chair for a long time.

"Paris?"

"Yes."

"It doesn't sound like you."

She kept her eyes where they'd been since she sat down—on the door.

"Paris?"

She jumped. "Yes!"

"Do not hang up the phone. This is Tobias and you've got to listen to me."

She pressed the receiver to her ear so hard it hurt. An insane wish for him to be here, now, brought a bubble of laughter into her throat.

"What's funny?"

"Nothing." She'd *actually* laughed aloud?

"Look, Blue, I just wanted to make sure you were okay."

"Yes."

"Earlier—"

"I'm in perfect shape, Tobias. I'm absolutely marvelous. I've never felt better. If I felt any better I'd fly away."

That silenced him. Another instant and he'd be launching into further analysis of how important women's breasts were to which particular men—and where she fitted into that scheme of things.

"Has something happened?"

"Happened?" Gradually, Paris leaned heavily back against the long, mahogany slats of the chairback. "Why would you ask me that?"

He was silent for some time before saying, "I'm not sure."

Steps were being taken to drive her into some sort of action. "Try and put it into words," she said. Someone wanted her to ask for help. Yes, to ask for help.

"You sound upset."

Her home had been violated but she had absolutely no proof. "In what way do I sound upset?"

"Just that. Can't you hear yourself? You don't talk that way. You sound spacy . . . aggressive."

"Aggressively spacy?"

More silence.

Out there somewhere there was a person or persons just waiting for her to make a move.

"How's your head, Paris?"

"Why?" Right now, whoever had taken a long look at one of her new designs must be expecting her to do something. "Why are you asking about my head?"

"Are you alone?"

"Yes . . . I mean . . . I really don't think that's any of your business."

"It isn't. But you don't sound well and I wondered if there was anyone there to take care of you."

"I'm not a kid."

His sigh echoed. "I didn't suggest you were a kid. What happened this afternoon was another disaster."

"Thank you for calling, Tobias."

"Don't hang up."

The bench had been cleared to allow room to make a sketch.

"The headache. The way you looked—tired, that is. That was all my doing, wasn't it?"

Aldonza's plaything must have been the evidence Paris needed to take to the police. She massaged a temple.

"Look, Paris. I'm sorry, okay? Why don't we get together in a civilized manner?"

"I've got to—"

"Work?" He laughed. "You know what they say all work and no play does."

"I'm already dull. I started out that way."

"Not in my book."

That must be why he'd lavished her with so much attention through the years.

"This afternoon," he said in his oh-so-mesmerizing voice, "I botched things, Paris. But you're not the kind of woman who doesn't give a man another chance. This is hard for me to say, but I think we may need each other. Could we meet and discuss that?"

He expected her to need him. Was that simply because he knew about the original problems with her collection and guessed she might be in deeper trouble than she'd confessed? "Thanks for the offer, but no, Tobias. Good-night." She hung up.

Had Tobias's call been timed to gauge her reaction to the intruder?

Crickets in tall grass.

White-blue skies.

Sweet, nose-wrinkling scents of drying hay and dryer warm earth.

Tobias came to crouch on the ground behind Paris and Cynthia. "It's their knees that make the noise."

Cynthia turned and batted his bare leg. "Is not."

"If you look really closely, you'll see their knees knocking together."

Paris giggled. "Go on, Cynthia. Do what Tobias says. Look close."

He rested a hand on each of their necks and pushed them, none too gently, closer to the waving yellow grasses. "See them now?"

"I can't even see any crickets," Cynthia complained. The sun had turned her nose a little pink under a smattering of freckles. "You're making fun of us."

"Making fun? Me. Would I make fun of you two, Paris?"

She looked into his gray eyes. He was fourteen and so much bigger than she was. When she thought about it, she liked him—not that he cared if she did. "I think you'd make fun of us," she said in a firm voice that pleased her.

"Why would a cricket's knees knock, then?" Cynthia said as a fresh burst of high-pitched clicking rose.

Tobias shrugged.

"Everybody knows that," Paris said. "It's because they're scared."

Cynthia leaned farther into the grass.

"You," Tobias told Paris, "are too smart for your own good, young Blue."

The thin white curtains she liked to draw at night fluttered, then billowed, filled with silver moonlight.

She'd been asleep. Now she was awake without remembering passing from one state to the other.

Her dream lingered. Seven years old in the Skagit Valley. At Pops and Emma's castle in years when there was neither a draw-bridge nor a moat—just an anomaly of a house that Pops loved and Emma hated.

And Tobias telling her she was too smart for her own good. And calling her Blue.

He had been very tall . . . even at fourteen he'd been very tall, and tanned and quite skinny in his T-shirts and cutoff-jeans. But she had liked him in the way she'd assumed girls liked their brothers; sometimes. The way in which she'd liked him hadn't begun to change until she was about thirteen and he was ancient—approaching twenty.

Paris smiled at the moon-filled drapes.

First love. How painfully sweet.

The scent in her bedroom was different. Different but familiar. Rising from the alley, probably.

Cigarettes. One of the French kind she remembered finding exotic when she was in Europe. Gitanes or Gauloises or some such brand.

People who chose Chateaux Alley billets for the night smoked generic castoff butts or the occasional treasured joint.

Normally no scent of a French cigarette filtered through thin drapes . . . And what she smelled was smoke from one of those cigarettes.

It was in the room.

Before she could repress the urge, Paris turned her head.

A pillow covered her face.

She thrashed her arms and legs, winding herself in the sheet. When she clawed at the pillow, a strong hand deftly trapped both of hers and pulled them up until she was helping her attacker do his work.

"Lie still."

Paris heard the voice. He wanted her to die quietly. He wanted her to be good while she died.

"*Still,* I tell you. I'm not gonna hurt you."

Blood pounded behind her eyes, but the voice sent an icy coat over her body. She stopped twisting.

"Good," he said. "That's it, baby. Relax. You're breathin', ain't you?"

She mumbled assent.

"Good. This is just because I wouldn't want you to get all excited. One look and you wouldn't be able to keep your hands off me. Happens every time."

She heard him drag on the cigarette and realized he'd been able to subdue her without taking the thing out of his mouth. Now he held her trapped with one hand and smoked with the other.

Thin she might be, but she was wiry and she was no wimp. Paris squirmed and tried to roll away.

"Shit!" The word sounded as if he'd clamped the cigarette between his teeth again. "Fuckin' bitch. Lie still or I quit this gentlemanly crap."

More than the pressure on her face, the prick of something needle-sharp stopped her writhing. Something needle-sharp delicately resting on the vulnerable, soft place where her collarbones met.

"Just listen, bitch. I got a message for you to take to your friend."

Paris held absolutely still.

"Oh, yes. That's very nice, baby. *You're* very nice."

She swallowed and the pricking grew a little sharper.

"This is nice." The point drew lightly downward and across the top of her left breast. She heard the tiniest *snick* and the thin strap on her nightgown fell away from her shoulder.

Panic soared. Still she didn't move.

"Very nice." The sharp knife—and she was certain it was a knife—left her skin to snag the bodice of the gown and bare her breast. "Yeah. Oh, yeah. Shit, a man's got to have discipline sometimes, but I ain't made of iron. God, I know what you can do with these things. And with your ass. Yeah, I want some of that."

A rustle came. He tongued her nipple and sucked it noisily into his wet mouth. Paris's knees jackknifed. Bile rose in her throat and she fought for breath.

His curses were a babble, but his disgusting lips left her breast. "Listen to me, bitch," he whispered hoarsely. "Listen good and remember every word."

Her heart thundered inside her trembling body.

"These are the words. Tell him time's runnin' out. Got that? You say, time's runnin' out and there ain't too much more to go. Got that?"

She nodded under the pillow.

"Good. And tell him how much you enjoyed meetin' with me."

Paris nodded again.

"Now I'm gonna take my hand off this pillow. But you ain't gonna move it till you hear the downstairs door slam. I'll slam it good and loud. You scream or yell before I slam that door and the next thing I do to you with this knife won't be so much fun. Got it?"

He waited for her head to move up and down.

"Good."

Slowly, pressure left the pillow.

"Easy," he told her. A fresh current of air crossed her body as he must have opened the door. "Not a sound, baby. Don't forget—I'll be glad to work out a way to get together for some more fun."

His shoes squished softly on the floor.

"I won't disappoint you, baby. Fun is my middle name and I *always* keep my word."

Thirteen

Third time lucky?

Tobias stood across the street from Paris's building and craned his neck to see the windows on the top two floors. He'd parked under the viaduct and walked up the block.

The entire building was in darkness.

She'd hung up on him. And he hadn't been able to do what should have been easy—tell himself he'd made an honest effort to apologize and put her out of his mind.

The front door opened.

Tobias almost started forward. Instead, he pulled deeper into the shadows.

A short, heavy figure emerged and ran swiftly down the three front steps, turned uphill and hurried to 'the corner. A car crawled north along First Avenue, slowed for the man—and Tobias could see it was a man—to get in, and then sped away.

The front door had been left open and no light at all showed from inside.

Tobias crossed the street slowly, automatically stepping over tram tracks and halting when he reached the opposite sidewalk.

A couple of hours after she'd hung up on him he'd tried to call again—and again and again.

A smart man would definitely give up.

Somehow, in the hours and days since he'd first set eyes on her again, giving up on Paris had come to represent a mixture between copping out on a challenge and walking away from the only woman to intrigue him since his divorce.

Miss Granola.

He frowned at the open front door. This wasn't an area of town where anyone should live so casually. Where was there an area, in any town, where people shouldn't be at least mildly concerned about intruders?

Driving here he'd used the cellular phone to try Paris's number once more. *No conversation on the line, sir,* the operator who had checked the line had told him. *Probably a phone off the hook.*

Tobias glanced in the direction the man had taken and then up at the silent facade of the apartments. He wasn't given to what they called presentiments of evil, but he felt the presence of evil now.

Paris had made it clear he wasn't welcome here. He ought to take the hint and leave her alone—leave this place—*now.*

There should be some light on.

What if . . . ?

To hell with caution. He walked into the building and up the stairs, by feel he walked up all the virtually invisible flights of stairs that took him to Paris's apartment.

Another door left open. This one wide open. Moonlight through the windows cut swaths across the unmoving scene. He took a step inside and said, "Paris?"

She'd sounded so unlike herself when he'd last spoken to her. Not that he was in a particularly good position to know exactly who Paris Delight was these days. Apart from a few brief exchanges after she'd returned from Europe and while he'd still been married to Cynthia, he'd never really known her as an adult.

Right now she was probably at the Blue Door with her crazy friends.

Hesitantly, he felt for the light switch and clicked it up. A single lamp came on. "Paris?" he said, louder this time.

If she came back and found him poking around it would be his own fault when he heard about it in the rumor mill.

He was going to get the hell out of here and forget the woman's name. She'd made it clear she didn't intend to help him with Pops. What did it matter if her delicate little feelings had been hurt by a man under pressure behaving like a man under pressure? He hadn't asked her to lie in wait for him when he was already stretched to his limit.

Not like a man under pressure—like a predator who'd been handed an easy mark. The truth sickened him.

Her scuffed brown wallet lay on a table near the rocking chair. Beside the wallet rested the receiver of a black telephone.

Why would she deliberately set the receiver aside?

To make certain he wouldn't bother her again.

And then go out without her wallet?

None of his goddamn business.

Tobias retraced his steps and went out onto the landing.

The sooner he got back to Union Bay the better. Tomorrow he was due to take in his proposal for the condominiums and to make some decisions on how to proceed up in the Skagit.

Who had left this building, left the door open, and been driven away in a big, gleaming, obviously expensive car?

He turned to the apartment again and located a corridor to the left of the main room. He set off at a firm pace. "Paris?" he said loudly, knocking on the first door he came to, then, again, called "Paris?" at the second. No response.

At the end of the corridor he found a flight of stairs leading upward to more darkness. He took the steps two at a time until he stood at the top.

This really was madness.

"Paris?"

The sound that came to him was muffled. A moan or a cut-off scream. Tobias's heart squeezed. He moved blindly forward until he reached yet another door, this one open. Again the moon was a lamp. Gleaming through softly billowing white drapes, the ghostly silver light wavered over a bed with a twisted sheet trailing from its side to the floor.

"Is there someone here?" Tobias said, careful to keep his voice level. "Hello?"

The strangled sound was softer the second time, but it came from this room. He pushed the door all the way open—and felt it make contact with something that gave.

A hiss of sharply indrawn breath shocked him. Gritting his teeth, Tobias crossed to the bed, switched on a lamp and turned around.

Slowly, the door swung away from the wall.

With her knees drawn up to her face and her arms wrapped around her legs, Paris huddled in the corner. "Oh, my God," he said. "Oh—my—God." He made to go to her but cast about for something to cover her with instead.

A white cotton blanket draped a chest at the bottom of the bed. Tobias grabbed the blanket and approached Paris. "It's all right," he said, absently crooning the words. "It's okay. I'm here. Only me."

She seemed to try to disappear into the corner.

What the hell had happened here?

The instant the question formed, a possible answer galloped to the fore.

Tobias's gut clenched. "Hush," he said, although she hadn't made another sound. "Let me put this around you."

He felt like a man with a net trying to capture a fawn. Paris's huge, blue eyes watched him over her knees and he believed she'd run if she could make herself move at all.

Her hair frothed about her face and shoulders. A short night-gown of pale yellow satin still had one thin strap intact. The other strap was gone. Paris held the gown to her breasts with her thighs—long, elegant, bare thighs. She had long elegant legs, but he'd noticed that detail on the houseboat.

Quick and matter-of-fact. Concerned but impersonal. That was the approach to take.

"You're going to freeze your—" *Good God!* "I'm going to wrap this around you."

She didn't help him. Tobias had to bodily shift her from the wall to drape the blanket and pull it together in front of her.

"May I help you up now?"

Paris clutched the cover to her neck. She didn't take her eyes off his face.

"Okay, okay," he told her. "Let me do this." Very carefully, he grasped her upper arms and began to lift.

Finally, her legs responded and a hand emerged from the folds of the blanket to catch at his shirt. She stood before him, hanging on, waves of shudders coursing through her flesh.

"Are you all right?" he asked her, knowing she was anything but all right. "Can you walk? I'll carry you."

She shook her head. "I'll be okay. The door didn't slam." Tears sprang into her eyes. "It didn't slam. I waited and waited but it didn't slam."

"Have you been attacked, Paris?" He held his breath.

"Yes," she whispered. "He came when I was asleep. He had a knife."

Tobias felt anger so harsh it was a crushing pressure on his lungs. Muscles in his thighs and back jerked solid until they hurt. When he reached for her he saw that his own hands trembled. "Come here," he said, pulling her into his arms. "Hold on, kid. You're safe now."

He wouldn't let his mind form the word he didn't want to think about. The previous night he'd all but forced sex on her. Tonight . . . He would not *think* that word.

Paris continued to cling to his shirt. He kept his arms around her and led her through the door to the landing then downstairs. "Where's the kitchen?" he asked.

"Other side of the workroom," she said through chattering teeth.

When he'd seated her at one of four chairs painted dark green and arranged at a round table he pulled another chair close and sat beside her. "I'm going to call the police. Is that okay?"

Her eyes ranged around the shiny painted kitchen with its high ceiling and old-fashioned white fixtures.

"Stay here." He got up, filled a kettle from a faucet that

gushed too hard, and set it on the gas stove to boil. "Tea," he said, more to himself than to Paris. "Tea's supposed to be good."

"Yes," she said quietly.

The smallest of a set of green ceramic canisters yielded some sort of herbal tea bags. Tobias located a mug. "Sit tight. I'll use the phone in the other room to call."

"They won't be interested." This time her voice was quite clear.

He went determinedly to the phone, depressed the cradle and dialed 911. A few succinct sentences brought the promise, "An officer is on his way, sir."

When he returned to the kitchen a jet of steam shot from the kettle spout and he poured boiling water over the tea bag. "Someone's coming," he told Paris, glancing at her anxiously. "Did you see him? The guy? Will you be able to describe him?"

She bowed her head. "No. He was in my bedroom when I woke up. I smelled his cigarette. I guess that's what woke me."

"And it was too dark . . . Hell, the police are going to ask these questions."

"He put a pillow over my face," Paris whispered. "Afterwards he said I had to wait till I heard the door close downstairs."

Afterwards.

Why hadn't he stopped the guy?

The crushing rage squeezed him once more. He remembered the short man and the open door. *"Would* you hear it? From so far away?"

Paris shrugged and put a hand out from the swathing blanket to pick up the mug he set before her.

His question was potentially answered by the sound of footsteps on the stairs to Paris's apartment. He hadn't heard sounds from the lower flights. Tobias got up and admitted two policemen from Seattle's bicycle squad. Dressed in yellow windbreakers and biking shorts, they removed their helmets as they entered.

"Officers Goethe and Wolfer," the first man through the door said. He and his partner made a swift visual check of the area. "You're Mr. Quinn, sir?"

Who was whom, and who belonged where, were quickly established. Both young officers sported bodies that should encourage any fitness freak to apply to the force.

They were all business. In the kitchen, the questions came. Paris answered and notes were taken.

"Did he hurt you, Ms. Delight?"

Tobias turned away.

"I struggled."

"Perhaps you'd best be examined by a doctor."

"He didn't cut me."

"Yes, but there was sexual contact?"

She hesitated and said, "Not . . . He didn't rape me."

For once it was Tobias who let his head hang forward.

"You're sure?"

Tobias swung toward the group at the kitchen table. "For God's sake! Wouldn't she know if she'd been raped?" The weight on his chest lifted but he wanted to shake someone, to threaten whoever had done this thing.

Neither policeman appeared fazed by his outburst.

"I wasn't," Paris said. She seemed small inside the blanket. "I think his only purpose was to scare . . ."

Her eyes lost focus and she remained quite still with her lips parted.

"Yes," one of the officers said when she showed no sign of continuing.

Paris looked at Tobias and coughed. "He told me to tell someone that time was running out. That's more or less what he said. So I guess he was trying to frighten both of us."

"You and Mr. Quinn?"

She hesitated before saying, "No."

"You and who else, then Ms. Delight?"

She reached up to push back the hair that had slid over her face. "I . . . He didn't give a name."

"Do you have any idea at all what he was talking about, or who he meant?"

The exchange continued. Tobias prowled back and forth. When his turn came he said he'd seen someone leaving the building but—other than mentioning that the phone had been off the hook—didn't elaborate on events leading up to his decision to come to Paris in the middle of the night. Obviously the men presumed Paris and Tobias were close friends.

"Doors should be locked, ma'am," Paris was told, and, "Someone will follow up with you."

Then Tobias was alone with her again.

"Nothing's going to come of that," she said.

He didn't say he agreed with her. "The first thing we're going to do is get a good lock on that front door and new keys. At the same time there'll be a new lock on your door and the intercom will be fixed. I'll have someone arrange to deal with it in the morning."

"I'll have to talk to the others first."

"It's going to be done or you're going to move out." He knew his mistake at once. "Sorry. I'm—"

"Used to giving orders," she finished for him, but smiled a little. As quickly as it appeared, the smile disappeared. "Why did you come?"

"You heard what I said to the police."

"That you tried to call me and couldn't get through."

"More or less."

She started to get up.

"Stay," he told her. "What do you need?"

"More hot water. I can do it."

He took her mug and refilled it. "Like I told the police, the operator said you probably had a phone off the hook."

"So you felt it was your job to get in your car—in the middle of the night—and come roaring over to tell me about it?"

Tobias lowered a fresh teabag and trailed it around. "Sounds bizarre when you put it like that."

"Not bizarre exactly." She arched against the chairback and winced. "Unlikely would be a better word."

"Does something hurt?" What would she say if he told her that being with her felt not only likely, but natural? It felt *right*.

"I ache," she said. "But it's nothing."

"You'd be more comfortable in your rocking chair."

She didn't cringe away when he put an arm around her and urged her to her feet.

As she sat in the chair the blanket slipped from her shoulders. Paris juggled to capture the bodice of her nightgown.

Tobias swallowed and set the mug beside her. All those shapeless, bland clothes she favored were very deceptive.

"Whoops," he said, smiling into her eyes, deliberately keeping his gaze on hers while he rescued the blanket and wrapped it around her as if he were a parent ministering to a child. "You need to keep warm. Shock can creep up on you after the type of thing you've been through. Drink some more tea."

Rather than pick up the mug, Paris caught his hand and held it tightly. "When did you try to call me back?"

"A couple of hours after the first time."

She drew his hand beneath her chin. "And you just thought you'd come here."

Tobias crouched beside her. "Yes."

"Why?"

"I . . . I did, that's all."

"And you saw a man leaving this building?"

"He left the door open and got into a car up on First."

She rubbed her cheek on the back of his hand. "I was so scared."

If he tried to touch her—really touch her—he'd ruin this spell. "I wish to God I'd tackled the sonovabitch."

"No!" Her fingers dug into his. "No. You weren't meant to. He had a knife."

She didn't want him hurt. He let himself test how that notion made him feel. Hopeful? "The man who lives here," he said. "Where is he?"

"Wormwood? He doesn't come back at night too often. Less and less often." Her eyes drifted shut. "Who am I supposed to tell? Who needs to know time's running out?"

Tobias murmured, "I don't know."

"Don't you?"

He willed himself not to snap a response, not to move a muscle.

"You and I have had some bad times, Paris," he told her. "I can't speak for you, but I've never felt as . . . *helpless* as I've felt in the past weeks."

"I feel helpless now."

"What I did . . . The way I treated you when you came to see me was wrong. That's what I've been trying to tell you. If I've finally managed to put the words together the way I intended to, would you please forgive me for coming onto you the way I did?"

Her eyes squeezed more firmly shut. Faintly, she said, "Yes."

"I know this is going to sound nuts, but I'm glad I decided to come and find you when I did—when I came and made my outrageous suggestion." He laughed uncomfortably. "I was clumsy—and inappropriate."

"You were desperate. I know how that feels."

He wanted, *desperately,* to kiss her. "Thank you, Paris. Can we forget that I came looking for you because I wanted you to do something for me?"

"I'd like to."

With his other hand, he very carefully smoothed back her hair. "Do you think we could . . . Could we try to get to know each other?"

"I'm not sure what you're asking."

She held him, let him touch her, because she needed comfort—nothing more. Tobias wound his fingers into hers and eased her forward. Paris came to him like a young animal seeking warmth and safety. She turned her face against his neck and sighed when he stroked the back of her neck and her shoulders.

The rush of emotion he felt was out of fashion—it was also as old as time, and he liked it. He felt protective.

"We'll take it slow and easy, Blue. We could start out by being friends."

"Friends," she repeated almost dreamily.

"I could really use a friend about now. If it's easier on you—with the family stuff and so on—no one has to know but you and me."

He thought she stiffened a little, but she didn't pull away.

"You're special. I don't want to overwhelm you, but I think you're the most special woman I've ever met." The strain of the night must have gone to his head. He cleared his throat.

"I know we've never—that is, we haven't had this—*that* kind of relationship. Maybe it seems sudden or something. But . . . Can we try?"

"I'm not sure I . . ." Her hand slipped from his and she sat upright. "Cynthia is my sister."

"I'm not married to Cynthia anymore, Paris. I haven't been for a long time. I'm single. Like you."

"But—"

"But, nothing. You and Cynthia don't have any blood relationship, if that's what's bothering you. Not that I'm asking you to be the mother of my chil—dren . . ." *Shit.* He made a pathetic attempt at a grin. "Not this week."

She blushed madly.

The clumsy-prize was definitely his. "I'm talking about friendship. Only. I'm not a monster, Paris. There have been misunderstandings in the past. I'm still dealing with some of them, but they don't affect you and me."

"No," she said, sounding more than uncertain. "I guess not."

One slender, shapely leg showed—all the way to lemon yellow lace at the indentation of her groin. Tobias would like to settle his mouth there, to breathe on that sensitive skin—to delve his tongue beneath the flimsy lace.

Paris gathered the blanket more closely about her. "I'm glad you came tonight. I'm glad you helped me."

He shifted his weight, dropped from a crouch to his knees. If the lady knew he had an erection she'd probably smack him for his help. "I'm glad, too. You ought to go to bed. I'll stay down here till I hear someone else come in. Then I'll make sure everyone knows what happened here tonight and you won't have to explain it all again."

"I don't know . . . Forget it. Thank you very much."

When she stood, he did, too. Tonight she felt different to him, less sure of herself and incredibly vulnerable. "What is it you don't know?"

Her lips parted and he saw her make up her mind to say, "Okay. I'm not sure there's any point in going to bed until I'm sure no one can walk in here in the dark again."

Tobias looked down into her pale, finely boned face. "Go

on." He gave her his best imitation of a brotherly bear hug and turned her toward the corridor. Close to her ear he said, "Go upstairs and sleep. I won't leave till it's light."

"But—"

"Will you do as you're told without arguing for once? I'm the oldest, remember."

She chuckled. "Boy, does that sound like an echo from the past."

"It is. I'm playing the big brother again. Away with you."

"Yes." With the blanket trailing behind, she started walking. "Thank you. I'll see to the locks first thing in the morning."

He would see to the locks, but he said, "That's great. I'll be down here on the sofa if you want me."

When he'd heard Paris climb the stairs, then walk across the floor above his head, Tobias stretched out on the nubby beige couch and propped his neck on the pillows at one end.

Forged jewelry. Attacks at knife-point in the night. She might not know it, but she'd trespassed somewhere she definitely wasn't wanted. Paris was on some sort of hit list.

He stared at the ceiling. Life wasn't complicated enough already, huh? Now he was adding an itch for the opponent's granddaughter.

Big Brother? In case she'd forgotten, Paris didn't have any brothers.

Fourteen

"It's me."

"Yeah." Conrad peered at Cynthia through the crack allowed by the chain on his studio door. The door slammed shut. The chain slid off and he stood back to let her pass. "Who knows you're here?"

"No one." The door crashed closed again with enough force to make her flinch. "No one even knows you've got this place, remember?" She remembered. She *paid* rent for it because a no-talent painter who hated tending bar could give her something she had to have.

His expression didn't change. "You're late."

"It wasn't easy to get away."

"You were with him?"

"It's been a week since I was there," she told him. "Nigel gets edgy if . . . Well, you know what I mean. He's used to—*being* with me."

"I don't give a shit if his dick falls off. You want something from me. You may get it. But not unless I get what I want first. Everything I want."

"You *will* do it?" She stood close to him and traced his bare pecs with a fingernail. Dressed only in jeans he was easy on the eye—and pleasantly taxing on other parts of her anatomy. The only furniture in the loft was a spool bed with a bare mattress. They might or might not use it. She said, "You haven't changed your mind, have you, Connie? You'll be ready when I say?"

He made no move to either touch her or to stop her from touching him. "Probably."

"You said you would."

"And you said you'd do something I wanted first. Something special."

Cynthia smiled. "And I'm going to. Tell me what it is and I'll do it." She'd been very good lately—no visits to Connie for almost two weeks. Sex only with Nigel—but tonight she was hot and Nigel hadn't been interested in repeat performances. Working with Tobias was important for Nigel, and even more important for Cynthia, but the poor boy wasn't used to daily toil—it tired him out.

Conrad walked across the loft with unconscious grace, his black eyes constantly on Cynthia—on her face, her breasts, her legs—insolently shifting but never entirely leaving her while he flipped the switch for a bank of track lighting.

European men turned Cynthia on. Conrad's roots showed in his olive skin and in the sensuously handsome arrangement of his features.

He waved her forward.

She didn't move. "You want it? Come and get it, lover." Maybe this time he would. Maybe this time he'd change his tactics.

"You know what I like," he told her.

Cynthia shrugged and strolled to an easel where a painting in progress rested. "What is it?"

"I'll tell you when you pay for it."

She turned her head to study a burst of black shapes blossoming from a blue center. "You like that, don't you? Having me pay for sex with you?"

"You pay for the paintings."

The paintings were the excuse for the money she gave him. He bragged that his work was becoming more and more sought after. The pieces left this room and ended up in storage at her condo. The money *bought* the sex that was the best part of every transaction.

Finally the track lighting took his attention away from her. He studied the way it shone on a vast sheet of blank canvas rolled out and clamped to the only full wall in the warehouse loft. The ceiling, and its four rectangular skylights, sloped sharply with the angle of the roof.

A tarpaulin covered much of the floor.

"That's too big," she said of the canvas. "I don't have a place to put it." The storeroom was crammed.

"This has been commissioned."

Cynthia crossed the space between them and caught his arm. "Who?" Jealousy flashed in too-familiar places. "I *own* you."

He looked at her hand and said, "You lease me, lady. And you haven't been around for quite awhile. Nigel has his needs. *I* have my needs."

"I called."

"And we're here, now."

"You'll do what I want?"

"Back to that?" He took her hand from his arm and guided it to his crotch. "You're going to have to persuade me—*tonight.*"

He was big but he wasn't hard yet, goddammit. She turned up the corners of her mouth and gave his cock a squeeze. "I'll persuade you. First I want your word you won't make a move till I tell you it's time."

His expression didn't even flicker—neither did anything else. "You already gave your orders, my lady."

Fear began to unfurl. "Tell me again." Nothing must happen before its time. Two major—and totally unexpected—wrinkles in her plans had come close to making her panic. Now she knew how to use those wrinkles to her own advantage. She needed Conrad, but she needed him to be absolutely predictable.

"There are things I want you to do, Cynthia. Different things, this time."

She shivered with anticipation. "Lay 'em on me."

His nostrils flared. "You're going to do the laying, baby. For a start. Undress me."

She barely stopped herself from pointing out that she always undressed him. "My pleasure." She unsnapped his jeans. This was part of the attraction, his incredible control and the challenge to make him break. He never had—yet. He could decide when he was ready to get hard, screw for hours without ejaculating—until she begged him to stop—then leave her panting and disappear into the bathroom to shower.

Just once she wanted to see him give away what he wanted to keep for himself alone.

His ass was like marble. Unyielding. Cynthia skinned his jeans down slowly, spreading her hands over his cheeks, kneading the backs of his rigid thighs and calves. When he let her toss the jeans aside, she settled the tip of a thumb in each groin, curled her fingers around his balls and sucked him deep into her mouth.

He flowered instantly, catching her off guard. At the moment when the driving head of his penis made her gag, he withdrew. "Up." Plunging his hands into the neck of her dress, he hauled, tearing seams as he lifted her.

Cynthia tried to tug his hand away. "Don't. You'll ruin it."

"Buy another one." He ripped the bodice in two. "I thought you wanted this. Didn't you say I never get angry?"

She stared into his fevered eyes and knew delicious dread.

Under his next onslaught, he shredded the bra she wore to please him. Her breasts spilled free. He laughed and Cynthia felt the liquid at her center. "Don't," she said, pretending to fend him off. "You're hurting me."

"Your tits are something, baby. "Tits and Ass." That song from *Chorus Line* could have been written for you."

In moments she was naked. And she was ready. She made a move toward the bed.

"No," he said, pushing her against the wall. "My pick, remember?"

Before she could respond, he uncovered a bucket and dipped both hands into red paint up to his wrists.

"What . . . No!" He came at her. "Don't. It'll get in my hair."

"Yeah."

"Stop it, Connie. Stop it!"

"My pick, Cynthia."

"Please."

"Yeah. You got it."

There was no escape. He caught her easily by the waist.

"It won't come off!"

"Sure it will. Have faith, baby." His hands were all over her. He dunked into the bucket again and slathered her thighs, then coated her breasts, playing with her nipples till she grabbed for him.

"Patience, Scarlet. All in good time. We're creating something unique here."

Next her face received his attention.

Cynthia shrieked and sputtered, tried to hit him, but missed. Full palms of slimy red hit the top of her head and drizzled down her scalp, aided by his combing fingers.

"You're mad!" she yelled.

Conrad went to his knees, slid his hands around her hips and foraged into her cleft with his tongue. Cynthia's head fell back and she clung to his shoulders. "Yes," she said through her teeth. "Yes, *yes. Yes!*"

Falling. Falling over the edge and burning up.

He drew back too soon.

"Not now, Connie!" He evaded her grasp. "Don't stop, *please,* Connie."

"Your wish is my command, lady. Let's go."

He spun her around, lifted her and thrust inside with enough sweet force to make her mind float.

Flailing to find purchase, she wound her ankles around his thighs.

"Beautiful," he said against her neck. "This is it."

She felt him carry her forward. Then her face and breasts connected with the wall—with the canvas. "What the hell?—" Automatically, her arms spread.

"Leave this to me, sweetheart."

The unbelievable pounding began. He thundered upward

into her and the hot blackness he made like no other man she'd ever known—except Tobias—broke.

When she would have sagged, he jerked her flat to the canvas and hammered some more, shifting sideways. "You're . . . scraping me," she moaned.

"This'll help," he told her.

He dismounted and daubed her skin with another layer of thick, red paint. The wild surging began. It began again, and again.

At last, when she couldn't stand alone, Conrad stretched her out on the tarp. "Okay," he said. "It's a deal. Give the word and I'll do what you want."

Cynthia fought for every breath. "Weird bastard."

He showed his teeth. "Me? Didn't you like it?"

She rolled onto her side and propped her head. "How the fuck am I going to get home?"

"You'll think of something."

Blinking, she stretched her eyes open and felt the paint drying on her skin. "This stuff—"

"Water-based. It'll wash off you." He'd picked up a can of lacquer and began spraying the canvas. "It won't wash off this. Ever."

Woozy, vaguely nauseated, she managed to sit up and watch him. Ranged across the wall were images far easier to interpret than any of Conrad's former paintings.

"That's *sick,*" she told him. "Sick."

The repeated blurred imprint of the side of her face, her hair, her hands and breasts, belly and thighs formed a repetitive mural. Between her splayed thighs rested the shapes of male thighs and knees.

Cynthia looked from the canvas to Conrad. "You said it was commissioned." Confusion seeped into her brain. "Who would commission this?"

"Someone who needs insurance."

"Insurance?"

"Against you changing your mind."

"But you can't prove that's—"

"You? Would you want me to try? Would you want me to go

to your money source, or find a nice public place and put it up with your name on it? Don't you think word would travel fast?"

"You wouldn't."

"Wouldn't I? And believe me, it wouldn't be tough to convince people in this town that it *is* you."

Cynthia got to her feet and promptly sat down again.

"Shocked?" he asked, smiling charmingly. "Don't be. Like I said, this is a commissioned piece. Commissioned by me. I'm really going to enjoy it. I already did. God, did I enjoy it."

"I thought you were going to help me."

"And I am. But I really don't want to be forgotten when you've got what you set out to get, Cynthia."

"I wouldn't—"

"You won't now. I'll enjoy this tonight. Then I'll put it in a safe place and it'll never be seen again—unless you decide to stop coming to me. Or to stop paying me. And the price just went up."

"You're going to blackmail me?" Disbelief dried out her mouth.

"No. Just make sure you don't neglect your commitments. I'm not going to neglect mine. All you've got to do is say it's time and I'll go to work with pleasure. I'm looking forward to it. Why don't you wash up?"

This time she made it to her feet and stumbled toward the bathroom.

"Did you bring any money?"

She looked over her shoulder at him. "Yes."

"Good. I need it." He took a brush and applied a few quick, deft strokes at the bottom of the canvas.

Cynthia turned around and approached slowly.

"Title," Conrad said, slipping an arm around her waist. *"Fucked.* Like it?"

Fifteen

"Hi, Sam." Paris hoped she'd covered her disappointment fast enough. "You got the watch, huh? You must be worn out."

Tobias had said he'd stay until someone else could take his place. She shouldn't have hoped to find him waiting for her—especially when she'd seen dawn break before sleeping and it was already past noon—but she had hoped.

Seated on the couch with his arms spread along the back and his tennis shoes propped on her glass table, Sam appeared more angry than tired. "Sit down," he said. "I want to hear about this from you."

"Didn't—"

"Quinn's an arrogant sonovabitch. I don't trust him. What in hell happened here last night?"

So much for Tobias's efforts to spare her a rehashing of a story she'd like to erase. "Some creep got in here and threatened me. Tobias hadn't been able to reach me by phone and he got worried, so he came over. Thank God he did. I . . . I was paralyzed, Sam. It was horrible." Once more her throat constricted with the urge to vomit.

Sam swung his feet from the table and got up. In jeans and

a slouchy, green cotton sweater, he was unrecognizable as Samantha. "What did the guy do to you?" His blue eyes glittered and muscles in his jaw flexed. "Did he—"

"No! And I don't want to go through all that again. The police came, Sam. Everything that can be done, *has* been done. I need to eat."

"I'm . . ." Sam put an arm around Paris's shoulders and rested his forehead on hers. "Sorry, kid. I feel protective, is all. Six years is a long time. I was here when you moved in, remember? You're like the sister I never had and I don't take kindly to some psycho sneaking up on my sister."

Paris's eyes stung. "Thanks, Sam." There'd been too much to get emotional about lately. "I couldn't ask for a better friend."

Briefly, they'd almost become more than friends, but that had been years ago, before Ginna . . . and before Michael.

"How come you're getting close to Quinn?"

"I'm not." *Liar.* "We have a lot of shared history. Right now there's some old family business to be dealt with."

"Does that give him the right to storm through this place telling everyone what they're *going* to do?"

"I don't think he would do that."

"I tell you—"

Paris hushed him. "Can we change the subject? It's important, Sam. I think someone else came in here earlier in the evening—before I got home. Or maybe it was the same person, but I don't think so. They moved stuff around on my bench. And a drawing was made of one of my new pieces."

Sam's hostile countenance softened. "You sure?"

"Well . . . Yes. Yes, I'm sure." She told him the general details of what she'd found and about searching the apartment—and the ball of paper that disappeared. "I wish I'd taken the paper with me."

"Are you sure you left it on the bench?" He looked around the room. "Could you have thrown it away?"

"Believe me, I put it on the bench."

"You're only guessing it was a drawing."

"Yes. But I feel it in my bones. That's why the space was cleared."

"I suppose *Mr.* Quinn has a great theory on all of this?"

"Actually, he—"

Mary, opening the door without knocking, created a blessed diversion. "Whoo!" Her thin cheeks glowed from exertion. Today she'd sprayed glitter into her hair and applied a red foil star high on one cheek. "Those stairs don't get any shorter."

"That's why you live on the ground floor," Sam said promptly. "You're too ancient for stairs."

Mary ignored him and headed for the kitchen. "Need the table," she said to Paris, swinging two canvas Does-R-Us bags by their handles. "That young man of yours is just right. Charming. And *so* handsome."

"Fucking con man," Sam said, not softly enough to evade Mary's perfectly good hearing.

"Don't you talk like that, young man," she said. "The new lock on the front door's in. New handle and all. Lovely, it is. Solid brass. A mint, that's what it must have cost. Won't hear of any of us paying a penny for it, either. And there're two keys for everyone. Each one numbered. Specially engraved. Mr. Quinn said to assign two numbers to each of us. I'm to see to that. And if anyone loses a key it's to be reported."

Paris, already following Mary into the kitchen, dared a glance back at Sam. He made fists and slammed them together.

"Tobias has access to the right kind of people to do these jobs," she said, casting about for a way to save the moment. "I—I mentioned we'd talked about the locks and so on but that we never seem to get around to doing anything about it."

"People like Quinn don't have any closer connection to locksmiths than you or I and you know it. I doubt if he even knows one end of a key from the other. He probably has someone who doesn't do anything else but open and close doors for him."

"Don't be silly, Sam," Paris said severely. "You're overreacting."

"Man's coming this afternoon to work on the intercom," Mary said smugly. If there was one thing the old lady enjoyed it was a little spirited argument. "Shouldn't be surprised if that Mr. Quinn hires someone to talk into *his* intercom for him. What do you say, Sam?"

"I say you're a meddling crone."

"I think I've been insulted again." Mary dumped the contents of her bags on the table. "I've got connections in the trade, Paris. Never had a need to mention them before, but now's a good time."

Circling, Sam eyed the collection on Paris's kitchen table. "Got any connections that pay for things like intercoms and solid brass door handles?"

"I told you Paris's young man's dealing with that," Mary said, fanning open a three-dimensional paper pumpkin. She opened another and another and a fourth, smaller version and heaped them on the floor. "I always did like orange. It takes people with strong personalities and vibrant coloring to make the most of it, though."

A growl from her stomach sent Paris to the refrigerator. "Great pumpkins," she said. Nothing looked good but she took a carton of yogurt and got a spoon from a drawer. "Any particular reason why we're decorating for Halloween?"

"Don't be coy with me," Mary said, selecting a length of white tulle from her treasures and arranging it into a series of puffs atop the table. Between each puff she placed a bluebird on a florists' pick. "Pretend the sticks aren't there. The food will be no problem. Black and orange has probably never been done before. All the better. One of my contacts will just take the idea and run with it."

Paris looked at Sam, who inflated his cheeks and shrugged. She tore the foil top from the yogurt container and ate a spoonful.

Mary stared hard at Sam. "Mr. Quinn's a very honest man. No doubt about what he wants. Honorable to the bone. I told him there were *some* who thought the type of affair he meant to throw wasn't what I thought it was. He said it certainly was exactly what I thought and he didn't have any interest in hustling Paris into bed."

Paris almost dropped the yogurt.

"No, sir," Mary continued, still glaring at Sam. "In fact, he said he had a particular fondness for Halloween."

"*Mary.*" Paris put the yogurt and spoon on a counter. "You *asked* Tobias if he . . . You asked if he intended to have an affair with me?"

Thin shoulders rose inside the jacket of a purple nylon jogging suit. "All that matters is that he doesn't intend any such thing. And he's buying a thousand pumpkins from me. I told him you get a price break at five hundred units and he ordered two of 'em. I haven't had this much fun since I don't know when."

"Why would he want a thousand pumpkins?" Sam asked.

With the flap of a hand, Mary dismissed him. "Another contact of mine creates to order. Little dressmaking shop in Kirkland. Wonderful work."

Paris found she needed to sit down.

"You can draw a picture." Mary's voice rose to a delighted trill. She poked at a bird. "But I can just see it all. Remember how the bluebirds carried the little flounces round her dress? It all makes such an interesting theme."

Propped against the counter with his arms crossed, Sam pointed a finger at Mary. "Are you talking about Cinderella?"

Mary pointed back. "You've *got* it. Cinderella. And it all goes together. The poor girl marries the rich prince. That's Paris— she's getting poorer by the minute—and Mr. Quinn. He's certainly rich. And the prince loves Halloween and buys a thousand pumpkins. And Cinderella's coach is made out of a pumpkin and that's what the theme's going to be for Paris's Halloween wedding. Pumpkins turning into golden coaches. And Cinderella marrying her prince."

When the silence had lasted a long time Mary sat down herself. "I knew you were going to love this. How about breaking with tradition. You could carry a wand with a star on the end instead of flowers."

Paris inhaled deeply and said, "This is unbelievable."

"I *knew* you were perfect for each other." Mary smiled ecstatically. "That's exactly what Mr. Quinn said."

* * *

Steam rose from the cobbles along Post Alley. The late afternoon sky showed as a livid violet strip. Paris, her hair wet from what promised to be the first of a string of squalls, dodged puddles and reveled in running—and in feeling optimistic again.

The rain had driven most customers away from little galleries lining the alley. Paris sniffed the sharp aroma of wet geraniums in window boxes, and dust turned to mud in a thousand crevices, and she smiled.

A good day.

A *great* day.

She reached The Blue Door and paused to catch her breath before pushing inside. Ginna and Conrad were where they belonged at five in the afternoon. Ginna sat at a table near the stage going over orders. Conrad was at work restocking the bar.

"Hey, *people!*" Paris shouted over the staccato pounding of Mrs. Lips—on her feet for the event—warming up with "Great Balls of Fire."

"Hey, Paris!" Ginna waved, squinting up from her books. "Come here and let me look at you. Sam wouldn't even let me go check on you while you were sleeping. Come here *now.*"

"I wouldn't let her in case she woke you up." Sam ambled in behind Paris and playfully tugged her hair. "I yelled at you out there. You were too busy running like a maniac to notice."

She whirled and threw her arms around him. "Sam," she said into his ear. "Finally, I'm getting a break. I think everything's going to settle down."

"Tell," he said, leaning away to look into her face. "Tell, tell, tell!"

"Only one time," she said, placing a finger on his lips to stop his protest. "Come on. I'm buying everyone a glass of water."

"Gee, thanks."

It took Sam, lifting Mrs. Lips's hands from the piano keys, to get her attention. She sat on the edge of the stage with Lips while the others crowded around Ginna's table.

Paris accepted a Coke from Conrad and drank thirstily. "What a day. What a bunch of days—and nights."

"We heard about last night," Lips said. "You should have come to get me."

She didn't remind him she'd hardly been in a position to get anyone. "Thanks. Let's hope there isn't a next time for me to take you up on the offer."

"Nice new locks, huh?" Lips remarked and guffawed. "Nice price, too. I like your friends."

"I don't," Sam and Conrad said in unison.

Conrad took a swallow of Paris's Coke and said, "Don't misunderstand me, Paris. I know we should have done something about security a long time ago. And you shouldn't have had to be molested to make us get on with it. But I don't like some stranger throwing his weight around and giving out orders about numbered keys. Bunch of bullshit."

"Quinn doesn't tell me what to do," Sam announced. "We're going to insist on paying for the work, and tell him to stuff his roll call."

"*You* can pay," Lips said. "For the price of what the guy's had done, we'll be thrilled to use his keys. Lighten up."

Sam got up. "You goddamn—"

"That's *it,*" Ginna said, narrowing her eyes. "After last night Paris needs some peace and support. She came in here saying she wanted to share some good news. Could we quit rattling sabers? I agree we can't let Tobias Quinn pay for the repairs but we'll make sure we're smiling and thanking the man when we ask for the bill. Anyone disagree with that?"

"Just because he owns—"

"*Anyone* disagree?" Usually the invisible force behind the partnership, Ginna cut Sam off.

Paris looked speculatively at the pair. Evidently Sam knew Tobias was Ginna's landlord.

Ginna reached for Sam's hand and he grasped her fingers. "Ginna's right as usual," he said. "I'm just jealous because Quinn owns this building and I wish I did. Then I could give it to my lovely lady. Pipe dreams. What's up, Paris?"

His honesty disarmed Paris—and rendered the rest of the group silent. Ginna bobbed up and kissed his cheek. "Keep on packing in the people, honey. We're doing just fine."

"Just fine," Mrs. Lips said. When she relaxed she was pretty and soft.

"Okay." Paris scooted her chair closer to the table and looked from face to face. "I got a call from the people at Fables. They asked me to go up there."

Her audience waited expectantly.

"First, I want to show you this." From the pocket of her skirt she produced a small padded envelope. She shook it upside down. A silver earring in the shape of a curving lily with a single pearl-tipped stamen tumbled to the plastic tabletop.

"One of my favorites," Ginna said, picking up the piece. "They'd be great with that necklace Sam had you make for me. I may still buy myself a pair. If they aren't all gone."

"That one's a copy," Paris said shortly.

Ginna turned the earring over and over.

Paris watched as the jewelry passed around the circle. "Not one of you would have known the difference," she said. "Only another jeweler who's familiar with my work would. That's plated, not solid. And I only use freshwater pearls—not cheap beads with the holes filled. I just wanted you to see how convincing this person is. She's good."

"Not as good as you," Conrad said, frowning over the lily.

"Pretty darn close. That's not the point. The designs are mine. Look at the signature."

Conrad lifted the piece toward a light suspended from the cavernous ceiling on a long copper pipe. "D," he said. "Geez, she's even copying your mark."

"Or he," Sam commented. "I'd like to get my hands on whoever's doing this. Is this why they asked you to go up to Fables?"

"Partly. A woman bought the pair and lost one. She went back to see if it could be matched—by the jeweler. They didn't tell her it was fake. I'm going to make another pair."

"Decent of them," Ginna commented. "At least, I guess it's a start."

Paris couldn't contain her grin any longer. "They apologized. They said they panicked and didn't think things through."

Conrad's dark brows slowly rose. "You're kidding."

"Nope. I'm still pinching myself but it's true. If anyone else returns something we're going to work it out. I won't be asked to pay anyone back. The woman—Eileen—she said she hadn't been fair to me."

Sam snorted. "She was right."

"The best part is"—Paris paused for effect—"They'll take my next collection! It can't happen twice. That's what they said. And Eileen said she hoped I'd be willing to carry on the way we did before because it's been such a good association."

"Big of them," Sam said while Mrs. Lips made a rare show of spontaneity and hurried to kiss Paris's cheek.

Conrad tossed the earring in his palm. "Sam told us you had more than one visitor last night. You think a drawing was made of a neckpiece."

Paris looked at her hands in her lap. "Yes." She didn't want anything to squelch her hopes again.

"So how can you be certain the next collection won't be pirated then?"

She avoided Conrad's questioning face. "Well, folks. Last year's grouping was copied after it was on sale. I guess that could happen again. But I don't think our forger's going to get away with actually beating me to the stores. Not with only one piece."

"What if he already got in and saw some others?"

Paris made a wry face. "Conrad, the devil's advocate. I'm going to make changes to everything I've done so far. And, thanks to the new locks some of you aren't ready to thank Tobias for, we may not have any more problems."

"Yes, indeed," Ginna remarked quietly. "Thank Tobias Quinn. Thank the man who really has a thing for our Paris."

"For God's sake, Ginna." Sam slapped the table. "The guy was married to Paris's sister."

Ginna stared at the order book in front of her and said, "Adopted sister," without looking up.

Sam wasn't deterred. "You know what Cynthia said about him."

"That's not our business," Ginna said. "But he's pulled some fancy strings—bet on it."

Seated at Ginna's left, Paris covered the pages in front of the other woman and waited until Ginna faced her before saying, "You think you know something. What?"

"Your Tobias must have had a persuasive message for the people at Fables."

"Such as?"

"Such as: Are you planning to renew your lease here?"

"Holy shit," Sam muttered.

"That's stupid." Paris frowned into Ginna's eyes. "You mean—"

Conrad pushed the lily earring across the table. "She means your new boyfriend is up to his old tricks. Manipulation. What does he want from you, Paris? What does he want badly enough to threaten people into seeing things his way."

"That kind of jerk doesn't need much of a reason to threaten," Sam said. "Probably looking for a way back into Cynthia's panties."

"Shut up," Paris told him.

"Somehow I don't think you've got it quite right, Sam." Ginna gently closed her book and got up. "But Tobias Quinn does own the Fables property."

Tobias paused inside the entrance to his Stewart Street offices and swore under his breath.

In midafternoon, when he'd arrived, an on-street parking spot near the market had been a rarity too enticing to resist. He'd arrived before the sky sprang a major-league leak.

He turned up his suit collar, ducked his head and prepared to dive—and saw Paris.

Soaked, her hair plastered to her head, her gauze uniform too wet to own a color, she leaned against the wall. Her arms were folded and she was looking straight at him.

Tobias forgot the rain. "Paris!" He stepped out and drew her farther under the green and white awning. "Hi. You're the best thing I've seen all day. But you're drowned."

"Always the last to leave," she said. There was no thrilled-to-see-you smile on display. "The lady was right."

"Me?" He reversed their positions, placing her in the corner and shielding her from blowing rain. "Someone told you I was always the last out?"

"A woman on the telephone."

"You asked to speak to me?"

"No. I said I had a delivery to make to Mr. Quinn if he was still in his office. That was two hours ago."

"I'm not getting this." He was getting her antagonism—in waves.

"I wanted to see you alone. But not *too* alone."

He straightened slowly. "We know I got off on the wrong foot with you. I thought we agreed to move on from there. Why didn't you come on into the offices? You're wet to the skin." Paris's skin never seemed far from his mind these days.

She took off her glasses and attacked the lenses with a fold of her damp skirt.

"Give them to me," he said and used the end of his tie.

"You'll ruin it."

"Silk doesn't scratch."

"I meant your tie."

"I don't give a rat's ass about my tie." Bypassing her outstretched hand, he placed the glasses on her nose and arranged the ear-pieces. "What I care about is why you're glaring at me like I managed to grow horns."

The slapping of rubber soles on wet sidewalks drew level and passed on the downhill grade.

When they were alone again Tobias said, "Paris, answer me."

Right on cue she bowed her head.

"Okay." He sighed, firmly took one of her arms and pulled her with him into the downpour.

"You can't manipulate me, Tobias Quinn," she said loudly, trotting to keep up. "You can't push me around and use me."

He only checked his stride an instant before setting his jaw and speeding up until she ran, panting, beside him. At the Jeep he opened the passenger door, all but lifted her in, secured her seat belt and locked the door again. By the time he was seated behind the wheel his suit pants clung to his legs and he could paddle inside his shoes.

Even the hardiest wanderers had abandoned the area. Tobias

drove north along deserted Pike Place and turned left toward the waterfront at Virginia Street.

"I want to get out."

He glowered through streaming glass at a darkening sky. "I'm taking you home."

"You aren't welcome there."

"*My* home."

"Stop."

"Why?" Glancing sideways at her, he turned the heater on low. "You've obviously got a burr . . . You didn't stand in the rain because you wanted to get wet."

"We can talk right here."

He ignored her and drove on toward the Seattle Center and Lake Union. "I want you to dry out, calm down and tell me who got you all riled up about me," he told her when they headed for the freeway overpass to Roanoke Street. "You can take a nice long hot shower."

"I don't think so."

At least she no longer sounded so certain. "How much sleep did you get last night?"

Her sigh filled the Jeep. "Plenty. Thanks for sticking around."

Now was probably the wrong moment to tell her what he thought of most of her housemates. "I'd have stayed till you woke up but I had a couple of meetings I couldn't cancel."

"You did more than you needed to. I really don't want to go to your houseboat."

"We're almost there. Relax, Paris. Regardless of what history and rumor suggests, I'm not into molesting unwilling women."

"Just willing ones?"

He laughed and thought she choked down a giggle.

They passed Roanoke Park on their left and soon the lights of the University of Washington shivered through the gray haze over Union Bay.

Tobias parked and got out without waiting for Paris's protests. She joined him before he could reach her door and walked ahead of him toward the moorages.

On his deck, he automatically checked the lines securing his

Zodiac dinghy. The view down the cut to Montlake Bridge was almost obscured. The rain showed no sign of stopping.

"Go on upstairs and shower," he told Paris when they were inside the house. "Get dry. Unless you'd like to get in the hot tub with me. Great in the rain."

"I'm here under duress. Just lend me a towel. Nobody ever died from a little rain water."

"I might." This woman—who had somehow managed to get well and truly under his thick skin—this woman was infuriating. He hopped on one foot to yank off a shoe, then reversed the process.

"The people at Fables called me today."

Tobias almost lost his balance. "Really." The shoes made a puddle on his wooden floor and his socks squelched.

"All's forgiven. Imagine that."

The socks came off and his jacket. "Congratulations. That must be a relief." His tie resisted his efforts and he yanked the ruined silk noose over his head. "Follow me. I guarantee your innocence is in no jeopardy."

"You aren't funny."

His shirt peeled away off in the manner of the skin on a not-quite-ripe kiwi fruit.

"Do you intend to strip?"

"Not entirely," he told her. "Not yet, anyway. I'm going to drop these in the laundry room. Then I'm getting a robe for me and a robe for you and I'm going out to the hot tub. If I were you I'd probably hide somewhere and put on the robe. Does that stuff shrink in a dryer?" He peered at her blouse.

"My shrinkage isn't your concern, Tobias."

"Right." He trudged to the laundry room. "Y'know, you didn't waste any time telling me what a rotten kid I was. Did I mention what I thought of you back then?"

That moved her. Tobias heard her behind him and smiled to himself. He took two white terrycloth robes from a pile in a cupboard and handed her one. "You can wait till I'm in the tub, if you like. You'll probably feel safer."

"I'm not . . . You aren't the first man I was ever around, Tobias Quinn."

"No?" Feigning surprise he unbuckled his belt and pulled it through its loops. "I guess that's a relief."

"I don't believe you thought anything at all about me when we were children."

"But if I did, you'd like to know what it was?" His zipper parted and he stepped out of his pants. "If you'll excuse me?" Naked, he walked outside.

Sixteen

Challenged.

Tobias had challenged her. Paris picked up the item of underwear that hadn't quite made it into the laundry sink and deposited it on top of his other clothes.

The kind of woman who turned into an aroused animal at the sight of a sexy male body would be imagining all kinds of possibilities right now.

There certainly were lots of possibilities.

She blushed—on the inside as well as the outside.

His body *was* spectacular. Not that she'd . . . Not exactly.

Cotton gauze did shrink—but it also dried quite quickly. If she spread her skirt and blouse out she'd soon be able to go home feeling more comfortable than she did now.

Fumbling in her haste, she skinned down to her bra and panties. With the warm, fluffy robe securely tied in place she was faced with a decision: to join him or not to join him?

Only cowards avoided harmless challenges.

Outside, the rain-cooled air raised goosebumps on her legs. Open to the sky and tucked into a niche, Tobias's hot tub was shielded from any curious eyes by a wooden screen covered with a shiny green vine.

A single spotlight illuminated the area. Tobias's broad back showed all the way down to . . . Paris looked away. She had to make sure he didn't think she was getting sucked into his trap. There was no reason why they couldn't have an adult conversation while he frolicked in his tub without her flinging herself upon him. Not that she really believed that could be what he wanted.

Evidently he would do anything to get what *he* wanted. She had to believe that now. And anything might well include using sex to wipe out her resistance.

Let him try!

Folding chairs leaned against a wall. Paris took one and set it beside the tub. She sat down and stared ahead at the dripping vine.

"You were a watcher."

Paris twisted toward Tobias. "A *watcher?*"

"As a kid. Always watching. You kept it up as you got older, too."

"Watching you?"

"Uh huh. Unnerving."

"I did *not* watch you."

"It's warm in here, Paris. With the rain on your face it's great. Come on in. It'll do you good."

Steam rose from the surface of the water. "I'm fine." She'd like to go in.

"Come *on*. I promise not to take you against your will."

"You're baiting me."

"But you're not running away. This feels good, doesn't it? The two of us here together?"

Whatever she did, she must not admit just how good. "Why did you make the people at Fables back down?"

With his eyes shut, he settled back, rested his head on the rim of the tub. His hair shone stark black. Moisture smoothed the black hair on his chest. A dark, silky swath arrowed downward. Beneath the lapping surface of the water, the dark line of hair diminished out of sight.

"I wish you could have seen yourself in the rain by my building."

Paris frowned deeply.

"You reminded me of a blue-eyed Italian sex goddess."

"Oh, right!" she sputtered, giving the end of the robe tie an extra tug. "I hear that all the time. You wouldn't believe how irritating the adoration gets."

"You don't know how beautiful you are, do you?"

"Come *on*, Tobias. This is me, Paris, the ugly duckling. If you're going to change the subject, please try not to insult—"

"In one of those scenes where a gorgeous creature rises out of a flood wearing a transparent white peasant blouse. Wet skin—perfect skin. Dripping hair. Begging for—"

"Don't insult my intelligence."

"I wasn't," he said mildly and eased deeper into the tub. "Do you ever wear white?"

"Not—" She'd almost said not on the outside. "Rarely."

"Hmm." He rolled his head toward her. "I like having you here with me—even if you won't admit you like it, too. I talked to the folks at Fables because I believe in justice. They kicked you when you were down. That wasn't just."

"Well . . . No, it wasn't. You threatened them, didn't you?"

"What I did or didn't do doesn't matter, sweetheart. Evidently you've figured out that's one of my properties. I gave a little lesson in the power of loyalty—my loyalty to you. Let's leave it at that."

She couldn't, but neither could she decide how to continue.

Tobias slapped the water beside him, sending foaming droplets into the air. "Sit with me, Paris. Life isn't simple at the moment. I could use your company." He straightened and offered her his hand. "Just company. Nothing else, I promise. Come on, Miss Granola. I won't take indecent liberties."

Baiting, always baiting. "I don't have a swimsuit."

"Do you have a bra and some panties on?"

She scowled at him. "You are so *personal.*"

"Well?"

"Yes, I do."

He snapped his fingers. "I'll hide my eyes if you prefer."

"Don't be ridiculous." She stood up and untied the robe. After all, how much difference was there between a bikini and her perfectly decent underwear?

The robe dropped over the chair.

She saw his gaze flicker over her lace and satin bra and matching panties.

Bikinis *were* different.

Expanding her lungs, Paris kicked off her sandals and put her hand in Tobias's.

"One step down," he told her. "That's it. Now tell me I don't have great ideas."

He had dangerous ideas and taking his hand had made certain she sat beside him rather than at a safer distance.

The swirl of bubbling water rose over her breasts.

Tobias continued to hold her hand. "I thought you said you didn't wear white."

His features were hazy. Paris squinted at him. "I don't."

"Why don't you take off your glasses?"

Her free hand went to her face. "I forgot!" She took off her fogged glasses and set them behind her.

"Still forgetful after all these years," he sang in a breaking parody of a Western tenor. "Some things never change. You're wearing white now."

"You weren't supposed to be noticing."

"I said I'd hide my face and you told me that was ridiculous. But I'm not *staring*."

Cynthia's accusations against her ex-husband wormed their way into Paris's mind. "What are we doing here?" she asked.

"Shutting out the world. Being with someone who knows us well. Enjoying not having to pretend we're anyone but who we are."

She didn't know who he was—not really. "We'd like the bill for the new locks, Tobias. Please don't make any kind of fuss about that."

He released her hand and slid his arm behind her neck.

Paris sat very still, every muscle in her back aching, every shred of reason in her being on alert.

Tobias curved his fingers over her bare shoulder.

"The others are very grateful—we're all very grateful to you for taking action on our behalf. But we can't allow you to pay for the work."

"Relax, Blue."

She tried to sit up. "I want to know why you call me that."

With minimal effort he landed her head on his shoulder. *"Relax."*

"Why Blue? You used to say I was a miserable little . . . Well, miserable."

"A miserable little toad? That's it. Blue, for miserable. I guess it stuck. The pick of your house buddies lives on the first floor. What a ball of fire."

Grimacing, Paris silently vowed not to talk about Mary.

"You think I'm trying to get you to have an affair with me, I understand."

The heat in her face had very little to do with the tub.

"You don't have to talk about it," Tobias said amiably. "I understand how you could make that mistake. Did Mary happen to tell you about my pumpkin purchase?"

"Yes. You didn't need to do that."

"I never do things unless I want to. I'm one of those people who enjoy the very old and the very young. We can learn so much from them."

She might as well get this discussion over with. "Like the virtues of Halloween weddings? How embarrassing."

"Like being old enough to be past embarrassment. And young enough to believe everyone loves you."

Paris tipped up her face to see his. "When did you get to be so philosophical?"

His black, spiked lashes lowered over eyes the color of steel. "If I am, it happened when I started wanting things that matter."

"How does a man like you decide what does and doesn't matter?"

Tobias regarded Paris with somber intensity. "Usually by being smacked over the head hard enough. Some people learn their lessons easily. Others have to figure out they may never get something important before they make a grab for it."

A little curl, deep inside Paris, was part pain, part pleasure. "Have you been smacked hard many times?"

"Mmm." He blinked against the rain and appeared to think deeply. "Twice. I'll tell you one of them. The other will have to wait. Maybe for a long time."

Without warning, he waded in front of Paris and lifted her to the rim of the tub. Tobias knelt on the seat below her and kept a grip on her waist.

His face was level with hers.

The water no longer shielded her body and she struggled with an urge to cover herself.

"You've smacked me, Paris."

In the moments that followed she heard her own breathing, and his, and the sound of raindrops on the wooden deck.

"Does that horrify you? Do *I* horrify you? Disgust you?"

"No!" There wasn't enough air in the night. "No, you don't."

He squeezed his eyes shut and a spasm, as of pain, crossed his rigid features. "I'm not quite as tough as you think I am," he said quietly. "Cut me and I bleed. Just like anyone else."

"I wouldn't cut you." No longer did she seem able to decide what to say.

"Somehow I believe you." When he opened his eyes something from within him smote her. "I believe you're the gentlest of women. And I believe that, gentle as you are, you'd fight to the death for someone you loved."

She whispered, "Yes, I would."

"But I also believe you're too vulnerable, Paris. You need to be loved. You need to be loved by someone strong enough to be there when you're ready to say you want him, and strong enough to allow you never to feel caged."

Carefully, wanting to touch him, yet afraid the touching might burn her, Paris stroked the sides of his face, pushed her fingers into his hair.

"Do you understand what I'm telling you?" he asked.

Did she? With slow precision, she caressed his neck and learned the shape of his shoulders and chest with outstretched fingers and flattened palms.

Tobias shuddered. He leaned to kiss her cheek, to wrap her in his arms and settle his face in the curve of her neck.

The hair on his chest brushed the naked swell of her breasts. Paris pressed closer. She rested her chin on top of his head.

Could this man be all the things Cynthia had said he was?

"I need you, Paris."

Her heart fell away. Cynthia warned her he was unscrupulous, single-mindedly ambitious, a man without conscience in matters of business—and in whatever else became his passion.

"It has to be a two-way street for me," he told her. "I've got to know I come first, too."

"First in everything?" she made herself say. "And what you want has to be first, too?"

"You know what I want." His lips found the hollow above her collarbone.

While Paris let her head fall back she longed for so much more. She longed for him to take off what little clothing she still wore. Parting her knees, she gripped his sides, slipped her feet and ankles back and forth over his solid, naked buttocks.

Unable to resist, she allowed her knee to drift around his groin.

His indrawn breath excited Paris.

If she'd been in any doubt before, Tobias's body made perfectly certain she did know what he wanted.

"Me, too," she murmured, nuzzling his ear.

"First?" he said, his voice rasping. "You understand what putting each other first means to me?"

She was slipping away. Reason was slipping away. She massaged his penis with the top of her foot. He was a big man—in every way.

Tobias held her waist in crushing fingers and made a sound that was a moan—and a growl. "I can't share you, Paris. If we're going to be together, it's going to be everything. No one gets in our way."

No one gets in our way. She forced in a breath and opened her eyes. Blood, rushing away from her head, made her dizzy. "Please tell me one thing. Tell me you aren't still trying to . . .

You never looked at me before. This isn't because you're trying to bind me to you?"

The tips of his fingers dug into her flesh. "Bind you?"

"Maybe . . . *Buy* me? My support? With Pops?"

He backed away so abruptly Paris slid forward and had to scramble to regain her balance. "Tobias—"

"Be quiet," he said, rising to his feet. "Just don't say anything."

He waded past her and climbed from the tub.

"I just wanted to hear you tell me the truth."

"If you'd been listening, you'd have heard it," he told her, catching up his robe as he went. "I'll take you home. First I need a shower."

He needed a shower.

This was where he came to shut himself away—and to forget.

Only the forgetting part wasn't working tonight.

At least he'd bought some time to collect himself. What in God's name had possessed him to pour forth all that drivel about unwavering love and understanding, and acceptance? To a *Delight?*

She thought he was still angling for her to plead his case with Pops. As if there was any chance the old bastard would back down from his vendetta even if his soul was on the line, let alone to please his granddaughter.

Tobias felt again the seductive caress of Paris's foot between his legs. How easy it would have been to take her then. Easy and pointless. Pointless, if she didn't trust him, and she didn't.

The shower door slid open behind him.

He braced his weight against the wall beneath the shower head and held still.

The door closed again.

Her fingers settled at the base of his spine.

'Tobias gritted his teeth.

With feathery strokes, Paris covered his vertebrae, one by one, climbing. And while her hands climbed she gradually layered herself against him, bracketing his feet with hers, pressing her thighs to his, her belly into his buttocks and settling her pointed breasts on his back.

He was so hard he throbbed from holding back.

She curved herself over him and behind his eyelids he saw them as if in a mirror. The image all but sent him to his knees.

"This is what I want," she said, her arms snaking around him. "I want you, Tobias." Her strong artist's fingers sheathed his penis.

Tobias jerked away from the wall and wrenched around to face her. "You don't *know* what you want."

Her mouth was open. The water pounded her face. He brought his head down and sucked her bottom lip between his. His teeth nipped the tender flesh and she whimpered.

"You don't know, do you?" His eyes locked on hers.

"Yes."

The thundering in his head and heart and loins deafened him, dulled him. He covered her breasts, pulled, rubbed. The ferocious leap of his manhood made him gasp.

"Tobias?"

"I want *all* of you," he said, hearing his own voice inside his head. His thigh, grinding upward between her legs, lifted her from her feet. She clung to him, her face contorting.

Pleasure.

Pleasure wasn't enough. Not anymore.

Gripped by her own drive, she rocked, urged him with every move to help with her release.

He made circles around her breasts, framed her uptilted nipples in the crook of his finger and thumb.

Her moan was a plea.

Drawn by her needs, and his own, he bent to take a nipple into his mouth.

She pulled his hair and rode his thigh, helpless to stop what she'd started.

"You don't trust me." Quivering with the effort it took, he unwound her fingers from his hair and lowered his leg. He eased her away from him.

Paris's eyes flew open.

Very deliberately, knowing he hovered between saving some-

thing he desperately longed for and risking it all for a few moments of blessed ecstasy—very deliberately, Tobias turned off
the water and opened the shower door.

Pink washed Paris's face.

"No," he told her. "Don't do that. Don't feel shamed."

"I am shamed. I've shamed myself."

"Because you're a wonderful, sexual woman? I don't think
so. I plan to do this all again, my darling. And next time nothing
will keep me from getting inside you."

She flinched, but took the towel he gave her. "I don't understand."

"I'll make sure you do." He had to turn away. "We've begun
something tonight. When you're ready to say what I want to
hear, we'll finish it."

Seventeen

"Jeesus," Nigel said. "Cameras, Toby. Fuckin' cameras."

Tobias turned around. "How did they find us?" Approaching across uneven ground, a shambling gaggle of men and women—two with camera equipment—homed in on the Quinn crew.

"It's the press," one of the engineers said.

Tobias surveyed the oversized bails of barbed wire that had been strewn along his property line during the night and made a rapid decision. "Come with me. All of you. Head them off. And don't answer any questions."

"No comment?" Nigel said under his breath. "Don't you think they'll manage to make something out of that?"

"Leave it to me." He smiled at a small, red-haired woman with Olympic track potential. Her brilliant mane flying, she sprinted to him over plowed debris. "Nice form," he said pleasantly.

"Melanie Evergreen," she said, not even mildly winded. *"Seattle Voice.* But you know that."

He didn't. "Nice to see you, Miss Evergreen."

"Call me Melanie. We'd like something personal on this situation. Tell me, Tobias, how does it feel to be fighting an old man who used to be your grandfather's best friend?"

"Call me Mr. Quinn."

Her hazel eyes hardened. "Fury rages in the Skagit Valley," she said into the tape recorder he hadn't noticed before. "Get a close-up in here," she told an arriving camerawoman. "Then the barbed-wire and the castle."

'Fuck,' Nigel said clearly.

Evergreen rewarded him with an encouraging grin. "You're the brother. The black sheep, right?"

Nigel grinned right back. "Baby, you'll never know how black."

A second cameraman and three more reporters arrived. "Baby" Evergreen crowded territorially close to Tobias. "Like I told you. The *Voice* is interested in the personal angle."

"War is it, Mr. Quinn?" one of the newcomers asked loudly. He indicated the barbed wire. "Battle lines drawn? Keep that dangerous old man at bay? Can we expect air cover?"

Tobias's crew began muttering among themselves. He sent warning stares in every direction. "There's no story here," he said. "You know the way back to the road. We've got work to do."

Someone laughed. "Completing the fortifications, would that be?"

Camera shutters cracked like mini-machine guns.

A flash of white captured Tobias's attention. The valley hadn't caught the rain front that had hit Seattle in the previous twenty-four hours. Wrapped in its own dust cocoon, a vehicle bumped erratically over dry terrain.

"Damn fool's going to ruin his suspension," Nigel said.

Slowly, Tobias's hands fell to his sides. "I don't think it'll be a big loss." He'd seen that old white Buick before—just once.

"Would you say desperation led to this situation, Mr. Quinn?" Melanie Evergreen asked. "Is it true that your brother's gambling debts and the money you're losing here are a threat to your entire company?"

His attention snapped away from the Buick. "You are full of

shit, Miss Evergreen," he said succinctly. "And you may quote me."

She raised her arched red brows.

"You employ a lot of people," a male reporter said. "This situation concerns those people—and the area in general. Do you have plans to downsize soon?"

He heard the words but his concentration was on Paris. She'd abandoned her car on the lip of a particularly cavernous rut and was scrambling toward him.

"Our lucky day," Nigel murmured. "We're about to be visited by She-who-sits-on-the-sun."

"Paris is all right." But she didn't look all right. When he'd taken her home in the early hours of the morning her face had been closed. She'd left him without a word. The closer she got now, the angrier and the more ready to attack she appeared.

In her left hand she held a tube. She held it like a relay baton and ran the last few yards to reach Tobias.

Her hair tumbled wildly about her face and shoulders. "I . . ." Her fingers closed on the front of his denim shirt and she tugged urgently. "I've got to see you. You made a fool of me."

"For God's sake, Paris." Bundling her through his men, he put himself between her and the press. "What are you saying? Those people are from newspapers. Don't ask me why, but they're hunting for any dirt they can find on me. Would you help me out by not giving them any?"

In an instant, tears swam in her eyes. She blinked, sending shining rivulets down her cheeks.

"Ah, *hell.* I'm sorry. I'm too wrapped up with this crap." He pulled her into his arms. "What's wrong?"

"Dirt?" she said against his chest. "They're *looking* for dirt?"

Her fists, pummeling his gut, caught him off guard. "Hey!"

"Why would they have to *look* for dirt?" The tube she held up was a rolled newspaper. "You already gave them enough to bury you in."

"Damn it, Paris. What—"

Without warning, she slapped the paper across his face and brought it down on his head.

"Stop her," Nigel said urgently, coming to his side. "For crying out loud, Paris, *knock* it off, will you?"

When Paris paused, her arm upraised, and looked at Nigel, Tobias saw distaste. The truth about Nigel and Cynthia had never been made public, but Paris knew. The thought sickened him.

Her mouth trembled. "You're trying to frighten Pops to death, aren't you," she said. "Barbed wire to keep him away? He doesn't come out, damn you. Why would you spread that stuff all around him?"

"He put it there," Tobias said. Red hair moved into his field of vision. "And made sure more of it was spread under a layer of soft dirt where it could puncture tires. It was here when my crew arrived this morning. I'm doing my best to keep this mess between us, Paris. To keep it private. *Help* me."

She put her hands on her hips. "Pops put the barbed wire there? He came out in the night and singlehandedly maneuvered that stuff? There's enough to fend off a beach invasion."

"She's got a point," Melanie Evergreen pronounced. "You must be the favorite granddaughter we heard about."

Nigel said, *"Shit,"* and glowered at Paris. "Keep your goddamn mouth *shut,* will you?"

"What happened here and how it happened is something we're going to discuss later," Tobias said. "Who called you? Who tipped you off that these buzzards were on their way?"

He heard her teeth chatter together. Shaking violently she unrolled the newspaper—the business section from *The Seattle Daily*—and held it in front of his face.

Tobias took a step backwards. TERRORISM IN THE SKAGIT VALLEY. He stared at the headline until Nigel snatched the paper away and read aloud, "Troubled Seattle development magnate, Tobias Quinn, is trying to smoke out his octogenarian foe." Nigel stopped talking but continued to scan the lines rapidly.

Paris looked over her shoulder at the miniature castle her grandfather had erected. A single, castellated tower, topped by radio antennas, fronted a structure that otherwise resembled an overgrown mole hill finished in gray stucco. Circular skylights dotted the top of the dome. A narrow but brimming channel of water surrounded the building and there was, indeed, a drawbridge. A white satellite dish formed the focal point on otherwise untended land.

To the left of the drawbridge, between the moat and the castle walls, lay the large wire pen where Pops's dogs exercised. Unfortunately there were no canines in sight this morning.

"Your grandfather and Mr. Delight were partners and the best of friends," Melanie Evergreen said. "Something happened to make them enemies. No one seems to know what the something was, but the suggestion is that your grandfather wronged Mr. Delight. This is your chance to tell the world your side of the story."

Tobias studied the sky.

"He's eighty-one," Paris said to him. "Couldn't you have left him alone?"

"I *am* leaving him alone."

"You've cut down trees!"

"Very few. It's hard to build on top of trees."

"Pops loved his trees."

Tobias scrubbed his face and silently prayed for guidance. "Pops still has *his* trees. The result of what we've done here will be that a new generation of people will learn how to make the best of the land."

"How to make the best of it for *you*, you mean."

Another reporter moved in. "Isn't that what you mean, Mr. Quinn?"

He could see the next set of headlines. This was going to crucify him. "This is a very personal dispute," he said, smiling at the man.

"Exactly!" Evergreen said. "And that's why I think you and I—and Ms. Delight, of course—should go somewhere and talk in private."

A barrage of objections arose from her companions.

The cameras snapped.

"I want to talk about your *humanitarian* efforts in Seattle," Evergreen continued, undeterred. "Your contributions to the arts. Particularly your deep understanding of important, of *meaningful*—"

"Fuck off," Nigel said. "And take the rest of these shits with you."

"I give up," Tobias told whoever wanted to listen. "If you'll excuse me, I've got business to conduct."

"Last night," Paris said, pushing her glasses up. "It was just like I thought, wasn't it?"

"*Paris,* don't—"

"You only wanted me because Pops is in your way here." She batted the paper in Nigel's hands. "It says right there that you've been trying to get Pops to pack up and move out so you can have everything."

Tobias heard the subtle whir of recording tapes. "I don't want his lousy acre."

"Yesterday you tried to make him let you in. You threw rocks at his door."

It all sounded so bloody crazy. "How else do you knock on a man's door when it's on the other side of goddamn . . . of a *moat?*"

"He's afraid of you now. Are you satisfied?"

Tobias narrowed his eyes.

"You're harassing an old man who only wants a little peace. He's threatening a hunger strike. How long do you think an eighty-one-year-old man would last on a hunger strike."

Nigel barked a laugh. "Too damn long, if I know that old bastard."

The recorders kept on whirring and pencils scratched faster than the cameras shot.

"Are you going over to comfort your grandfather, Ms. Delight?" Evergreen asked.

"Maybe you'd rather comfort Mr. Quinn?" a snide masculine voice suggested.

Tobias turned on Melanie Evergreen. "Paris can't comfort her grandfather because she can't damn well get *in* to comfort him. Anymore than anyone else can get in."

"Is that right?" Melanie asked, her eyes wide.

"Pops is a very private, very independent man," Paris said.

"He won't let her in," Nigel said, sounding satisfied.

"Tobias"—Paris waited until he faced her—"I'm not going to stand by and watch you destroy Pops."

He had the fleeting thought that he'd like her to be as protective of him. "Why don't you follow these nice people off my land, Paris?" Any thought he'd had of a liaison between them had been madness from the beginning.

"You're not listening to me," she said. "You won't do what you're trying to do because I'm going to stop you."

"Toby—"

He raised a hand to silence Nigel. "That's it," he told Paris. "That old man has cried wolf one time too many. Now he's going to find out who's the dirtiest player around here. And so are you, Blue."

Cynthia's red Porsche was already in the garage when Nigel drove in. He hit the button to close the doors before getting out of the Lexus.

She'd better come through or he was a dead man.

"Cynthia?" Spreading dirt from his boots with every step, he hurried through the upper floor of Tobias's house. "Where the fuck are you?"

He got his answer soon enough. Stretched out on her stomach atop the big master suite bed, she was engrossed in one of her porno flicks.

And she was bare-ass naked.

It might be nice to come home to a surprise.

"Turn that thing off," he told her. "Now."

Her lovely bottom rose a few inches from the bed and gyrated.

"Cynthia—"

"I'm busy."

"The movie can wait."

"Masturbation can't."

He took the remote from beside her and aimed it at the giant-screen TV. The picture faded without his registering what he saw. "Tell me who's paying for information about Tobias."

She wasn't listening.

"Damn it, Cynthia!" Nigel sank a hand into the hair at her nape and pulled.

Panting rewarded his effort. He slapped her rear and her howl was pure pleasure before she convulsed and rolled to her back.

"For god's sake," Nigel said. "Couldn't you have waited?"

"For what? Anytime you're ready, I'm ready, lover." Looking at him upside down, she reached her arms back to surround his hips. "Unzip for me, sweetie. I'm hungry."

Nigel averted his eyes from the tempting vision of her flushed breasts and the triangle of golden hair between her thighs. "Who is it?"

"Don't shout at me."

"Answer the question."

Her long fingers pressed at his crotch. "You don't need to know. Why are you so angry?"

"I've got to have the money, Cynthia. I'm out of time. They're going to come for me if I don't pay."

"You'll get the money. I'm not allowed to tell you who's paying us. That's part of the deal."

He didn't trust her. But he was helpless. "Did you know Tobias was having a thing with Paris?"

Her fingers slowly went limp and dropped away. For several moments she lay, staring up at him, her arms above her head. "A thing?" she finally said. "What the hell does that mean?"

"He's been seeing her. They were together last night."

Cynthia rolled to stand up and moved in close enough for him to feel her body heat. "Together? As in, *together?* That's not possible. Paris wouldn't . . . She's too much of a prissy tight-ass."

"She said otherwise—in front of me and a crew of about twenty. And a selection of Seattle's brightest newspaper types. And from Tobias's reaction to her, I'd say they're more than casual acquaintances right now."

Cynthia's pointed tongue made a circuit of her lips. "I've got to talk to her."

"No!" Clamping a hand on her upper arm, he hurried her to a cream-colored divan near the windows and pushed her down. "The last thing we can afford is for you to let Paris know the two of us are involved. She and big brother are on the hate end of the love thing right now. But all it'll take to push them together is the news that *I* came running to tell you what happened today."

"Let me get dressed." She stood up.

Nigel made sure she connected with the divan again. "I want to talk to the money man myself."

"No."

He wasn't a violent man, but she made him feel violent. "You aren't hearing me, baby. I need—"

"And I've got it." Smiling, running her hands up his thighs and cupping his balls, Cynthia rose, uncurling up his length like a sinuous, red-gold serpent. "All I wanted was to have a little fun with you before I gave it to you."

Relief sent a wave of heat under the surface of Nigel's skin. "Oh, thank God, baby." He hugged her, stroked her smooth back and squeezed her bottom. "Give it to me."

"There's time." Nimble fingers worked the buttons on his shirt.

He caught her wrists and held her off. "I want you to give it to me now. Then I want you to go home while I attend to business."

"Nigel—"

"Do as I tell you. I'll come for you later and we'll celebrate. *Really* celebrate." The proximity of a full reprieve piled up his sexual arousal as if his body was a dam holding back a tidal wave. If he touched her now he wouldn't be able to stop. "Where is it?"

Grumbling, she went to a closet and produced a bulging green plastic garbage sack. "Do I *have* to leave?"

Nigel opened the sack, found it was double, and saw bundles of notes inside. "Yes, you do. This is great, honey." He turned her around and gave her a playful swat. "Off you go. Make sure you're ready and waiting when I come."

Cynthia giggled. "Aren't I always?"

* * *

Someone was setting him up.

With his jean jacket slung over his shoulder, Tobias walked along the dock toward home. In late afternoon, when he'd returned to the office, he'd been confronted with a heap of messages and Gladys's huffy outrage on his behalf.

Inquiries from worried clients, inquiries from worried potential clients, a dozen requests for media interviews—all awaited him. And Gladys, bless her faithful heart, had insisted upon manning the phone until eight when he'd made her go home.

Then he'd tried to talk to Paris.

She'd hung up and when he called back later one of her male buddies answered and told him to do something he didn't think was possible. His final call, at something past midnight, had been picked up, and cut off as soon as he spoke.

He reached the houseboat. Unlike last night, he could see lights along the length of the Montlake Cut and the bridge was a black silhouette against a charcoal sky speckled with stars.

If he could, he'd turn back the clock and be sitting beside Paris in the hot tub again. He'd be satisfied to hold her hand and feel her arm against his—and the rain on his face.

Regardless of what blocks her family threw between them, the way he felt about her wasn't going to go away.

He'd fallen in love with another Delight. He'd fallen so hard he knew, without a doubt, that he'd never really been in love before.

And the last words he'd spoken to her, face-to-face, had been a threat. And she'd threatened him in return.

Flapping noises came from the deck. Tobias went aboard and walked around to the front of the houseboat. The gloom didn't stop him from seeing that the dinghy had slipped one of its moorings. Still attached by a single line, the rubber craft teetered over the water.

Tobias dropped his jacket, gripped a cleat and leaned until he could snag the loose line.

The blow hit at the same moment as he smelled cigarette smoke . . . a moment before he slid into the black water.

Eighteen

Where was he?

Paris hurried past a wall of aquariums in the hospital entrance.

"He's been hurt. We don't know how badly."

No, no, no. Not Tobias. He could not be badly hurt.

The reception desks were deserted.

Spinning around, she searched for signs. *Emergency.* She should have gone to the emergency entrance. Following green arrows she started to run. Faster and faster. Her throat burned.

More aquariums. Fish and plants an orange-green blur. Doors swung open without assistance.

Then the silence was behind her. Ahead everything moved—fast. Doctors and nursing staff were about the business of dealing with another city-night's dramas and their purposeful coming and going closed out trivial interruptions.

The first familiar face she saw was Nigel Quinn's. He paced before a room with large windows. Beyond the windows Paris could see curtains drawn around a bed.

"Nigel!" She reached him and touched his back. "Nigel, thanks for calling me. How is he?"

He spun around and the compression of his lips formed a white line around his mouth. Nigel had never liked her, but this was no time to confront old differences.

"Nigel?"

"Calling you was Tobias's idea, not mine." He indicated a couple sitting in two of a row of chairs against the opposite wall. "Remember Bill Bowie and Vivian?"

Disoriented, Paris saw a worried blond man and a dramatic Latin-looking woman who held his hand as if comforting him. "I don't . . . Perhaps. Did I meet you at Tobias's?"

The woman raised her face. "I'm Vivian Estes," she said in fluid Southern tones. "Bill and Tobias are very old friends. I think we met once when Tobias was married to Cynthia."

"Yes, I do remember." At the house on Lake Washington. But that had been years ago. She returned her attention to Nigel. "What happened? Where's Tobias?"

He inclined his head to the room behind him. "The police are with him. They kicked us out."

"Police?" Paris clutched, and closed her fingers around air before the man called Bill sprang up and guided her to a chair. She tried to smile at him as she sank into it, but failed. She buried her face in her hands.

Without looking, she knew the cool stroke on the back of her neck came from Vivian Estes. "Put your head down," the woman said.

"Do you always pass out at the mention of the police?" Nigel asked.

"Be quiet," Vivian commanded. "Go and ask someone for a cold wet cloth."

"I'm not a goddamn nursemaid."

"We'd appreciate it if you'd do that, Nigel." Bill Bowie spoke for the first time. An ordinary voice but one with the kind of authoritative edge that suggested he didn't expect or tolerate many arguments.

The woozy sensation cleared from Paris's brain. "I'm all right." She sat up but Nigel had already gone in search of the wet cloth.

Bill Bowie and Vivian Estes sat, one each side of Paris, watching her with a mixture of curiosity and concern.

"What happened tonight?" Paris asked.

An unreadable glance passed between the two before Bill said, "We're not sure yet. Evidently he was attacked."

Paris gripped the seat of her chair and stared ahead at the windows.

"I didn't realize you and Tobias had kept in touch," Bowie said. "Sly dog, our Tobias."

Rather than drop her face, Paris leaned back in the chair. "Tobias and I have been . . . We've known each other since we were children."

Bill arched an almost white brow. "I know. I just never guessed the association had continued. Given the—well, frankly, I'd assumed—"

"Honey," Vivian said, leaning across Paris and caressing the man's neck in a way that left little doubt about their relationship. "There could just be a whole lot you don't know about Tobias. There are things a man doesn't even tell his best friend." She smiled knowingly at Paris who realized she might be looking at the most beautiful woman she'd ever seen this close.

The door to Tobias's room swung open and two police officers came out with a nurse at their heels.

Paris instantly jumped to her feet.

"He should rest for another hour or so," the nurse said, approaching Bowie. "Dr. Nolan wants to check him again before he releases him."

The policemen set off toward the exit.

"All right if I go in?" Bowie said.

"If you can stop him from losing his temper again," the nurse responded, smiling faintly. "He doesn't like being on the receiving end of a bunch of questions. Let's keep it to one visitor at a time until Dr. Nolan says otherwise."

Vivian moved forward in her seat. "You aren't admitting him to the hospital, then?"

"Doesn't look like it." The nurse walked away, passing Nigel on his return.

"One at a time," Bowie said, indicating for Nigel to go into Tobias's room. "Tell him we're here."

Paris screwed up the courage to say, "Me, too."

Nigel gave her another tight-lipped stare before handing over a wet cloth and a towel and going to see his brother.

Paris sat down again and suffered a cool compress to be applied to her neck and then her forehead. Vivian had a firm but gentle hand. At any other time Paris might have enjoyed being ministered to by such comforting hands. Tonight all she cared about was the man on the other side of the windows.

Only minutes passed before Nigel reappeared. Bill made to go to Tobias but Nigel caught his arm. "He wants to talk to her first." He indicated Paris.

"Go on, honey," Vivian said softly. "And don't mind the protective little brother. He's had a bad scare, too."

Avoiding Nigel's malevolent stare, Paris followed Vivian's instructions and went cautiously through the door. "Tobias?" she said uncertainly when she reached the curtains around his bed.

"Shut the door behind you and come here." He cleared his throat. *"Now."*

She dealt with the door, found her way through the curtains but stood as far from the bed as possible.

"I'm not going to bite."

But he looked almost capable of biting—hard. His black hair was rumpled against the white pillow. The glint in his gray eyes held pure impatience tinged with—anger? Pallor underlay his tan, but he still appeared disgustingly healthy and out-of-place in the sterile bed. Blue-covered packs of ice were piled beneath his shoulders.

"I told you to come here," he said, far too quietly this time.

Paris approached. "They said someone attacked you? Where did it happen?"

"Closer," he ordered.

Another step brought her in range of his very strong hand. He landed her on the bed beside him. "They don't like people sitting on patients' beds," she told him. Her heart thudded too hard.

"Bullshit. It's all the thing now. Haven't you seen how new fathers get into bed with their wives and babies?"

Paris eyed him suspiciously.

"No," he said, sounding almost wistful. "I haven't just had a baby."

"Should I get the nurse?"

"Not if you want to live."

"Tobias—"

"An attempt was made to kill me tonight. When I went home, my Zodiac had been conveniently loosened so I'd have to lean over the water to pull it all the way aboard again. That's when I was hit with something hard enough to convince me the guy meant business." He moved against the ice and winced. "The bastard missed my head but he made a hell of a dent across my shoulders."

"Thank God he missed," Paris said. She visualized him slumped on his deck in the darkness and felt sick.

"Thank God he did part of what he set out to do. He sent me into the water and somehow I managed to keep it together long enough to hang onto a fender and keep out of sight. I know he watched to make sure I wasn't coming up again. I heard him when he did leave. If something had gone wrong and I'd landed on the deck, he'd have made sure he didn't miss a second time. I don't quite remember how I made it out of the water and inside to call for help."

Paris looked at his hand on her wrist. "You asked Nigel to let me know you were here."

"Yeah. I think someone should have hit me hard a bit sooner. It made my mind clearer."

He wasn't making a whole lot of sense but Paris found she didn't care as long as she was here and he was very much alive. "Nigel seems angry with me."

Tobias's smile was the last thing Paris expected. "What?" she asked him. "Why are you smiling?"

"Do you know what I believe?"

She shook her head.

"You would if you thought about it. I think you and I are

linked somehow. I think we're being set up as public enemies. Or should I say, enemies in public?"

"Shouldn't you be resting?"

Tobias lifted her hand and studied her unadorned fingers. "I'm going to make a proposition. Are you ready for that?"

"This morning we were threatening each other," she reminded him, almost certain his brain had been knocked a little loose, almost afraid it hadn't. "I'm still mad at you—and probably getting madder."

"I know. You're as hard-headed as that old man."

"Don't talk . . . You're injured. I'll wait until you're on your feet, *then* the war will resume. I'm only here for humanitarian reasons. For old times' sake. Kind of in your mother's place." Too late, she regretted the reference to the woman who'd dropped out of her husband's and son's lives to follow a man to the other side of the world.

If the comment bothered Tobias, he hid it well. "Funny," he said, with every sign of deep consideration. "I have difficulty seeing you in a motherly role—when it comes to me, that is."

"Pops isn't talking to anyone, Tobias. Not even my grandmother. She's as furious with you as I am."

"I'm sorry to hear that. Emma was always a favorite of mine. I miss her."

"Don't evade the issue. We're going to have to deal with it."

"Not right now, my sweet." Tobias took her fingers to his lips and, while her stomach did not-so-tiny flips, he kissed the end of each one. "We've crossed a line, Paris. It's that line you can't turn back from."

She met his eyes.

He said, "You know the one, don't you?"

Paris cleared her throat. "We haven't . . . Not exactly."

"A technicality." His smile was the old, wicked smile. "From here on it's a matter of when, not if."

"I want, so badly, to believe in you." The words were out before she could stop them.

Tobias pulled her over him, slid his free hand around her neck and kissed her.

For the space of a breath she fought him. As quickly, she gave in. Closing her eyes, she let him mold her to his solid chest.

"Oh, what you do to me, lady," he said, when their lips finally parted. "How about climbing in here with me."

Struggling for breath, Paris put her fingers over his lips. "As you said, you didn't just have a baby. We've got to concentrate, Tobias. What happened tonight was evil. There are evil things out there. Don't forget—"

"That a man attacked you a couple of nights ago? Hardly. Same guy, sweets. Same guy."

She pushed to sit up and winced when he grimaced. "Sorry," she said, touching his beard-rough jaw. "What do you mean?"

"I almost missed it. Remember the smell of the cigarette?"

Paris shuddered and folded her arms around her ribs. "I'm never going to forget."

"The guy who hit me tonight was smoking one of those French cigarettes. Too much of a coincidence, wouldn't you say?"

She averted her face. "What are we going to do? Did you tell the police?"

"I told them. They haven't turned anything up on what happened at your place yet. They'll do their best but this isn't an amateur production, Paris."

"It could be . . . No, I guess you're right, it couldn't be a coincidence."

"Someone's going to come in at any second. Please just listen to me. How did you get here?"

"Wormwood was at home, thank God. He dropped me off."

"Okay." Tobias laced the fingers of their right hands together. "I'll ask Bill and Vivian to take you back on their way home. Bill will go up with you and check things out. Then you use that nice new lock on your door and don't come out until we talk."

"I can't—"

"I'm a sick man. Humor me."

She had to smile. "What if you're still here in a week?"

"I'll be home before morning. But you haven't heard my proposition. We're going to keep the world thinking we hate each other's guts."

Paris frowned. "You'll have to expand on that."

"I think you got pulled into a mess that was only supposed to involve me. The mess with Pops may not be the issue, not really. He didn't come up with this plot to make me look bad all on his own. I've got someone out there who's trying to wipe me out professionally. Evidently it wasn't happening fast enough. They decided things would speed up with me dead."

"If you're right . . ."—and she wasn't convinced—"Well, then why was I attacked? What do *I* have to do with any of this?"

"I thought I didn't know, but now I think I do. When I had my brilliant notion to come begging at your door, I must have given my personal Machiavelli a thrill. He was presented with a whole new line of approach. We're supposed to suspect each other of conspiracy. I'm out to frighten you into helping me with Pops. You're in league with whoever *they* are to ruin me because of an old family feud—and because of Cynthia, I suppose. And the result is that we keep each other too busy for me to look elsewhere for my villain."

Paris said, "We're going to have to deal with the issue of Cynthia, aren't we?" They couldn't avoid something so raw.

"Yes. And we will. I don't intend to knock her to you, Paris, but . . . Later, okay?"

"Okay." It had to be. "At least I may be past watching my designs get ripped off—thanks to you."

Tobias let out a slow breath. "Let's hope so. Whatever happens, you aren't on your own with any of this."

Reading too much into what he said would be easy.

He squeezed her hand. "Not anymore. Is that a deal?"

This time she had to hold onto her heart. "We'll see."

"No . . ." He must have read the reservation in her eyes. "Have it your way. For now. If I begin to feel I can't be sure you're safe, I'm going to move you."

"I'm not going anywhere," Paris said, then, "No, no, Tobias. Don't try the heavy-handed male bit with me. I've been on my own too long. I admit you may have stumbled onto an answer to a lot of things, but I can't play the helpless little woman."

"Another discussion for later," he said, but he did grin. "You will take the precautions I've asked you to take?"

"Yes."

"As far as anyone knows, you still don't trust me. You think I'm a grasping opportunist who's out to victimize Pops."

"I certainly do."

He had the sense not to turn that into a joke. "And the less I see or hear of you, the better I'm going to like it."

"Sounds about right to me."

"Yeah. Sounds like a pain in the ass and a waste of good time, to me. We each need someone we can trust in case we can't make contact for ourselves."

Avoiding his eyes, Paris said, "Nigel doesn't like me. As in, he *really* doesn't like me."

"Nigel heard that fiasco up in the Skagit. He already has you convicted of attempted murder. *My* attempted murder. He'll come around in time, but I think I'll let him keep on thinking I've got you in here to scare the hell out of you."

"Is that what he thinks?" Paris's mouth remained open.

"That's what I told him, so that's what he thinks. Bill probably makes the most sense. At least he won't question me when I ask him to take you home. But he's not long on imagination and he could put up a fuss about my theory." A sound at the door made Tobias try to rise closer to her. He fell back and whispered urgently. "My secretary, Gladys. She'd never let me down. If need be, we can trust her. How about you? Who would you use?"

Paris took her hand from his and stood up. She massaged her eyes beneath her glasses and said, "You won't like this, but Cynthia."

"God, no!"

"She's selfish. We both know that. But she wants me to be happy and I'm not going to tell her . . . I'm not telling her anything but the frightening stuff." Perhaps she should tell him she'd exclude only the *really* frightening stuff—that she was falling in love with a forbidden man.

"Hey, Tobias." It was Bill Bowie's voice, lowered to sickroom pitch. "Okay if I come in now?"

Tobias brushed the backs of his fingers down Paris's thigh.

A shiver followed in the wake of his touch.

"As long as I don't say we're madly in love," Paris whispered.

"Honestly, I know Cynthia would do anything to help me if I needed her."

He caught the tip of his tongue between his teeth, kept his gaze steadily on hers, then visibly made a decision. "We'll go with your instincts. Cynthia it is." he raised his voice. "Come on in, Bill."

Nineteen

Sitting cross-legged on the floor, Paris bent over the table in front of her couch. She tried to concentrate on sketches for a sweater pin of braided silver—and she tried to ignore the irritable tapping of Cynthia's toes.

"I still think Tobias is up to something."

Paris lifted her coffee mug and drank. "You say that at least twenty times a minute."

"Don't exaggerate."

"Twenty times every time we talk, then."

"There was another article in the paper this morning." Cynthia examined a fingernail which evidently met with disapproval. "It said Pops isn't talking on the radio at all anymore. Speculation is that he's really starving himself up there."

"And this is when Emma decides to take a cruise to Alaska." Paris shook her head. "I suppose I could . . . Scratch that idea. I'm not asking the police for help with anything. They already think the Delights and the Quinns are the crime world's equivalent of hypochondriacs."

"Tell me again what that creep who broke in did to you?"

Paris rolled the mug between her hands and looked reflectively at Cynthia. "We'll drop that, if you don't mind." Her sister's preoccupation with sex, particularly if perversion was involved, troubled Paris.

"I need you with me at that party tonight," Cynthia said, not for the first time since she'd arrived—shortly after breakfast.

Paris had guessed—correctly—that only something personally imperative to Cynthia would rouse her at an hour of the day she considered uncivilized.

"Paris?"

"I can't." She hadn't seen Tobias in the week since they'd been together at the hospital, but they'd talked on the phone daily . . . and nightly. "Tobias may be wrong about this conspiracy theory of his, but I was attacked and so was he. And there's no doubt it was by the same man."

"I don't see why insisting you stay shut up here is going to keep you alive until you're three hundred and ten. Hell, a plane might crash into the building."

"You know that's not the point."

"I know you'll be perfectly safe going to a party with me tonight." Sliding to the floor beside Paris, Cynthia arranged her legs and smoothed her black jumpsuit over her thighs. *"Eve-ryone's* going to be there. You'll have an opportunity to make some good business contacts."

"I don't understand why you want me. Get a man to go along. We both know that would take about ten seconds to arrange."

Pouting, Cynthia rested her elbows on the table and turned her head to see what Paris was drawing. "I know you don't understand, but I'm still off men. In time I'll be ready to try again, but not yet."

In her present mood, Cynthia made it hard for Paris to avoid spilling every detail of the times she'd spent with Tobias. She bit back the questions: *Are you sure he did all the things you said he did? Couldn't you please tell me you exaggerated—just a little?*

"Come with me tonight, Paris."

Tobias was a very sexual man—but Cynthia reveled in her sexuality, too. Surely the same man could be different with different women.

Paris rested her forehead on the rim of her mug. Thinking

about Tobias with other women made her crazy. The fact that it made her crazy made her scared.

From a distance she heard Cynthia say, "There's going to be a publisher there. I know if I can get someone to read this book they'll buy it. I don't trust agents. If I can work without one, I will."

"Don't you think working with an agent would be safer?" Paris said absently.

"Why pay someone else when I can do it myself?"

"Aren't contracts—"

"I'm not a fool. I know what I will and won't sign."

"Whatever you say."

Cynthia turned Paris's sketch toward her. "This is pretty. Will you come?"

"I've got so much to do if I'm going to have a full line ready by September." And she'd promised Tobias she wouldn't go anywhere while they waited for someone to make another move against him.

"You've worked like a dog all week. What harm could it do to take a few hours off?"

Paris dropped flat on her back on the floor. "All right, I'll go! Would you please leave me alone now?"

"*Yes!*" Cynthia bounced to her feet. "All kinds of gallery people will be there. And theater types. And *money*, Paris. *Big* money."

"So how do you intend to sneak me in? As your maid?"

Cynthia poked her with a toe. "Wear some of your own jewelry. And that horrible red chiffon thing. No one has to know it came from a flea market. We'll pass it off as *avant garde.*"

Paris snickered. "As long as whoever wore it in the ice follies doesn't show up."

A threatening glare was Cynthia's only response.

As soon as she was alone again, Paris returned to her sketches. The past week had been remarkably productive. Rather than attempt to scrap every new design, she'd made minor but dramatic changes. Her first project had been to actually work on the collar she was certain had already been pirated. A distinctive transformation was accomplished simply by replacing the amethyst with a large, deep green tourmaline, and spinning several silver threads up and over the stone.

Aldonza's loud purr broke the peace. Curled in a ball, the cat snoozed in a shaft of sunlight that shone through a blue vase to dapple white markings with violet.

Beside the vase sat the phone.

She didn't owe Tobias an itinerary of her every move.

Surely he'd understand that going to a party with Cynthia was safe.

Paris scooted closer to the phone. She had promised to let him know if she had to leave.

He cared.

Cynthia had been horrified at the idea of Paris believing a word Tobias said.

Paris snatched up the receiver and dialed the direct line into his office.

He picked up at one ring. "Quinn."

She started to hang up.

"Hello?"

Slowly, she returned the phone to her ear. "This is Paris."

"Hi! Hold on."

She heard footsteps and a door slamming before he returned and said, "Is everything okay?"

"Terrific."

"Nothing's happened?"

"Not a thing. Tobias, I—"

"You must have heard my mind. Are you blushing?"

"Blushing?"

"You blush at anything and everything. I was thinking about long hot showers in the morning—with you. And long hot swims off a tropical beach at night—with you. And a number of other long, long hot ideas. Remember that technicality we haven't dealt with yet?"

She was blushing.

"Of course you do. Paris, I want to make love to you. I want to see you naked again. You're perfect. You *feel* perfect."

"Tobias."

"No one's listening at this end. Do you have someone with you?"

"No. It's just that—"

"You want me to make love to you, too. I know. Want to discuss the ways?"

Paris put a hand to her brow and found it burning. Her heart did erratic things and she pulsed in places that weren't likely to be reached soon.

"Such a quiet thing," Tobias said, his voice soft and low. "I bet you won't be so quiet when we—"

"Don't."

He laughed.

"I mean it, Tobias. I called because I promised to tell you if I intended to go out."

At last he was silent.

"Cynthia and I are going to a party tonight."

"Are you out of your mind?"

She got up. "I didn't have to call you."

"The hell you didn't! We have an understanding."

"And I'm adhering to it." A week trapped inside the apartment was too long. "This isn't anything to do with your kind of people."

"My kind of people? What the . . . What does that mean?"

Paris almost pulled the phone off the table. Trapping it before it fell, she said, "Just what I say. Cynthia needs my support and I'm going to give it to her. It'll also be an opportunity for me to make some contacts in the business. The kind of people I deal with move in different circles from yours."

"Yeah. Circles that forge jewelry."

"Rather than try to kill people?"

"As far as you know."

"I think—"

"Did you see the latest in the *Voice?*"

"Cynthia mentioned something about it. We're having a real problem dealing with Pops. Actually, we're not dealing with him at all. He still won't speak to us. For all we know he could be ill."

His sigh reached her. "His wolves looked pretty healthy yesterday."

"Dogs."

"Don't go to that party tonight, Paris."

She hung up.

* * *

The view was three-hundred-and-sixty degrees of glittering city. Beyond the glass walls and dome of the twenty-sixth floor condominium a cloud-streaked moon spread lemon frost through skies as sheer as indigo tissue.

Paris shifted her weight in the ruby slippers she'd bought to match the cast off red chiffon costume—and because she'd always wanted a pair of "Dorothy" shoes.

A serious man in a black velvet jacket and floppy green bow tie spoke across Paris to a slight woman banded in orange lycra. "It's expensive," the man said. "But *anime* is the coming thing."

Cynthia, standing between the man and woman, made owl eyes at Paris who grinned and said, "I thought you were in publishing, Mr. Hunter."

"I am," he responded. "But these Japanese comics are going through the roof. I feel it in my bones. Today laser discs and Internet discussion groups. Tomorrow . . . well, who knows?"

"What do you see as the hottest new trends in publishing?" Cynthia said. Her white dress was a minimalist masterpiece; stripped down to bare essentials.

"Publishing's soft," Hunter pronounced over his beaked nose.

Paris swayed a little to the new-age music and put her brain into neutral. Cynthia had been right when she'd said there would be big money present tonight. The condo belonged to Astor Burken, a prominent Seattle socialite and patron of the arts. Luminaries from the theater and music scene mingled with gallery owners and a select group of artists. Melanie Evergreen of the *Voice* was the sole recognizable media type—no doubt on hand to snap up the "personal" angle on something particularly obscure but desperately meaningful.

Only the artists—and Paris—weren't wearing the stuff of best-dressed lists.

The bejeweled guests glittered like the skyline. Rich colors and subtle colors and spangles and beads. Some wandered out to a large terrace where water in a swimming pool rippled a luminescent *crème de menthe* shade in the moonlight.

"Bill." Paris heard Cynthia say excitedly. "Paris, it's Bill Bowie."

Paris automatically turned her head toward the elevators that deposited arriving guests. Cynthia was already in motion across white marble tile toward Bill Bowie. He was alone—that surprised Paris more than actually seeing the man in this setting.

Confronted by Cynthia, Bill paused in the process of greeting Astor Burken. Even at a distance, Paris saw the man frown. Then Astor's attention was diverted. Cynthia wound an arm through Bill's and nodded toward Paris who couldn't hear a word over the music and babble.

By the time Cynthia arrived with Bill, the Japanimation enthusiast had wafted away with his silent companion in orange.

"Can you believe this?" Cynthia said. Her breasts overflowed the tiny strapless dress to press into Bill Bowie's upper arm. "Do you remember Bill? We used to be inseparable."

Bill, immaculate in black tie, shook Paris's hand. "Paris and I met again recently," he said, neither encouraging nor discouraging Cynthia's clinging attention. "Does Cynthia know what happened to Tobias?"

"Yes—"

"Paris and I tell each other *everything,*" Cynthia said. "Oh, I can't tell you how wonderful it is to see you, Bill. We shouldn't have become such strangers."

"Things changed," Bill said, glancing down the front of Cynthia's dress without a flicker of reaction in his ice-blue eyes. "Between you and Tobias."

Cynthia pouted on cue. "But not between you and me. D'you know I haven't been sailing once since you and . . . I haven't been out since I went with you."

"Vivian and I enjoyed that day, too," he said. A nerve flickered beside his left eye.

"Come and see the pool." Undeterred, Cynthia urged him down two steps toward the doors leading outside. "Coming, Paris?"

"No, thank you." Cynthia's performance with Bill fascinated her but she'd rather avoid the unprotected roof.

Paris watched them go. A breeze from the open doors flipped the multitude of red chiffon points that floated free from the flapper style dress she wore.

She looked down into her barely touched champagne. All about her people were with people. Couples. Groups. Normally she didn't care that she no longer had someone whose name was linked with hers. And if she cared, now she no longer wanted the other name to be Michael.

The drop in conversation stole up from behind her. New Age had given way to Mannheim Steamroller. *Sunflower.* Paris hummed and felt the softness of the music calm the frenetic shifting around her. Sunflowers—or perhaps a field of yellow corn waving beneath blindingly blue skies.

She stood at the top of the steps. Below her every green leather couch and seat held guests. More people stood in knots.

All laughter had ceased. The cornfield faded.

Paris felt silence and expectancy. The small hairs on her spine rose. Slowly, holding her glass to her chest, she turned around.

The man who had arrived was taller than the rest, broader, leaner and darker, and more intense. His silver-gray eyes found her over the heads of the watching throng. He was oddly, silently menacing.

"Quinn," someone nearby whispered.

He was promptly shushed.

Tobias's gaze never left his target. Looking neither left nor right, he walked toward her. As he walked, the crowd parted as if cut in two and rolled aside by a paring blade.

Then he stood before her, looking down—looking all the way down, over the thin floating red chiffon to her spangled red shoes and back to her eyes.

Paris dropped a hand to her side and fidgeted with a flimsy point of fabric. "My McFadden's at the cleaners," she said. "With my Romeo Gigli pantsuit."

"Good," he said, loud enough to be clearly heard. "I wouldn't have missed you in the red number. Your hidden personality emerges."

Heat began its ascent of Paris's neck.

Tobias deliberately stared at those who stood closest until they broke into awkward conversations. Even hovering Melanie Evergreen pretended disinterest.

"I told you not to come here," Tobias told Paris in low tones. "Do you realize how vulnerable you are?"

"In the middle of a hundred people?"

"Coming and going from this place."

"I came by car. Cynthia drove me."

"How did you think you were going home?"

"I *am* going home with Cynthia. She'll drop me off."

He searched the room. "If she remembers you're here." A corner of his mouth jerked downward.

"Of course she'll remember."

"And drop you off? And, of course, nothing could happen to you on the way into that . . . You could be picked off in front of the building, Paris."

Her heart pummeled, but she glared up at him. "You make it sound as if there were snipers on the rooftops just waiting for me. Why would anyone want to hurt me? Tell me that."

Her voice had risen and she met the curious stare of a pale woman in gray silk who leaned toward her partner and said what Paris guessed to be her own name. "You're making a spectacle of us," she said through her teeth.

"Really." Tobias sank his hands into the pockets of his tuxedo pants and pretended interest in his surroundings. "One more fund-raiser. New museums for new art, hm? I understand that's what this do is about. How much did you sign up for?"

"They didn't seem too interested in ninety-nine cents," Paris said grimly. "I'm here for Cynthia's sake."

"I thought you said you might make some contacts."

"Cynthia said . . . I've met some interesting people." Not an entire lie, but close.

"Speaking of the lady, here she comes." His features hardened. "Good God! What the hell's she doing with Bill?"

Before Paris could respond, Cynthia and Bill reached her side. Once more the hubbub sank to a muted current of sound. Paris could feel avid anticipation in the air.

"Hello, Toby, darling," Cynthia said, still using Bill's arm like a hitching post. "What on *earth* are you doing here?"

"I came to find Paris," he said, far too distinctly. "Bill. How's it going?"

There was more in the question than the obvious. Bowie said, "Great. How's the neck?"

"Healing rapidly, thanks."

"All kinds of surprises tonight, hm?" Bill made a subtle attempt to dislodge Cynthia—without success. "Cynthia's been reminding me of how long it's been since she saw me."

Paris was mortified for Cynthia, who continued to smile seductively at Bill. "I've been telling him how much I've missed the company of a man who knows how to live," she murmured.

"Yeah, you must have been through some tough times," Tobias said. His cool, strong fingers closed on Paris's elbow. "Let's go."

She held back.

Tobias pulled her toward him. "I said, let's go, Paris."

The room blurred to a whispering mass of colors. He moved and breathed and exuded power, yet a stillness—a cold stillness reached out from him.

Without warning, Cynthia flapped at Tobias's fingers on Paris's elbow. "She doesn't want to go. We're having fun. You still haven't learned to have fun, have you?"

Horrified, Paris set her glass on a tray held in the paws of a bronze tiger.

"Bill?" Cynthia's voice was shrill. "Don't let Tobias bully Paris. He was always such a bully. I can't stand to watch him treat Paris the way he treated me."

Paris closed her eyes and prayed to wake up—somewhere else.

"Don't be silly, Cynthia," Tobias said smoothly. "You know I'm a pussycat."

The pressure Tobias exerted on her elbow meant she either went with him or raised even more of a fuss than they had already. As it was, this scene would be the stuff of gossip all over town by tomorrow.

Paris turned on a smile and walked beside him.

"Bill?" Cynthia whined behind her.

Tobias halted, but not in response to Cynthia. "There you are," he said softly to Vivian Estes. She must have slipped into the party while Paris was engrossed.

Vivian, swathed in a floor-length creamy satin cloak, extended a honey-tan hand and let Tobias take it to his mouth.

"I wondered where you were, my dear," Tobias said, still in a low voice. He moved aside, taking Paris with him.

Vivian was confronted with the vision of Cynthia's white breasts spilling softly against Bill's chest, her long legs all but astride one of his.

"*Shit,*" Tobias muttered.

Cynthia sprang away from Bill and all but rushed to Vivian. "*Darling.* God, what a marvelous night this is turning out to be. First Bill, then you. And you *look* spectacular, of course."

Avoiding Cynthia's impending embrace, Vivian swept past her and accepted Bill's long kiss. They kissed, and kissed, until Cynthia tossed back her hair and smiled unseeingly in all directions.

A male chuckle or two reached Paris's ears and she heard Astor Burken announce a dessert buffet by the pool.

Bill and Vivian parted.

"I'm taking you home," Tobias said to Paris. "Right now."

Vivian smiled and said, "Good to see you again, Paris." She slipped a crystal button through a satin frog at her neck. The cloak parted, revealing gold lining and a matching gold sheath beneath.

A mandatory admiring pause followed before Cynthia said, "What a fabulous outfit, Vivian," in breathy tones, followed by a squeal. "Oh, look, Paris. She's wearing a Delight. Look, everybody. Did you ever see anything more beautiful? Vivien's wearing the latest *Delight.*"

Vivian's smile held genuine pleasure. Her hand went to her throat.

She wore a silver and gold neckpiece . . . Several strands of silver wound upward to cradle a single, large, deep green tourmaline.

Twenty

"Nice job," Tobias said, knowing this bluff probably wouldn't wash. "You had everyone believing you hate my guts."

Paris pressed herself into a corner of the elevator—the corner farthest from where he stood—and watched the descending numbers on the lighted panel.

He'd never met a woman so unaware of her physical allure. Tall, taller in her sparkling red shoes, she was lithe and leggy and softly untamed. The dress had taken his breath away—or rather, what Paris did for the dress. Floating with each tiny move, points of chiffon, each one tipped by a single red bead, swirled about her. Beneath the chiffon he could see a thin, body-skimming shift that ended high up her thighs.

He knew her body was his ideal, but what it did for that shift . . .

He also knew all about her legs, but watching them play peek-a-boo through red chiffon . . . Tobias envied the chiffon.

Her hair was braided and wound sleekly around her head. A simple pair of gold and garnet earrings were the only pieces of jewelry she wore. Lipstick the same color as the stones emphasized the pale smoothness of her skin.

Tobias looked into her eyes and realized she'd been watching him watching her. He gave her his best you-caught-me grin and said, "I thought we could go to my place and talk."

"Forget it."

"You didn't get to finish your champagne. We'll crack open a bottle."

She folded her arms tightly around her middle.

"Paris?"

They bumped to a soft halt and the doors to a mahogany-lined foyer slid silently open. A liveried doorman came forward and ushered them out onto Fourth Avenue.

Paris turned and hurried away.

"For . . ." Tearing off his jacket, Tobias caught up and flung the coat around her. Before she could shrug it aside, he clamped an arm over her shoulders. "Calm down, will you?"

"You made a fool of me in there."

"Bullshit."

She checked her stride. "You've got a foul mouth, Tobias Quinn."

He had to laugh. "You said that to me when I was seventeen and you were ten. In exactly the same tone."

"No, I didn't."

"You *did.* I fell over your feet—which, by the way, were too big for you at ten—I fell over them and said, *shit.* And you said: You've got a foul mouth, Tobias Quinn."

"I remember." She tried to toss off his arm.

Tobias pulled her against him and set a course for the Jeep. "Do you remember what I said to you next?"

"My feet are still big."

"Your feet are delectable." He turned her left at Vine Street. "I said *you* wouldn't say *shit* if your mouth—"

"I remember that, too. We're going the wrong way."

Why, oh why couldn't his life—in particular his love life—be simple? Why did he have to become infatuated with impossible women? Admittedly this woman was impossible for quite different reasons than the objects of any of his previous adventures of the heart—or whatever it was that became involved.

Tobias concentrated on keeping his imagination above his belt. Good God, maybe he was the freak his ex-wife had accused him of being. His life was on the line. The woman he wanted in his bed had already gathered her share of fallout from the threat against him . . . He still wanted her in his bed. In fact he wanted her right here on the moonlit sidewalk.

"What did you say?" He'd heard her voice as if from a great distance.

"I said you had no right at all . . . In fact you had less than no right at all to embroil me in that mess back there. You had no right to follow me. You make me as *mad* as hell!"

"And you're not going to take it anymore?" he offered winningly.

Paris didn't play along.

They reached the Jeep. Tobias kept his arm around her shoulder while he unlocked the passenger door. "Yet again, I'm kidnapping you," he said, laughing at his own reverse psychology while he hoped she'd think he was only finding the moment amusing. "Will you come quietly, miss?"

In the gloom, her eyes were black—as black as her braided hair. "Because I don't want to walk all the way home in these stupid shoes, I'd be very grateful for a lift," she said formally.

He helped her into the high seat and ran around to jump in beside her. Feeling this happy and expectant because she was letting him drive her home was yet another sign he was in deep trouble with this woman.

Slipping the Jeep through the quiet streets, he hoped she didn't notice how slowly he drove.

"It may work out just fine that you went tonight," he told her.

"Approval? Why, *thank* you." Sarcasm flowed.

"We furthered our cause. Did you see Evergreen's face? She was drooling. I bet her little tape recorder was running somewhere inside her party dress."

"Damn you, Tobias!"

Already slowing for a streetlight, he braked harder than he'd intended. He shot an arm in front of Paris as she jolted forward.

She clutched his shirtsleeve, slammed backward and withdrew her hands as if he'd burned her.

"Okay," he said, making no attempt to drive on even when

the light changed to green. "What's with you? I thought you and I had a deal here."

"The deal wasn't that I would become your prisoner."

"*Prisoner?* All I did was show responsible concern for you. I damn nearly got killed a week ago. I've still got a welt to prove it. And we know the same maniac all but raped you a few days earlier."

"Don't."

"And don't you avoid the truth. We don't have the luxury of pampering finer feelings here."

"I think he mistook me for someone else."

Tobias looked sideways at her. "You always were a dreamer. If you think there's another woman in my life right now, you're wrong."

She met his eyes. "I'm not in your life."

"Aren't you?" He saw the faint tremble of her mouth. "Even if you don't think so, you've got to know that man did. You already said there couldn't be a reason for someone to attack you other than as a random act. It wasn't a random act."

Her eyes were luminous. "It could have been."

"Sure. A random act by someone who didn't actually rape you but who *threatened* to rape you next time and who gave you a message to give to someone else. This is about me, sweetheart. End of story."

"But you didn't understand what he—"

"No, I didn't know what he meant. But that doesn't change a thing. And you *are* in my life. I want you there."

A street-cleaning vehicle lumbered close behind them, forcing Tobias to make a turn and head south toward Paris's place. "Look," he said. "Bear with this plan of mine, will you? At least until we see if it draws—"

"You aren't the only one with problems." Her voice rose. "Don't you . . . Can't you imagine, just for a minute, that I might have things on my mind that have nothing to do with whether or not my poor old grandfather gets in the way of you making an even bigger fortune than you already have?"

The length and vehemence of the speech left him grasping for a response.

"Well I *do* have troubles of my own, Tobias. I have big problems. I have *huge* problems. Not that I want your help. I'm not blaming you, but you already tried to help and that's probably made everything worse."

She was on the verge of tears . . .

"Please drive faster."

"What's happened?" He drove slower again, not faster. "I thought things were better."

"They're not. They're awful. Worse than I could possibly have imagined. I'm scared to death."

Tobias frowned at her, touched her shoulder and set his jaw when she jerked away. "Spit it out," he said shortly. "How am I supposed to know what's eating you if you don't tell me?"

"I want to know where Vivian Estes got that neckpiece."

He looked ahead at the road. "The one Cynthia screamed about tonight? I assumed it was a commissioned piece."

She snorted. "It wasn't."

"Then I suppose she must have bought it. Your stuff's in several places around town."

"Not a piece from the new collection—a piece that hasn't even been *released* yet."

He barely stopped himself from braking again. "You mean Vivien was wearing a *stolen* piece?"

"No. I'm pretty sure it's a copy. But it's a copy of a piece I changed in the last week. I didn't mention it, but earlier on the same night when that awful man came, someone got in and sketched the collar. Actually they made two sketches, I think. One was balled up and left on the floor. It disappeared while I was checking the apartment."

"You never said a word about that."

"I forgot. If you'll remember, I was slightly shocked by the other event."

Tobias turned onto South Main Street and pulled up in front of Paris's building. "You said you changed the collar after that, though."

She nodded emphatically. "Yes. Exactly. I changed it and Vivien's wearing a copy of it *after* the changes."

"Oh, *shit.*"

"I wish you wouldn't . . . The point is that someone wants me out of business."

"Or out of your apartment."

It was Paris who frowned this time.

"How easy is it for you to keep up this place—financially, I mean?"

For a moment he thought she'd tell him to mind his own business, then she said, "It's paid for. But you know that. The taxes and so on are high and so are the costs of my materials. I'm still building my reputation and clientele. My reserves are almost zero. So I don't have any fat to trim, if that's what you mean."

"I'm not sure what I mean. I'm just thinking aloud. I wonder how many people realize you have to make a success of your work to survive."

"So much for the wonderful new locks," she muttered, ignoring his last comment. "They didn't keep anyone out."

He stiff-armed himself against the wheel. "Which suggests whoever's out to get you has a key."

"You did your little numbering job."

"I mean your crook lives right here in this building."

Her seat belt clicked undone and shot into its retractors. She hauled his jacket free and set it aside. "Now *that* is bullshit, Tobias Quinn. Don't you ever say a thing like that about my friends again. Locks can be picked and that's what's happened here."

"Put your seat belt back on."

Her hand was on the door handle. "I'm getting out."

"No." Tobias locked the doors. "You're going to listen to me. I want you away from here."

"Bullshit."

"Damn it, Paris. I hate it when you swear. It doesn't sound right."

She shook her head and pressed it into the headrest. "How many times am I going to have to tell you this is my home and I'm not going anywhere?"

"I won't get a wink of sleep with you here."

"That's bull—"

"Don't say that again. If you're afraid I'll ravish you, forget it. I wouldn't touch you with a fifty foot pole."

"Thanks."

"I've got a spare room."

"No, thanks."

He craned forward to look up at the facade of the building. "What's the big deal. It's a dingy dump."

"It's very desirable real estate and you know it. Let me out."

His throat closed. He couldn't allow her to know he never recalled feeling as panicked as he did at the thought of her alone here. "Will you please let me look after you?"

"That's crazy. No. No, *thank* you. Now if you'd unlock the doors, I'm tired and I do intend to sleep."

"Paris—"

"And when I wake up in the morning, the first thing I'm going to do is find out Vivian's number and call her. I intend to track down whoever's doing this to me and stop it."

Another premonition of evil flowed over Tobias. For the second time in recent memory his skin crawled with dread—and both times had been as a result of Paris Delight.

"Unlock."

"All *right,"* he said tightly and released the latches. "I'll come up and look around."

"You'll get on with your life and let me get on with mine," Paris said, climbing out. "Thanks for the ride."

Grief—woman-type grief—was behind him. He'd decided that detail when his marriage had failed and there was no reason to change his mind now. Tobias paused long enough to watch Paris enter the building before flooring the accelerator and screeching away.

To hell with her.

The first thing Paris did after carefully locking the door to her apartment was check on the neckpiece. A silvercloth bag taken from an emptied institutional-sized can for dried potato flakes revealed what she'd expected: silver and gold, and a gorgeous, bullet-shaped green tourmaline. The neckpiece shone softly in her hands. And this was *her* work.

She replaced the can in her clever hiding place beneath the

kitchen sink, then felt foolish and took it out again. Opening a brown paper sack, she placed all her finished pieces inside, closed the can again and put it back under the sink.

A thunderous crash sounded somewhere overhead.

Paris stood still, the bag of jewelry crushed in her arms. This time she wasn't playing Nancy Drew. This time she would get herself a nice, big Hardy Boy to take the fall.

On the toes of her ruby slippers, she tapped from the kitchen into the workroom. Very carefully, she set the bag on the couch, depressed the telephone cradle while she picked up the receiver, then let the cradle rise up quietly. By the light of the lamp she'd turned on when she got home, she punched in the Lipses' number and heard the distant ringing from below.

Four. Five . . . seven, eight, nine.

She depressed the cradle again. Sam and Ginna wouldn't be back yet. Neither would Conrad.

Tobias.

Paris wrinkled her nose and longed for Tobias's big, strong presence. He wouldn't be home yet and she didn't know the number for his car phone.

The door to the roof! Shoot. The door to the roof—of course. Laughing weakly, she crumpled onto the couch beside her jewelry. That afternoon she'd gone up to cut a big white dahlia for her bedroom. She'd become engrossed with weeding the frames and come down carrying a plastic bin filled with yard waste.

She'd left the door ajar and now the wind had slammed it.

The clock showed three in the morning. Wormwood wouldn't be back now, not that he ever was anymore. Paris put the new chain on the door and took her brown paper safe upstairs.

In the corridor leading to the bedrooms she was met by a heavy current of air. The roof door had slammed wide open, not shut.

If there was one thing she absolutely did not want to do, it was climb to the roof now—in the wee hours—when she knew someone had managed to get into the apartment this week while she was *in* it.

The wind could just as well catch the door and throw it back into the jamb. And it could do it when she was asleep. Paris wasn't sure how much more her beleaguered nerves would take.

Hurrying, she tossed the bag on her bed, darted along the corridor and up the stairs to the roof. The wind was definitely cooler.

She stepped outside and pulled on the doorhandle.

Nothing budged. The wooden wedge she sometimes used to keep the thing open must be rammed in place.

This was a conspiracy to rattle her until she broke. Determined to get past the fear, Paris took a deep breath and went behind the wide-open door. Just as she'd thought, the wedge was the problem. She bent down and had to use both hands to wiggle it free.

With the job done, she stood up to grasp the handle.

She missed.

The same wind that had thrown the door open, did indeed force it shut again.

Her teeth chattering, Paris almost managed to smile at her own paranoia. All around her, the darkness felt soaked with living, reaching things.

She turned the door handle and pulled. The door didn't move. Using two hands, she turned the opposite way and tugged again.

It was jammed. With her heart pulsing in her throat, Paris jiggled and yanked.

Not a millimeter of give.

The muscles in her throat constricted. Tugging some more, she rested her forehead against a panel—and grew still.

From the other side, distinct on the uncarpeted steps, came the *squish, squish, squish* of feet. Feet in rubber-soled shoes. Feet going down . . .

Paris flattened her arms at her sides and backed away.

She couldn't open the door because someone had locked it . . . locked her out here . . . locked her up here.

The wind wasn't strong enough to have taken the door. Why hadn't she figured that out? A gusty, chill breeze, not a strong wind. A breeze that whipped her dress, tapping the little beads together.

Paris swung around and backed up until she stood pressed against the door.

He was behind her.

The whole night and the sucking space beneath the parapets were before her.

Breathing through her mouth, she edged around the sloping roof housing—away from the door and the creature in soft shoes who might be waiting.

Waiting?

Paris sank down on the pebble-strewn tar paper that covered the roof. Would he come back up? Was he waiting for her to scream, to bang on the door, to beg? Did he know she was afraid of heights, that she suffered from vertigo?

Faintly, rising with each fresh burst of breeze, came disjointed bars of dixieland jazz. The same breeze snatched the notes away again.

Waiting.

Beneath her hand, beneath the thin chiffon bodice, her heart chattered. She had to make a noise. She had to catch someone's attention. But not the one who might be waiting for that noise.

No one would hear her. Not unless she shouted to someone in another building, or in the street below.

Paris closed her eyes and felt the world spin slowly around inside her head. *Look at an upright.* A voice she didn't remember, a voice from the past told her to stare at something that didn't move. That meant opening her eyes. Paris didn't want to see.

Rustling swelled. It chilled her bones. She made herself look and focus on the tubs of bamboo. Beneath a sky torn to ragged, sooty banners, the bamboo swayed and bent, its sun-dried leaves caressing each other as would papery fingers.

The rubbing fingers changed to parched laughter, a demonic chuckle.

Beyond the snickering host, emptiness loomed. The space between the tubs and the parapets. Paris covered her ears and hummed tunelessly, shutting out the night's sounds.

Move. She must move, confront, and act.

On legs that had no blood, she rose slowly but didn't straighten her back.

He had been in her apartment when she came home. While she'd checked her designs, he'd crept up to slam open the roof door, then hidden—perhaps in the spare bedroom—until she fulfilled his plan and came up here.

Locks weren't keeping him out. Or keys.

Keys could be copied.

Paris took off her shoes and set them down, careful to make no sound. In the six years since Emma gave her the apartment, she'd never been within feet of the edge of the roof. Now she approached the screening bamboo, and pressed herself between two tubs.

The canes clattered. As smooth as ivory, they knitted into finely meshed bars that smacked her face and upraised arms.

Then she was beyond the clinging cell.

The fire escape.

She had looked up from below. At this level, a ladder paralleled the brick wall to reach within dropping distance of the metal platform outside the bedrooms.

Pebbles jabbed the bottoms of her feet. Paris didn't care. She closed her eyes again and tried to remember where the ladder would be.

The ladder, old and unused and attached to the wall by . . . she didn't know how it was attached.

Still crouched, she approached the parapet and dropped to kneel before it. The pebbles were little knives in her skin now.

Keeping her face down, she reached over the short wall and felt about. Nothing. Walking on her knees, feeling and feeling, she swallowed rising bile.

The sound of the bamboo swelled. This time she was outside its circle. The laughter rose to a howl.

Feeling, feeling. Groping along rough brick and old, crumbly mortar.

The tips of her fingers connected with peeling metal. One upright, and then another. A rung between. Stretching her wrist and elbow brought her in touching distance of a second rung.

She'd found her escape.

Five floors to the sidewalk. Paris crouched and hooked an arm over the parapet. Her lungs swelled until her ribs ached.

"Dopey, Paris. Dopey, Paris can't climb a silly tree." Nigel Quinn had chanted the words at her, dancing a circle about her beneath an old maple up in the Skagit. He'd grabbed her wrists and flung her around and around until her feet swung off the ground. Then he'd dropped her and left her with heart pounding, a pain in her middle where breath used to be, until, finally, she could crawl away and cry.

Paris used the wall and her arm to pull herself up. Panting now as she'd panted on that long-ago day, she forced her body down along the top of the parapet and swung a leg over.

The air she sucked into her mouth tore her throat and went no farther. She grappled to keep her purchase on the safe side of the wall.

All the night seethed with chirpings and scratchings. The bamboo clamored for attention and the breeze sawed in and out of her ears.

The wall grazed the tender insides of her thighs. She was astride it now but with her body still stretched flat.

She would fall.

Even if she gained the ladder, unseen claws would pluck her away and spread her in the air like an ungainly red bird.

Fall. Fall for so long before the shuddering, shattering impact upon the cracked sidewalk. And then there would be more red. A river and a lake of red.

Dry heaves rammed her stomach against her diaphragm.

Something crashed nearby, crashed with splintering force.

Footsteps joined the cacophony inside her brain, footsteps that ran, and paused, and ran on.

He'd come to finish her. Below waited the hard street. Here, a few yards away, waited the tormentor who had done what he set out to do; terrify her to death.

She heard a force charging through the bamboo but couldn't look. Wrapping her arms over her head, driving her face into the unforgiving stone, Paris stopped thinking.

A male voice said, "There you are."

She screamed.

Twenty-one

"There you are." It sounded so bloody inane.

Paris was screaming. And screaming.

Tobias hovered, wanting to run and grab her, afraid to move at all in case she slipped over the wall.

"Paris," he said gently, taking a single step toward her. "It's okay. Keep still. Please, keep still."

The scream dwindled to a choking sound.

My God, why would she be trying to climb off the *roof*? Or jump from the roof? . . .

Another step, and another and he could almost reach out and touch her. "Hush," he said. "Hush, Paris. Everything's going to be fine. It's going to be great."

The next sound to reach him was sobbing. She was sobbing between raking gasps.

He had her!

Clasping her waist, he lifted. At first she kicked out, fighting him with a foot while she clung to the wall, but he tore her free, swung her back to safety, slammed her into his chest.

Her fists came up. Tobias trapped them, gripped her wrists and shook hard. "You fool! You little fool!" He shook until her head jarred back. The braids had slithered free to flap like a kid's pigtails. "What the hell did you think you were doing?"

Her teeth clicked together. Her eyes didn't focus.

Tobias wanted to strike her. "Why?" he shouted. "Why would you want to do a thing like that? Nothing's so bad it can't be fixed."

As suddenly as if someone had hit the backs of her knees, Paris slumped.

Fury pumped madly at Tobias. He hauled her up, gathered her in his arms and carried her, pushed past the bamboo and strode inside, down the steps to the floor that held her bedroom.

He had to sweep a brown paper sack to the floor before dumping her in the middle of the mattress and sitting beside her hips. Leaning over, he held her wrists down at shoulder level.

Paris, her mouth open, stared at him and through him.

"Damn you!" His rage drove her hands deep into the mattress. "What in God's name would possess you to . . . Why would you decide to jump off the roof?"

Small meaningless sounds broke from her.

"Damn you! I . . . Damn you, Paris." He felt the totally alien smarting of tears in his eyes. "Whatever it is, tell me. I'll *fix* it. D'you hear me?" He shook her again. "D'you *hear* me?"

"I wasn't," she whispered.

"You weren't *what?*"

"Trying to jump. I was trying to get down."

"You're not making any sense." And he was shouting again.

"The fire escape." Her swallow clicked and she winced. "I found the fire escape. But I couldn't . . . I couldn't."

"I saw you," Tobias told her. "You were halfway over the goddamn parapet. Five or six floors up. Another couple of inches and you'd have been dead." His next breath expanded to all but choke him.

"I went up to close the door. Then it shut while I was outside and I heard someone going back down the steps. He locked me out. I thought he was waiting to come and get me up there. The fire escape was the only way I could think of to get down."

She began to cry soundlessly. "But I—I c-couldn't make myself do it. I tried, Tobias. I couldn't put my feet on the ladder."

The adrenaline wouldn't stop spurting through him. "The door to the roof wasn't locked. The door to the apartment wasn't locked—or the front door."

Paris shook steadily. "I locked everything when I came in. And I put the chain on my apartment door. And the roof door *was* locked."

He buried his face in the pillow beside her head. "I thought you were going to jump."

"I'm so terrified of heights. The bamboo is up there so I don't have to see the edge. I get sick. The world spins around. I thought I was going to die."

"I'll *kill* the bastard." He had to find him and stop him—for good. "You're *mine*. Do you hear me? *Mine*. I don't let anything happen to my own people."

He lay half over her. His body responded to fear and anger and desire. He needed her. He needed her now. They were both alive and they needed each other.

Paris twisted a hand free and pushed her fingers into his hair. She held his face fast to her neck. He saw the rise and fall of her breasts and saw, for the first time, that the red dress was tattered and ruined.

Taking both of her hands above her head, he straddled her hips. His urgency shook him but he didn't want to tame it. Bending down, he kissed her, rocked his face over hers, opened her mouth and drove his tongue deep into her mouth. Paris's chin came up and he felt her response, a response that started with her tongue meeting his and coiled down to the arcing upward of her breasts against his chest and, finally, her legs wrapping around his hips.

When he released her hands she raked short nails the length of his back and pressed them into his buttocks, lifted her pelvis and rubbed insistently against his erection.

He was losing it.

Making an inch of space between them, he tore at his shirt and felt Paris come to his aid. Together they struggled until he was naked to the waist. His belt came off and hit the wall when he threw it aside.

The dress fastened at the back. Tobias lifted Paris against him and wrestled the zipper down. He should have saved the effort. Their breathing soughed together, louder, while the dress all but disintegrated in his hands. Tossing it away, he studied for a long moment the scrap of a red silk bra with narrow lace edging that didn't cover her pink nipples. Matching panties, cut up at each side to the lace band that rested smoothly beneath her navel, and sheer red stockings with wide lace tops completed what was left of her party clothes.

"Paris," was the only word he could form. He kissed the tops of her breasts and willed himself to slow down. With the tip of his tongue, he followed the revealed, puckering half-moons above her nipples

Her hips jolted higher off the bed and she pushed a hand down inside his pants to tangle in thick hair.

Tobias ripped open his fly. Paris delved and brought his penis free. Her thumb worked over the smooth head. Her fingers slid down the rigid length of the underside to cradle the distended weight of him.

He squeezed her thighs together between his knees. Once more he rose up to take her mouth, to kiss her eyes and nip hungrily at the lobe of an ear. "Paris. I won't let you go away again." Dipping, he snaked his tongue beneath the bra to circle a thrusting nipple and she cried out. Her free hand tore at his hair, but she was urging him closer, closer.

The bra went the way of the dress. Her breasts were high and pointed—and her rocking shoulders let him know how they ached for him to lave each peak. Tobias nibbled and sucked—and reveled in her moans.

Paris pushed at his pants, pushed them down over his hips and scratched his skin in the process. She jack-knifed her legs and used her feet to scrape the fabric away.

Tobias palmed her mound and bared his teeth in triumph at the damp silk he met. She was as hot and ready as he was. He brought himself against her, nudged aside the scrap of material.

She trembled and arched beneath him, her eyes glittering bright, her moist lips parted. *"Yes,"* she told him, the word low and sexy as hell. "Now, Tobias. I want you now."

With a single surge, he entered Paris's slick passage and buried himself in her to the hilt.

Her cry touched the edges of his brain and shattered away. *Slower.* Reason urged what his body couldn't deliver.

Again he drove inside, and again, and he heard her cry out with each thrust. She was small. Her muscles hugged him close, squeezed him.

They rolled until it was Paris who sat astride Tobias's hips. With his hands under her arms, his thumbs pressed to her nipples, he lifted her almost free and brought her down upon him.

His was the next cry he heard.

Tobias held her on top of him. Their sweating bodies fused together, her breasts to the thick hair on his chest, her arms looped around his shoulders, her thighs stretched along the length of his. His hands splayed wide over her bottom, pressing her to him.

They were still joined.

His chest rose unevenly beneath her. She felt the strong beat of his heart and his breath moved escaped hair across her forehead.

She and Tobias had made love.

Paris squeezed her eyes tightly shut and knew she would never be the same again because of what they had just done.

"I'm sorry," he murmured.

"What?" She would not open her eyes. As long as they were closed, the moment could not be broken by anything outside.

Tobias stroked her hips and back. "I yelled at you when you were scared. But I was scared. My God, Paris, you'll never know how scared I was when I saw you on that wall."

She tilted up her head until she could kiss the side of his neck. He tasted of salt and smelled cleanly male. The other scent that reached her was the faint essence of the sexual union they'd shared. Her heart beat in time with his.

"That wasn't the way it was supposed to be," Tobias murmured, nudging until he could kiss her brow. "I took you like a wild man."

Paris smiled. "We took each other like wild people." Her grazed knee scraped the sheet and she dragged in a hissing breath.

"What is it?"

She attempted to find a more comfortable place for her damaged skin and failed. "Nothing."

Without another word, Tobias eased out of Paris and turned her to her back. With one hand resting on top of her head, he looked into her eyes and frowned. "You're in pain. I hurt you."

She held her bottom lip in her teeth and showed him the torn palms of her hands.

"*Shit!* I mean, hell." He shot from the bed and stood over her, holding her wrists. "You're torn to shreds." Then he saw her knees and when he lifted one, the long grazes on the insides of her thighs. "I've made it worse. There's grit. You're bleeding. Damn, I'm not an animal. Why didn't you stop me?"

"I couldn't." She knew her heart and soul were in her eyes. And she knew her vulnerability to this man might destroy her. She didn't care anymore.

He looked over his shoulder. "Is that the bathroom?"

"Yes. Stay here. I'll sponge off the cuts."

"You won't move another muscle." Tobias lifted her as effortlessly as he'd lifted her before. "And from now on, I'm not letting you out of my sight until that madman's behind bars."

He carried her toward the bathroom.

Paris rolled her breasts against his chest. "I love the feel of you."

"Enough," he ordered. "I've got to keep a clear head—for both of us."

"Why did you come back tonight?" How could she put into words her gratitude that he had ignored her rejection and come for her?

Tobias paused at the foot of the bed. With the hand that held

her side, he lightly fingered the underside of her breast. "I
thought that was obvious."

"Tell me anyway—just in case I guessed wrong."

"I don't like unfinished business." He smiled down into her
upturned face. "I remembered we hadn't dealt with a certain
outstanding technicality."

This wasn't the way it should have worked out.

*First that self-satisfied piece of shit, Quinn showing up and almost
catching him inside the bitch's apartment. Then some fool woman hanging
around in the doorway of this building for so long it could be too late to
see anything now he'd finally made it to his hiding place on the roof.*

*If Quinn hadn't shown up the fun would have begun by now. Wait-
ing had become boring. Waiting for orders that never came, orders he
was supposed to be ready to carry out when he knew the one supposed
to give those orders wouldn't have the guts when the time came.*

He was giving his own orders from now on.

The night glasses gave him a clear view of the roof across the street.

*Fuck! Quinn must have found her. Light that had to be shining from
the stairwell through the open rooftop door cast a glow behind the bamboo.*

Quickly scanning downward, he froze, his prick instantly on alert.

*The whore was naked. Naked in Quinn's arms and plastered around
him like hot syrup.*

*Closing his eyes, he unzipped his pants and pulled his prick through
his shorts. Inside she would be like hot syrup, too. Prissy, private, cun-
ning whore.*

*Jacking off while he kept the glasses trained on the man's hand—
pawing her breast—took only seconds.*

*Quinn started to move. He carried the lying slut out of sight. They
were going into the bathroom.*

*He was ready again. Leaning against a chimney stack, he pumped
himself. Quinn would fill the tub and climb in with her. He'd take her
in the warm water, and again on the floor. Quinn was seeing what she
hid so well from everyone else.*

The time had come. No more waiting.

* * *

"I can do this myself," Paris said. Sitting naked on the toilet lid, she felt awkward.

With no evidence of self-consciousness, Tobias leaned over the bathtub, testing the heat of the water as it ran in. "You probably could do it yourself, but I'm going to. I want to." He slanted a slit-eyed glance back at her. "I need to atone for being callous."

"All I had to do was say I was hurting and you'd have stopped."

"I didn't give you a chance."

"I didn't want a chance."

He turned off the faucets and offered her his hand. She took it and steadied herself while she climbed into water just the right side of being too hot. "Thank you. Now go and nap while I dig pebbles."

"Leave you to have all the fun? I don't think so." He pushed her knees down and held her legs under the water while she smothered a yell and fought to rise up again. "Hush," he told her. "It'll calm down in a minute."

He was right, but the skin still stung. "Ouch, ouch, ouch," she said through barely parted lips.

"I know. When we're done, I'll blow on them."

Paris checked his face and found him looking not at her knees, but at her breasts. His eyes rose to hers. Rather than smile, he leaned over the tub and kissed the flesh he'd watched, slowly and thoroughly. Sliding a hand under her bottom, he supported the weight of one breast and drew the nipple deeply into his mouth.

Paris gasped. Loose from its tail, his hair fell forward. "Tormenting pirate," she murmured. "I . . . Tobias, stop."

"Don't want to," he said, his voice muffled. But then he did stop.

Plunging her deeply gouged palms and scraped fingertips beneath the surface of the water, he located a washcloth and soaked it. "We've got to make some plans," he said, dabbing at a palm and peering close to flip out embedded pieces of dirt. "First we attend to some other business, then we decide how to proceed."

"Other business?"

His eyes met hers briefly and his smile was wickedly, heavily sensual. "The only business I want to deal with right now."

The cloth, squeezed over her head, sent a gush of water over her face and left her gasping and trying to scrub at her eyes.

More water, wrung from the freshly soaked washcloth, ran first over her back, then from her neck, downward between her breasts. Soap, applied by Tobias's circling hands, joined the water.

Paris made futile grabs for his wrists. Giving up, she took her own revenge. She rose far enough out of the tub to flick her tongue over a flat, male nipple until he held her off. Then she slithered away and gripped a far more sensitive part of his anatomy.

"That's *it,*" Tobias shouted, laughing. "You asked for this."

Sending a tidal wave onto the tiled floor, he landed on top of her in the tub.

Cuts and grit lost their fascination.

Twenty-two

Nigel rested against the pillows on what had formerly been his dear, stupid brother's nuptial bed and watched Tobias's ex-wife dress.

Shortly before dawn she'd come to him in a foul mood and he'd learned new angles on the depth of her rapacious appetite for perversion. He massaged the burns made on his wrists by strips torn from a sheet. Long sleeves would be mandatory for him for a few days. Thank god she'd decided her pleasure would be greater if his ankles *weren't* tied to the bed.

"Ready to talk about it now?" he asked her.

In the hour since she'd arrived, she hadn't spoken. Rather than break the silence now, she stood up, wearing only a deep pink garter belt and ivory-colored stockings. She approached the end of the bed and braced her weight on her arms, allowing her big breasts to jut suggestively in his direction.

Nigel sighed. "Baby, you may be ready for more, but I think I've about had it."

Cynthia swayed a little and her beautiful flesh moved just as she wanted it to. Her areolae were huge and her nipples became erect under his scrutiny. "Are you sure you've had it?" she asked, all husky invitation.

Nigel touched his almost flaccid dick and shrugged. "You've drained me dry, sweetness. I'm just going to have to work at recovering by tomorrow."

She pushed upright. *"If* I decide I want you tomorrow."

He was supposed to be angry at the thought of being deprived of her attention. Nigel couldn't quite dredge up enough emotion.

"I want you to speed things up," she said, all business. "My friend is in a hurry now. That information I told you about last week is important. More than important. Make sure I get it tomorrow."

Nigel turned on his side and propped his head. Cynthia caught up the scrap of a white dress she'd arrived in and stepped into it. He hadn't been surprised to discover that all she wore underneath was the garter belt that held up her hose.

"Do you understand?" she asked, wiggling until the dress was bunched around her waist.

"Mmm."

She worked the skirt down until the red hair at her crotch disappeared. By Nigel's calculations, there'd be no way she could raise a knee one inch without giving the world a view it wouldn't forget.

"Nigel?"

"It felt good to call that creep Piggy and tell him I had the money," he said. "I've had it with slogging through dust and playing the humble reprobate. I figure I can string brother Tobias along for a stake and be out of here."

Cynthia paused with her bodice pulled taught under her breasts. "What does that mean?"

Despite himself, he was getting hard again. "You're changing my mind about being tired. Come here."

Taking her time, working the tight fabric upward with excruciating slowness, Cynthia gradually encased lush flesh until the top of the strapless dress covered her nipples—just. "You aren't going anywhere, Nigel," she said, reaching back to check the zipper she'd closed before replacing her bodice. "Don't even think about it."

"I gave information. I was paid for it."

"You didn't give enough information. And you were paid too much for it. Now the work really begins. Try to duck out and we'll blow the whistle on you. Not that we'll have to."

Nigel swung his feet over the side of the bed and stood up. "I think it's time you learned I won't be pushed, baby."

Her chin came up. "What are you going to do? Hit me? Wouldn't that be smart? Wouldn't that get you a long way? Do as you're told. I'll call tomorrow."

"I may not be here."

"Oh, I think you will. By my figuring, you're overdue to find out you're not going anywhere yet."

Muscles in Nigel's belly jerked. "What have you done?"

Catching up her purse and pulling out a set of car keys, Cynthia didn't bother to look at him. "You'll find out. Get me what I want by tomorrow and I'll make sure you're okay. No"—she raised a hand to silence him—"don't ask anymore questions. Just do as you're told and you'll be okay."

When she'd left the room he stared at the open doorway for several seconds before going into the bathroom. Moments later he heard the rumble of a garage door and the muted sound of Cynthia's Porsche engine.

What the fuck was she up to now?

Bending over the sink, he ran cold water and sluiced his head and neck.

He was rubbing his eyes when the point of cold steel settled between his shoulderblades. "Keep your eyes shut," a familiar voice grated out. "Keep still and listen."

Nigel hovered between vomiting and emptying his bowels— or both. "Piggy," he whispered. "How'd you get in here?"

"I been in here, lover boy. You are one lucky fucker—so to speak."

"Where?" Nigel asked, cracking his eyes.

"As if I'd tell you. Keep the baby blues shut—if you've got plans to use 'em again."

Nigel shook, but he didn't try to open his eyes.

"All the money wasn't in the bag," Piggy said.

Nigel's thighs locked. "It had to be. You got it right after I . . . Right after I got it," he finished.

The needle-sharp blade kissed a line, vertebra by vertebra, down Nigel's spine. "Right after you got it and helped yourself to a little finder's fee before handing it over?"

"No." He shook his head emphatically. "Honest to god, Piggy, it was all there. I swear it."

The knife traversed one buttock. "Maybe. Maybe not. Maybe this is what the little lady meant just now. Only she's not so little, is she? Oh, yeah, she looks different standing up."

Nigel couldn't think straight anymore.

"You gotta do something for the lady to get the rest of the money. That's how I read it. Only now you're late with your payments again, so the price went up."

"It can't," Nigel moaned. "I've got to get out of this. I can't do it. Don't you understand?"

"Oh, cry," Piggy said in falsetto tones. "I *love* it when you cry. And you got such cute buns. A tight little ass. It's been a while since I got it off with a boy, but this job's taken longer than planned. I could be gettin' desperate."

Nigel straightened.

The point of the blade traced rapidly down his groin and flipped under his dick. "Get the money," Piggy said, caressing Nigel's butt with fat fingers. "You were ten percent short and the interest just went up ten percent."

"I'll get it," Nigel screamed.

"That's better. You've got five days. Screw up this time and I'll pay another visit to the sexy girlfriend. I'll give her what she wants, *loverboy.* What you don't know how to give her."

The tiniest jab sent searing pain into Nigel's balls. His feet slipped on black marble tile and he caught his jaw on the sink before he hit the floor.

Doubled over, cradling his throbbing head, he waited for the voice and the knife. Neither came. "I'll get it," he said, panting out the words. "I'll get the money. Okay?"

There was no response.

Minutes later, minutes that felt like hours, Nigel opened his eyes. Piggy had left as silently as he'd arrived.

"Screw this up and I'll pay another visit to the sexy girlfriend." He pushed wet hair off his forehead. Another visit? Cynthia and Piggy working together against him? Cynthia *with* Piggy? Tobias had once said she'd fuck anything that moved.

A warm stickiness touched his thigh. Nigel looked down and saw a hair-thin trickle of bright blood.

Twenty-three

"Ah, ah." Paris moved just fast enough to stop Tobias from fumbling across her to pick up the phone.

He blinked slowly. "It's ringing."

"It's not your phone. You're still asleep. Enjoy it."

He didn't appear entirely convinced but he fell back to the pillows and closed his eyes.

Paris picked up the receiver, scooted up a little and settled herself more comfortably. "Hello?" She pulled the sheet up to her neck.

"I talked to Vivian."

Cynthia? Paris glanced at Tobias then craned to see her clock. "You aren't up yet."

"I haven't been to bed. Too much to think about. We writers do some of our best work in the middle of the night."

Paris looked down on Tobias's relaxed face. *"I'm* not up." And lying in bed beside Tobias while talking to Cynthia on the phone felt bizarre.

"Bill wanted me last night."

Tobias's eyelashes were thicker than any man's should be. In repose, his mouth had an almost sweet tilt. His hair, soaked by the time they'd come to bed, had dried in wavy tangles.

"You saw how he looked at me," Cynthia said.

"Hm? What?"

"Bill Bowie. Doesn't he turn you on? All that whiplash sinew and hard strength. I bet he can keep it up for hours."

"Cyn—You say the darndest things sometimes."

Cynthia giggled. "I want to find out and I'm going to. If Vivian hadn't shown up last night I think he'd have asked me to sleep with him."

Paris was horrified. "But you *wouldn't* have. He and Vivian—"

"*Aren't* married. Not that it would matter."

"For—" Paris stopped herself from saying anymore.

"Oh, don't be such a prude. What you need is a man, and I don't mean Tobias Quinn. Tell me what happened after you left with him last night, then I'll tell you what Vivian said."

"Nothing happened," Paris said promptly and crossed her fingers. She *detested* lying. "Why did you call Vivian?"

"Not so fast," Cynthia said. "I couldn't believe you allowed him to march you out of the party."

"In case you've forgotten, I don't like being embarrassed, particularly in public."

Cynthia let out an explosive sigh. "You are too worried about what other people think. I suppose he took you home."

"Yes."

A short silence followed before Cynthia said, "And then?"

"Tobias is concerned about—you know what he's concerned about."

"I find it hard to believe. After all, darling, he was never exactly attentive to you before he needed some help with Pops, was he? I seem to remember that he completely ignored you."

How true. Paris couldn't stop the shreds of doubt. "Let's get back to Vivian." She had to get past the old tapes. Tobias hadn't faked his concern for her last night—or what had followed. He couldn't have . . .

"Didn't he bring up Pops again?"

"No. I did have another visitor after I got home." She wouldn't explain everything now, but she had promised to tell

Cynthia anything she ought to know. "We'll talk about it later. What made you decide to call Vivian?"

"I'm not completely oblivious, darling," Cynthia said. "I realized that neck thing was the one I saw you changing. It was, wasn't it?"

"Yes."

"And now Vivian's got it."

"She's got a copy."

Another silence met Paris's announcement.

"The original is still here. Someone must have worked very hard to produce what we saw last night from a quick sketch. I intend to talk to Vivian about it myself."

"I think it would be more interesting if you didn't."

Tobias stirred, rolled toward Paris and threw a heavy arm across her. Paris waited until his breathing settled again before saying, "Why don't you tell me what you're thinking. I'll just listen."

"Vivian doesn't know she's got a copy," Cynthia said. "To be honest, I thought it was stolen. It's good, isn't it?"

"Very."

"All I did was have a friendly conversation with her. Wasn't it lovely to see each other again. That kind of crap."

Paris thought about the glint in Vivian's gorgeous green eyes when she'd seen Cynthia with Bill. "That must have made for cozy conversation."

"Oh, you don't know how to move with the grownups, do you? Vivian didn't think anything of me being friendly with Bill."

"If you say so."

"You'll be proud of the way I handled the collar thing. I said I didn't know she had a piece of your jewelry and she said she never had before. Cool as that. But when I asked where she bought it, she clammed up. What d'you think of that?"

"What am I supposed to think?"

"She *didn't* buy it. Someone bought it for her, only she's not saying who, but *I* know. And I've got to hand it to them. They timed it beautifully, didn't they?"

"You've lost me."

"Oh, give me *patience*. You are so simple sometimes, Paris. You do know Tobias and Vivian have had a thing *forever* don't you?"

Paris studied the man's sleeping face once more. There was a great deal she didn't know about him, but she wouldn't be making any more snap judgments. Last night had changed her forever.

"Well they have," Cynthia continued. "Will you promise me you won't go to Vivian yourself? I really think I can get more out of her than you if you'll let me help."

"I'm confused."

"Couldn't I be the one to . . . Well, couldn't *I* be the big sister for once and watch out for you? I'd like to help you. Do you understand?"

"You've never—" Paris had always assumed the lead because she was supposedly the steady one. "I think I do understand." Maybe being responsible for someone else for a change would be good for Cynthia.

"This is my take on the thing," Cynthia continued, sounding excited. "Tobias got the new locks put on, right? Right, well, he also arranged for the keys. In control, as always. He knew about the attack and he knew someone was going to do something about making sure the building was secure, so he made certain he was the one to do it."

"I don't—"

"Well, *I* do. And he had someone go in and make a sketch of your necklace, *after* you changed it. Then he got the copy made and when he found out you were going to the party last night, he got Vivian to wear it there to make you panic again."

"Why don't you stick to writing mysteries?"

"Fact is stranger than fiction," Cynthia said, completely seriously. "Take it from me. If you wrote some of the things that happen in real life everyone would say they were farfetched."

"There are holes in this," Paris said, keeping her voice low.

"I expected you to say that. I don't believe Vivian expected to see Bill there last night. Bill told me he'd only dropped by because Astor begged him to. He'd been at some cigar club bash at the Four Seasons. He was on his way home but changed his mind and stopped by."

"You seem to forget that . . . You were the only one who knew I was going."

"Wrong. You told Tobias."

"Not what party or where."

"*Think*, Paris. He showed up, didn't he. He found out where you were going."

Paris squinted at a picture of fields of wildflowers on the opposite wall. Without her glasses, the painting was a fuzz of bright color.

"Well? He did, didn't he? *He* arrived. Obviously looking for you. And Vivian—in the necklace—was right behind him. He wants you to turn to him, I tell you. He wants you dependent on him. The press is on his tail over the Skagit thing. He's got *huge* money tied up there and nothing's happening."

Gradually, Paris's building dread receded. Tobias had said he thought someone wanted them to suspect each other. And he'd told her they should pretend they did. And they had. Between the press reports and the rumors that would spread from their encounter at the party, the story that Tobias Quinn and Paris Delight were enemies must be all over Seattle.

"Paris? Do you see where I'm heading?"

Cynthia was only voicing—and taking a step further—what lots of people thought.

"Paris?"

"I see. Yes." Tobias stirred and she stroked his hair.

"The crews aren't working up there because of something or other. He *needs* a Delight for a friend and he wouldn't lower himself to come to me. You were his only chance—*are* his only chance."

Tobias rolled onto his back and opened his eyes.

"Has he offered you a loan?"

Paris looked down into clear gray eyes, shadowed by dark lashes. He raised a hand to stroke her cheek. Where he touched her, she tingled. And she tingled in a lot of places he wasn't touching.

"Paris? Has he?"

"Why don't I call you back later."

"Paris . . . Oh, God"—Cynthia's voice dropped to a theatrical whisper—"Is he with you?"

She couldn't answer, couldn't do anything but watch Tobias and rub her face against his fingers.

"He *is. Jeesus,* Paris. Are you mad? Don't tell him this is me. Okay?"

"Quit worrying." She tried to avoid his steady gaze but failed.

"*Shit,* I'm going. Be *careful,* Paris. Just say you will."

"Yes."

"You'd better be. I know him. You don't."

Paris turned away to replace the receiver.

"Who was that?" Tobias asked.

With her back toward him, she slid down into the bed.

She couldn't have resisted the arm that pulled her back into the cradle of the very male body behind her. Tobias fitted Paris's bare bottom into his lap and rubbed his hair-roughened thighs against the smooth backs of hers. "Let me guess. Cynthia. Mm? I'd rather not say that name here—or anywhere."

"I don't talk about Cynthia. I mean, I don't say things about Cynthia."

He kissed her nape. "You, my love, are one of the world's honorable people. A select group. I intend to take appropriate care of you."

Paris closed her eyes tightly. "How did you know where to find me last night?"

"Gladys—my secretary—is quite the sleuth. She found out what was going on where. Then she went after the guest lists and came up with Cynthia."

"And you went without an invitation?"

"No. I had an invitation. I get one every year. I just don't usually go."

"Did you ever go with Cynthia?"

"Yes."

She drew a deep breath and let it out slowly.

"That's history. This isn't." Gently, he smoothed her hair away from her face. "This is now and—and we're not going to let anyone spoil it for us. We can decide that, Paris. Sweetheart,

I don't want to spend time on recriminations but I'm not a monster. I am what I am with you. That's what I've been waiting to become without knowing it."

Paris wriggled until she could settle on her back and stare at the ceiling.

"You're still afraid to trust me, aren't you?" he said, propping his head. "I thought you were beginning—"

"I am," she told him. "This is new. It's almost impossible to believe. Why would you *want* me?"

His laugh made her peer into his face.

He sobered, with obvious difficulty, and kissed her nose. "Of course you would ask that. Why would I . . . Why would I want a lovely, honest woman who also happens to be the sexiest woman in the world?"

Her face heated. "Be serious."

"Oh, I am." His touch on her cheek was gentle. He studied her as he might a blueprint—very closely. "I've never been more serious about anything. You'll never know how much I wanted you to say you believe in me. Thanks, Blue. May I hold you?"

He had a wretched habit of bringing tears to her eyes. Paris turned into his arms and hid her face in his shoulder.

His big hand covered the back of her head. "Are you crying?"

"No."

"Ah. No, of course not." He drew her to rest on top of him and pulled the sheet over her. "You have the most endearing way of not crying."

Her next breath shuddered. Being with him, like this, was a numbing mixture of erotic awareness and strangely natural comfort. He was fully aroused yet he held her carefully, soothed her because he sensed her distress and he was strong enough to contain his desire.

Concentration threatened to become impossible. "I don't think I'm going to ask Vivian about the collar." She wanted to tell him why, but she had to give Cynthia the chance she'd asked for. "It would only embarrass her."

"One way or the other we're going to have to track down your forger."

"I know. And when we do, I'll find a way to make sure Vivian gets the real thing. In the meantime, will you promise not to say anything to her?"

He rubbed her shoulders. "I'm not sure you won't change your own mind on this when you've got time to think, but I'll promise. For now. If you promise me something."

Paris didn't want to think about how she'd deal with explaining Cynthia's theory if she ever had to. "I will if I can," she told him.

"Fair enough. I don't want you to feel threatened. Do you think that would work?"

"That's what you want me to promise? Not to feel threatened?"

His chin was hard on the top of her head. "I want you to promise to believe me when I say I've fallen in love with you."

Walking beside Paris's oddball renter did nothing to quiet Tobias's leapfrogging nerves. True, he'd only seen Wormwood a couple of times, but he should have noticed before that the guy was all brown.

Brown and with the type of personality that went very nicely with the word *dun*.

For the third time since Wormwood—answering the new intercom at Paris's apartment—had said he was, "Going where she was," Tobias tried to establish voice contact. "Nice of you to let me come along."

Wormwood shrugged. In fact, Tobias had waited for the man to appear at the front door and fallen in beside him without an invitation.

"How long have you been living at Paris's?"

That bought him a sidelong brown glance. "Long time."

"You're a painter."

An eloquent shrug raised bony shoulders.

They walked at a leisurely pace past the bust of Seattle's founding father, Chief Sealth, on the sidewalk in front of Doc Maynard's. Another hot afternoon had brought a standing-room-only crowd to the tables outside the old pub. Cold beer slaked parched throats and laughter rose against the irritable banter of the bargain-booze-in-brown-bags groups gathered on benches beside the street.

Tobias ducked a launching flight of pigeons and tried again with Wormwood. "Have I seen any of your stuff?"

The other man wiped the back of a hand over his mouth. "I paint on furniture. Chairs. Tables. Anything that takes my fancy." He turned his expressionless eyes on Tobias again. "Anything I think will take someone else's fancy. Paris makes wearable art. I paint usable art. I like doing stuff for kids. Pigs jumping over the moon."

"Cows," Tobias said automatically.

A flicker of a smile came and went. "Pigs. Kids know the way it goes, too. They like paradoxes. They like to be the ones to point out how things ought to be."

The idea raised pictures of delightedly scornful little faces. "You could be right." Tobias wasn't sure what to make of the painter, but there was definitely more to him than first impressions suggested. "You're sure Paris will be at the Blue Door?"

"She'll'be there."

Muscles in his neck relaxed a little. Just the thought of seeing her softened the edges of the wound his professional pride had suffered since he left her a few hours earlier. Tobias realized he was smiling. Either he was losing his mind—or love had begun to make him mellow.

Love. He'd been the man who would never allow the word to pass his brain, to say nothing of his lips. He'd been the man who had pronounced love a myth. But today he'd told a woman he loved her.

He'd told another *Delight* he loved her.

No matter how crazy the entire notion might be, Tobias needed to be with Paris. He *needed* Paris, period. Sharing what had happened to him with her had become as necessary as breathing.

First he had to get her to move out of her apartment.

"You and Paris," Wormwood said in a monotone. "You're sleeping together."

Tobias shot the man a frown. "That's a hell of a question."

"It was a statement."

"She told you?"

"I know. Everyone does. She's gotten different."

"Is that bad?"

Wormwood made the turn into Post Alley. He stood aside for a contingent of cyclists in very little, very bright biking gear. "I don't know about those things," he said when they continued on. "She seems fine to me. Paris is a special lady."

"You don't need to convince me of that."

The painter put his hands into the pockets of his loose brown trousers. "I wouldn't want anything to make her unhappy. She's been good to me."

The Wormwoods of this world were an enigma to Tobias but he liked the guy's sentiments on the present subject.

"Word has it you were pretty rough on Cynthia."

Tobias stopped an automatic retort. "Cynthia is Paris's sister. I gather she's also friendly with the rest of you. That makes it tough for me to defend myself. Let's just say I'm not known as a mild-mannered man, but I am known as a fair and civilized one. Shall we leave it at that?"

"Suits me."

They didn't reach the Blue Door an instant too soon for Tobias. Inside the windowless club only the lights nearest the stage were on.

Sam, or Samantha or whatever the hell his name was, lounged in a chair on the stage, his legs crossed, directing a monologue at Paris and Ginna. Dressed like any other average American male who'd developed a thing for frosted wigs, every exaggerated mannerism was at odds with the man's decidedly masculine body.

The topic was the possibility that Prince Charles of England might decide to follow in his great-uncle's footsteps and spurn the throne. "That was Edward VIII, darlings," Sam said. "He was Charlie's hero. Well, Charlie's as good as told me I remind him of Wallis Simpson. So it follows, doesn't it? They'll make him Duke of something really *marvy* and you can call me *Duchess.*"

Ginna and Paris laughed before Sam looked over their heads

and saw Tobias approaching with Wormwood. The impersonator's arms became anchored over the back of his chair. "We've
got company," he said, managing to sound as if "company"
was something like "clap."

Both women turned and both smiled. It was Paris's smile that
turned Tobias's heart. A surprise in white shorts and a shirt
tied at the waist, she came to meet him. He knew better than
to do more than take her hands in his and kiss her cheek lightly.
"There ought to be a law against you *ever* covering those legs,"
he said softly. "I've got to get you alone."

"Soon," she told him. "I've found something out, Tobias. At
least, I'm almost sure I have. I want to tell everyone. Okay?"

It wasn't okay, but he didn't have the right to say anything
but, "Sure. Something happened I need to tell you about, too.
Alone. How long will this take?"

"Conrad should get off soon and the Lipses are on their
way."

Keeping impatience out of his eyes wasn't easy. "They all
know about us, don't they?"

She looked at the others. "Did Wormwood say something
like that?"

"Uh-huh."

"Then I guess . . . Here's Conrad and Lips."

Tobias observed the latest arrivals with mixed feelings. Dark
and too good-looking for comfort, Conrad moved with agile
strength—and he looked at Paris as if he was hungry and she
was the only meal that would fill him up.

"Hiya," Conrad said, to everyone in general and to Paris in
particular. "You call. I come. Mrs. Lips is going to close up the
stand for me. Lips said she could." With Lips towering behind
him, he wiggled his eyebrows at her. "You've got our full attention, kid."

Paris pulled Tobias with her to Ginna's table and urged him
to sit. "All of you, sit," she said and he could see her breathing
was shallow.

Taking off his wig, Sam climbed down from the stage and
joined the others around the table.

Paris remained standing. "I've been getting my hands on as

many forgeries of my pieces as I can." She lifted a canvas shopping bag that had been hung on the back of her chair. "As many of *certain* pieces as I can. Most copies aren't any good—to me."

There was a subtle forward motion among the listeners.

"Look at these." Rather than cascading jewelry onto the table, she produced a handful of tissue-wrapped packets from the bottom of the bag and offered them. "Look at them very carefully and tell me if you notice anything."

Two single gold earrings, a silver and gold pin and a simple silver necklace of flat links inset with purple jade discs.

Tobias noted that Wormwood and Conrad concentrated on the task intently, turning and turning an ornament—and shaking their heads. Lips, Ginna and Sam watched. Tobias didn't know enough to look for anything.

"Come on," Sam said impatiently. "What are we supposed to see?"

Paris's eyes remained on Wormwood and Conrad.

"They're fantastic," Conrad said at last, glancing from Paris to Wormwood. "Am I wrong or are these—" He turned suddenly and surprisingly red.

"Yes," Paris said. "You're right. I almost didn't spot them. At first I thought they *were* mine."

Wormwood silently placed the necklace on the table.

"Well?" Paris said to him. "What do you think?"

"Someone ought to die for this."

Tobias felt shock in the pause that followed.

"Shit," Sam said. "I do believe the man's got feelings after all. I'm with you, friend." He offered a hand to Wormwood, who ignored it.

"I don't think we should carry things quite *that* far," Conrad said. "What we do have to do is get organized. Where do we start? Really start to look for this guy—or woman?"

"It's a man," Paris said.

Every face turned up to hers.

"First it was the fact that they almost fooled me that got my attention. Then it was this"—she put the pin on her palm and pointed to the signature "D"—"this gave him away. He was proud of these pieces. His ego got in the way."

She had the rapt attention of her audience.

"Does anyone remember a man who called himself Coeur?" Ginna wrinkled her forehead. "I don't think so."

Sam and Lips shook their heads.

"Fuck!" Conrad waved a finger. *"Coeur.* Hey, Wormwood, wasn't he the guy—"

"Yes." Wormwood was on his feet. "Partner in Seattle Streets. About . . . About five years back. Hot gallery for a while. They had some of the best stuff in town."

"Drug bust," Conrad said. "He was busted for dealing. Geez, I was a snotty-nosed kid fresh out of art school, but I remember."

Wormwood pushed in his chair. "What'll you bet me he isn't back in town and strapped for cash?"

Tobias's patience snapped. "Will someone tell me what you're talking about."

"Coeur designed jewelry," Wormwood said, all traces of languor wiped out. "He was good. Some said he was the best. This isn't his style, but he made it." He held an earring between finger and thumb. "And I'm not coming back until I find out where he's working."

Sam reached for Wormwood's arm but Paris said, "Let him go, Sam. If anyone can find out where Coeur is now, it's Wormwood. He knows more people in the business than any of us."

"Okay," Sam said, very deliberately. "So let him go play tracker, but would you explain—for the fools' gallery—how you happened to settle on this poor bastard?"

Paris pointed to the signature on the back of the necklace. "Not a "D," see? He fell in love with some of them and he couldn't put my mark on them. These are open and swirled at the top. Narrow at the bottom. Almost my mark, but not quite."

"Oh," Ginna said, leaning over to look close. "A heart!"

"You've got it," Wormwood said, already in motion. "A heart. And that's how he signed his work. With a heart for his name, for the French, *coeur."*

Twenty-four

He'd told her he loved her.

Even while Paris hugged the knowledge to her and felt the curl of warmth it brought, she was afraid to believe some fantastic joker wouldn't hop from the shadows and shout, *"Fool!"*

She stood awkwardly in the middle of Tobias's living room. He'd given her two choices: be with him here, or at her place. The decision had seemed simple. For the first time, she didn't want to be in her apartment, and she wanted to be with Tobias anyway.

That was before she'd packed a bag, gathered everything of value, and ridden beside him in his jeep to the houseboat.

What would Cynthia say? And Emma when she found out? And Pops, *if* he ever found out?

Tobias returned from taking her things upstairs to the spare bedroom. She'd declined his offer to show her where it was.

"Help me decide on our gourmet dinner," he said, offering her his hand. When she didn't move, he dropped his arm and studied her, his head on one side. "Sorry you came?"

"No. Not sorry. Just confused that I'm here and not sure I should be."

He'd told her he loved her. She loved him, but couldn't bring herself to tell him in return.

"Would you turn your back on a desperate man?"

Rather than toss back a flip answer, Paris scanned his features, noticing what she'd been too self-involved to notice before—there was something different about him, something edgy. No sign showed of the humorous tilt to his mouth. The skin drew tight about his eyes and over his cheekbones. "Are you desperate?" Paris asked. Not thinking about Cynthia's warnings was impossible. "Is it something to do with Pops?"

"You're direct. That's something else I like about you. I think it may all be something to do with Pops. With the Skagit project, at least. But . . . It's warm in here. Too warm to think. Will you sit outside on the swing with me?"

"You never could stand being inside for long," she told him and then she did hold out her hand and wait for him to clasp it. "I'd like to go outside with you." She'd like to go everywhere with him. Most of all, she'd like to stop looking for reasons to doubt him.

Tobias shut the front door behind them. Seated on the porch swing, they rocked gently. His dock extended farther into the bay than the rest and no other houseboats were visible. This was quite a different evening from the last she'd spent here. No rain tonight, only a clear, black, star-crusted sky about a million miles distant. Lights strung along rigging cast a twinkling web around the Seattle Yacht Club and the University's buildings wore a clear, bright halo.

"I hope your friend, Wormwood, can track that guy," Tobias said, lacing their fingers together and carrying them to his mouth. "If the phone rings we'll hear it out here."

"Never mind me." No one had seemed surprised when she'd said she was leaving with Tobias. They'd call the minute they got any news—if they got any news. "Tell me about you. Today."

"*AnaisAnais,* that's what you wear sometimes."

"Don't change the subject."

"You and I make a great pair. Someone's out to get you. Someone's out to get me. We think they're different people, but we think the fact we came together may have given someone a bright idea to use—against me, anyway. But we're both in deep shi—Deep *trouble*."

Paris chuckled. "Nice save."

"I try. I lost a deal today. I shouldn't have."

She looked at his profile. Bowed over her hand, he touched her knuckles to his lips. If there were to be a moment that never ended, this would rank high among the ones she'd choose.

"Bill Bowie's as floored as I am. He threw his hat in the ring, too, but more out of courtesy than anything. I was a shoo-in for something that size. Big condo complex downtown. I'd get the financing together *and* deal with the contracting for the outfit with the property. Very few people can handle what I'm talking about on this scale and still offer an attractive deal. Gunter Williams should have been the closest contender, but he wasn't."

"Bill got it?"

"No. Some Californian outfit. We don't know anything about them. New apparently. But something's wrong. Really wrong. I think I've got a rotten worm in my apple barrel, Blue. They weren't keen on doing it, but the owners let me see what beat me out. Just enough under on price. And a dead match for every incentive—plus one or two extras only a fool would offer. A fool or someone who doesn't care if they take a bath on this one."

"Can people afford to do that?"

"I'm damned if I know how this group can." He shifted until he could pull her head onto his shoulder. "The only reason to do it is obvious. A direct attempt to push me off the top of the ladder. That doesn't take any brain to figure out, but from what we can find, they may not make it through this one project, so what's the point?"

Paris breathed in the scent of him, absorbed the feel of him. "I wish we could just seal off this swing and never go back out there."

He played with her hair, giving little, preoccupied tugs. "One day it's going to be over. And we're going to be sealed off. Together. That's all I care about. Where, isn't a big deal to me. In the meantime I've got someone leaking inside information and I've got to find out who."

"I don't understand why the property owners would choose

an unknown over you. Even if they're a bit cheaper, surely going with a solid company like Quinn would be safer."

Tobias didn't answer immediately, when he did his voice was tight. "They said that with my very public difficulties elsewhere, they felt it was prudent to go with a *competitive* bidder. This competitive bidder—according to these people—wouldn't be likely to go under because they had everything tied up in another project that might never get off the ground."

Paris sat up and turned to face him. "The Skagit? Is that true? You've sunk so much money up there that the delays could—"

"*No*. It's a nuisance. A damn great nuisance. But we are absolutely solid."

"Then tell them."

"I have. They're not listening. Hell, I could let this one go and not blink, but what about the next time it happens. And the next. I can't even cry foul because there's no proof. I know I've been ripped off, but the outside group isn't about to tell me who gave them the information."

"You'll *have* to do something."

"My lawyers are on it. Unfortunately, it's so damned subtle. Pinning it down could be a long process. And we could come up completely empty-handed."

Paris touched his sleeve. "I could try talking to Pops for you."

He hauled her onto his lap and looped his hands around her neck. "Did you just say you really do trust me?"

"I do trust you."

"Did you maybe say—sort of—that you might love me, too?"

Michael had sworn he'd never stop loving her and she'd made the same promise. This time could be different, but she still wasn't ready to say the words. "I might," she told Tobias and quickly kissed his lips. "We ought to fix that gourmet dinner before one of us faints."

His arms tightened about her. He rested his forehead on hers. "Okay, Blue. We'll do that." Gripping her waist, he lifted her in front of him and stood up. "The menu is staggering. Everything from chicken pot pies to baked potatoes stuffed with broccoli and cheese-food sauce."

"Yuck!"

Tobias laughed as he opened the door for her. "The best of everything in the one-dish variety. Low sodium. Reduced fat. Then there's banana cream pie for dessert."

"Reduced fat?" She followed his lead and smiled past the uncertainties.

"Of course not," he said seriously. "But it's still frozen so that probably helps, don't you think?"

"Undoubtedly."

The phone beside the couch rang and the force of their twin starts showed how phony their relaxed act was.

Tobias answered at once. He flipped open a notepad and took a pen from a table drawer. "Yes." He wrote rapidly, glancing up at Paris only once. "You're sure? . . . Okay. How long ago? Thanks. We'll leave now. I'll get back to you."

"Wormwood?" Paris asked when he sat rereading what he'd written.

Tobias shook his head. "Conrad. He remembered someone who might know where to find Coeur. Someone who used to work at Seattle Streets."

"And he found them?"

"Yes." He gave her the notebook. "And the guy showed him where Coeur lives. That's his address."

A few stars still dusted the heavens but they no longer seemed a million miles away. The sky's canopy pressed down on the tops of gracelessly aged buildings. In the morning's small hours, a Lower Queen Anne area side street—near the Seattle Center—held all the appeal of nightfall after a riot. Marauding bands of looters—dashing between the hulking structures on the Center grounds to invade lifeless dwellings—might have appeared at any moment.

Tobias had cruised the area several times before finally parking. Paris hadn't questioned his reason. They were both playing a game with rules they'd never learned. Thinking time could only be a smart advantage to grab.

They stood on a narrow sidewalk where the roots of gnarled

old trees had cracked and lifted stones into a lumpy, crazy-paved trap for the unwary.

"Will you change your mind and let me do this on my own?" Tobias said.

"Absolutely not." The building in front of them was only three stories high with a flat roof and dark paint peeling away from a crumbling stucco facade. Stone steps led up to a recessed front door. "I'm the one who talks his language."

"Have you thought about what you're going to say in that language?"

She hadn't, but she did now. "I think I'm going to tell him I'll blow the whistle if he doesn't stop."

The fingers of one of Tobias's powerful hands grasped the top of Paris's left arm. "That's it? You'll do something if he doesn't stop stealing your designs?"

"Yup. That's it. You can't take nothing from nothing and this man's got nothing. Look at the place. And think about what he's been doing. He's not making big bucks."

"He's been ruining your life and I don't believe he chose you by accident. I still think someone put him up to it. There's another mind working behind the scenes."

Logic was impossible to deny. "I'm going in," she told him. "He'll be scared out of his mind when we confront him. Maybe we can do a deal on some information."

"Plea bargaining, home-grown style? You've been watching too many courtroom dramas."

Paris started up the steps, pulling Tobias with her. "I'm calling the shots," she said, while her heart did pole vaults. "I'm very glad not to be alone with this and I wouldn't want anyone but you with me. But I've got to do what feels right."

"We'll see," Tobias said grimly. "First we need to get him to let us in."

A faded strip beside one of three buttons announced, "C. Merk." Paris promptly jabbed the button and listened for the response from the rusted intercom grill.

Minutes and several unheeded jabs later, Tobias pressed his brow to the filmed glass in the front door. "Holy shit. What a dump. If he's in, he's not rolling out the welcome mat."

Footsteps on the sidewalk came close to stopping Paris's heart from beating at all. A heavy man, reeking of eau-de-bar, shambled up the steps and came to a full, rocking halt in front of Paris and Tobias.

"Hi," Paris said, too scared to be ashamed of the squeaky sound she made.

"Piss off," the man said, sniffing while he patted and poked through his clothing to produce a key.

"We're here to see Mr. Merk," Tobias said, so pleasantly Paris's mouth fell open. "He called to say he's under the weather and needs help. The fever must have made him too groggy to answer the door."

At last the smelly, swaying body located the lock, scrabbled to insert his key and thrust the door open. "Piss off," he muttered again, disappearing inside the gloomy entrance.

Tobias neatly wedged a toe in the door, stopping it from closing, and waited for the other man to shamble away into the interior of the building.

"Come on," Paris said when she couldn't tolerate another second of waiting. "Let's get this over with."

In the hallway, the smell of stale grease, decaying food and other assorted unpleasantness brought her stomach plowing up under her ribs.

Tobias put his mouth to her ear. "Hold your breath and follow me. One floor up."

On the stairs, she clutched a handful of his shirt from behind. He reached back to hold her wrist.

"Christ!" he muttered as every tread whined.

By the time they reached the next floor the darkness was absolute. The layout helped. With the steps placed to the right of the structure, turning left was the only option. Feeling his way along the wall, Tobias kept Paris behind him while he made slow forward progress.

Paris tugged at him and he stopped.

"What?" he whispered.

"He could be armed," Paris responded. "This is dangerous."

"Conrad said the man's a nut, but not the kind to turn physically vicious. Conrad also said he'll join us here as soon as he can fire up one of your famous vehicles."

"Oh, yeah," Paris muttered. "Nothing's running too well. The Buick—"

"We know what happened to the Buick. I do have a gun."

Speechless, Paris gulped. "You do?"

"You bet. I'm not that much of a hero—or a fool. Do we go on, or not?"

"On."

"There's a door where my hand is. I'm going to knock. I want you to back off a bit and be ready to run if you have to. Take the Jeep and get help. The keys are in the ignition."

Her stomach had made its way to her throat where it collided with her heart. "Knock," she said, with no intention of leaving him.

She felt him reach inside his shirt. He'd taken out the gun. Then he knocked and for Paris the sound rivaled any gunfire.

"It's open," Tobias said softly. "You artists like to live dangerously."

Paris ignored him. The door swung slowly open, crackling over papers and debris strewn on the floor. Faint light shone from some interior room.

"Mr. Merk?" Tobias said, but not very loudly. "Hello, Mr. Merk. This feels bloody stupid."

"The man's probably sleeping."

"It stinks in here," Tobias commented. "And it looks like an after-the-bomb scene."

As her eyes adjusted to the gloom, Paris saw piles of cardboard cartons spilling contents, unframed canvases propped along walls, chaotic stacks of books, rumpled magazines, tangles of clothing, blankets, discarded shoes, a table consisting of a sheet of wood on cinder blocks and littered with carryout food containers and beer bottles. The stench of rancid Chinese vegetables threaded through a dense aura of old human sweat.

"He could be out." Paris didn't doubt that Tobias guessed how *much* she hoped Coeur was far away.

"Stay here," Tobias commanded. He went silently forward,

picking a path around obstacles, to reach another door from which the vague light issued.

He went through the door and disappeared.

Paris counted to ten and followed.

If possible, the second room was a bigger disaster than the first. The general rubble was duplicated but with the addition of a bed—and a jeweler's bench heaped with disorganized tools.

Swinging gently from the work light clamped to one side of the bench, a faceted crystal strung on nylon thread flashed minute spots of vivid color.

The man who should have been in the bed at that hour sat instead on the floor before a sheet of glass used for the same purpose as the wood in the other room.

Dressed in a ragged T-shirt and olive drab fatigue pants, he sat cross-legged, his feet bare. His arms rested, palms turned up, in an attitude of meditation.

His eyes were closed.

Tobias saw Paris and waved her back.

She walked to his side and said, "Coeur? Snap out of it. We've got business to deal with."

The man gave no sign of hearing her. Paris glanced at the detritus on the makeshift glass table. Prominent was an open book in some foreign language, but it was the needle that demanded her complete attention.

"Drugs," she whispered.

"I noticed," Tobias told her. "He's so far out of it he's still got the tube on his arm."

"Couldn't that be dangerous?"

"This guy only lives for dangerous," Tobias said. "I don't know why we're whispering. He's listening to better music than we're playing. I guess I'll take off the tubing before he looses his damned arm."

Still holding his gun on the man, Tobias crouched beside him and loosened the rubber drawn tight a few inches above the right elbow.

The instant he pulled the tubing, Coeur, if that's who he was, gradually toppled sideways to slump, his legs still crossed, on the floor. One knee connected with the table, sending the syr-

inge rolling across its surface to muddle with other items Paris
didn't recognize.

"We'd better get some help," she said, looking around for a
phone. "He must have overdosed. He could die."

Tobias pushed three fingers into the man's carotid artery and
settled his eyes on Paris's. "The phone's over there," he told
her. "Better make it the police. This guy's already dead."

The predawn chill stung Tobias's eyes. Back on the sidewalk
in front of the Lower Queen Anne apartment building, he and
Paris stood beside a policeman who appeared as bored as they
were tired. A silent ambulance bearing Coeur's body had only
recently slipped away from the curb.

"I thought the detective said we could leave," Paris said.

The officer stirred. "He's on the phone checking something
with downtown. As soon as he's got what he needs he'll release
you. You could have waited inside."

Paris shuddered. Tobias turned her to face him and enfolded
her in his arms. "Somehow we decided to pass on the comforts
of home," he told the cop. "After all, staying for three hours
when you weren't invited in the first place might already be
considered excessive."

No response was offered. For three hours after calling for
help, Tobias and Paris had answered questions, watched the
machinery of the law deal with a dead man, and answered more
questions. They'd both protested treatment that suggested they
were criminals rather than victims looking for justice.

"Trespassing," Paris said glumly. "Wait till the papers get
hold of this. Quinn and Delight caught trespassing in the home
of a dead junkie—while the dead junkie was in residence."

"Should do great things for our reputations. Was it my imagination, or did my gun permit cause a hint of disappointment?"

Behind her glasses, Paris's blue eyes showed only bleak exhaustion.

"Thank God Conrad showed up to support our story." Tobias
felt as uncomfortable with the guy as he ever had, but Conrad

had arrived and told the police he'd tracked Coeur's address and passed it on to Tobias.

"I'm glad he went back to tell the others what's going on," Paris told him. "I've got to get there as soon as I can. They'll be worried sick."

All Tobias wanted was to get her back to the houseboat and into bed—preferably his bed. All he wanted was to hold her and forget this disaster ever happened.

Scattering a host of foraging birds, a figure arrived at the street corner and walked purposefully toward them. Tobias slowly took his hands out of his pants pockets.

"Wormwood!" Paris ran to meet the man. She threw her arms around his neck and he hesitated before patting her back. "Oh, Wormwood. Coeur's dead. We found him."

Wormwood unwound her arms and promptly sank his hands into his own pockets. With Paris at his side he approached Tobias. "Conrad brought the news. I asked questions all night and didn't get anywhere. Poor old bird's bought it, huh? Years ago the word was that he dealt but didn't use." Still dressed in the same brown of the previous afternoon, Wormwood also wore the lines of deep fatigue on his face.

"The police asked us a million questions," Paris said as if the cop were deaf. "You'd think we'd killed the man and then called for someone to come and catch us."

Tobias rubbed his gritty eyes and prayed for dismissal. "How'd you get here?"

"Walked," Wormwood said offhandedly.

Tobias stared at the man. "Long stroll."

"I'm used to walking. What's going on in there? I thought you'd be gone."

"So why did you come?" Tobias asked, more sharply than he might have.

Wormwood's blank expression didn't change. "Just in case you were still here."

"Thank you," Paris said, casting a reproachful glare at Tobias. "As soon as they say we can go, Tobias and I will take you home. I've got to let the others know I'm okay."

A herd of footsteps thundered on the stairs inside the building and the detective arrived with the remainder of his entourage.

Detective Dean peeled away from the uniformed contingent. Donning a gray fedora that did nice things for his lean, intelligent face, he strolled to confront Tobias and Paris. "This a friend of yours?" He inclined his head to Wormwood.

"A good friend," Paris said promptly. "He came because people are starting to worry about us."

The detective opened a stick of gum, folded it precisely in half and wedged it inside a cheek. "You'll be home with Mom and Dad soon. Okay if I talk in front of your friend?"

Paris's eyes opened wider and she said, "Yes," as if she'd like to say, *why?*

"A fraction of the pure stuff he probably used would have killed him. Know what I'm saying?"

Tobias crossed his arms. "You mean he used uncut . . . Whatever he used wasn't cut?"

"Heroin. Yeah."

"Isn't that dangerous?" Paris asked.

A dour smile lifted the corners of Dean's straight mouth, a mouth some women might find appealing. "I'd say you've analyzed the situation perfectly. He was a longtime user. They don't make that kind of mistake."

"But he did," Paris said.

Tobias drew her beside him.

Dean took his time studying their faces. "He didn't make a mistake. The way we figure, someone brought Chinese food and a present for dessert. Evidently he didn't question what was in the dessert."

"Murder?" Tobias said, mostly to himself. "The timing's too convenient."

"Exactly what we said." Dean shifted the gum between his teeth and chewed in earnest. "We've got your addresses. Got a way home?"

Tobias nodded.

"Right. We'll be in touch as soon as we're ready."

"Just a minute," Tobias said. "Are you making some sort of suggestions here?"

Sharp, light blue eyes regarded him steadily. "No suggestions. Must have been frustrating for Ms. Delight to see her jewelry copied like that. Pretty difficult to prove without the sketches or witnesses. Enough to make anyone mad."

Paris's pale face flushed crimson. "Not mad enough to kill someone!"

Helpless to take back her words, Tobias set his teeth and kept right on looking into the detective's eyes. A flicker of satisfaction showed. He touched the brim of his hat and walked around the hood of an unmarked car at the curb.

When they were alone with Wormwood, Paris said, "They think we killed Coeur. How could they?"

"No, they don't," Tobias said. He didn't tell her what he thought, that the police were weighing the possibility. "Let's go to your place and drop Wormwood. If anyone's still awake, you can give them a rundown." And then he wanted to get her out of there—permanently, if he had his way.

Paris resisted his attempt to shepherd her toward the Jeep. "Don't try to protect me," she told him. "I've just been warned. They suspect me of murder."

Stretched along the length of Paris's couch, his head propped on one arm, Tobias appeared fast asleep. Aldonza watched him narrowly—from a perch on the back of the couch.

Conrad, slumped over the table, held his eyes open with his fingers.

"This is the craziest thing I've ever heard," Sam said, pacing. He called to Ginna who was brewing more coffee in the kitchen, "Have you ever heard of something like this, honey?"

"No, Sam." Ever diplomatic with her lover, Ginna didn't tell him he'd already asked the question more than once.

"See?" The only apparently wide-awake member of the group, Sam waved his arms triumphantly. "We don't have anything to worry about. You read too much into what the cop said, Paris. He was just going through the motions."

From her place near the window, Paris saw Tobias's eyes shift beneath his lids. Neither of them had read too much into Detective Dean's cryptic comments and Sam had swung between panic and philosophical reassurance ever since they'd walked through the front door.

He ran a hand over his hair and retraced his path. "Lips and his lady aren't missing their beauty sleep."

"Nor should they," Paris told him gently. "You should all go to bed. Especially Mary." The old lady snoozed in the rocking chair.

Wormwood reentered the room from the direction of his own quarters. "I'll take her down," he said. "Come on, Mary."

Grumbling, Mary let him pull her to her feet. "Go over the border, that's what I say," she announced quite clearly. "We'll put you in the back of a delivery van and drive you over."

Tobias's eyes were wide open.

"Let's go," Wormwood said with his rare, shadowy smile in place. "You'll need some rest before you drive any getaway vans."

"I'm not driving," she said irritably, jerking away from Wormwood on her way to the door. "I've got contacts. When those fools figure out what's what, we'll get you back again. I've ordered the pumpkins."

By the time Wormwood had managed to urge the woman through the door and close it, Conrad had given up on his eyes and rested his head on his arms. Paris listened to the clump of shoes going down the stairs and, finally, silence.

"So," Sam said. "What are we going to do? Wait here for those assholes to come and throw more accusations around?"

"No," Ginna said, coming in with mugs on a tray. "We're going to drink this, then go away and leave these people in peace."

Tobias swung his long legs down and accepted coffee. Avoiding eye-contact, they all drank.

"Conrad should have gone with you," Sam said. "He should have made sure I went, too."

"No fucking car," Conrad remarked, blinking. "Should have taken a cab earlier."

"Why didn't you come to the club and tell us?" Sam demanded.

"Shit!" Conrad's tanned complexion darkened. "I told you I was trying to start one of the cars. Don't lay—"

"That's enough," Ginna said. "There's nothing any of us

could have done to change this. Arguing isn't going to help a thing. We all need some sleep. Things will work out."

"Yeah," Sam said. "We'll hope they work out without Paris getting arrested."

Paris set her mug down hard and covered her mouth with a shaking hand.

"Keep your mouth shut," Conrad said to Sam. "Can't you see what you're doing to Paris?"

Sam started to respond, but looked at her and grimaced instead. "Geez. Sorry, Paris. I never was long on tact."

Conrad pushed to his feet. "Okay if I use the bathroom?" He didn't wait for a response before ambling along the corridor.

"Well, children," Tobias said, draining his mug. "I suggest we carry out our many threats to get some sleep."

Paris met his eyes and felt warm. Tired as she was, arousal stirred. Upstairs in her bed, or at the houseboat, they would make love again soon. The unspoken understanding passed between them and her body quickened.

Conrad erupted from the corridor, a piece of paper in one hand. "Stop him!" he said, already on his way to the door. "Don't let him leave."

He tossed the paper toward Paris and ran out. Sam scarcely hesitated before hustling after Conrad.

It was Ginna who reached the folded sheet of paper first. She flattened it and read. Paris and Tobias went to look over her shoulder.

"Dear Paris," Wormwood had written. "Give this to the police. I was in a jam but I should have thought of another way out. I made the sketches and had Coeur copy them. He was a buddy of mine once. We never lost touch. When you came to the Door yesterday and said you'd figured out who the forger was, I panicked. Coeur died the way he'd have chosen. Oblivious. His heart just stopped. You shouldn't have been dragged in. I didn't expect Conrad to get the address. I killed Coeur Merk. It's over now. Thanks for everything you did for me. I'm sorry for the way I paid you back. You won't have to worry anymore. It's all over." The note was signed, "Richard Wormwood."

Tobias took the note from Ginna. He went to the phone and punched in numbers.

"Richard," Paris said. "I never knew he had another name."

Twenty-five

Blackmail.

Four months ago, when he'd first been contacted, he'd come close to fainting. The caller told him he'd been seen picking up a teenage male prostitute on Second Avenue. If he didn't do as he was told, his lover of fifteen years would receive photographs.

He should have stopped it all then. He should have confessed the miserable, squalid little truth and risked losing the man he loved.

Now it was too late. It was even too late to as much as write a note to the one human being who had ever really returned his love.

Scarcely able to see through eyes too dry and blurred for tears, Wormwood made his way south by feel. It was better to leave without making contact again. At least his partner might be spared the pain of knowing he'd been betrayed.

One careless act, one urge to try a beckoning boy in a muscle shirt and tight jeans, and fifteen years of loving and caring had been blown away.

The great ridged circle of the Kingdome roof loomed ahead.

Wormwood set his fading gaze on the graying roof of the sports arena and shoved his feet forward, onward, one and then the other.

Not far now.

Luck had never been his friend. An artistic talent that fell just short of great had consigned him to also-ran status. And the one beautiful constant ever to come his way would never know why his lover walked out of his life without even saying goodbye. It was better that way.

He reached the dilapidated section of gray buildings near the dome. Traffic rumbled steadily past him on First Avenue.

The sound of the engines bored into the cells of his brain. Roared.

He walked into a woman on the sidewalk. She yelled at him but he didn't hear the words.

If only he'd never been weak enough to talk about himself to anyone—even someone persuasive and sympathetic. But he had. He'd opened up and shared his joyous relationship with just one person. And that confidence had been twisted and used against him like a club.

Some judge of character. He'd confided in a blackmailer.

If he'd walked past the boy . . .

If he hadn't been seen with him that night . . .

If he'd refused to be blackmailed . . .

If, if, if, if . . .

A block away from First Avenue, two freight trains hammered together. The linkage clanked and rolling steel wheels gathered speed.

He started to run, stumbling into walls every few steps.

"Watch it, buddy!" The mouth in a passing face stretched wide and slid past too slowly.

Loser. "You're a loser, son."

How many years since his father last looked him in the eye and said, "You're a loser, son. A fuck-up." The old man's baseball cap had been pushed up on his sweating red brow. Beer from a can glistened on his lips. *"Who'd of thought I'd whelp a friggin' pansy?"*

He'd picked up the boy and gone with him to a room. But

then all he'd done that night was watch him undress. The kid preened and posed . . . and enticed. Innocence an illusion. Innocence long lost behind the pretty brown eyes.

"You okay?" A workman in a yellow hardhat loomed in front of him. "You need help?"

"No. No!"

He needed forgiveness. He needed peace. He needed what he could never have—to turn the clock back and walk away from the boy on Second Avenue.

At last he saw his destination. Above him on the multilaned Viaduct, morning traffic flashed past in a thunderous stream. The steady thud, thud of tires over seams pulsed at his temples.

The sun didn't warm him, yet sweat soaked his back and ran cold down his face. Every gulp of air tore like acid down his throat. His lungs swelled against his heart. His arms were numb, and his legs. Numb legs that pushed on, on.

A car horn blared.

The sign at the on-ramp to the elevated highway ordered: *No Pedestrians.*

Upward.

"Can't you read?" A face through a pickup's open window. "Dumb shit!"

Dumb shit.

"Who'd have thought I'd whelp a friggin' pansy?"

At the top of the ramp he stood, filling his mind with sun chips on Elliott Bay and the soaring peaks of the Olympic Mountains in the distance.

The sunlight flashed on windshields—a never-ending rush of windshields past his left shoulder.

Wormwood faced the windshields and stepped off the narrow curbstone.

Blinding flashes beckoned—like the beautiful boy.

He counted his steps. One, two, three, four . . .

Twenty-six

Paris stepped out of the shower in Tobias's "spare" quarters and dried herself on a huge yellow towel. "August first," she said into the steamy air. "And I hadn't even noticed we'd run out of July."

The sky of another nightfall showed through twin skylights. This had been a day filled with revelation, with horror, and with a new coming-of-age for Paris. One more piece of her innocence gone. Believing in the essential goodness of others would be tougher from now on.

She rubbed her hair and fought with the accumulated tangles of almost two days until it hung straight and wet—and cold—against her skin.

The shoulders of the chaste white cotton gown she donned were instantly soaked. With her heavy hair restrained in a towel turban, she put on a matching robe.

Each small chore: pushing arms into sleeves, tucking in a pocket turned out by the wash, threading satin-bound buttons through tight buttonholes—she accomplished every task as if hampered by deep water.

There had never been exhaustion—or desolation—like this.

A tap on the bedroom door startled her. She'd assumed Tobias must already be asleep.

Paris walked into the simply furnished bedroom and said, "Yes," before removing the towel and hanging her hair forward.

"Only me," Tobias said.

She turned her head to the side and continued drying her hair. With his hair as wet as hers, he stood in the doorway dressed in a white T-shirt and soft, ancient jeans. "I thought you were going to bed," she said.

"I'm having trouble turning my brain off."

Paris straightened and absently folded the towel. "It's August first," she said.

"Is it? I hadn't had time to notice."

"Every year on this day I'm going to think . . ."

He rested one bare foot on top of the other. "People die every day. August first is as good as any other day."

"I can't believe he did it. He walked up that ramp and kept right on walking into the middle of the highway until he was hit."

"I thought you were going to say you couldn't believe he did what he did to you."

Paris tossed the towel onto the bathroom counter behind her. "Wormwood died today. Doesn't that make you feel at all bad?"

Tobias leaned against the doorjamb. His gaze lost focus. "I feel numb. I feel confused and worried. I feel angry that you've been through so much when you don't deserve to be touched by something as sick as this. The guy murdered a man. He murdered a man he hired to make forgeries of your jewelry. We may never know exactly why he needed the money, but he chose to victimize you—the woman who'd been nothing but good to him. And he obviously went running to knock Coeur off because he was afraid you'd manage to track him down and if you did you'd probably find out the truth."

"But when he realized the police might blame me for the murder, he confessed," Paris said. "I know everything he did was wrong, but . . . I thought he was a friend."

"Yeah." Tobias walked across the room and turned down a handmade quilt atop the cherrywood spool bed. "Come on. I'm going to tuck you in and you're going to get some sleep. It's almost ten at night and you've been up since yesterday morning."

"So have you."

"Get in."

"Did I ask someone to feed Aldonza?"

"Ginna. Come on."

Dutifully, Paris unbuttoned the robe and took it off. "You need to get to bed, too," she said, not looking at him, yet feeling his eyes upon her. "Promise you'll go now?" She didn't want him to leave her.

"I'll go."

She hovered beside him, then sat down on the edge of the bed and swung her legs onto the mattress. Instantly, the covers settled over her.

Paris closed her eyes and lay in a rigid line—waiting. Surely he could feel how much she needed to be held—really held.

The sheet pulled under her chin.

The light clicked off.

"Sleep well, Blue."

"Thank you."

She felt his breath on her forehead. Her mind forgot to be tired.

Tobias brushed her cheek with a forefinger.

Paris's breasts tightened, and the muscles between her legs and deep in her belly.

He kissed her brow.

She stopped breathing.

His jeans rustled against the quilt.

"Tobias?"

"It's okay," he said. "Just let go. I'll be right across the hall."

The door opened and closed very quietly.

Paris held still in the darkness. Within moments the flush left her face . . . her body remained afire.

He would be right across the hall? Paris set her jaw. She was too old for games. Tobias Quinn was no fool, he couldn't have stood beside her and *not* felt her desire for him. The little comforting act he'd just performed was designed to arouse her—and to let her know he could still walk away. He was overdue to find out he couldn't call all the shots.

Without bothering with the lamp, Paris threw aside the covers and got out of bed. She stalked to the door, whipped it open and marched *right across the hall.*

She didn't have to open his door because he hadn't completely closed it. And she didn't knock. "I've had it with you," she said, pushing into the room. "Why am I here, anyway?"

With his back to her, Tobias—very slowly—finished pulling the T-shirt over his head. Muscles flexed in his back and shoulders.

Tobias's broad shoulders and slim hips were of no interest to Paris. Neither was the fascinating way his straight spine arched—nor the sharp delineation of oblique muscles from armpit to waist.

"You can go to hell," she told him.

He turned around. "What brought this on?"

"I wanted you to know how I feel about you. Now, answer my question. Why am I here?"

Unzipping his jeans on the way, Tobias went to turn down the dark red quilt on his bed.

"Were you always so goddamn tidy?"

His face snapped up. Sharp light shot into his steely eyes. Just as quickly the expression softened. "You'll get over it. All it'll take is time."

"Damn you." The force of her disappointment speeded her breathing. "There's absolutely no reason for me not to be in my own home now. Thanks for the hospitality. I'll call a cab."

She felt the atmosphere in the room change shape and flinched. In the second her eyes were shut, Tobias crossed the room. He backed her to a wall and stood near enough to give her a close-up of a hard-set, darkly stubbled jaw.

Paris cleared her throat. "Excuse me, please."

"Excuse you? Where the hell do you think you're going?"

"Back home," she said very quietly.

"Are you out of your . . . Don't answer that. Forget that. You've lost your mind. I'm putting you to bed."

"I'm not your goddamn kid!"

"Why are you swearing like a . . . Why are you talking like that?"

Paris pressed her lips together. They absolutely could not tremble now.

"You're here because it isn't safe for you to be at your place. There. I didn't want to say that, but if you're going to behave like a little idiot I don't have any choice."

"Of course it's safe." Her mouth *was* trembling. "Wormwood's . . . dead. No one's going to be creeping around making copies of my work anymore."

"Well, then," Tobias said, bracing his arms on the wall at the level of her temples. "Then I guess there's not another thing to worry about. *Christ!* Wormwood was only part of the problem."

"Don't."

"Oh . . ." His chest expanded. "Let's go through this in simple steps. Just so you'll get it. Yes, we can check off a forger and the guy who fed him. But you were attacked in your bed. You were also shut out on the roof by someone who—at the very least—intended to scare the *shit* out of you."

"But—"

"But nothing. We know we were both attacked by the same guy. He definitely intended to put me on the bottom of the bay—permanently. We don't know who *he* is. He hasn't been stopped. *You* are not safe. I'm not letting you out of my sight. Got it?"

Paris snapped her mouth shut.

"Good," Tobias said. "Very good."

"That's *it.*" Rapid blinking didn't do a thing for stinging eyes. "There may be women who really get off on the old domination routine. I'm not one of them."

"You aren't leaving."

"Wormwood was the one on the inside. The man on the outside does *not* have keys. He walked in."

"Not the night you almost found out how well you *don't* fly."

Paris refused to meet his eyes. "That *was* Wormwood. I'm sure of it. When he heard me coming he must have run upstairs to hide. Then he shut me out so he could make some more copies. He didn't know I'd taken all my stuff out of . . . Well, I took it out from under the, er, safe. He'd have let me out later and pretended he just happened to come back and hear me or something."

"Maybe. We still have someone unaccounted for. This isn't about domination. It's about being smart."

She looked directly up into his eyes. "And you think doing what you just did to me was smart? Did you think it was clever? Does that kind of thing turn you on?"

The corners of his mouth twisted down. "Turn me on? What the . . . You're going to have to spell this out for me."

"If I'd done it to you I'd have been a *tease*. It's the double standard that gets me. A woman tries to explain herself and she's nagging. A man browbeats a woman and he's *explaining* his point of view."

His eyes narrowed. "What point?"

"Don't play dumb. *Sleep tight. Don't let the bedbugs bite.* Tucking me in. *Turning me on.* Walking out and leaving me wanting you so you could have the last laugh."

He pushed his fingers into her hair so suddenly, her head banged the wall. "You are out of your mind," he said through his teeth. "The last *laugh?* Make up your mind. You're the one who sent me to bed. All you had to do was ask, sweetheart."

"Ask?" She made fists against his rigid chest. "I was supposed to ask you to . . ."

"Say it."

Paris glared at him and shook her head.

His fingers tightened against her scalp. *"Say* it."

"Okay! I wanted you to make love to me!"

The edges of his teeth showed. Paris noticed tiny things, like the hint of overlapping eye teeth, the vertical dimples beneath his cheekbones, the thin white scar above his eyebrow.

His body hit hers without warning. He flattened her aching breasts, jutted his pelvis into her belly, proving beyond doubt that she wasn't the only one with an urge. She felt him through the flimsy cotton nightie. Iron-hard, heavy and hot, Tobias had a big urge.

"Your wish is my command," he said, his voice husky. "I wasn't planning on sleeping anyway."

A thrill of exquisite fear stiffened her nipples.

Tobias's hooded eyes made a leisurely downward pass. "Nice," he said. "You like wet clothes?"

Paris glanced down involuntarily. Her nightgown, damp from her hair, clung transparently to her breasts. Her pink nipples pouted through the cloth.

With his thumbs, he raised her chin and lowered his head to kiss her neck. Paris plucked ineffectually at his arms. Tobias answered by playing his tongue over the tip of a nipple.

"Tobias."

"Uh-huh?"

One of his hands stroked her length, worked the gown up and slid to cup her mound. His fingers probed.

Paris rolled her head away.

Cool air slid over her legs and belly. Tobias held the nightie about her waist and dropped to his knees. She felt his tongue snake into the slippery flesh his fingers had aroused.

There was no time to protest, to even get a handhold on his hair or shoulders. Her climax rolled, split her with fire . . . broke in wave after wave.

"Ah," was all he said. Then he was on his feet again, lifting her, wrapping her legs around his waist and thrusting inside.

The wall burned her back but she didn't care.

Tobias was iron driven by raw, surging power. Paris clung to his neck and clenched down on each stroke. Sweat slicked his body. Cries jarred from his throat. His buttocks heaved beneath her heels.

His release came and Paris smiled even as she gasped.

"Ah, hell," he muttered. "Too fast. You do that to me."

Paris slid down his length until her toes met the floor. Panting, he held her against the wall and layered open-mouthed kisses over her shoulders and the tops of her breasts. Rolling her nipples beneath his palms, he took her lips and delved deeply.

When he rested his face beside hers, he said, "Too damn fast, Blue."

Trying not to grin, she dropped beneath his arm and made for the door. "Some things take practice," she told him. Her legs wobbled. "One day you may reach my level of control."

Tobias whipped around and reached for her.

Shrieking, she attempted to evade him and landed, face-down, across his bed.

"Control?" He caught her hips and pulled her toward the edge of the mattress.

Paris clawed but failed to find anything to grip. "Yes, control. You wouldn't want to lose it."

Once more her nightie was pushed up, giving Tobias a perfect perspective on her naked and vulnerable bottom. And that's where he held her. He held her and he entered her again.

Paris reared up. Already he was engorged like pulsing granite. Filled with him, she sobbed her pleasure. Tobias folded himself over her back and the beautiful inner beating flowered. His hands came around and he filled them with her breasts.

"Tobias." His name—and hers on his lips—and the rippling flood of another climax washed through blood and bone, nerve and skin.

She was perfect. He was never, ever going to let her go. Even if she refused to say the words, he'd felt her love—seen her love for him.

Afraid he'd crush her, Tobias rolled off Paris, pulled her, still face-down, to his side and maneuvered the quilt over them. He rubbed her back, her arms, followed her spine, skimmed her waist.

Paris didn't move or speak.

Tobias crooked a knee on the backs of her thighs and stroked, tangling his foot between hers.

With his tongue, he found her ear and she sighed.

"I'm too long for this," he whispered.

Paris giggled. "Braggart."

"Braggart?" He grinned and nipped her earlobe. "You don't think so, huh?"

She squirmed until she could find his penis.

He wasn't ready.

"I'll take your word for it," she said.

He tickled her until she batted him away, then said, "I was referring to the way we're lying on this bed, ma'am. Care to join me in the right direction?"

"I'm ashamed to admit it." She sighed. "But I'd probably join you in any direction."

Tobias laughed. Clasped together, they wriggled around like mating fish until their heads arrived on the pillows.

"We match, y'know," he told her, smoothing her hair away from her face, glad they'd never got around to turning off the lights.

Paris traced his lower lip with a short fingernail. "I think most people would say we're complete opposites."

"Because you wear brown gauze and I don't?"

She landed a light punch in his midsection.

"I was thinking we're both perfectionists in our own way," he said. "I've spent my life making Quinn the best. You've spent yours making Delights the best."

Her blue, blue eyes rose to his. The smile he saw wasn't on her lips but it was deep inside those eyes. "That's the last thing I would have expected you to say. I'd never have imagined you'd compare what I do to what you do."

"Different but both important," he said. "What you make is timeless. It'll be important forever. Unfortunately what I make will keep having to be replaced by better and bigger and better yet."

Her long, slender arms slipped around his neck. "You surprise me every day, Tobias. Thank you. You, on the other hand, will be the one who keeps doing things bigger and better."

He kissed her forehead and closed his eyes, breathing her in. "Do be careful what suggestions you make at the moment, Blue. I'm not sure I can live up to them—not immediately."

She chuckled softly and scooted up until she could play her lips over his.

The playing turned to kissing and the kissing to deeper kissing.

"The other thing I was talking about," Tobias said before fresh arousal could deaden reason. "I was talking about how well we fit together."

"Oh." Paris held quite still. "That seems to be true."

"You are absolutely perfect for me. Is it threatening to you for me to say that?"

She stared him directly in the eye. "I'm not sure."

At least that was something. "You can take as long as you like to decide. As long as you do the deciding while we're like this."

"Nice offer."

"I thought so. There is something different about you and me. Appearances."

Paris raised her arched brows. "No kidding?"

"Yeah. I'm a simple guy. What you see is what you get. Put me in a suit or in jeans. Take 'em off again and there aren't any surprises."

"Ooh, I don't know about that." Her naughty smile delighted him. "You've managed to surprise me a few times."

There was so much he wanted to say. The timing had to be right. Everything had changed so rapidly—the decisions he thought he'd made for a lifetime, and what he'd thought about this woman only weeks ago.

"You're one constant surprise, Blue. I . . . I may have become addicted to the wonder of you."

"Maybe—" Flattening a hand on each side of his face, she studied him intently. "Maybe we'll be lucky."

Tobias swallowed. He enfolded her closely, gently, and stretched to turn off the lamp.

Timing was everything. This was the time to say nothing.

Paris smelled fresh coffee. Her nose twitched and she squinted into blades of sunlight through vertical, white fabric blinds.

Fresh coffee and warm syrup.

She nestled deeper into the pillows. Must be Sunday. Ginna

usually made pancakes on Sundays and the smell of the syrup wafted through the building like a memory from warm summer mornings of childhood.

High summer. High, pale blue skies. Soft, cool early wind through sweetly drying grass. And crickets.

Paris's eyes opened wide.

She was in Tobias's bed, on Tobias's houseboat, and childhood was a long, long way behind both of them.

And it wasn't Sunday.

He'd left the bedroom door open. Muffled kitchen noises reached her. *"We match, y'know."* Was he really saying what he appeared, so transparently, to be saying—what he had actually said once in the sensual, sexual aftermath of intimacy?

The sound of a raised voice wiped away all traces of sleep.

Paris pushed the sheet from her face and listened.

A female voice. Then the rumble of a male reply.

Paris was consumed by the illusion of being caught where she had no right to be. She couldn't see her nightgown. She couldn't really see anything particularly clearly. A terrycloth robe hung on the edge of the bathroom door.

Scuttling, she unhooked the robe and closed herself inside the bathroom. Wrapped in the white terry that reached her ankles, she felt safer—another illusion. The fright that confronted her in the mirror brought her nose close to the glass.

Hopeless.

On tiptoe, she went to the top of the stairs and instantly knew her mistake.

Turned up to hers was Cynthia's lovely, reproachful face. Naked to the low waist of his jeans, Tobias stood wiping his hands on a dishtowel.

Paris wrapped the robe tightly around her and sat on the top step. "Morning," she said.

"Afternoon," Cynthia responded. "What a sickeningly domestic scene. How did I guess you were here, I wonder?"

"Does it matter?" Tobias commented, pleasantly enough.

Cynthia ignored him. "I've been trying to call you for hours. Finally I gave up and went over to that . . . I went over to find you. You weren't there."

"Do you know what happened yesterday?" Paris asked. If she could, she'd have saved Cynthia this awful moment.

"That crazy Mary told me. I don't appreciate having to waste my time on old loony tunes just because my sister's shacking up with my husband."

"Ex-husband," Tobias said, still mild. "You haven't learned much about kindness yet, have you, Cynthia?"

She gripped the banister and kept her gaze on Paris. "I'm glad for you. It must be a relief to have that man dead. That doesn't mean I have to enjoy hunting all over town for you and then finding you *here.*"

"I should have had the guts to tell you what was happening between Tobias and me," Paris said. "But I'm not glad Wormwood's dead. It's a relief to feel safe again, but I wish no one ever had to die to make someone else safe."

"You are such a sodding goody two-shoes," Cynthia said venomously. "You can't begin to know how sick I am of you being the Cinderella to my wicked sister act."

Paris felt sick and puzzled. "I don't know what's making you act this way, but let's cut the nastiness. You've found me. Say what you came to say."

Dressed in a short green tank dress, Cynthia placed her hands on her hips and expanded her bosom. "I'm amazed you can concentrate long enough to ask."

"Cynthia," Tobias said, warning now.

"All *right.* I got a message because you were *otherwise* engaged. Some dippy ham-radio shmuck tracked me down. Pops sent out an SOS for you this morning."

Paris was instantly on her feet.

"Get your butt up to the Skagit," Cynthia said, obviously relishing each word. "That's the message. Pops is getting weaker and he's too old to go without food for so long."

"I didn't think he'd really do it," Paris said, her heart beating threadily.

"Well, he has. And he says you're the only one who can give him a reason to go on living."

Twenty-seven

Family "togetherness" had already grown old. The sight of Cynthia, her dress hiked up to the lace tops of her stockings, infuriated Tobias.

The radio-equipped van was too small, the quarters too close. Cynthia sat in the driver's swivel chair, one leg crossed over the other and bobbing. Beside her, Nigel cleaned his nails with a toothpick—and watched her legs.

Paris hovered over the radio operator. A gauze blouse and skirt were in place—apple green this time—and her attempts at hastily subduing her hair had failed. A brown barrette pulled a center section straight back from her face. The rest showed signs of having been slept in.

"We've been here three hours," Nigel remarked. "He's not going to speak to us."

Tobias bent to look through dark-tinted windows at Pops Delight's castle. "You weren't forced to come," he told Nigel. He hadn't even been *asked*.

"This is a family thing," Nigel said. "I belong here."

Tobias closed his eyes but didn't waste time praying for patience.

"What if he's too weak?" Paris said. "No one's seen any provisions delivered for weeks. He could be failing because there *isn't* anything to eat in there and I don't even know how we'd go about getting in."

"Storm the castle," Cynthia said and snickered.

"Shut up," Nigel snapped, gaining himself a point or two with Tobias.

"Mr. Delight," the radio operator Tobias had conscripted, spoke into a microphone. "Mr. Delight, I'm leaving the line open. Your family's here."

"I don't have a family."

Tobias straightened, hit his head and smothered a curse.

"*Shit,*" Cynthia whispered. "Finally."

Paris slipped into the seat the operator quickly vacated. "Hi, Pops. It's me, Paris."

"I expected it of the rest of them," Pops Delight said in his gravelly voice. "But not you, Paris. You were always my girl."

"Tell me what you want me to do, Pops," Paris said.

Silence met the request.

"Always *my girl,*" Cynthia muttered, casting up her eyes.

Tobias crouched beside her and said, softly, "What's eating you? Why are you picking on Paris?"

"I'm worried, too," she snarled. "I may not have been born into this family, but it's the only one I've ever really known."

He felt a twinge of pity. "Paris thinks the world of you. You know the old man always had a soft spot for her. People are like that. They shouldn't, but they do have favorites. Don't punish her for it now. She's been good to you."

Cynthia jerked her foot sharply. "I'm uptight," she said. "Like the rest of you. Believe it or not, I care what happens to Pops. *He's* been good to me, too."

Tobias raised a hand and almost patted her thigh. He thought better of it and got to his feet. "Sure. Okay. So let's all cool it, shall we?"

Nigel continued to work his toothpick under snowy nailtips. His creamy silk shirt and cinnamon-colored trousers bespoke the casual elegance to which he was accustomed. Tobias barely stopped himself from snatching the toothpick.

"You there, Paris?" Pops asked abruptly.

"Here," she said. Her capable fingers made her hair even more of a mess.

"I'm not eating, y'know. Nothing to eat here anymore."

She turned to look from Cynthia to Tobias. For once he couldn't think of anything to say.

Paris turned back to the microphone and said, "Just tell me what you want me to do."

"Is it true Cynthia's with you? And those good-for-nothing Quinn brothers?"

She rested her head in her hands. "Tobias arranged for this radio van, Pops. Nigel and Cynthia are here."

"Then you can all hear this at the same time. No one's going to build a thing on any land I can see from my home. Is that clear?"

Paris shot out a hand to silence the beginning of Tobias's retort. "You sold the land all around you, Pops."

"A park. That's what I understood. Tax write-off."

"Convenient memory," Tobias muttered.

Cynthia leaned forward. "It's me, Pops. Cynthia. I'm worried about you."

"Just like your mother," Pops said. "No brain. You married one of them."

"We're divorced," Cynthia said, grinning up at Tobias. "I came to my senses."

Paris whipped around in her in her chair. What Tobias saw in her eyes was hurt—and disgust. He liked that. He liked that a lot.

"Paris," Pops said. "One of my radio buddies has been reading the papers to me."

It was Tobias's turn to mutter, *"Shit."*

"It's all lies, isn't it?" Pops asked. "He hasn't been trying to use you, has he?"

"I've already told you I think you should talk things through with Tobias," Paris said. "When Emma put me through to you from Seattle, remember?"

"Papers say he's been trying to buy you off. Trying to help

you with some sort of business difficulty in return for persuadin'
me to give up."

"The papers say a lot of things that aren't true."

A hollow cough crackled through the receiver. Paris's hand
went to her own throat. "Pops? You all right?"

"Getting weaker," he said and coughed again.

"Talk to Tobias," Paris said. "He's right here and he wants
to work things out."

A muffled curse hissed into the van. "If I hear that vandal's
voice I'm out. And you won't hear from me again."

Tobias crossed his arms. The radio operator met his eyes and
shrugged.

"This is what I want," Pops said. "I want *you* to do this for
me, Paris. Get Quinn to write me out a paper. A legal paper.
His lawyer and one you get for me will see to it. Understand?"

Rubbing her palms on her skirt, she sat back in the chair.
"No," she said. "No, I don't understand. If there's something
you want done between lawyers, why don't you get *your* lawyer
to deal with it."

"Don't have a lawyer anymore. Don't believe in them. Why
pay someone else to do what you can do yourself?"

"But you want me to hire a lawyer for you now?"

"Just for this. I want a paper that says there'll be no building
in my lifetime."

"You old buzzard!" Tobias shouted, ignoring Paris's beseech-
ing gesture. "What the . . . You think you've played this perfectly, don't you? Sell me a fortune in land. Take the money,
then threaten to starve yourself to death if I *use* what I bought."

"You *owe* me," Pops roared. "You owe me for what Sam did
to me."

From the corner of his eye, Tobias saw Nigel slap his knees
in disgust.

"Someone's coming," the radio operator said. "In a pickup."

Tobias ignored him.

"God no," Cynthia said on a sigh. "That's all I need."

"What d'you say?" Pop asked.

Expecting the press—blessedly absent so far—Tobias peered

toward an approaching battered red and white pickup with a homemade wooden canopy on its bed.

The vehicle bumped to a stop beside the van.

Bulk is Best, read a hand-lettered sign on the side of the cab.

"Bulk is best," Cynthia said mutinously. "Sounds like an ad for a fucking laxative."

"Cynthia!" Paris said, scrambling from the chair to throw open the door. "What's got into you? It's Dad!"

Tobias smiled at the relieved, almost little-girl pleasure in Paris's grin. She leaped to the ground and went to meet the tall, slightly-built man who had passed on thick dark hair and blue eyes to his only biological child.

"If Beryl's with him, I'm going to puke," Cynthia said, yanking her skirt over the tops of her stockings. "What the hell made them show up now?"

"I think I'll take a walk," the radio operator said and did just that, heading in the direction of the site boss's empty trailer.

"I think it might be a good idea for you to tone it down, love," Nigel said to Cynthia. His face expressionless, he stabbed the toothpick into the back of her hand, waited for her shocked, "Ouch!" and fixed her with a hard stare.

Before Tobias had to stop further bloodshed, Paris led Maurice Delight into the van. She put a finger to her lips and returned to her seat before the radio. "Sorry, Pops," she said. "I've got someone here who wants to speak to you."

"I don't know what's going on there," Pops said. "I'm getting weaker by the minute and you keep me hanging around while you argue. I'm not talking to anyone but you. And I've told you what I want. A legal paper signed by Quinn. No building on my land in my lifetime."

"It's not your—"

"Any land that *was* my land."

"That's outrageous," Paris said.

"What Sam did to me was outrageous," Pops said. "I've waited a lot of years to pay him back. Time's come. Either young Quinn does what I ask or I'll make sure he goes out of business."

If that wasn't an admission of some sort of conspiracy to ruin him, Tobias didn't know what would be.

Gently but firmly, Maurice Delight put his daughter aside and leaned to talk to his father. "This is me, Dad. Maurice."

Tobias got a mental image of Pops Delight's sagging jaw. The man didn't respond.

"I do keep an ear open to what's going on with you," Maurice said. His was an older version of his daughter's clever, distinctive face. "Word of this latest nonsense reached me yesterday. I've driven all night."

"*Nonsense?*" Pops sounded on the verge of apoplexy. "Damn me, but I'm not listening to my own son insult me in front of an audience."

"Sounds good to me," Maurice said. "You're behaving like an old fool. If you don't want the world to know what's really behind this, you and I had better talk. Save that ornery pride of yours, Dad. I'm on my way over. Let down the bridge. We'll have this out without the audience."

He didn't wait to hear his father's reply. With a pat on Paris's shoulder and a kind smile in Cynthia's direction, he left the van and plodded determinedly toward Pops's acre.

"Pops?" Paris said.

They all heard the line go dead.

Maurice Delight's back was straight inside his rough, tan cotton shirt. A woven leather belt settled his worn work jeans on lean hips. The scuffed brown boots he wore had seen a few summers and winters in Idaho dust and mud.

"You're like him," Tobias said to Paris. "Not just to look at. Why didn't I notice that before?"

Gnawing her bottom lip, Paris watched her father find a path through bails of barbed-wire and cross onto Pops's property.

"I've just realized something," Tobias said. "You're Pops's favorite because you're Maurice's double."

Behind her glasses, her eyes showed no surprise at the comment. "He misses Dad," she said quietly. "He can accept in me what he couldn't accept in a son. I'm not really ambitious—not in the usual way—and I don't care about . . . *things.* I guess that's what it is. Dad's the same."

Cynthia's stocking tops came back into view and the sandaled toe resumed its impatient wiggling. "Pops can't stand Maurice because he's a loser. Where's Beryl?"

"Your mother's running the co-op," Paris said sharply. "Dad said they hope you and I will get over to visit soon."

"Over my dead body," Cynthia retorted.

"You don't even sound like yourself," Paris said. "Are you angry about something?"

"Stow it," Nigel ordered. "What does Maurice think he's going to do? Swim the moat and scale the walls."

Cynthia giggled. "Maybe he can get in through the dog door."

"Nope," Tobias said, lowering himself to sit on the top step in front of the open van door. "Take a look at that, sports fans."

The drawbridge, a steel grill monstrosity, jerked out from the castle wall and descended, a few shaking inches at a time, until it slapped into place. A cloud of dust rose.

Maurice Delight marched on, crossed the drawbridge and disappeared inside the pocked concrete mound.

And the drawbridge rose again.

An hour passed before Paris heard another sound from the radio. "Paris," her father said. "Come on over and bring Tobias with you."

Cynthia got to her feet instantly. "About time," she said. "My butt's ready to fall off from sitting here."

"Just Paris and Tobias," Dad said. "Stay by the radio, Cynthia. You, too, Nigel. I'll get back to you as soon as I can."

"Cynthia," Paris said, holding out her arms. "Pops is being . . . He's being Pops. Melodramatic. Be patient."

Avoiding Paris's proffered embrace, Cynthia turned her back. Paris hesitated, then left the van and walked beside Tobias toward the castle. "I wish Pops wouldn't treat Cynthia as if she was second best," she said, while she also wished she wore something other than insubstantial flat sandals that trapped rocks and dry dirt. "It really does hurt her."

"She wasn't always treated second best," Tobias said. "When

you were growing up, Pops and Emma bent over backward to be fair. Cynthia forced them away from her. And I don't mean by marrying me."

She couldn't deny that Cynthia had been in enough scrapes, both at home and in New York, to try any parent's or grandparent's patience. "It's time to let all that go."

"You're forgiving. That's nice." He didn't sound as if he thought it was nice at all. "Here comes our bridge. I never thought I'd see the inside of this place again. Maybe I should have brought my gun."

"Tobias!" She stopped in her tracks and waited for him to face her. "Who's being melodramatic now?"

His grin was pure, delighted wickedness.

"This is no time for jokes," she told him severely.

He didn't argue and they crossed over the ringing metal bridge that took them to an open door so low both Tobias and Paris had to duck to enter. Inside was the rounded cavern of an entrance hall plastered an eggplant color.

Tobias groaned. Paris found his hand and squeezed. Tobias shared the commonly held opinion of Pops's masterpiece: an unforgivable eyesore. Paris enjoyed the childlike exuberance of her grandfather's toy.

Hanging onto Tobias's hand, Paris left the foyer by a door leading into a large funnel that opened to the sky. Pops's idea of an atrium contained a bed of white rock relieved by a story-high, red and green flashing neon cactus in a huge green plastic pot.

"Gruesome," Tobias muttered.

"Unique," Paris countered and stopped, too amazed to bring her teeth together again.

Tobias threaded his fingers through hers and said, "Emma? What a surprise. Nice surprise, I should say."

"Emma," Paris echoed. "You're on a cruise. On the inland passage."

Emma, an anxious pucker between her brows, hurried forward. "I fibbed. I didn't go."

"Never would have noticed," Tobias commented.

"I *had* to come and look after him," Emma said. "And he wouldn't let me if I told anyone I was here."

Paris started forward. "He's in really bad shape, isn't he? Should we get him to a hospital?"

"Perhaps you ought to talk to him," Emma said. "He's ready now. Maurice always had a way with his father—whenever Edward would *let* him speak his mind."

Breaking into a run, Paris tried to pull free of Tobias. He held on and loped beside her.

"Use the kitchen door," Emma called. "I'm coming."

"I'm never going to forgive myself for not taking him seriously," Paris said, out of breath from anxiety rather than running. "He's too old for so much excitement—and for starving himself."

The kitchen was the center of activity in the castle. Pops, who had made up for Emma's dislike of cooking, could invariably be found there.

A zigzagging passageway led from the atrium to a swinging half-door into the kitchen.

Maurice sat on a clear plastic chair at a circular, pink Formica table. Facing him, but with his back to Paris and Tobias, was Pops.

Pots and pans and a vast array of cooking implements crowded counters and shelves. Pops's radio equipment nestled on a desk high surface flanked by clear canisters of assorted dried foodstuffs.

"Pops!" Paris cried, rushing to his side and looping her arms around his neck. "We're all so worried about you. We can work something out and get you back on your feet."

Another pair of eyes as blue as Paris's stared serenely up at her. "Don't get in a lather," he said. "Sit down. And have him sit down, too." He jabbed the fork he held in Tobias's direction.

Paris planted a kiss on her grandfather's cheek and remained standing. Tobias, on the other hand, strolled around the perimeter of the room poking at cardboard boxes with the toe of a sneaker.

"Sit down," Pops repeated, spearing a chunk of chicken, a

piece of pastry soaked in gravy and scooping them into his mouth. "I don't like people fidgeting when I'm eating."

"You got him to eat," Paris said to her father. "Oh, thank goodness. You look fine, Pops."

"He looks more than fine," her dad commented.

"Marvelous," Tobias added. "Might want to watch the gut, Pops. Sneaking up on you a bit, isn't it?"

The fork became a pointer once more. "That's enough from you, young Quinn."

"What's all this, then?" Tobias asked, passing Emma as he continued his inspection of the boxes. "Just delivered by helicopter, was it? Canned salmon. Canned fruit. Dried fruit. Cereal. Pasta. Sauce. Canned pâté de foie. Dehydrated chanterelles. And here we have, caviar? Fading away, are we?"

Pops continued eating his chicken pie.

"My father misunderstood a few things," Paris's dad said to Tobias, indicating for Paris to take a chair beside him. "He didn't realize you and your grandfather were two different people."

" 'Course I did," Pops said benignly. "I believe in the Bible. Sins of the father, m'boy. Sometimes the end justifies the means."

Tobias looked blankly at Pops whose thick hair had turned white but had yet to recede. A handsome man, he carried more flesh than Paris's father.

Pops jutted his chin in his son's direction. "*You* know what I'm talking about."

"Dad's been pulling a fast one," Paris's dad remarked, almost offhandedly. "Seems he's ready for a ten-year siege and he's only just warming up to the idea of starting to miss a few meals."

"A smart man lays in supplies against disaster," Pops said defensively. "What would you do? I couldn't have anyone see food being delivered. Emma brought rations in at night, just in case."

"Emma?" Paris turned to her grandmother. "You've been doing this all along? Living in Seattle and playing a game?"

"No," Emma said. "I wasn't coming back, but I got worried about your grandfather. Once I'd decided to make up—at least

temporarily—I owed it to him to help him with what he'd decided to do."

"To lie and try to ruin Tobias?"

"You don't understand," Emma said. She glanced at Tobias.
"Neither of you do. But it's over now."

Pops waved his fork. "Go ahead and tell 'em, Maurice. Might
as well hang all the dirty family washing out. Tell 'em about
your mother and Sam Quinn."

"Oh, Edward," Emma murmured. "Why—"

"This is so ridiculous," Maurice Delight said. "Get over here,
Tobias." When Tobias had come, obviously reluctant, to sit op-
posite Paris, Maurice continued. "Now, Mom. It's your story.
You tell it."

"Only if this mealy-mouthed reprobate promises to let bygones be bygones." Emma, as smart as ever in a beige silk suit,
planted her feet apart. "Promise, Edward. If you do, I'll stay in
this wretched prison of yours—as long as we can keep the
bridge down."

For the first time, Pops's expression changed. He turned a
suddenly younger face toward his wife. "You'll stay?"

"I'll stay. Yes. I love you, you old idiot."

Paris's heart turned. As she looked at her grandfather she
felt the start of tears.

He swallowed visibly and said, "Well, then. I'm glad you've
come to your senses."

Emma's toe tapped the white concrete floor. "Tobias, your
grandfather and I had a bit of a fling once."

After the slightest pause Tobias said, "When?" and stared at
Paris.

A horrible idea unfurled. "When?" Paris demanded.

Emma yanked on the bottom of her suit jacket. "Before I was
married to your grandfather, of course."

"We were engaged," Pops said, his heavy brows drawing
down.

"Promised," Emma countered. "You hadn't given me a ring.
And you hadn't spoken to my father."

"Promised should have been good enough. It wouldn't have

been so bad if you'd told me yourself. But you never said a word. I had to hear it from Sam Quinn."

"Why would my grandfather tell you that?" Tobias said.

"To rub my nose in it," Pops said. "He and your grandmother had your father nine months to the day after they were married. Maybe not quite nine months, if you ask me."

"Edward," Emma warned.

Paris and Tobias shared a relieved glance. At least they weren't related!

"Everyone wants the truth," Pops said expansively. "They're going to get it. Emma and I took a bit longer to have Maurice, here. Sam was so full of himself he said—"

"He'd had too much to drink," Emma interrupted.

Pops pushed his empty plate aside. "No excuse for trying to cast doubt on a friend's manhood. Sam said my Emma wouldn't have taken so long to get pregnant if she'd stayed with him instead of marrying me."

"He said it thirty-five years after you two had been married," Maurice said, every word thinned by exasperation. "And you let it separate you from the best friend you ever had."

"They were both responsible," Tobias said, surprising Paris. "My grandfather never learned to let go of a fight, either."

"And now he's dead," Maurice said. "No kissing and making up. Right, Dad?"

Pops folded his arms over his considerable paunch.

"Whose idea was this vendetta?" Tobias asked, so evenly Paris didn't immediately realize what he'd said.

"What's that, boy?" Pops said.

"You heard me. Who put the bee in your ear to pick a fight with me?"

Paris prepared for a salvo from Pops, who prided himself on following no man.

The salvo never came. Pops belched mightily. He hauled himself to his feet and crossed the kitchen. "Maurice," he said. "Get over here and give me a hand."

Pops pulled a deep bottom drawer all the way out and waited for Maurice to help him lift and set it on the table. Tobias barely snatched Pops's empty plate away in time.

With all the flourish of a magician producing a rabbit, Pops whipped away a green garbage sack that had been tucked over the contents of the drawer. "See that?" he asked, triumphantly pointing. He looked to Tobias. "See that, boy?"

They all saw what the drawer contained.

"Don't believe in lawyers," Pops said. "Don't believe in banks anymore, either. That's what you paid to rent my land, young Quinn. Ever see that many thousand-dollar bills in one place?"

Tobias shook his head slowly. "Rent?"

"Foolishness," Emma said. She picked up a kettle and filled it. "I think we all need a cup of tea."

"I don't believe you came up with the idea of making my life hell all on your own," Tobias said. "Someone got to you and said it would be a good idea."

"You saying I need someone else to think for me?" Pops asked sharply.

"I'm saying I don't think you're the type of man who leaks lies to the press. Oh, you tell lies easily enough. We've seen that today. But someone else has been working on the outside while you've been holed up in here."

For an instant Paris thought Pops would snap back an answer. She saw him change his mind and pick up a bundle of thousand-dollar bills instead.

"My men didn't put that barbed wire out there, Pops. You know it and I know it."

"I don't know any such thing," Pops thundered, his face turning florid. He was a tall man and the extra weight he carried made his size impressive. "You suggesting I put it there?"

Rather than shout back, Tobias relaxed in his chair. "Nope. I'm suggesting someone put it there for you—to make me look bad. Your radio buddy must have read it to you out of the local rags. Poor old recluse taunted with bails of barbed wire. Sound familiar."

A pugnacious scowl brought Pops's brows and nose closer together. "Damn foolishness," he said. "Over now. Here you go, son." He shoved the money he held into Maurice's hands. "Never gave you a thing because I never thought you'd make anything of it. You're a decent man. That'll help you and that silly wife of yours get ahead faster."

Maurice took more than a moment to react. When he did, he tried to push the money back at his father. "Beryl's a good woman," he said, his mouth a tight line. "Good values. We share the same values. We don't expect anything for nothing."

Pops promptly shoved the wad into Maurice's hands again. "You're not getting it for nothing. It's part of what's yours by right. Now, I don't want to hear anymore about it."

The sound Paris heard was Emma sniffing. Holding a handkerchief to her nose, Emma Delight smiled through a film of tears and said, "Take it, Maurice. Your Dad and I mean it."

Pops riffled through notes in the drawer as if they were index cards and he had no particular reference in mind. "Sick of this place," he grumbled. "Been here too long. About time I sold it."

"What?" Tobias laughed aloud. "You impossible old devil! All the grief you've given me and now you want to clear out?"

"Where do you fancy going, Emma?" Pops said as if Tobias had never spoken. "Still want to do that Alaska trip?"

Emma was too tearful to do more than nod.

His chest expanding with his air of satisfaction, Pops took another bundle of money from the drawer. "Alaska first. Then I fancy going around the world."

Tobias rested his elbows on the table. "You're not going to tell me, are you?"

"No," Pops said shortly. "Nothing to tell. You and Paris got something going?"

Paris felt Emma and her father look at her. She studied her hands in her lap.

"Well?" Pops said loudly. "Simple enough question, young Quinn. What are your intentions toward my granddaughter? Think we ought to know, don't you, Maurice?"

"I think Paris is old enough to make her own decisions," Maurice said, but there was nothing neutral about his tone.

"Paris?" Tobias said and when she raised her eyes to his he added, "Do we have *something going*?"

Blood rushed to her face with blistering force.

He grinned and slid a hand across the table toward her.

Hesitantly Paris reached out to touch the tips of his fingers with her own.

"Damned peculiar," Pops commented gruffly. "Young people today are damned peculiar."

"Do we, Paris?"

She remembered to take a breath. "My intentions are honorable," she told him, ducking her head.

"Damned peculiar," Pops muttered.

"Bluebirds and pumpkins?" Tobias suggested. He wasn't smiling anymore.

Paris's heart seemed to stop. "I don't know. Maybe turkeys?"

"That long?" Tobias said and his disappointment showed.

"We'll see."

Pops threw down his wad of bills and went to put an arm around his wife. "Strange way of sparking if you ask me. I reckon they're saying there's something between 'em though, Emma."

Maurice put a work-worn hand on top of Paris's. "Whatever you decide will be fine with Beryl and me. We want what's best for you." He glanced at Tobias. "Do it right this time."

"You can have this place as a wedding present," Pops said, bringing a fist down on a pink countertop. "There. I can't do more than that, can I?"

Paris didn't dare meet Tobias's eyes but she heard his sucked-in breath.

"Alaska first, Emma. Then the world. Better see it while I'm still young enough to enjoy it."

Twenty-eight

"So," Nigel said, leaning against the passenger door in the Jeep and watching Tobias while he drove. "It's just the four of us now. Cynthia and I are dying to know what went on with Pops."

They'd ridden in the radio van as far as Everett—north of Seattle—where Tobias had left his own vehicle. He wanted Paris beside him. And he didn't want Cynthia breathing the same air with them. But the arrangement was the best they could manage until he could drop Nigel and Cynthia off.

"Come on," Nigel prodded. "The two of you have hardly said a word since you came out. Is the old man at death's door or what?"

"Pops will be fine," Paris said.

"Where can I take you two?" Tobias asked.

"My place," Cynthia said promptly. "Paris and I need to talk."

"I meant you and Nigel." He moved into the fast lane. "Your place it is. Paris and I have plans."

The atmosphere of venom that followed his statement brought him a great deal more satisfaction than it should have and certainly a great deal more than would make Cynthia happy.

"You take Cynthia home, if you don't mind," Nigel said, evenly enough. "I'm going back to the office to finish up some work. This little jaunt has put me behind."

For the second time in only a few hours, Tobias warmed toward his half-brother.

There was no way to tell Paris what he was thinking, but Tobias deliberately took Nigel to the Stewart Street offices before doubling back toward Cynthia's apartment. Last night, Paris had brought up the question of the copied necklace Vivian had worn to Astor Burken's benefit party. Almost in the same breath she'd mentioned, not quite offhandedly enough, that there were rumors he knew Vivian more than casually.

When Tobias had asked, bluntly, if Cynthia had suggested he had something to do with Vivian wearing the necklace, Paris's head had made a dip and he'd abandoned the subject—for the moment.

The best way to explode any efforts Cynthia might make to sabotage what he and Paris could have together was to force a confrontation in Paris's presence.

When he announced his intention to "see Cynthia safely into her apartment," Paris smiled with pleasure. Cynthia made a fist against her middle and went ahead of them into the building.

"You don't need to come with me," she said at the elevator door.

"We *want* to," Paris said.

"We want to," Tobias echoed. "You and I have been enemies for too long, Cynthia. Why not bury the hatchet?"

Her nervousness showed in the nibble of sharp little teeth along her bottom lip as the elevator swept them upward.

Outside her door lay a long florist's box. Cooing, Cynthia swept it up and peeked at yellow roses through a cellophane insert as she let them into the home she'd chosen after the divorce.

Tobias had never been there before. He never intended to go there again.

The roses buoyed Cynthia's confidence. "Come and help me

put these in water." Her mouth curved smugly. "We could all use a drink. You'll do the honors, won't you, Toby?" Carrying the box in the crook of her arm as if it were a baby, she trotted into her gleamingly unused kitchen.

"There's wine in the refrigerator," she said. "Reach that crystal vase for me first, would you, darling?"

His toes curled inside his sneakers. If she could hurt him, she would. And if she could hurt him by suggesting to Paris that she could still pull him around by the collar, she'd enjoy the experience doubly.

Paris retrieved the tall, heavy crystal vase Cynthia had indicated and filled it with water.

Tobias made no move to find wine. "We wanted to talk to you about the neckpiece Vivian wore to Astor's party." He hitched himself to sit on the low counter beneath the wall phone. "Paris got some sort of impression my name may have been linked with Vivian's at some time. Would you know anything about that?"

"Whatever gave you that idea?" Pushing back her hair, Cynthia avoided looking at either of them. She lifted the lid off the flower box and set it on the black marble surface beside the sink. From the top of a bank of steel-fronted drawers she produced shears and began trimming the ends of rose stems.

"Does that mean you've never heard a rumor about me and Vivian?"

"Never." She snipped, and dropped a bloom into water.

Tobias noted she showed no interest in the envelope accompanying her considerable tribute. "Aren't you going to open the card?"

"Oh." She caught her tongue coquettishly between her teeth. "I know who they're from." Her smile at him was conspiratorial.

He hadn't thought his heart could grow colder toward this woman. He'd been wrong. "Well, why not share your secret with us. Paris and I want to know every happy detail of your love life, don't we, Paris?"

Dear Blue—beautifully, adorably bedraggled, Blue—held her

troubled heart in her shadowy eyes. She didn't deserve this nonsense, especially when she'd been through so much.

"Never mind," Tobias said briskly. "The neckpiece. Something Paris said made me think you might have an idea how Vivian came to be wearing it."

"*Paris!*" Cynthia rounded on her. "You didn't tell him?"

"No." Paris's eyes were round now and she took a backward step. "At least, I suppose he may have gotten some idea you and I had discussed it. Did you talk to Vivian again?"

"You promised." Cynthia pouted.

Paris breathed in impatiently. "*Did* you? You asked me not to do anything until you had."

"Oh, go ahead and say anything in front of him, why don't you?"

Tobias met Paris's eyes. She raised her jaw and said, "Yes, I will do that. Have you talked to Vivian?"

In a flurry of furious activity, Cynthia haphazardly lopped off rose stems and jammed them into the vase. "You were never someone I could trust to be on my side," she muttered. "Always waiting around for a chance to make me look bad."

"Cynthia?"

"I've been too busy!" She glared at Paris. "I've got my own life to live. While you've been busy fucking my ex-husband, I've been trying to write a book."

Paris blanched and put a hand over her mouth.

"You are a—" Tobias pushed past Cynthia and put an arm around Paris. "Paris and I are going to be married. Because she seems determined to keep up a relationship with you, I'll do my best not to rip your heart out right here. But get in my way again and I may forget to restrain myself."

This time it was Cynthia's face that turned white. An icy rim formed around her lips. She looked unseeingly at their faces, then at the empty rose box, empty but for a long, narrow padded envelope with her name typed on a label.

When she picked up the envelope, it shook. "You can't," she muttered. "You're not going to do this to me." She tore at the heavy tape that closed the envelope and sank a hand inside.

"Please," Paris said. "Can't we be kind to each other in this?"

Cynthia's dry eyes glittered with rage. "Liar," she said. "Cheat. Miss Purity on the outside while you're filth on the inside."

Tobias took a step toward her. Paris's restraining pressure stopped him.

"What is it, Cynthia?" Paris asked.

He frowned at her, then looked to Cynthia. Expressions ran over her face in dissolving waves. Her eyes lost focus. Her mouth slackened. Taught skin over cheekbones and jaw turned putty soft before his gaze.

Slowly, she withdrew her hand from the envelope.

Paris screamed.

"Shit," Tobias muttered. He moved fast, grabbing Cynthia's wrist and the envelope and swinging both over the deep steel sink.

The stench had been held in by a thin plastic bag that Cynthia's long nails had punctured. Old, dark blood and a tangled mass of animal organs slithered onto shining steel. More brown blood oozed down the skirt of Cynthia's pale green tank dress and her ivory silk stockings. Drops pooled on the white tiles like plum gelatin.

"Open the card, Paris."

She snatched up the envelope, tore it open and read: "Enemies must be chosen more carefully than friends." Holding the card by the corner, she stared vacantly at him. "That's all. What does that mean?"

"It's a death threat!" Cynthia shrieked, trembling uncontrollably. "Voodoo. And you thought I should try to talk to that woman?"

Tobias turned on the faucet and held her slimy hands under the stream. "What woman?" he asked, layering satin into the question.

"Vivian! Who else is into black magic?"

"I don't know anyone who is. And why would she want to threaten you?" He knew she'd been frightened beyond caution.

"She's jealous. She knows Bill wants me now. She knows he's going to come to me as soon as he can get rid of her."

"If she doesn't kill you first," he said in a tone he might use if reading from a gravestone. "Paris, I think we should leave Cynthia to gather her wits."

Paris didn't argue. She went with him and stood silently aside while he closed the apartment door behind them.

The next sound they heard was Cynthia's scream. She screamed and screamed.

Paris reached for the doorhandle but Tobias stopped her. "She'll get over it. We both know she screams whenever she throws a tantrum. And tantrums are something she's perfected. I should know. I think we should pay Vivian a visit."

Bill was out of town on business, a maid had informed them, but Ms. Estes was beside the pool.

Only a mile from the house Nigel now called home, Bill Bowie's multilevel house also faced Lake Washington. The rooms were furnished with the beautiful antiques Vivian had brought with her from New Orleans. There was an aged patina to the interior that complemented ivy-covered brick on the outside.

In an elegant room opening onto an enclosed courtyard, bowls of lush, fully opened white roses cast glistening reflections on a grand piano, a massive, claw-footed mahogany table, and into a soaring gilt-framed mirror above a delicately plastered fireplace.

The roses scented the air that slipped in from a humid late afternoon.

As she walked over priceless silk rugs and gleaming wooden floors, Paris was conscious of the dust on her sandaled feet.

The maid led them to the courtyard and withdrew.

Tobias held Paris's hand and stepped outside.

A circular pool dominated a courtyard paved with irregular green slate. Urns spilling vines and riotous flowers topped a brick wall. Beyond the wall, sun sparkled on Lake Washington.

Paris felt like the little match girl who'd accidentally wandered out of the snow and *through* the window on Christmas Eve.

Vivian, long, sleekly voluptuous and honey-tan, stretched out in a chaise beside the pool. A hot pink swimsuit fitted her without a wrinkle. Her toenails and fingernails were the same shade. So were her lips. She raised her nose from the book she'd been reading, pushed her sunglasses up, and waved.

"Tobias!" She dropped the book and clamped a wide-brimmed straw hat more securely on her head. "Come here at once. Who *is* that you've got with you?"

Paris muttered, "The ugly duckling."

Tobias chuckled and placed a firm hand at her waist. "My fiancée," he said. "Paris Delight. From the hospital? You've met a few times, Vivian, love."

"Ooh!" Vivian flowed to her feet. "Ooh, how lovely, darlings. Ooh, a wedding! Oh, I can't stand it that Bill's not here. Marie!" She pattered toward the door where she met the maid who'd showed them in. "Champagne, please, Marie. And three glasses. Hurry."

With the maid dispatched, she administered sound hugs and kisses to both Tobias and Paris. "I may not believe in marriage personally, but I *love* the *idea*. It's so romantic."

Paris felt entirely eclipsed by this shimmering creature.

"Thank you," Tobias said. "We're glad you approve. Did you send a bag of chicken innards to Cynthia?"

Vivian paused with her arms outstretched. "Ah." She let her hands fall to her sides and sauntered back to the chaise. "Pull up chairs, loves. Be comfortable."

"Did you?"

"Why would you think such a nasty thing of a nice girl like me?"

Paris saw Tobias control a grin. "Because you have a certain reputation and I don't know anyone else in these parts with a similar reputation."

"Hm." Vivian examined her nails. "Which either means I did it or that someone else did it expecting me to take the rap."

"Fair assessment."

"And," Vivian said, looking at them over the tops of her glasses, "As long as Cynthia learns a lesson from whoever *did* do the dirty deed, it really doesn't matter who it was, does it?

I wouldn't be surprised if she chose the wrong enemy this time, would you?"

Paris sat on the chair Tobias swung forward.

"I wouldn't be surprised," he said. "But it might be nice to be sure the only intention was to frighten—"

"The shit out of her?" Vivian finished for him. "Don't worry that handsome head of yours. You and Paris have better things to think about now. Leave Cynthia alone and she'll get the message. I really think she may become a much better girl after this."

In other words, by not denying the fact, Vivian admitted sending Cynthia the sickening bouquet. While she felt relieved, Paris was aware that this was not a woman she'd care to count as an enemy.

The champagne arrived in a silver bucket. Vivian poured it into shallow glasses herself. "No flutes in this house," she remarked. "Silly modern ideas. One needs surface to let the bubbles expand."

Paris took her word for it and smiled politely at a simple toast for love, health, and happiness. She drank and recognized that this was no generic brut from the grocery store.

"There was something else Paris and I needed to discuss with you," Tobias said. "The neckpiece you wore to Astor's."

"Good heavens, yes." Vivian sat up straight in the chaise. "Do you know, I didn't have a clue you'd made it, Paris. What marvelous work you do."

This was the part they should have rehearsed. Paris caught Tobias's faint shake of the head. "We wondered where you bought it," he said. "Paris was surprised to see it that night."

Vivian took off her glasses. "This is so strange. I didn't buy it."

Paris set down her champagne glass. "That's what Cynthia said. She spoke to you about it, I understand."

Vivian's green eyes turned blank. "Briefly. We won't be speaking about anything again." She handed Paris's glass back to her and smiled. "I like you. I have a feeling you're going to be exactly what Tobias needs."

"Thanks," Tobias said. "I hate to push on this, but where did the neckpiece come from?"

"That's just it." Vivian hunched her shoulders and spread her hands. "I thought Bill had sent it because he knew I was wearing the gold dress that night. He hadn't. Neither of us knows *who* sent it to me."

She refused to be swayed an inch. But he would try again. Tobias settled his hands loosely around Paris's neck and kissed her until she gasped for breath.

"Change your mind," he begged.

"I can't." She'd unlocked the front door of her apartment building. "Aldonza has probably already divorced me. And I need to organize myself and do some thinking."

"Thinking?" He accomplished a mighty frown. "Thinking about what? Changing your mind and not marrying me?"

"We have a great deal to discuss about that yet," she said, but she smiled. "One of the first things to be dealt with is the dividing line."

He ducked to peer closely into her eyes. "Dividing line?"

"Between your independence and mine."

"I don't want any independence."

She laughed, tilted up her chin and laughed.

"Well," he said, feigning woundedness. "I don't. I'm surprised you do."

"Only in certain areas. Like in the bathroom from time to time—and right now when I've got to get organized."

"I'll give you the bathroom—from time to time." He was suddenly serious. "I don't want to leave you here tonight, Paris. It doesn't feel safe to me."

"Well, it is. *I* feel safe. I grant you that it seems someone tried to do you harm."

"Seems?"

"They did try. But everything's in the open now. We're going to be okay. You're going to be okay. Pops has backed off, so the Skagit project can go ahead. We're even going to own a castle up there!"

He shuddered. "Don't remind me."

"I'm going in, now, Tobias. I'm going to touch bases with Mary and anyone else who's around. When everything's under control I'll call."

"And then I can come and get you?"

"Not tonight."

He let his shoulders slump. "I won't sleep without you."

"Yes, you will."

"You don't intend to walk to the Blue Door tonight?"

"No, you old worrier, I don't."

"Why can't I stay here with you?"

She kissed him, so quickly he had no time to prolong the event. "Because if you do I won't get anything done."

"I'm telling you I won't sleep without you."

Paris pushed the door open and stepped inside. "Go home. I'll call later."

"How much later."

"In time to talk you to sleep."

She closed him out. Tobias backed down the steps and looked up the front of the building. Dusk had begun to draw shadows over stained brick and to cast a secretive gloss over windows.

It wasn't cold, yet a shiver ran through him.

This had been an endless day. He got into the Jeep and turned the key in the ignition.

Paris belonged with him, not here in this place where he felt a terrible, nameless threat.

He couldn't suffocate her. Reluctantly, he eased away from the curb.

Home. A drink. Then he'd wait by the phone.

Twenty-nine

Paris hadn't told Tobias, but she'd needed to deal with being in the apartment alone in the aftermath of Wormwood's death.

His note had been ambiguous in that he told her nothing about what had driven him to betray her. But she couldn't bring herself to believe he'd done so lightly.

For once Aldonza allowed herself to be cuddled. Wrapped around Paris's neck like a smooth, warm collar, she rode along from room to room until Paris returned to the couch with a battered cardboard box in her hands.

From inside, she removed furniture designed for a doll house, furniture Wormwood had not only painted, but made by hand. It had been a gift to her the first Christmas he'd lived in the apartment. *One day you'll have a little girl of your own,* he'd said. *In the meantime, you're still a little girl yourself in some ways. See? The dish ran away with the fiddle.* Paris smiled through tears. *Spoon,* she'd corrected him. *Not on that table,* he'd told her, grinning with pleasure as he'd introduced her to his own form of child's play.

"Idiot," she said softly. "Why didn't you come to me? Why didn't you let me help you?"

She looked at her watch. Eleven. Very soon she'd call Tobias. Maybe she'd have him come and get her after all.

The apartment had smelled musty when she came in. Now, with the window open, the heavy evening perfume of her potted flowers stole in from the fire escape.

What a day. What an incredible day.

Tobias had actually seen what she'd guessed a long time ago. Pops could accept and even admire her refusal to embrace competition with anyone but herself. The same traits in his son had been labeled as weaknesses—until now. At the castle today she'd seen the miracle of an old man recognizing his son's strengths for the first time.

Paris loved her dad. His quiet, unshakable sense of honor never changed. He'd found his little piece of bliss in Idaho— with a simple life in simple surroundings. Paris understood his needs but she preferred to live simply in the city. And she was going to marry a man who wanted her for herself and without any changes.

Marriage.

Michael had become nothing more than a tiny piece of her past. Tobias was her present, and her future.

He made her proud. Only a big, generous man would have left Pops with his dignity intact—*could* have left him with the secrets Tobias must itch to pursue.

Her stomach flipped and she closed her eyes. Superstition was outside her experience yet she was afraid to believe this dream could come true, that Tobias would not change his mind or simply tell her she'd read too much into what he'd said.

But he loved her. He'd told her he did.

Tapping at the window shocked her so much her neck hurt. She sank to the back of the couch and stared.

The window rose all the way and a head was thrust into the room.

Paris's hand flew to her throat and she laughed hysterically. "Darn it, Sam. You scared me out of my wits."

"Doing a spot of watering," he said, holding a can aloft then turning back to set it down by the pots. "Came up from the outside. Didn't know you were home. It's been hot. Wouldn't want your daisies to wilt, would I?"

"You're so good to me."

"You don't do heights. But you want to look at the flowers—and smell the flowers. Whatever Paris wants, Paris gets. *Voilà.*" Anchoring the neck of his suit jacket, he gave a short bow. "Paris's carefree flower patch."

"Sam."

"Samantha, please, darling. I'm between shows."

Hiking up a pleated, black chiffon skirt, he climbed into the room.

"It's dark out there," Paris said. "You could break your neck on those stairs."

Wearing a new brunette wig, he threw himself into her rocking chair and spread black stocking-clad legs. "Got my mountaineer's crampons securely in place," he said, raising one incongruous black running shoe. "Paris, kid, I must be getting old."

She put Wormwood's miniature table back into its box. "Tired?"

"Tired and disappointed."

Paris dislodged Aldonza. "That doesn't sound like you." Neither did he look himself. She leaned forward. "You went on without makeup?"

"Took it off." Sam rocked the chair violently. His voice rose. "Have you ever thought I might hate it? The makeup? The jibes?"

"No." She hadn't. "I thought—"

"You thought. A lot of people think they think. They don't. Neither do you. You know who I really am under the fool's suit. I'm a *man.* But you're like the others. You don't *see* me."

"Oh, *Sam.*" In a rush, she went to him and knelt beside the chair. "Of course I see you as a man. You're a wonderful, strong, incredibly attractive man. Wow—I don't know how to tell you everything. You're so good at what you do. You make people laugh. The gear is flamboyant, but the humor is subtle. You *are* tired. That's what this is about."

As abruptly as he'd begun to rock, he became quite still. His blue eyes regarded her without a flicker. Paris felt a panicky fluttering in her stomach. "Should I get Ginna?"

A nerve twitched beside his mouth. He parted his lips a little and settled a large hand upon both of hers on the arm of the chair. "I don't want Ginna," he said, massaging her fingers with a thumb. "You understand these things. You're two people. Pure and plain on the outside. So different where it doesn't show. Will you help me, Paris?"

A breakdown? Could Sam actually be having an emotional breakdown, or collapse or whatever? "Tell me what to do." He might not want Ginna, but Paris did. Ginna had a magic touch when it came to calming people down.

"I've got to get away for a while." Sam's gaze didn't falter. It's intensity became uncomfortable. "Will you help me do that?"

"Ginna—"

"Not Ginna!"

Paris jumped. His fingers dug into the backs of her hands.

Sam averted his face. "Please. I can't think about Ginna now. It's all so destructive. Do you have anything to drink? Scotch?"

"I . . . No. You know me. All I've got is the condemned wine in the refrigerator."

"Great. I'll take it. I'm sorry, kid. Really sorry to do this to you. It's just that . . . Wormwood . . ." He propped an elbow and covered his eyes. "We argued sometimes. But I can't believe he's dead."

Paris swallowed. She'd shed too many tears in the past two days. "I know." She stood up and rubbed the back of his neck. "I'll get us both some wine. Maybe we should drink a toast to him? Say goodbye? Forgive him? He wasn't a bad man, not deep down."

Sam pulled her hand from his neck. "So good," he said, but his smile unsettled Paris. "Such a good little girl."

"I'll get the wine."

On legs that trembled, she went rapidly into the kitchen. Wine wasn't what she needed. She put on a kettle before opening the refrigerator. The open bottle of fumé blanc had been moved from the back of the door. Pronounced undrinkable by all, Paris kept it for cooking.

She opened the door wide and bent to search through the contents of the shelves. "Fumé blanc, where are you? Come out, come out, wherever you are."

The squish of soft footfalls came from behind her. Tiny hairs rose on the back of her neck but she didn't turn around. She was being silly. It was only Sam. "If I didn't know better," she told him. "I'd think someone stole our priceless vintage."

"People can be so unkind."

"Ah. There it is. All the way at the back." Her fingers closed on the green bottle and she began to straighten.

A blow to the side of her neck crumpled her knees. "Sam!"

"Not to worry, ducky." *Twisting.* Fingers twisting in her hair tore at her scalp. She couldn't turn around. "Trust Sammy to look after you."

"Sam! What—?"

Rustling close to her head. *Plastic bag.* It descended over her face.

Her hands flew out, clawed the air. Wine exploded from the bottle she dropped, rose in a miniplume laced with fractured glass.

Suffocate.

The refrigerator door smashed wide open.

"Stop it!" Her voice roared inside her head. "Stop . . . it!"

Scrabbling, she clawed at the plastic.

The arm that held her, trapped her elbows to her sides.

Light dimmed.

Heat, red heat burst inside her brain and she screamed, *"Sam. Sam."*

Blackness rippled in at the edges of her vision, slid over the heated red.

"Can't . . . breathe. Can't . . ."

Surprise parties had never ranked among Tobias's favorite pastimes. This one was different. For this one he didn't have to pretend to be a good sport.

He hoped Paris wouldn't be upset at having her quiet night at home disturbed for a party designed to cheer her up. Only, the apartment wasn't her home anymore. She belonged with him and after tonight he intended to make damn sure she *stayed* with him.

The building immediately opposite theirs, Sam had told him on the phone. Park a couple of blocks away so Paris wouldn't see the Jeep and be suspicious something was going on.

Enter by the front door that would be unlocked, and go directly to the fourth floor apartment. Mary, who insisted upon playing a big role in the event, would come up with an excuse to get Paris across the street.

Following Sam's directions, Tobias went through the door into the building opposite Paris's. He winced at ear-splitting heavy metal that rang from the ground floor apartment. On the second floor, gold stenciling on glass panels announced, Schmidt, Schmidt and Waverly, Attorneys-at-Law. No lights showed through the glass.

Tobias took the next flight two steps at a time and reached another suite of silent offices.

On the fourth floor he paused, suddenly wishing he had a gift to give her. A ring. He hadn't thought about it until now. She wore almost no jewelry. Thinking of her capable, unadorned hands, he smiled. The lady made beautiful jewelry but she rarely considered how she looked for long enough to wear some herself.

He loved the way she looked. They'd choose the ring together and he'd put it on her in private. Yes, very much in private.

As promised, the fourth-floor apartment door stood open and he walked inside. "Hello?" he said softly. "I've forgotten the password, guys."

"Over there." Sam's voice was hushed. "They're all in the bedroom."

"I hope she doesn't have a heart attack on us," Tobias said. He couldn't see the other man. "Maybe we should turn on the lights and be milling around. She'd like it just as much."

"No way. That'd ruin everything."

Tobias shrugged and crossed the shadowy room. He couldn't make out the shapes of any furniture. "Whose place is this?"

"A friend's," Sam said shortly. "I borrowed it. Hurry, will you?"

"Smells like a tomb."

Sam coughed and muttered something unintelligible.

"Are you sure Mary's going to manage to get her over here?" To Tobias this began to seemed less of a good idea.

"Positive," Sam insisted. "Go on in. You're the last to arrive. I'll stand watch and sound the warning when I hear them coming."

These were Paris's friends. For once he would bury his aversion to loud display and go along.

"Hurry," Sam said. "I think I hear footsteps."

Tobias stepped into the room Sam seemed to indicate and peered through a darkness thicker than the one he'd already left. The sickly smell of mildew increased. "Hi," he whispered, edging forward. "I don't want to step on anyone's toes."

No response.

"It's Tobias."

Creaking sounded, a rocking squeak like rusty hinges.

A flood of white light from a naked overhead bulb blinded him. *"Jeesus,"* he muttered. "Who did that?"

"A better man than you," Sam said behind him. "Move. And *don't* turn around."

A sharp object poked his spine, pushed him farther into the room. Tobias registered a gun at his back an instant before he saw the bed—and the woman on the bed.

He started toward her but the cool steel of the gun barrel smacked against his ear.

"Far enough," Sam said. "We've got a great view from here. Any closer would be greedy."

Spread-eagle, her wrists and ankles lashed to the tubular metal head and foot of the bed, Paris's eyes were open but glassy. A saliva-soaked gag of some green fabric ensured her silence.

Tobias started to turn around.

"Straight ahead, you dumb asshole." The barrel cracked along his cheekbone.

Paris moaned.

"You *son-of-a-bitch*," Tobias said, trembling with fury. "What have you done to her?"

Sam's voice took on a sing-song quality. "I've made her pay. I've made her show her real self." Grinding the gun into Tobias's face, he shoved him across the room, past the end of the bed and along the window wall to the corner at a level with Paris's head. "That's what she really is. Bitch. Teasing bitch."

He had to hold on. He had to think very carefully. The gag had been torn from some part of Paris's skirt or blouse, both of which lay on the floor.

The twine that bound her was thin. Raw, swollen flesh showed purple and shiny where she'd struggled. Her hair, wound into a rope above her head and knotted around a rung in the bedhead, served as another vicious restraint.

She wore a low-cut blue lace bra and panties—and her sandals.

"I watched you from my place," Sam said. "You dropped her off and I waited. Then I left so Mary would see me and think I was going back to the club. It was all perfect. Just the way I planned it. Around the corner. Up the fire escape. I used a plastic bag. Didn't take long. As soon as she was unconscious I carried her down the fire escape."

Her eyes rolled and found him. Tobias tried to put strength and promise in his expression.

"Getting her across the street was the hardest part. I put her arm around my neck and dragged her. I sang and made a fuss, like we were both drunk—like she was paralytic." He laughed and hiccuped. "I wore a dark wig just in case nosey Mary was looking. I never wear a dark wig. It worked. It *worked.*"

"God." Tobias shook his head with what he hoped was amazed admiration. Flattery was the only weapon he could think of. "Brilliant. What a mind you've got."

The gun dealt another blow. "Shut up, smarmy bastard. You can't get around me. I've waited too long. This part wasn't in the agreement, but Cynthia doesn't get to call the shots anymore. She promised me money I never got. She'll have to pay me now or I'll sing."

Tobias stared into Paris's wide open eyes. He didn't trust himself to say anything.

"She hates Paris, too," Sam said. "Just like I do. Always everyone's little darling. The perfect one while Cynthia took the fall for everything just because she was human."

Tobias's stomach jammed somewhere in his throat. "Cynthia said she'd pay you to do this to Paris?"

"You've got it. I'm going to kill her, y'know."

Bile rose in an acid rush. "For Cynthia?" He could not compute this.

"For me. I kidnapped her for Cynthia. Scared her shitless. All Cynthia wanted was to persuade her dear sister to leave their apartment so it could be sold. Worth a small fortune, that place. Cynthia wanted her share. And she wanted Paris to suffer. She wanted to break her. Sly, cheating bitch. Lying bitch."

"Don't—"

Sam kicked the backs of Tobias's knees, sending him to the bare floorboards. "Shut *up*, fucker. I wouldn't have had to wait so long if you hadn't showed up. You gave Cynthia ideas about getting back at you through the slut. Spreading rumors in the papers. That slowed me down. But now I'm getting what I want and I'm giving Cynthia *both* of you for the price of one."

Paris gurgled deep in her throat.

"She's choking." Tobias crouched, desperate to free her, terrified to move at all.

Her body arched up off the bed.

"She wants me," Sam said. "She's offering it to me. Begging me for it."

The gurgles turned to retching croaks. Tears streamed from Paris's reddened eyes. Every jerk must tear her hair at the scalp. A rivulet of blood coursed from her left wrist to stain the bare and already filthy mattress.

If he did nothing, this crazy would kill her anyway. Tobias threw his shoulders backward, connected with Sam's belly. He fell, cursing, flailing to regain his balance. A peeling cane chair broke his fall, then fractured and flew apart.

Sam's head thudded into the water-stained wall and Tobias was upon him. Dressed only in black satin boxer shorts, his tanned torso, arms and legs oiled, Sam bared his teeth and struck back.

Grappling with a slippery arm, Tobias fought to smash the gun loose.

Sam revolved beneath him, slithered like a mud wrestler and bucked his rear into Tobias's gut.

Tobias had the weight advantage but he only stopped Sam for an instant. Screeching his glee, Sam turned over again, this time with a chair leg in his left hand. He rained bruising blows on Tobias's head and shoulders. The surprise bought Sam the time he needed to leap away.

"Move and she's dead," he said, his voice shrill.

Wiping blood from his nose and mouth, Tobias stayed on his knees. "You'll get caught," he said through swelling lips. "They'll lock you up. Know what they do to men who go inside for what you're doing to a woman?"

"Shut the *fuck* up, asshole."

"Yeah. I think you've got some of the words right for what they do. I hear showers with the boys are lots of fun. They may even beat sleeping with the boys."

"Shut up," Sam screamed. He put the bed between Tobias and himself and pointed the gun—complete with silencer—at Paris's face. "Listen to me. I'm in charge. You hear? *I'm* in charge. Not you, rich man. She didn't want me. The spoiled rich girl who played at being friends with the little people didn't want me. She pretended. Hear me? She pretended she was too *pure* to fuck a little man like me. She had her *actor.* I know all about that. I know everything she did with him."

Tobias went to get up.

"Stay, Spot." Sam brandished the chair leg. "Roll over and play dead—until you *are* dead. Stay, or she dies now. Before you. You're both going to die, only it's going to be you first, Quinn, so I can finish my fun."

"Take off the gag," Tobias said. "She's choking, for God's sake."

Sam's pale eyes slid to Paris's face. "I don't want to hear her voice."

"She won't say anything, will you, Blue? Shake your head."

Her eyes found his again. They registered no comprehension. She retched against the fabric jammed between her teeth.

"Shake your head, Paris. Then Sam will take off the gag."

Her gaze cleared. She rolled her face to look at Sam.

"Shake your head!"

Finally, she did as he asked.

"Fuck you." Sam forced the chair leg through the rope of hair and turned. Her body convulsed and he yelled, "Choke on your own puke. I don't give a shit, bitch."

"Kill me," Tobias shouted. "Kill me, but let her go."

Sam waved his gun between the two of them. "So touching. I'd like you to watch what I'm going to do to her, but you'd be a nuisance. So, I'm going to shoot you through the mouth. Then I'll fuck her brains out before I shoot her, too. A sick murder, suicide. That's what they'll call it. And Cynthia will testify to her poor ex-husband's perversion. She divorced him for it. Now his business reversals have made him flip all the way out. So sad."

"Cynthia doesn't have money," Tobias said. His temples pounded, and his right ear. He tasted his own blood. "Not the kind of money you want."

"She knows someone who does." Sam grinned, narrowing his eyes to ice-hot slits. Suddenly he knelt on the bed beside Paris. "She's paying me because someone's paying her."

"Who? Who's paying her for this?"

"Not for this. For something else. But that's not my business, is it? This is my business." With his free hand, he freed his erect penis from his shorts.

Muscles coiled in every inch of Tobias's body. He forced himself to remain still.

Watching Tobias's face, Sam stroked his shaft along the underside of Paris's outstretched left arm and over the exposed top of her breast. "She's ready for me. Know how I know? She's wearing the lilies. She always wears the lilies when she wants it. Lilies like the ones I keep so nice for her."

Her eyes closed.

"Look at me!"

He dragged his penis up her neck and along her jaw.

"Look at me!" His shoulders convulsed, hunched over.

And Tobias launched himself. His fingers closed on the gun and rammed backward. The snap he heard was bone.

Sam bellowed. The chair leg shot away and clattered over the floor. He shrieked and overbalanced from the mattress.

He overbalanced into Conrad as he barreled into the bedroom.

Staring at them both, Tobias leveled the gun at Sam's heart. "Your lives are a luxury," he told them. "Breathe. You do anything else and you die."

Tears streaked Sam's face. He cradled his right wrist against his chest and sobbed out his pain.

"Mary saw you come in here," Conrad said. He opened and closed his mouth repeatedly. "Shit, I *can't* breathe. What's happened here? Paris? My God, what's happened here?"

The gun didn't waver. Awkwardly, Tobias searched for the knot securing the gag.

"Mary said you came in here," Conrad told Tobias. "She said Paris came home, but when I went up there she wasn't in. I could hear the kettle whistling in the kitchen. It just kept on whistling. Mary thought you might know where Paris was and she'd seen you coming—"

"Yeah," Tobias snapped. "I get the picture."

"Let me help with Paris. Please let me help. You're taking too long." Disregarding the gun, Conrad picked up the discarded green clothes and spread them over her. He began working at the twine around one of her ankles. "Sam did this?"

"Yes. No time for that, now. Are you together enough to hold this on him?"

Conrad recoiled. "The gun?"

Tobias nodded impatiently. "I've got a penknife in my back pocket. He may be hurting too much to do anything. But I've got to be sure and I need both of my hands for this."

"Okay." Conrad wiped his palms on his jeans and took the weapon. Holding it with two hands, he pointed it at Sam who continued to sob and rock.

"Blue, Blue," Tobias muttered. "Why did I let you talk me into leaving you? You're almost out of here, my love. Hold on."

He cut away the gag and didn't pause before freeing first her hands, then her feet.

She remained as she was, arms and legs outstretched, her lips parted. Welts scored her face from the corners of her mouth to the angles of her jaws. Both of her wrists, and ankles bled.

"You making it, Conrad?" Tobias said without glancing at the man.

"Just look after Paris."

Cutting her hair was out of the question. Concentrating, separating tangles, he gradually released her final bond.

"I'm afraid to move her," he said. "I'm afraid to do anything. Stay while I get help."

Paris's hand shot to grab his shirt. "No," she whispered.

"Carry her," Conrad said, not taking his eyes off Sam's huddled form. "She's too frightened to be here with this creep. Get her out."

Tobias didn't argue. Shutting out her whimpers when he couldn't avoid contact with her cuts, he gathered her up and went to the door. "I'll take her to Mary and call the police from there."

"Do it," Conrad said. "But make it fast. I'm a painter, not a gunman."

Murmuring nonsense into Paris's hair, Tobias set off through the dark room leading to the landing.

A muffled shot sounded before he reached the top step.

He hesitated.

"Help!" The cry was Conrad's.

There wasn't a choice. Tobias lowered Paris to the floor and ran back the way he'd come.

Conrad, the gun hanging limply from his grip on the tip of the butt, pointed blindly at Sam. "He came at me. He crawled and threw himself at me." Looking at the dangling weapon, he said, "It went off."

With the toe of one shoe, Tobias poked Sam. The man didn't move, didn't speak—or cry. Dropping beside him, Tobias felt his neck for a pulse, then turned him onto his back.

There wouldn't be a pulse.

The bullet had made a clean hole between his staring eyes.

* * *

"You hurry up, young man," Mary said. With one of her bony
arms clamped around Paris's shaking shoulders, she glowered
at Tobias. "Bring those things here. Then, outside with you."

Huddled beneath a comforter, Paris watched him approach
from the bed in Mary's pink chintz-festooned bedroom. The
grim set of his jaw left her in no doubt that he didn't intend
to go anywhere without her.

"I found these." He held up a purple fleece robe Paris had
forgotten she owned, and a pair of backless green slippers.
"This stuff's soft and comfortable."

The sound of sirens froze them all.

"They'll want to talk to us," Paris whispered. "I can't yet."

"No one's talking to you until you've been to the hospital,"
Mary said, pinching her mouth into a wrinkled circle.

"You're right," Tobias said. "Mary, I'd like to take care of
Paris myself, if she'll let me."

"Well, I don't think that's . . ." Mary stopped in midsen-
tence. "Well. After all, it's not as if I wasn't young myself once."

There was a tap on the door and Ginna's face appeared. "Is
something going on?" she asked. "What's happened?"

Paris felt her jumping heart slam into her sternum. Tobias
sat down beside her on the bed and found her hand. He
squeezed tightly.

"You're . . ." Paris cleared her aching throat. "You're back
early."

Ginna approached the bed, her brows drawing together at
the sight of Paris's bruised face. "Something . . . Someone did
that to you?" She brought her shoulders up. "Oh, *no.* I got one
of those awful feelings. You know how I do sometimes?"

"Yes." Paris knew. She also knew Ginna was special, too special for the shock and pain that awaited her.

Mary went to Ginna. "You're a strong girl," she said. "You're
going to accept this and carry on. We'll help you, won't we,
Paris?"

Paris looked into Ginna's beautiful eyes and saw her concern
flare into stark horror. "Ginna, Mary's right. We're here for

you." Her own terror dimmed. The man she loved wasn't dead and she would recover from this night.

"Sam," Ginna said, staring around wildly. "It's Sam, isn't it?"

"He . . ." *He intended to kill Tobias, then rape and kill me.* "Stay here with us," Paris said.

"Stay," Tobias echoed.

"Where is he?"

Mary took both of Ginna's hands in hers. "I'll make some tea. No. A glass of sherry. That's what you need."

"Paris," Ginna said, ignoring Tobias and Mary. "You're hurt. Someone hurt you."

Paris looked away.

"Sam hurt you?" Ginna whispered.

When she got no answer, she said, "Please tell me where he is. Has he gone? Has he left me?"

The tears that squeezed from Paris's closed eyes burned the raw patches on her cheeks.

"Come with me," Mary said. "Young man, you take care of Paris. I'll make sure Ginna's all right."

The bedroom door closed, and the door to the entrance hall, before Paris remembered to breathe again.

She sat, unmoving, aware of Tobias's fingers wound together with hers.

Finally he said, "I've got to take you to an emergency room, Blue. You're going to feel all those bruises later. I want you completely checked over. There's a lump on the back of your head and your ankles and wrists need to be dealt with properly." Mary already washed the cuts but they throbbed with every move.

"Can you put on the robe?" Tobias asked. "Or would it be okay for me to help you?"

Paris raised her eyes to his. "It was so horrible. He already had my ankles tied when I came to. I couldn't do anything."

Tobias raised a hand. He hesitated and said, "Is it all right if I touch you? I want to hold you, sweetheart."

She nodded. Her mouth trembled and she pressed her lips together.

He stroked back her tangled hair. "I've never been that scared in my life."

She laughed shakily. "Not even when you got banged on the head and thrown overboard?"

"Not even then. It happened too fast. I wish Ginna didn't have to go through this."

"She's really something," Paris said. "I think she'll hold on. Nothing was ever handed to Ginna. She's done it all herself."

Tobias eased her head onto his shoulder. "You like her, don't you?"

"Yes." Paris breathed in his warmth and strength. "I've liked a lot of people. How could I be such a rotten judge of character?"

"You're not." He gave a short laugh. "Put it down to a streak of bad luck in the friend department."

She knew he was deliberately avoiding mention of Cynthia. "Maybe my luck'll look up now." Thinking about what her sister had done would have to wait—at least for a little while.

A deep breath expanded Tobias's chest. He let the air escape slowly. "You may want to talk to someone," he said.

Paris lifted her head. "Talk?"

"Mmm." Very carefully, he framed her face. "About what happened. About how it makes you feel."

She smiled—and winced, and rested her fingers on his lips. "Do you really love me?" The blush that rushed to her cheeks made her duck her head.

His strong hand covered hers and he brought it to his chest. "Feel that?" he asked.

Beneath her hand his heart beat strongly. "Still alive," she said, but couldn't laugh.

"Only because you are. Even if that . . . Even if he hadn't shot me, I'd have died if something happened to you over there."

Paris began to cry softly.

"Blue?" Tobias raised her chin. "Sweetheart, I do love you. Don't you know that yet?"

She drew in a breath that seared her raw throat. "I know. I don't need to talk to anyone but you. Hold me, Tobias. Keep on holding me."

Thirty

Facing the bay from Tobias's deck, Conrad sat in the dinghy. Paris and Tobias had waited until the police finished questioning him to explain Cynthia's apparent involvement with Sam. Conrad had taken the news badly, but seemed to understand Paris's reluctance to take action against her own sister.

A short while earlier Conrad had returned from an after-lunch walk with gravel crammed into the pockets of his jeans. This he now tossed, piece-by-piece, into the water.

The pain-killers Paris had been given at the emergency room worked well enough, but her face still ached. Her tongue felt swollen and she couldn't swallow without wincing.

"Waiting isn't going to make this any easier," Tobias said. He'd propped Paris comfortably on the swing while he sat on a folding chair taken from the hot-tub courtyard.

Conrad shied a pebble high into the air and they all watched it fall, splash, and send a delicate series of rings across the smooth, dark green surface below the deck.

"How're you doing, Connie?" Paris asked. He hadn't complained, but she and Tobias were certain the police had been tough on him. "Conrad?"

"Numb, I guess." He pulled up his knees and rested his chin. "What a mess. First Wormwood. Now Sam . . . and Cynthia. Who'd of thought it?"

Tobias scooted his chair closer to Paris and rested a hand, carefully, a few inches above her bandaged right wrist. "Cynthia has to face up to the consequences," he said, as he'd already said several times. "She would do anything to get what she wants—including killing both of us."

An old ketch chugged by under engine. Its rust-colored sails flapped dispiritedly. Paris followed its progress toward the cut and said, "I don't think she intended him to go as far as he did. He as good as admitted she didn't."

"The police are going to dig some more and they'll turn her up, Blue. If we can get her to go in on her own it'll be easier on her."

"Poor Cynthia," Conrad mumbled. "Poor, beautiful, mixed-up Cynthia."

Paris looked gratefully at his back. "That's it. She is mixed-up. And she's my sister. How can you ask me to turn my own sister in to the police?"

"Seems to me a lot of people are mixed-up, or *messed*-up because of her. Your buddy, Lips, told me Ginna's convinced she should have been able to do something to stop what happened. She deserves to know Sam had help coming up with his scheme."

"Ginna has to take responsibility for her taste in bed-partners," Conrad said. "And she will. Ginna isn't in this equation. I'm going to keep an eye on her. I'll make sure she doesn't feel alone."

Tobias smoothed the hair at Paris's temples. He'd refused to leave her side since Sam had been shot. "I want to put this behind us as badly as you do. What Cynthia did won't go away. *We* have to find a closure for ourselves and the only way we're going to do that is by confronting her and forcing her to confront herself."

"She'd go to jail," Paris said.

"If she really didn't intend for anyone to die, things won't go too badly for her."

A shower of little rocks hit the bay like shrapnel. "Can I make a suggestion?" Conrad reversed directions on the central seat of the dinghy and faced them. "Give it twenty-four hours. Call her today if you feel like it, but make arrangements to talk to her tomorrow. You both need to sleep on it first. Hell, I know I'm past making any sane decisions until I *do* sleep."

Paris raised questioning brows at Tobias.

He puffed up his cheeks thoughtfully.

"The decision's yours," Conrad said, climbing out of the dinghy. "I'd better go check on Ginna. Then I'm gonna crash. The cops will be back, you can bet on that."

"They'll be here, too," Tobias said. "What you say makes sense. Except I don't think we should call Cynthia. She's going to hear about Sam. If we give any hint we think she was involved with him she might bolt."

The phone rang and he hopped up to grab a portable and bring it outside. He covered the receiver and said, "Nigel," before listening again. His eyes screwed up as if with pain. "This isn't a good time, brother. I could use you there to cover for me." Resignation flattened his mouth. "I told you why when I called earlier."

On tiptoe, Conrad headed for the dock. He waggled his fingers at Paris and mouthed, "See you later."

She nodded and waved.

"No," Tobias said. "Out of the question. When we're through here, put Gladys on and I'll tell her what you can have. She'll get a check cut and signed for you. Good luck. I'm not holding my breath; but I always wish you the best, Nigel. Give me Gladys. Goodbye." He waited, said, "Hi, Gladys. Go down to Tom and have him cut a check for twenty-five thousand. To Nigel . . . You certainly did tell me so. See you in the morning, Gladys." He used a thumb to break the connection.

Paris let him decide what to say and when to say it. At last he set down the phone. "Why would I be disappointed when history repeats itself? Why would I think Nigel would change? He's cutting out again. New York this time. Everything's happening in New York, he tells me. Someone's asked him to go in on a club that's going to make a fortune. Will I lend him half a million?"

Paris gasped.

"Yeah. No piker, that brother of mine. I said no and he seemed surprised. You and I really lucked out in the sibling department. Will you come to bed with me? I want to be unconscious, but only if you're there with me."

She looked at his bowed head. "To bed? In the middle of the afternoon?"

"Yes."

"What will the neighbors say?"

He raised his eyes to hers. "Probably something about us sleeping through a great opportunity."

All men were bastards.

Cynthia couldn't believe Nigel had managed to slip out and leave her with only one possible escape. *Don't hang around,* his note had said. *The man who works for the people I owe money to (still owe money to, thanks to you) will be back. Today's the day I'm supposed to pay up. I'm out of here. This is all I'm giving you, lady. He already made threats against you so don't be at the house when he shows up. And I do think he'll show there. He finds his own way in. Nigel.*

One chance.

Earlier in the day Conrad had phoned to issue warnings, too: disappear or risk getting pulled into what that fool Sam had done. Her instructions to him had been to kidnap and frighten Paris. When and if she decided that there was no alternative. Nothing more. He'd gotten impatient and he'd gone too far. Now he was dead, but not without spilling his guts to Tobias.

One lousy chance.

She smoothed a wrinkle out of ivory stockings. Mirrored closet doors in what had once been the bedroom she shared with Tobias assured her she'd chosen her outfit well.

Laughing softly, she turned and looked at herself over a shoulder. If a creamy lace bustier and hose with wide lace tops could be called a perfect outfit, then she was perfectly dressed.

With three-inch-high sandals on her feet, Cynthia left the bedroom and made her way through the house at a leisurely pace. She took the spiral staircase to the basement and mixed herself a rum and Coke at the wet bar.

Clinking ice cubes together, she spread a towel on the weight bench, stretched out on her stomach and crossed her heels in the air. A click of a remote control, and the movie Nigel had never returned, one of her favorite schoolgirl dramas, came to life on the TV screen.

When a hoarse, flat voice asked, "Can you swim?" she almost dropped the glass.

Cynthia arranged herself on her side and controlled a gasp of horror when she saw the man who approached. "Hi," she said, the breathless whisper real. "I've been waiting for you."

Purplish lips parted. Tiny colorless eyes fixed on red hair at the apex of her thighs. He appeared to have no neck, no shape at all. Sandy hair was slicked straight back from a low forehead that rolled into a lumpy overhang to those evil eyes. He was as wide as he was tall. The jacket of his wrinkled white linen suit flared from thick sloping shoulders to hang loosely over his hips.

A monster. Nothing could have prepared her for the disgust and fear that roiled in her belly.

"Where's lover-boy?"

Fighting to control shallow breathing, she scowled. "He's on the run. He knows he still owes you money but he's ducked out. Look." From one stocking top she removed Nigel's note. "He left this."

The foul, parody of a man took the note into bloated pink fingers and read—and tucked the paper into a pocket. "So why are you still here? I didn't think you liked it when I paid you a visit."

Cynthia's gorge rose. She swallowed and got up. His face was on a level with her breasts and that was where his attention fixed. "I played a little trick," she told him, sauntering slowly away to begin a trail around the pool. Nigel had brought her to this. She must not allow her revulsion to show. "Remember when you called here and spoke to the maid? You asked my address?"

He watched her every movement and his tongue darted around his lips. "She told you?"

"She *was* me. I only pretended to be the maid. That was my sister you cozied up to. Boring, huh?"

He shrugged.

"I'm not boring," she said. "And you're not boring. You're exciting. I've never known a man like you."

"You sent me after your sister?"

"That was before I knew what I was missing." *God, what was going to happen to her?*

"How did you find that out?"

"My sister told me about the night you went to her. It should have been me, sweetheart. We'd have had a ball. We still can have a ball if you want."

Without appearing to move, he produced a knife and flicked open the blade. "I asked if you could swim."

He confused her. "Sure. Why?"

"Swim."

"I—"

"Swim."

She hesitated while he pulled a chair close to the side of the pool and squished himself into it. When she started to undo the top hook on the bustier he waved the knife for her to stop. "Leave it," he said. "And the stockings. The shoes can go."

Cynthia kicked off her sandals. Her heart hammered so hard she was sure he could see it beat in her breast. He was a thing, not a man. His sandy hair was like orangy yarn stiched to the head of a fat, pink doll. A horrible doll.

Her only chance.

He inclined his head and she dived into the water.

"This side," he said loudly. "Breast stroke."

She stroked past him in the short lap pool without looking up, but felt his tiny eyes on her.

Her fingers met the wall and he called, "Crawl."

"Butterfly," came next and this time he heaved to his feet and stood at the end of the pool where she could see him every time her torso rose from the water.

Her stomach revolted. If she vomited, she'd never pull it off and get what she wanted—what she *had* to have.

"Backstroke!"

Why hadn't she ever thought of this? The idea fled as quickly as it had come. For once in her life she didn't feel sexy.

She reached back, touched the wall and felt a shoe descend on her fingers. Panic twisted her gut.

"Out," he said, withdrawing his foot.

He made no attempt to help her climb from the pool. When she stood in front of him, pushing her streaming hair away from her face, he spread his short legs and studied everything but her face.

"Like what you see?" she asked.

"Maybe." With the tip of his needle-bladed knife, he touched first one nipple, then the other. "Tell me why you waited for me."

She began to tremble. The knife tip repeated its tiny torture. "D'you have a woman?"

"Why did you wait?"

"I want a new life." Screwing up all the courage she could find, she said, "I want you to take me with you when you leave Seattle."

"Why?"

Because she was broke and knew she couldn't have long before the police would come for her. "Because you're exciting," she said. "We'll make a good team."

"I don't need a partner."

"No, no," she said quickly. "I mean I'll take good care of you. I know a lot of things and so do you. We could have great times together."

"You want to be with me?"

"Yes. Wherever you go, I want to go." *Straight into hell.*

He narrowed his eyes until they almost disappeared. "Prove it."

Cynthia gasped with relief. "I hoped you'd say that. Anything you want."

He put the knife away. Bunching the fingers of each hand

together, he grasped her nipples and pulled. "Look at that, baby. Sitting up and begging. Like little cocks ready to fuck."

Her stomach turned and turned. "They want you."

His fat hands spread and he squeezed her breasts until they hurt.

Cynthia kept on smiling.

"On your knees."

She got down and he parted his jacket. His pants were already unzipped and she saw the proof that everything about this man was thick. She closed her eyes and opened her mouth.

He was ready.

"You're hired," he said, blessedly quickly. "Cross me and . . ."

"I'll never cross you."

"They call me Piggy. I like it."

Her ticket out was aptly named. "Okay, Piggy."

Twilight glowed beyond the windows. Half-asleep, Tobias felt Paris leave the bed. They'd slept through the afternoon, eaten the soup he'd heated and brought upstairs, then slept some more.

Just lying with her in his arms had brought him the kind of peace he'd have scoffed at finding only days earlier.

She went into the bathroom and stayed so long he swung his legs from the bed and got up. Naked, he crossed the floor to knock on the door. "You okay, Blue?"

"Yes!"

Her sharp tone wiped away the last traces of sleep. He backed up, sat on the edge of the bed and waited until she appeared. He flipped on a lamp.

"Hi," she said. "I didn't mean to wake you."

"Obviously." She wore a sweatshirt and jeans. Her jeans. His sweatshirt. "Going somewhere?"

Paris slumped against the wall. "I've got to. Go back to bed and I'll do this as quickly as I can. Trust me, please. I'm making the right decision."

Tobias got up and began pulling on clothes.

"No," Paris said. "Please let me do this on my own. It'll be best."

"You're not waiting for tomorrow. You're going to Cynthia's now."

"Yes. And of course you don't need second sight to figure that out."

"Fine. I understand, but I'm coming with you."

"She'll only be mad."

He yanked a sweatshirt over his own head and paused. "Do I care? Do *you* honestly care if Cynthia is mad?"

"She's been found guilty without a trial, Tobias. We're not supposed to do things that way in this country."

He didn't waste breath on further argument. Slipping his feet into deck shoes, he picked up a set of keys from the bedside table and ushered her ahead of him from the houseboat.

Traffic was still heavy, the city alive. Small crowds gathered on sidewalks outside coffee bars and taverns. Paris cracked the Jeep window letting in snatches of laughter and shouting and a current of warm air.

They drew up beside Cynthia's building just as another vehicle pulled out of a parking spot. "Just call us lucky," Tobias muttered.

"We may need more than luck here," Paris responded, getting out of the Jeep before he'd taken the key from the ignition.

In the lobby, the concierge glanced up and smiled when she saw Paris. "Evening, Ms. Delight."

"Evening," Paris said, going directly to the elevators.

Once the doors closed them inside, Tobias settled his hands on her shoulders and looked down into her eyes. "This isn't going to be nice."

"I know."

"Don't get upset. Don't let *her* upset you. I'm here and I'll make sure everything turns out okay."

"There are things you can't fix, Tobias. But I'm glad you're with me."

He had to be satisfied with that.

Cynthia didn't answer Paris's repeated rings at her door.

"Either we camp here," he told her. "Or we go home and keep calling until she gets back."

Paris pushed a hand into her pocket and removed a key. "Or we go in and wait for her." She unlocked the door and walked straight in without looking back.

Tobias closed and locked the door behind them. It couldn't hurt for Cynthia to arrive home *not* expecting to find them there. An unlocked door might send her running in the opposite direction anyway.

Paris called, "Cynthia?"

He walked into the large, too white living room. Paris passed him on her way from the kitchen toward another room. "Cynthia? Are you home? It's me, Paris."

Something felt different from the last time he'd been here. Bare shelves. He frowned at glass shelves lining one wall, then at the twin tables in front of the couch. Cynthia's mammoth collection of crystal miniatures no longer crowded each surface.

Frowning even more deeply, he followed Paris and found her standing in the middle of a bedroom that showed signs of a possible bombing. "Holy shit," he said. "Will you look at . . . *Damn.* She's gone. Somehow she found out her number was up and she's cleared out." Clothes and shoes, costume jewelry and cosmetics, were strewn everywhere. Every drawer gaped.

"Where would she go?"

He brought his fists down on top of a chest. "Where do you think? Probably with Nigel."

"Oh, they aren't still—"

"We don't know that." He picked up a handful of underwear trailing from an open drawer and stuffed it back inside. "Who else but Nigel . . ."

"Uh-uh," Paris said softly. "You didn't tell Nigel what Sam said about Cynthia, did you?"

"You know I didn't. You were there when I talked to him."

"Then she may have decided to take a trip that doesn't have a thing to do with what happened to me."

Tobias knew she was saying aloud what she wanted to believe. He pointed to a flashing light on the answering machine beside the bed. "Someone else must think she's still here." He punched the message button and listened to the tape rewind.

"You have four messages," the canned voice informed Cynthia.

After a beep, a man's voice said, "Call me," and hung up. Next, the same voice said, "Call, damn you." "You owe me," was followed by, "I'm coming over. Be there," together with the time the call had been made.

"She must have left with him," Paris said. She was too pale to please Tobias. "What shall I do?"

He checked his watch. "If she'd left with him we'd probably have passed them on the way up. That last call was made twenty minutes ago."

The front door slammed and the voice from the answering machine shouted, "Cynthia?"

A walk-in closet stood open behind Paris. Tobias caught her around the waist and half-lifted her inside and behind the door. "Don't make a sound," he said into her ear.

Running footsteps criss-crossed the condominium and, eventually, skidded to a stop in the bedroom. *"Bitch,"* a familiar voice said. "Fucking *bitch.*"

Paris's fingers ground into Tobias's arm.

The man left the room but he didn't leave the condo. He went into the living room and they heard him dragging something across the floor, then repeated pounding against a wall. The pounding stopped and his footsteps receded to the far side of the unit. The noises he made then were too muffled to identify.

"I'm going to get you out," Tobias said. "Call the police."

"No way. I'm not leaving."

"Please. It may be—"

"Dangerous? What a concept. Stop telling me what I should and shouldn't do. I want to know what he's up to."

They left the closet. Tobias tried to put her behind him but she shoved in front and crept to peer through the crack in the bedroom door. Shaking her head, she walked softly into the living room and stopped.

Tobias bumped into her and saw what she'd seen. Over one

wall stretched a large, unblocked canvas. Representational hardly applied. Realism covered it nicely. The equivalent of a potato cut—using a woman's body rather than a potato—dipped in red paint. A woman having sex with a man who stood behind her—again, and again, and again, and again.

Paris's violent shudder snapped his concentration. He followed her stare to two words at the bottom of the painting. *Cynthia* had been printed in six-inch high black letters, followed by *Fucked,* in the same red used for the rest of the piece.

The sound of drawers opening and closing captured their attention. Paris leaned near to whisper, "office," and point.

"Come on, come on!" the man ground out. More drawers slammed. "Sonofabitch. You left it on the hard drive, you little fool. You *left* it." A whoop followed, then the sound of a computer keyboard being slowly tapped.

Before Tobias could stop her, Paris walked directly to the open door of what must have been Cynthia's office. He joined her and stood, watching while a single keystroke started a laser printer humming. Within seconds sheets began sliding across the top and into a holding tray.

Paris moved, but Tobias was quicker. He put her firmly aside and reached the man as he started to turn around.

Tobias launched himself like a guy with a low batting average and home base in sight.

"Shit, man!" Conrad yelled at the point of impact with the pale polished floor. Air rushed from his lungs in a loud, "Oomph!"

Tobias pinned his arms.

"Get off me," Conrad begged. "Get *off* me."

Conrad was younger. Tobias was bigger and in better shape. Not trusting himself to speak, he whipped the other man to his stomach and twisted his hands behind his back.

"What's happening?" Paris cried.

"It's called clean-up time," Tobias told her. "I think we're gathering in the last pieces here."

"My arms," Conrad screamed.

Tobias tore off his own belt and cranked it several times around the other man's wrists. He dragged him to his feet, shoved him back into the computer chair and used what was left of the belt to buckle the prisoner in place.

"When the press gets hold of this you're gonna wish you were never born," Conrad said, his face twisted with pain. "Stop him, Paris. He's gone nuts. Cynthia knew he was crazy."

Paris wasn't listening. She'd picked up a stack of sheets from the printer and begun to read.

"That's mine," Conrad said. "Cynthia let me use her computer for a project I've been working on."

"Nice project you just decorated the living room with," Tobias commented without inflection. "You do interesting work."

Conrad's brown eyes glittered. "That's personal," he said.

"A gift, maybe?"

"You've got it."

"Kind of an *in-your-face* gift, maybe."

Conrad shifted and winced. "Whatever you say."

"Must have been fun to do."

"It was." A lift of his jaw held defiance. "We both thought so."

"You don't have to convince me."

"Tobias," Paris said. "Oh, my God. I don't understand. It's all here. Everything that happened. All of it. She even used the real names."

"That was just a joke," Conrad said. He slumped and Tobias felt the last remnants of fight go out of the man. "She'd have changed the names in the end. But she ruined everything. Silly bitch even took time to bring it up to date before she took the floppies and deleted the file from the hard drive."

"But she didn't," Paris said, holding out the sheaf of paper and gathering more from the tray. "It's here."

"She forgot the backup file." Conrad's smile was lopsided. "I thought I'd hit pay dirt. I could have made her pay for that forever. I never did get any real luck."

Side by side on Cynthia's white leather couch, with Conrad begging for release every few minutes, Tobias and Paris read not a mystery noyel, but a film script by Cynthia Delight Quinn entitled *Pure Delights*.

"Cast," Paris read aloud, running her finger over her own

name, and Tobias's and Sam's, each entry spelling out their past sins in Cynthia's eyes and how they would be paid for. "She does hate me. I'm the reason her family doesn't see her for the worthwhile daughter and granddaughter she really is. But Sam was supposed to kidnap me, not kill me."

"Wormwood," Tobias said. "Poor devil. She saw him picking up a kid on Second Avenue. She threatened to tell his lover if he didn't help her ruin you and drive you out of the apartment." The list went on, covering innocent people with familiar names. Cynthia called them "supporting cast."

Paris jabbed Conrad's name. "She wanted him to kill you," she whispered. "She paid him by buying his paintings."

"And she brought it up to date," Tobias said, incredulous as he read, *"The fool smoked a French cigarette while he bungled it. Thought it was brilliant to pretend to be Piggy."*

"Who's Piggy?" Paris asked.

"The guy doing the collecting from your violent buddy's brother," Conrad said. "He was the one who paid you the friendly night visit. Cynthia told me about it. She arranged that, too. That's what gave me the idea about the cigarette, just in case anything went wrong."

Tobias stared at Conrad and realized he'd begun to lose control. He'd delivered his self-incriminating information with belligerent pride. "Sam didn't attack you last night, did he?" he asked softly. "You murdered him to stop him from telling anyone about Cynthia. If he pulled Cynthia into it, she'd pull you right along with her."

"Prove it!"

Riffling through pages almost to the end, Paris located a speech delivered by one Conrad: *"I killed him for you, Cynthia. I killed him for us. We're safe because no one's ever going to know you were involved with Sam."*

"Bizarre," Tobias said. "Unfortunately for both of you, Sam had already said his piece. We're going to call the police now."

Paris groaned. "Detective Whatsisname is going to be *so* pleased to hear from us again." She got up and went heavily to a phone.

Blowing the whistle on Cynthia would cost her a great deal,

Tobias knew, but he also knew she'd do what had to be done now.

He turned back to the list of characters in the "script," and read through to a second page. His eyes went to the bottom entry for *The Money Man*. This man had paid Cynthia—to help him ruin another man. He'd paid a ransom to Cynthia's lover to get information on his rival, information already responsible for the loss of a major deal to a dummy company set up in California. He'd also arranged to fire up *the crazy in the Skagit* and use him. An old feud made it easy to persuade Pops Delight to go along.

Tobias heard Paris talking to the police but he stopped listening to her words. Just as he knew he was the "rival" in Cynthia's piece and that Nigel was the "informer," he knew the name he'd find linked to *The Money Man* would be Bill Bowie.

The rest was Cynthia's unfulfilled dreams of riches in the wake of bringing Paris down and helping Bill steal Tobias's position in his field. Evidently Conrad, like Sam, had moved before Cynthia gave the word. Tobias should have bitten the dust only shortly before she disposed of poor Vivian and became the new love of Bill's life. Cynthia had even included a note about arranging a copy of one of Paris's new designs and sending it to Vivian anonymously for her to wear at Astor Burken's party.

Only Cynthia's present whereabouts were missing from the drama—and whether Bill knew he'd been caught. Those were questions the police could take up.

Tobias reached the final sheet of paper and grew cold. Paris returned to his side and looked over his shoulder. She made a strangled sound. *Intro:* was the heading. *Night. A man's voice narrating. Camera gradually goes in for a close up:*

His rubber soles made no sound on the fire escape. When the time came, he would climb up this way again and it would all be so easy . . .

Thirty-one

"Are you beginning to feel as if the rest of the world's got it backwards?"

Paris had been staring blankly past the houseboats toward the University of Washington campus. She glanced at Tobias. He finished locking the Jeep and faced her. His hair was rumpled, two-days' growth of beard shadowed his cheeks and jaw, and blood from Conrad's nose spattered his stretched-out sweatshirt.

Even with dark slashes beneath his eyes, slashes that appeared blue-gray in the early morning light, he looked irresistible.

"Backwards? The rest of the world?"

Looking at his keys as if deciding what to do with them, then shoving them into a pocket in his grimy jeans, he reached for her hand. "Backwards. They go to bed at the damndest times. At night usually. Then they get up in the morning and go to work! Imagine that!"

Paris was too exhausted to do more than grin weakly. "Imagine. Loony, every one of them."

They stumbled down the ramp to the dock and scuffed to

climb aboard Tobias's deck. He let them into the houseboat and immediately headed for the stairs.

Paris hung back. She heard him reach the bedroom and go inside shouting, "A shower, a shower, my kingdom for a shower. I'd better call the office. They'll think I've died."

A habit. That's what all this was, a habit. Without warning, tears swam in her eyes and overflowed. Blindly, she turned toward the door, poking in her jeans pockets for a tissue.

"Hey!" Tobias's feet thundered on the stairs. "Come on, Blue, before we both collapse. I'll scrub your back if you'll scrub mine."

A stupid sob erupted.

His hands descended on her shoulders but she shrugged him off. "You're crying. Blue, you're *crying*. Sweetheart, speak to me. *Look* at me. Oh, for God's sake I am such an ass. You've really had it, haven't you."

She hunched over and wept afresh. "Such—a—*mess*. Bill. *Cynthia.*"

A bunch of tissues magically appeared in her hands. "Please try not to worry about things you can't change," he told her. "I'll get used to what Bill did to me. I don't even know if I hope they catch him before he can leave the country. Whether they do or not, something tells me he'll wish he was dead when Vivian gets a shot at him. And you've done everything you possibly could do to help Cynthia. You can't help her now and it isn't your fault she's messed her life up."

"It's . . . not . . . that."

Tobias rubbed her back and she cried louder.

"Okay, okay. Relax. Let me get you up to bed. When you've had a good sleep everything will look better."

"It won't. I'm a lousy judge of people. I'm dangerous to be around."

"That's it. You're getting maudlin. Up the stairs with you."

"I'm going home."

"For . . . I will *not* lose my temper with you because you aren't yourself. You *are* home."

"This is *your* home, not mine." She settled a hand on the

doorhandle—and found herself spun around so fast she grabbed Tobias to stop herself from falling.

"Knock it off," he said. His lips thinned. "This is your home until or unless we decide to live somewhere else. Together."

"I've caused you nothing but trouble."

He brought his face closer. "I like trouble."

"You kind of *fell* into a relationship with me. You never, ever looked at me as anything but someone who was . . . *around.*"

"That was before." A dangerous light entered his eyes.

Paris was past caution. "When you came to me all you wanted was my help—not a lifetime commitment."

His arms folded over his broad chest.

"It's not fair for you to get stuck with me out of some stupid sense of duty."

"Duty? *Stupid?*" His shoes had already been discarded and he rocked onto the balls of his feet. "Most people avoid suggesting I do stupid things."

She bowed her head. "You're not stupid. You're kind and dear—and now you feel you've got to stick with me because my family jumped to some conclusions."

"The *hell* I do."

"I think I should do the right thing and put some distance between us."

"The *hell* you will."

"I hate it when you swear."

He made fists on his arms. "Do you love me?"

An instant overflow of tears cascaded and she was helpless to stop it.

Tobias said, much louder than he need have, *"I love you.* I thought we'd got that straight."

"W-we haven't d-done the usual things."

"What usual things, goddamit?"

She began to tremble. "Oh, I don't know. Little stuff. We've never been on a picnic. We've never *danced* together. You know, the usual . . ."

"We picnicked as kids," he said tightly. He kept an eye on her while he backed up and hit buttons on the sound system. "You want to dance? We'll dance."

"I don't want to dance," she told him in a small voice, but he pulled her into his arms.

Celine Dion and Clive Griffen, singing slowly, hypnotically, about falling in love, wound around Paris's heart as seductively as Tobias wound his body around hers. He hummed against her cheek, swaying, then swinging her around.

Paris looked up into his face.

"When I fall in love," he said, "It's going to be for keeps." He bracketed her feet with his own and rocked her. "I've fallen in love, Blue. Can't undo it now."

She framed his jaw and murmured, "When I give my heart away, it'll be the only time."

"When?"

"I already did."

His eyelids lowered. "Good. We're doing one of those usual things. Notice? Dancing. I like dancing with you."

"We're swaying and massacring a beautiful song."

"It never sounded this good to me before."

Paris settled a forefinger on his lips. "Not to me, either."

The song ended and Tammy Wynette's breaking country voice launched into a husky demand for a woman to take care of her man.

Tobias grinned. "Yeah," he said, spinning her away from him and rolling her back in. "I want that from you, baby. Always be there for your man."

Too tired for gymnastics, Paris clung to him. "I love you, Tobias Quinn. I really love you."

The lean lines of his face changed, grew tense. "Was it so hard to say?"

She looked into his eyes. "What was hard was knowing it for so long and not daring to say it."

He led her upstairs and undressed her. She watched him take off his clothes before putting an arm around her waist as they went into the shower.

Tobias washed her back and she washed his—before they washed every other inch of each other.

She was first in bed. He stretched out beside her. Paris closed her eyes.

Moments ticked by.

Tobias hadn't turned the stereo off. From downstairs came the smoky strains of a Nat King Cole song.

"Are you asleep?" she whispered.

"No."

"Me either."

His hand settled on a breast and he stroked. "Would you slap my face if I said I want to be inside you?"

Her breasts felt heavy and hot—and raw. She grew wet and achy and *needy*.

"Blue? You gonna slap me?"

Paris smoothed the backs of her fingers down the mat of hair on his chest, past his navel. His belly jerked and the place between her legs contracted in response. Her fingers closed on him. "I'm not going to slap you," she said, her voice husky, "As long as you don't keep me waiting."

Tobias didn't answer. He rolled to position himself between her thighs. Slipping into her, sighing when she crossed her legs around his waist, he made love to her slowly and for a long, long time.

"It's not because you're so serious," he said, kissing her open mouth.

"What?" She couldn't think, only feel now.

"Blue. It's your eyes. It was always your eyes. Bluest eyes I ever saw."

Later she'd probably tell him how sweet he was.

They were watching a flame-colored sunset streak the sky. Tobias rocked the swing a little and played with Paris's hair.

When footsteps approached along the shoreside deck they both stopped breathing.

"Just us," Mary said, arriving with Ginna at her heels. "Came to make sure you were managing all right."

Tobias clamped Paris against him. "More than all right," he said. "Just terrific, thank you."

Ginna nodded. "I noticed. Mary talked me into bringing her